The DRAGON'S HEART

ALYSHA KING

The Dragon's Heart

First published 2019

ISBN: 978-0-6485003-2-2

For my friends and family, whose lives
have inspired me to no end.

And in memory of my wonderful Aunty Liz.
May you burn brighter than any star out there.

Other works by the author

The Order of the Rose

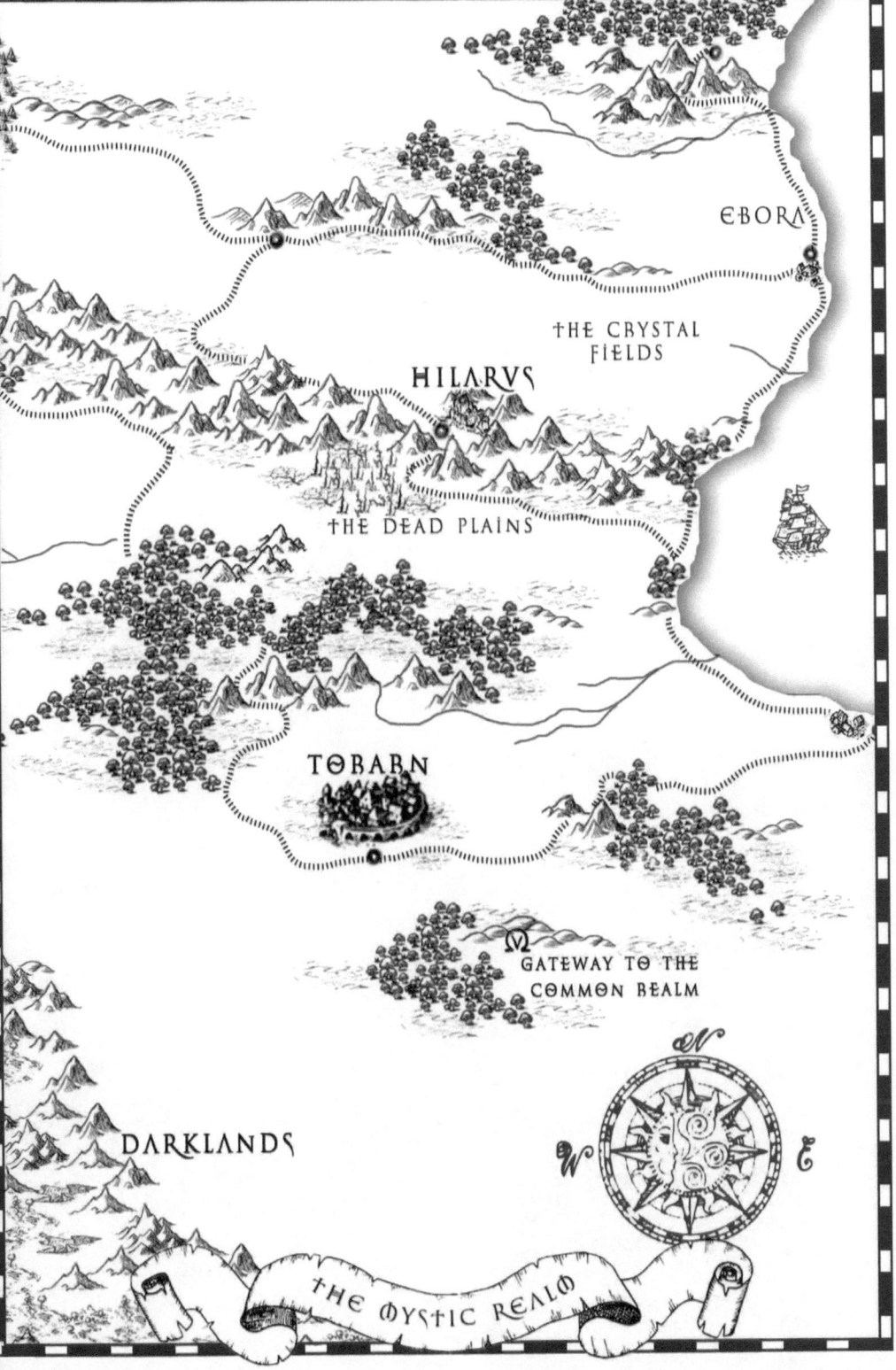

EBORA

THE CRYSTAL
FIELDS

HILARVS

THE DEAD PLAINS

TOBARN

GATEWAY TO THE
COMMON REALM

DARKLANDS

N

W   E

THE MYSTIC REALM

Prologue

I thought the fall of the Empire would make everything easier.

I would have my family; I would be released from my defensive duties as a Seeker and perhaps even be able to live an almost normal life. I do not know which thought was more foolish — being able to leave the life of a Seeker behind, or ever being able to be anything that might resemble *normal*.

Instead, everything has become so much more complicated. A number of senior Imperials managed to elude capture after Malevolence's fall and escaped to the Dark Lands where they have more willing aid and allies. Worse still, lone rebels and rogue armies of creatures that had been given certain *privileges* under the Empire are now attacking unprotected villages. My parents are constantly being called to arms to fight these Imperial loyalists. I fear that, having just gotten them back, I may lose them again. It's not that I lack faith in their abilities — their powers are almost unparalleled. It's simply that I know the deceit and levels to which Imperials will sink. I should know this better than most...

With no sense of loyalty or compassion for those he once considered allies, Jeremy Schultz used every vindictive source available to him to further the Empire. He'd used his ability to Shapeshift to impersonate someone I had held dear. He'd taken Ji's face and used it against me. Hearing of his death, I had expected some kind of relief — I certainly felt no remorse. Instead, he has left even more questions in his wake. The pain he had caused certainly did not diminish with his departure, which for all concerned, has never been fully explained. There is a part of me which is almost anxious to know how he died, yet there is something within my heart which wills me to forget him, to be content with the fact that he is gone. It still confuses me.

Jeremy is not the only Imperial who continues to aggrieve me. I am afraid to sleep, to even close my eyes for fear of being confronted yet again by Saar. He has not let on who he is or what his exact plans are but I know it is only a matter of time before he leaves the realm of dreams and confronts me in the real world. If he spoke the truth of his powers, there may be nothing that could stop him.

I am yet to tell anyone about him. I am not sure, perhaps it is because I know so little about him, or maybe it is because he exists, for now, only in my mind and my dreams. What help could be afforded to me, when I can't even be sure the threat is real? No. Perhaps the most I can do for now is to find out as much as I can about this *Twilight Travelling* and how I can control it. It is, after all, my power. If anything, with everything that is still going on, I should at least be able to have control over that.

~Chapter One~

Interrogation and Extinction

T he sound of dripping water echoed off the damp floor. The light from the single candle reflected eerily around the dull green cave, its long wax drippings flowing down the rock. The small pool that stretched along the far wall was still; only the smallest amount of candlelight shimmered across its surface in a vain effort to break through the oppressive darkness. Stalactites hung perilously from the low roof, long and sharp, bearing down on the cave's single inhabitant. Bound only feet from the water, the mermaid's head was bowed reverently, her only sound a slight rattle as her gills struggled for oxygen. Her long, blonde hair hung limp over her drooping shoulders, and a ringlet of tiny delicate shells clung lopsidedly to her crown. Her skin was dry and tight over the bones of her chest and her spine; salt encrusted and flaking in great web-like patterns. Her silvery-blue tail was dull and cracked, and dried blood clung to her scales like weather-born rust. The mermaid's eyes were closed, her face drawn with pain and exhaustion.

A drop of water slid down a stalactite, landing with a loud *smack* on the pool's surface. The mermaid's eyes snapped open, immediately alert. They flitted over the water's surface then moved about the cave, searching. Her gaze paused on the cave's dark entrance; she watched, waiting.

She only had to wait a moment before it appeared.

The figure was shrouded in a hooded travelling cloak, the hem brushing noiselessly along the floor. He stooped as he made his way slowly to the side of the small pool, sitting carefully on the edge of a large rock. The mermaid watched her visitor carefully, neither surprised nor wary. Instead, she observed him with growing defiance. For a tense moment, the pair simply stared at each other. Then, the visitor raised his hands and lowered his hood. A pair of silver eyes shone like the edge of a dagger, slashing through the semi-darkness. The corner of his mouth curled up into a smirk as he continued to eye the defiant mermaid at his feet. She narrowed her eyes ever so slightly, waiting.

Finally, Saar spoke.

"You're not looking too well, Your Highness," he said in a low voice, the smirk lingering on his lips. "Obviously land does not agree with you..."

He cocked his head to the side, waiting for her to answer. The mermaid continued to stare.

Saar turned his eyes to the pool of water, the surface still once more. He sighed melodramatically.

"This needn't be, Your Majesty. You needn't suffer," Saar whispered as he leant forward and ran his fingers over the surface of the water.

The mermaid's gaze was drawn by the ripples drifting lazily towards her, and her pulse quickened. She could hear it whisper, feel its pull. Her head spun with longing, but with great effort, she pulled her eyes from the pool and faced her tormentor once more. She took a short, rattling breath, trying to still her mind, and said nothing. Saar lifted his fingers from the water, droplets falling from the tips with soft *plinks* upon the rock. He moved closer to her, searching her face.

"I admire you, My Queen. Your strength is truly admirable. But is this really necessary?"

The mermaid was adamant in her silence, tightening her lips. Saar maintained his smirk, but his eyes flashed momentarily with annoyance. He drew closer, lifted a hand to her face and brushed aside strands of her salt-caked hair. She flinched as Saar gently stroked her dry flaking cheek, his damp fingers leaving a fleeting trail of jewel-bright colour across her moisture-starved skin. Her breath hitched, the coolness of the water awakening the primal urge within her that all mermaids felt for the ocean. Saar's grin widened at her reaction and he held his fingers at her jaw, clearly relishing in the effect he was having upon her.

"Such beauty. It is such a shame..." he purred, and her cheeks flared with humiliation.

When she spoke, her voice was hushed from disuse, broken by the dryness that had taken her over.

"Do not think that by appealing to my vanity you will draw what you need from me," she croaked as her gills flapped desperately. Her head still swam with longing and it took all her self-control to ignore the burning desire the water had invoked. She needed her wits about her. "My... physical deterioration is not nearly as disturbing to me as what my subsequent betrayal would be."

Her brilliant green eyes burned with such fervent determination that Saar's confidence slipped along with his grin. Recovering from his moment of frustration, he diverted his attention, taking a piece of her hair in his fingers and twisting it almost absentmindedly. Salt coated his fingers at the touch, the tiny white flakes trickling to the floor. There was quiet again, the silence punctuated by the odd drip that resonated softly from somewhere within the cave.

"I beg your forgiveness, Your Majesty. I was merely commenting. I would never believe such slight a compliment would compel you to speak," Saar said, examining the tress in his hand with undue devotion.

The mermaid's lip curled in abhorrence at the thought of forgiveness and was very much on the verge of pulling away from him. However, she remained quite still, enduring his unwelcome touch. Saar spoke again.

"My Queen, dear Asselia. Do not think that I am unaware of your situation," he said in a hushed voice. "I cannot possibly imagine the inner turmoil you must be dealing with at this moment, the dilemma which you have been forced to face."

Queen Asselia's eyes narrowed further.

"Forgive me if I am wrong, but you are yet to name an heir, are you not?" Saar asked in an overly polite manner, continuing to examine the lock of hair entwined in his fingers. "A fairly important part of Mermaid hierarchy, no?"

The mermaid queen's breathing quickened but she did not concede. Saar dropped his hand and raised an eyebrow.

"Now, my knowledge of mermaid lore may not be the most complete so please feel free to contradict me, but is it not said that should a queen die without either producing or naming an heir, then that queen's clan shall perish along with her? My, what a terrible thing, being responsible for so many. You have certainly risked much, not doing so earlier. Why, look where you are now!" he said, indicating with a small flourish at the cramped little cave. "Is your clan not one of the largest in the realm?"

Queen Asselia burned at his words and the flippant manner in which he spoke. She leant towards her captor, her breath short and sharp.

"You knew the lore long before you lured me here. *You* created this. Your knowledge therefore comes as no true revelation," she hissed.

Saar's face fell, his lips turning down in a pantomime of regret. He leant over again and this time dipped his entire hand below the surface of the water. Breathing hard now, the mermaid queen struggled to keep her mind from reeling, anger and fury burning alongside a deep and almost uncontrollable yearning. She pulled against the iron manacles clamped about her red and raw wrists, fighting against the urge to throw herself at this repugnant human. Saar's burning silver eyes watched her despair with ill-disguised glee.

"Then surely you know what will happen, should you fail to tell me what I want? Are you truly ready to sacrifice not only yourself but your entire clan for something as inconsequential as a fulfilled prophecy?" he asked, lifting his hand from the pool and raising it over the mermaid's head.

The water splashed down upon her and he watched as she writhed, fighting against its affects. Her body was ablaze, her mind torn asunder.

"Stop," she found herself begging, her voice rough. "Please…"

His face was close to hers now, whispering softly in her ear, "Then end this. Why keep this going? I want only for the prophecy. After all, like I said, it has already been fulfilled, so there would be no harm—"

"My clan needs me…"

"And you know how to save them," he purred, brushing her hair back from her taught face with his wet hand. "Besides, it is all in the past."

"It is not, though…"

Queen Asselia's eyes widened in horror as the words slipped from her mouth. She had not meant to say it, but the water… Confusion, fear, and dismay welled up inside her. Saar pulled away, triumph on his face.

"Finally, something true. Thank you, My Queen." He turned his head and looked at the wall, his eyes unfocused. "*Not* in the past, then, meaning she has not yet fulfilled the prophecy," he said pensively. "I suppose this means that the Empress is not yet truly defeated. This is… good news…"

Asselia fought back the tumult raging within her, her body shaking as she fixed Saar with a furious glare. She balled her fists in her metal cuffs and spat, "You know nothing of mermaid prophecies. If you knew the truth then you would have no need for me and you would have your answers. This is no more than a show of how truly limited your knowledge is."

Saar paused in his thoughts and smiled hopefully. "Then please, Asselia, enlighten me. Tell me the truth of your prophecies. As they say, *the truth will set you free.*"

"Certainly not in this case. The truth will not be revealed by my tongue, no matter the threat."

And with this proclamation, Asselia fell silent once more. She shook from the effort of ignoring the trickling beads of water still coating her skin, but she remained defiant in her gaze.

Saar waited, then sighed again, only this time in earnest.

"As you wish, My Queen. It does not matter, though. All will proceed. Your silence was never going to stay my plans. Unfortunately, neither will it stay my hand. If you are willing to make this sacrifice, then at least it will not be on my conscience."

Queen Asselia straightened at these words, but Saar paid her no attention. He stood and straightened as much as he could before rearranging his hood so that only his luminous eyes were visible from beneath it. He gave the mermaid one last piercing look before turning for the entrance. The queen watched as he left. The oxygen passing through her gills was now sharp, almost cutting, and the droplets upon her scales were drying rapidly. There was almost no water left in her body. She knew she would not see him return.

~Chapter Two~

Revelations

The sound of metal upon stone reverberated around the high walls of the dungeon. Carey ducked just in time to miss the heavy spear as it swung over her head and hit the wall behind her. The ringing in her ears was deafening, but she ignored it. She retaliated with a swing of her sword, aiming at her opponent's stomach, but he jumped back, just out of reach. With a quick shifting of his body, he swung his spear around for another attack, its tip barely missing her throat.

Stumbling backwards, Carey gripped her sword tightly to stop it falling from her hand. Despite the cobbled ground, she found her footing and squared her shoulders, sword out in front. A bead of sweat slid down her cheek to catch on her upper lip, salt tingling on her tongue as she swiped it away.

They faced each other, still for only a split second before he lunged at her again. Carey wasn't quick enough, and the tip of his spear glanced across her cheek. In surprise, she lost her footing and fell into an awkward roll, only just managing to hold onto her sword. Sharp pain spiked through her elbows and knees as she crashed down, but she shook it off as she tried to correct her stance, knowing her attacker was right behind her. As she turned, he bore down on her, gleeful in his advantage. She threw her sword up and felt it shudder as it connected with the spear. It was mere inches from her face and her hands trembled, the force of her opponent's weapon bearing down on her. Carey winced as her muscles trembled. Pushing his face close to hers, he grunted, "Give up?"

Despite the pain, Carey gave a bark of laughter.

"Not in this life."

With one swift movement, she curled her knee up into her chest and struck out at his kneecap. Her foot connected with a heavy crunch and he let out a cry of pain. Taking advantage of this moment of weakness, Carey jumped to her feet. Knocking aside his spear, she forced him to one knee, grabbed at his shirt, pulled his back against her chest and drew the blade of her sword across his throat.

"Got you," she hissed in his ear, and she could have sworn she saw the hint of a smile lift at the corner of his mouth.

"Bravo, Carey!"

The two combatants broke apart at the sound of applause. Carey lowered her weapon and wiped her brow, pushing back light brown hair from her face. A short, stout figure came in from her left, still clapping in apparent approval.

"Very good work, I must say, very good. Been practising, Carey?" the sword master, Sir Garrow, inquired.

"I'd have to say yes," came an amused murmur from below.

Ji was still on his knees, panting slightly from his recent defeat. Carey let out a small gasp.

"Oh! Sorry Ji!" She apologised, holding out a hand.

With a strange smirk on his lips, Ji reached out and Carey pulled him to his feet. Her hand tingled slightly as she glanced up at his face, his rumpled brown hair falling over his clouded blue eyes as they gazed just past her left ear. An instant later, however, he had relinquished his grip, his head turned towards the sword master. Carey felt her face flush, her cheeks burning as she turned from him, sheathing her blade aggressively. Jaw clenched, she strode from the training floor, brushing her hair back. Sir Garrow signalled to Kat who had been watching their spar eagerly from the sideline. She smiled at Carey as she walked onto the floor, her dark wavy hair bouncing about her shoulders. She was decked out in her favourite sparring gear — a thick leather corset over a loose top with billowing sleeves, fitted pants and high black boots. A small scarf was knotted at her throat, covering the goat's head brand placed there by Imperials. Carey thought she looked

10

rather like a pirate. At least, those she had seen in books.

"Good fight, Carey. He almost had you though," Kat noted as she pulled out her weapons of choice — a pair of long, pointed sai, each fashioned with three viscious-looking prongs — and twirled them expertly in her hands.

Carey nodded slightly. "Almost. You've got a challenge on your hands."

She watched as Kat crouched low opposite to Ji, ready to strike. Ji had his spear at the ready, completely still so that he might sense Kat's vibrations.

This was daily practice for them now. It was more than an expansion of their defensive knowledge; the three of them had recently been made aware of lands within the Mystic Realm that required this kind of combative knowledge. These lands were known as the Dead Plains. Blackened and barren, they were the by-product of some of the largest and nastiest battles that had raged during the first years of Malevolence's reign. The land had been scarred beyond redemption; no animals inhabited it and the plants that had once grown there no longer did.

More importantly, the Dead Plains were completely devoid of magic. As a result, witches, wizards, and any other magical race found themselves unable to use their powers within the borders of these lands. Recent rebellions by Imperials still loyal to Malevolence had led them to these wastelands and, not wanting to find themselves defenceless against an enemy, the Council had ordered any who might be called to arms to be practised in hand-to-hand combat. A large section of the castle's dungeons had been converted into a training arena for them, lined with all manner of weaponry, and Carey found herself visiting them for a good two hours at least every day.However, this was nothing compared to her two best friends.

The training had brought out an insane competitive streak between Kat and Ji. Wanting desperately to prove himself and to show that he was just as capable as anyone else, Ji spent endless hours doing extra training with the sword master. His ability to *see* the vibrations of those around him had expanded phenomenally, and as a result his fighting had become more accurate. Carey was always in a state of awe when watching him spar with Kat; when she was fighting him there was no time for such emotion. Ji's hearing capabilities had compounded to compensate for his lack of sight and every move and noise Carey made only aided him. He called it his *unfair advantage*.

Kat, never to be upstaged by Ji's commitment to anything, matched his training patterns and had taken to mentally documenting Ji's every strength and weakness. Ji had specifically asked them to not hold back during their training sessions which, in Carey's opinion, Kat was a little too eager to oblige. Then again, this only fuelled their competitive egos, for Ji would never admit that Kat was overdoing it. Carey found that if she did hold back, she would invariably find herself on her back with the tip of Ji's spear at her throat. She could not underestimate him.

Sir Garrow signalled and Kat immediately launched herself at Ji. He reacted equally fast and there was a resounding clash of metal as he blocked Kat's attack.

Turning from the violent scene, Carey lifted her sword and placed it back on the wall where it would stay until her next session, removed only to be tended to by the swordsmiths. Sir Garrow was standing nearby, watching Kat and Ji's fight with a critical eye. When Carey came to stand by him, she found herself looking down at his balding scalp. It truly drove home the lesson of never underestimating one's opponent. Sir Garrow had earned his title of Sword Master with his flawless skills and impenetrable defences. His reputation was second to none, but it also made him an unwilling target of Kat's fervour. She was determined to beat him some day; Ji and Rupert had a bet going just in case she ever did.

"Can I help you, Carey?" he asked, keeping his eyes on the fight.

Carey couldn't help smiling. She liked Sir Garrow. He was one of the only Council members who didn't insist on calling her *Your Highness*.

"Would you mind if I excused myself, Sir Garrow? I feel the need for some fresh air," Carey asked as she watched Kat tumble gracefully before pouncing, cat-like, once more at Ji.

"No, of course not. I'll see you tomorrow," he answered, still watching Kat and Ji. "Oh, good block, Ji! Just watch your footing!"

Bringing his spear around to the side, Ji steadied himself, his face a mask of concentration. Without a second glance, Carey stole from the room, glad to get away from the others. *No, not Kat,* she told herself, *just Ji.* He had caught her by surprise and she silently chastised herself for allowing it.

The pain and confusion Carey associated with Jeremy had compounded with his death. No one had managed to solve the mystery of his demise, which, despite its suicidal façade, contained a number of unexplained anomalies. How could anyone, in a bound room where no magic could be used, with nothing more than the clothes on their body, manage to cut themselves and stay conscious long enough to write a message on the wall in their own blood? It sickened and angered Carey beyond all reason whenever she thought about it. She felt cheated by how Jeremy had managed to escape. Murder or suicide, it made little difference to her. Carey had wanted to see him; talk to him despite how repulsive the idea was to her.

She wanted to know why he had done it, why he had betrayed them… And why he had misled her. Jeremy's death had deprived her of this opportunity, sinking her further into the deep dark hole he had created. She felt a deep sense of unexplained anxiety any time she thought of him but even worse, this anxiety had transferred to Ji also. Since they had returned, the feeling had grown steadily until the very thought of being in the same room as Ji made her feel queasy.

Even after the Spring Ball, when she had glimpsed a moment of hope for them, it had become increasingly difficult for her to even talk to him. There were strained silences and awkward moments, not unlike that which she had just experienced in the training hall. She hated feeling this way. Even if Jeremy had simply been playing on her emotions the whole time and that connection Kat spoke of didn't actually exist, she wanted nothing more than to be friends with Ji, to be able to speak with him freely and enjoy being around him as the others did. But every time he spoke, every time he laughed or joked, all she heard was Jeremy. Everything came back to him and it infuriated her.

Fists clenched; Carey grimaced at these dark thoughts as she strode absentmindedly down a corridor.

It was mid-afternoon and she saw only a few people, all of whom murmured acknowledgement as she passed. Carey nodded vaguely, so lost in her own thoughts that she was unaware of where her feet were carrying her. The adrenaline from the fight, and more noticeably, from those few moments with Ji, was finally ebbing away. Those instances were few and far between, but they always happened when she least expected it. With great mental effort she pushed her emotions aside. She needed to focus.

She was turning another corner when she heard a voice come from behind.

"Carey, dear! Sweetheart," it called, and Carey spun around.

Her mother's smiling face greeted her; all bright eyes framed with grey-streaked honey-brown hair. She hurried down the corridor and gave Carey a hug. Her mother was still wearing her heavy travelling cloak over her usual slacks and high leather boots. A sign that she had only just returned. Carey had not seen her mother for near two weeks, and her sudden presence sparked a flicker of happiness inside her.

"Darling, I have the most wonderful news. We found her — we found Seramina!" Jenny Lee said with a wide grin.

Carey's mouth spread wide with surprise, all thoughts of Ji and Jeremy instantly wiped from her mind. "You did? When? Where? Is she here now?" she asked.

Her mother laughed pleasantly. "Don't worry. She'll be here soon enough. She was hiding with a band of travelling witches and wizards. You might know them. Does the name Anoueshka ring any bells?"

Carey grinned. Of course she remembered. Their brief encounter and her unimaginable kindness had touched her deeply, and she was instantly glad that Seramina had found them.

"That's fantastic. Certainly unexpected, but fantastic," Carey said, her happiness producing a quiver in her voice.

Jenny nodded. "Indeed. They certainly looked after her well. *You* should be proud though — your little bit of magic saved her life."

"It did?" Carey asked, relief rushing over her. She could not remember a day in recent times when she hadn't worried about the young witch she and

Kat had helped to escape from Imperials. She did not share Kat's confidence in her abilities, and Carey had feared that her magic had not been enough. The very notion that she might have failed in saving yet another innocent had almost been too much to bear.

"She's an unusual one though, quite unique," her mother reflected. Carey frowned.

"How so?"

"Well, from what you told me, I was under the impression she was only just beginning to understand her skills as a telepath."

"Yes, that's what I understood from her diary entries," Carey said with a slight frown.

"It would seem she is a little more skilled than we first thought," Jenny said thoughtfully. "Apparently she heard we were searching for her. She said that was how she knew we weren't Imperials. I mean, I have encountered mind-readers before, but they have always been limited in their abilities, only able to focus on a single person at a time and never so skilled as to differentiate one from a crowd without knowing their target first. Seramina was able to find us amongst the entire camp and distinguished us as friends."

"Huh. I didn't know," Carey muttered, intrigued.

Silence fell over them for a moment, each lost in their own thoughts when Jenny started suddenly.

"Oh, but she'll be arriving any moment! Your father is bringing her but I came ahead to let you know. They will be here soon so you must go down to the entrance hall to meet her. It will be a comfort, I feel, for her to see a familiar face. I'll go and fetch Kat and Ji in the meantime," she said as she began to head down the corridor from which Carey had emerged.

"Are you sure?" Carey hesitated.

But Jenny had already walked off, waving for her to move. "Yes, of course. It's no problem. You go and meet Seramina. We'll be down soon enough."

Carey's mouth turned down into a frown again but she turned on her heel and hurried to her room to change. She felt her heart clench with the expectation of seeing the girl they had saved. The man they had entrusted her with had reportedly been taken by Essedarian not long after the fall

15

of the Empire, and Carey had feared that Seramina had fallen to the same fate. She and Kat had wanted to aid in the search for her, but Jenny had denied their request, fearing they may be too easily recognised. So, they had waited. They threw themselves into training and other activities in order to keep their minds from dwelling on it for too long, but the anxiety was still there, humming in the background.

Having changed from her training gear to a white linen top and a pair of dark, fitted pants, Carey ran to the stairs, feeling an enormous weight beginning to lift from her chest. It drifted from her, caught in a draft as she passed the great stained-glass windows. With all the bad, it felt wonderful to have something good finally occur.

She skipped lightly down the huge marble staircase. The entrance hall was empty, except for the guards by the door. They straightened upon her approach. Carey rolled her eyes.

"At ease, Jensen, Faren, it's only me," she said, holding the bottom railing of the staircase's banister. The guards relaxed.

"We know, Carey. It's just habit," said Jensen who was standing to the left of the door. He was tall and broad-shouldered but with a kind face and bright eyes.

Faren, a shorter, slighter figure with sharp features and a shock of ash-grey hair, agreed. "Yes, habit. Not all Council members are as lax as you, Miss Carey."

Carey's mouth twitched at the edges. She had managed to persuade most of the guards, as well as the castle staff, to forego using her formal title and standing at attention when she would appear. Some Council members frowned upon this, but Carey cared very little for keeping the castle hierarchy defined. She didn't need to satisfy her ego by having people grovel at her feet.

Carey shifted impatiently, watching the courtyard beyond the entrance. Kat and Ji had not yet joined her — she hoped they would finish their spar soon. Those two would go for hours if Sir Garrow let them.

A call echoed from the castle walls; the herald announcing an arrival. As Carey squinted, a small group of people appeared at the castle gates

16

and began to cross the courtyard. The shortest of the lot was hooded and cloaked, but Carey knew it had to be Seramina. Robert Lee, Carey's father, was walking protectively by her side. Carey didn't move, waiting and watching as the convoy crossed the threshold. As soon as they were within the confines of the castle, the shrouded figure threw back her hood to reveal a head of bright red hair and a wide grin.

"Carey!" Seramina cried as she ran across the marble floor.

She flung her arms around Carey's neck and hugged tightly. Carey grinned as she returned the sentiment.

"I'm so glad you're safe," she said as Seramina pulled away.

The young girl looked vastly better than Carey remembered. The cuts and bruises had since healed, and the only evidence of her torture were a few small white scars on her face and arms.

Her hair had grown slightly too; it was now a short bob, still as bright as ever, a luminous red against her pale skin. Most importantly though, was her presence. Carey could feel something different about Seramina. Apart from the fact that she was no longer terrified, there was something deeper. It was like the hum that filled Carey's fingertips when she summoned her magic, but constant. Seramina was surrounded by it.

Seramina grinned. "I'm so happy to see you again. I was so scared. When those Imperials came for the Councillor, I was so sure they would find me too, so I ran. I didn't know where to go until I found Anoueshka. I was so glad when she said she knew you, and your magic worked perfectly," Seramina babbled happily. "And then your mother and father came. I didn't ever think that would happen. I heard about the Empire's fall, but I didn't know what that meant. I didn't know if you and Kat and Ji were all right. But Anoueshka said you'd be fine. I couldn't help believing her; she was always so nice. Where are Kat and Ji? Are they here too?" She searched the hall but they had not yet appeared.

"Don't worry, they're coming," Carey assured her, "but just be careful with Ji. He's changed since you last saw him."

Seramina's brow creased. "Changed? What happened?"

Carey shook her head, cursing herself for saying anything. "It's nothing.

17

We'll explain later. We're just happy to have you here."

Seramina nodded. Her eyes moved past Carey's shoulder and her face broke with excitement. "Kat!"

Seramina rushed past Carey and up the stairs to where Kat and Ji had just entered. Jenny left them and came down to where Carey stood. Robert, pulling his cloak from his shoulders and running a weary hand through his short, light hair, embraced his daughter as she welcomed him back.

"She seems happy," Carey's mother commented, watching the young witch as she chattered excitedly with Kat.

"Yes, she does, considering," Carey agreed, pulling away from her father. "She'll be staying in the castle, won't she?"

Robert smiled. "Of course she will. Did you really think we'd allow otherwise?"

Carey didn't answer; she still felt very protective of the young girl, despite their short history. "Well then, I expect Kyna will be happy. She keeps moaning about not having any friends her age in the castle," she said, referring to Rupert, the Head Healer's younger sister.

Jenny and Robert laughed, and they watched as Kat re-introduced Seramina to Ji. A waiting servant hurried over to them, taking cloaks and other travelling things from the Emperor. Robert thanked the man, his voice warm and grateful, sending him off with the request for a warm bath to be drawn in his quarters.

"Now, we're having a formal dinner tonight with the Council. Everyone is going to be there. I trust you'll be able to find something suitable to wear?" Jenny said with a sly smile.

Carey rolled her eyes, knowing full-well that her mother was teasing her. "Very funny. Yes. I'm sure I can find something. Is it for Seramina?"

"Partly. It's also for an old friend. He was an advisor to your grandmother back when you were young. After her death, though, he went into hiding with his family. He was a targeted man, so we did not begrudge him for that. His son was very young so we understood his compulsion," said Robert.

Seramina, who was obviously not held back by the fact that Ji could not remember her, was now babbling away about her time with Anoueshka.

"So, he'll be returning with his family?" asked Carey as she watched the bubbly redhead.

At first neither Jenny nor Robert answered, causing Carey to look away from Seramina and turn to her parents. Both had stopped smiling now, a hint of sadness in their eyes. Carey's smile slid from her face.

"They're not coming..."

Jenny shook her head. "The hidden city where they were hiding was attacked by Essedarian. His wife and son did not escape."

It was an all too familiar story and the usual feelings of despair bubbled in her stomach, though now only bitterness seemed to penetrate through to the surface now.

"What's his name?" Carey asked, fighting to hide the edge to her voice.

Jenny's eyes flicked searchingly over Carey's face, narrowing slightly.

"His name is Lord Acheron. Kat and Ji would remember him from when you were younger. He is one of our oldest friends and we're so grateful he is coming back to us." She placed a gentle hand on her daughter's shoulder. "Darling, is everything all right? When I caught you before you looked... frustrated."

Carey could tell her mother was being kind with her description. She thought of a number of things that she would like to say to her mother, to earn her comfort and wisdom, but she shook her head.

"No, I'm fine. Just thinking about training — Ji nearly beat me, so I was just going over my strategies," Carey lied effortlessly, surprised at how easily it came to her. Then again, she should have expected it after weeks of feigning emotional sanity.

Her mother didn't seem convinced, but she didn't push, and Carey was grateful. Her parents were particularly liberal, which suited her just fine.

"You had better go prepare for dinner then. It will be starting at seven, so that should give you plenty of time to locate your shoes," Jenny teased.

Robert had started up the stairs and Carey saw him grin at her mother's words as he turned away from her.

"Thanks," she said with a huff of exasperation. It wasn't her fault she could never remember where she put her shoes.

Jenny clapped her hands together. "Seramina! Come — we have a banquet to dress you for," she called, holding out her hand for the young girl. Seramina gasped in excitement.

"A banquet? What am I going to wear? Will Carey and Kat and Ji be there too?" she gushed as she joined the Empress.

"Of course they will. Now come with me, we shall see what the seamstress has waiting for you. I'll see you in the banquet hall," Jenny said to Carey over her shoulder.

She led Seramina down the corridor to the right at the top of the staircase, Seramina's excited voice echoing back to them. Carey couldn't help smiling.

"Banquet, hey?" Ji said, he and Kat coming down to stand with her. "Think you've got enough time?"

With a cry of disbelief Carey threw her hands over her head and stormed back up the staircase, Kat and Ji's laughter following her.

*

"I'm impressed. Dressed, with shoes *and* on time. I'll have to make a note of this," Kat commented, eyeing Carey with a hint of a smile as she entered the banquet hall.

Carey had decided on a dark blue velvet dress with sheer sleeves that draped from her elbows right down to the floor. A belt of pearls and crystals sat about her hips, the ends folding over at the front and running down the length of her skirt. At her hip hung a short dagger, ceremonial in its appearance with its gold hilt and sapphire settings, but its edge was sharp beneath its sheath.

She gave Kat a withering look, though casually admiring the floor length green silk number she was wearing; beautiful gold embroidery weaving its way across Kat's chest and down the right side of her skirts.

Drawing her eyes away from the tiny gold-stitched birds at Kat's hip, Carey straightened the circlet on her head unnecessarily. It was worked into her honey brown tresses, the majority of her hair swept over the back of the tiara in an elegant twist. "I really wish I didn't have to wear this thing on my head, though. It drives me mad."

"What, your *crown*?" Ji smirked, interpreting her point of frustration correctly as he came to stand at her other side. "Well, you will be a princess." He was wearing a smart dark suit with a tailcoat, a hint of a plum red vest peeking through at the waist. His collar was high and the cream shirt beneath was slightly ruffled.

"Yes, because I absolutely begged for it. I'd much prefer a title like yours and Kat's — *Keeper of the Realms*," Carey grunted in agitation. "At least it sounds less pretentious than *princess*."

Kat and Ji rolled their eyes.

"You're wearing that necklace, I see," Kat commented, nodding at Carey.

Carey put a hand to her throat, where the blood-red stone lay against her skin. She had swapped her Seeker necklace for the necklace she had found hidden beneath her bed, much to Kat's annoyance.

"We've studied it, Kat. It doesn't seem to do anything," Carey said defensively.

"Doesn't mean it won't, though," Kat interjected.

Carey dropped her hand in exasperation. "Seriously, you need to relax. You would think that if it did something it would've done it by now. I've tried everything on it so if it does do something special, it sure isn't doing it for me."

Kat grunted, unconvinced. "I don't know about that. Why did somebody hide it? People only hide what they don't want others to find. I think it's dangerous."

"Maybe it was just something special that this person wanted to hide. It doesn't have to possess magic to be worthy of being hidden, you know," Carey argued, crossing her arms.

Kat opened her mouth to retort but Ji interrupted. "All right, you two. We've already been over this. I don't like the thing any more than you, Kat, but if Carey wants to wear it…" he said in a low voice.

"But, Ji—"

"Just," he stopped Kat, "Just leave it. Besides, do you really think this is the time?"

Kat looked at the necklace; Carey could tell she wanted to say more. She was working her bottom lip between her teeth furiously, but after a moment of what seemed like intense internal debate, she turned away.

"Fine," Kat said, looking over the heads of the crowd gathering in the hall. "Then while we're waiting for dinner to begin, I'll go and speak to Sir Garrow about something. I didn't get to talk to him after our session today." And with a swish of her emerald green skirts, Kat left them behind in search of their Swords Master.

Ji *humphed* as Kat made her way across the room.

Carey turned to him. "Thank you. I can't believe—"

"Don't," he said shortly. "I might have stopped Kat from harping on about it, but that doesn't mean I approve. I just didn't think it was the time or place for another argument."

Carey felt her cheeks burn and she turned away, folding her arms again.

They stood in silence, Carey watching the other Council members mill about the hall as they waited for the guests of honour to arrive. Carey played with the necklace absently, annoyed with Kat and her incessant badgering with regards to it. Carey wasn't stupid enough to wear something dangerous; she had tested it thoroughly, trying everything and anything she could think of. To date, it had done nothing unusual or spectacular. The tiny, red swirling cloud within continued to churn, unchanged and seemingly oblivious to her efforts. The only conclusion she could come to was that it was a rare gem, for try as she did, she could not coax any magic from it. Carey thought Kat might have a little more faith in her.

Several Council members greeted her as they walked past. Lady Marksis, a particularly knowledgeable woman with a brilliant shock of short white hair and a penchant for speaking much too fast, stopped and spoke with her for some time. She had been a friend of her grandmother's long ago and always told the most interesting stories. Lord Carron, her brother with whom she shared a magical talent for trickery and deception, accompanied her. According to Kat, they eluded and infiltrated the Empire so many times that they had become almost legendary.

After Lady Marksis and Lord Carron had moved on and she had

acknowledged a few other Councillors, Ji cleared his throat loudly, breaking the silence between them. "I hear you'll be sitting next to Lord Acheron at dinner tonight," he said casually.

Carey whipped her head around so fast she heard her neck crack. "What? Why am I sitting next to him?" she asked, rubbing her neck.

Ji shrugged. "Hierarchy, I suppose. You're usually at the head of the table with your parents, then, I guess, the guests come next," he reasoned.

"But I don't even know this man. What am I supposed to talk about? I'm absolutely terrible with these sorts of things," She groaned at the inevitable awkwardness that would undoubtedly ensue. Ji laughed softly.

"Carey, there are about… twenty other Council members here. I'm sure Lord Acheron will find himself engaged in conversation with at least one other person besides yourself. I think you'll have little to worry about. Keep it to general topics — the Council, how well the Centre City is recovering. The weather…"

"The weather?" repeated Carey in disbelief.

"Exactly," said Ji, his teeth flashing as he grinned.

Carey bit her lip pensively. "My mother said you and Kat knew him back in the day. Do you remember much about him?"

Ji frowned in thought, his eyebrows knitting together and his lips pursing. "I don't remember too much about him. He was a very good friend of our parents. He was always around. Other than that, I can't say much more."

"Oh, come on, Ji! You must remember more than that. What was he like?" Carey asked, pleading for more information.

"I don't know, Carey, it's been more than a decade. I suppose he was nice, but seriously, I was too busy trying to play practical jokes on you and Kat to notice anything more. I was, after all, only about six-years-old or so. You can't expect too much."

Carey chewed her tongue in disappointment, unhappy with the lack of information.

"Ji!"

Kat's voice punctured the air so suddenly that Carey jumped in surprise. She could see Kat standing with Sir Garrow and Ji sighed.

"She wants me over there, doesn't she? I'll bet anything that she's trying to set up more training sessions. That girl never lets up. I'll be back soon, all right?" he said to Carey, lightly touching her arm before making his way over to where Kat stood impatiently.

Carey's watched him weave his way carefully across the room, hands alighting gently on elbows and shoulders as he navigated the crowd.

Suddenly, a head of red hair appeared at her shoulder; Seramina was beaming up at her.

"Hello Carey!"

Seramina was wearing a periwinkle blue dress with short, fluttery sleeves. Someone had put three small white flowers in her hair so that she looked positively angelic. She spun around, causing her skirt to flare out from her ankles.

"Isn't it pretty? Do you like it?" she asked Carey happily.

Smiling, Carey nodded. "It's very pretty. It looks good on you."

"Kyna helped me get dressed. I like her. She's funny."

As Carey watched Seramina smooth her gown tenderly, she felt glad that her premonition of their friendship was coming true. Seramina needed a friend.

"Carey? I wanted to say thank you," Seramina said quietly.

Carey turned to her. "Thank you for what?"

"For… for saving me. It was a trap, you know. The burning. They wanted you to come and I… I couldn't do anything…" Seramina said, and Carey could see this was difficult for her.

"Seramina, you don't have to—"

"No," Seramina exclaimed softly. "I want to. You could have been caught! *They* could have caught you and then, just think… But you came. You still came and you saved me. I… I just wanted to say thank you."

Seramina fidgeted uncomfortably; Carey couldn't even begin to imagine the memories this gesture was dredging up.

"You shouldn't be thanking us, Seramina. It didn't matter that it was a trap. We weren't going to let you die for something that wasn't your doing," said Carey, trying to ignore the guilt that clawed at her chest.

She couldn't bear to accept Seramina's thanks, knowing that it was her very existence that had led to the death of Seramina's family. Seramina's family, who had been mistaken for members of the Order and the Patronis, who had sheltered her from the Empire and paid the ultimate price because of it... How many countless others had suffered because of them... because of her? It was a startling trend that Carey was all too eager to put a stop to, and she knew she could never do enough to atone for what had happened.

"You still saved me," Seramina answered quietly. "And I don't blame you, not at all."

Carey ignored the burning in her throat and forced a smile. "I appreciate that," she accepted, knowing she would be less inclined to forgive herself that easily.

There was a lull in their conversation and Seramina picked idly at some embroidery on her skirt as Carey watched, just as preoccupied — something her mother said sprung to mind.

"Seramina, before your arrival, my mother told me how they found you. She said you heard them through the crowds, that you knew who they were before you even saw them. Could you do this before?"

At her words, Seramina seemed to regain the fervour with which she had entered.

"I couldn't, no! At least, not on purpose. My father was trying to teach me but I could only ever manage talking with those around me who were also telepaths. My family was like me, so I could talk with them, but anyone else..." she shook her head. "But now, I can hear and talk with anyone!" she said with a mixture of excitement and incredulity at her new power.

"Really? Can you hear *everything* other people are thinking?" Carey asked, less out of curiosity and more out of fear for what Seramina might overhear.

Seramina pouted in thought. "At first, no. It was slow — it didn't happen all at once. In the beginning, I thought I was hearing everything, but then I realised it was just when people were thinking directly about me. They would look at me and so I would hear what they thought. Words and emotions, all together. I'd never been able to feel emotions before..."

"Is that still telepathy, if you're feeling another's emotions?" Carey asked.

25

Seramina bit her lower lip in thought. "I don't know. Anoueshka used the word *empath* when I described it to her."

"So, you're an empath as well as a telepath now?"

Seramina's brows knotted together and her lips came together in a small pout. "An empath *and* a telepath... I suppose..."

"Tell me what you hear," Carey prompted gently.

Seramina paused momentarily before answering carefully. "I can... *hear* words if that is what someone is thinking. I can also *feel* what they're feeling in that moment. It's almost as though their emotions are being transferred to me. Or pictures, what the other person is seeing. Unless someone is actually thinking my name, I just sort of *feel* that they are thinking about me. If someone were to think actual sentences, then I would hear that because we don't always think words, you know? This is so hard to explain... *You* understand though, right, Carey?" she asked hopefully.

Carey smiled at her reassuringly. "I think so, even if it is... unusual. I've never heard of this before, although, I wouldn't put too much stance in that. There is a lot I haven't heard of. Maybe... maybe you're just getting stronger. Or maybe this is something special that only you can do."

Seramina's eyes popped. "You think so? You think I have a special power?"

Carey looked into her eyes. *"Seramina? Can you hear this?"* she thought, testing her.

She grinned as she heard Seramina's voice ring clearly through her mind. *"Yes! I can hear you! Does this mean I'm special?"*

Laughing out loud, Carey took Seramina's hand and squeezed it gently. The same tingling buzz she had felt before floated up her arm, and Carey quickly released her, surprised by the sudden surge of power. Seramina's laughter died away and she looked down at her dropped hand, her forehead creasing as Carey gazed at her with a mixture of puzzlement and surprise.

"Is something wrong, Carey?" she said quietly, and Carey jumped as she realised Seramina had felt her astonishment. But before she could say anything, an announcement rang through the hall, heralding Lord Acheron's arrival.

Distracted, Carey and Seramina turned their attention, along with everyone else, to the entrance. They watched as Carey's mother entered, arm linked with a tall bronze-haired man obscured by the crowd. Carey pursed her lips, let out a long-suffering sigh, and straightened her crown.

"Excuse me, Seramina. I have to go meet our other guest," she said.

Seramina promised to find her again later, then wandered off happily to find someone else to talk with.

Carey wished she didn't have to leave Seramina's company; it was far more preferable to having to converse with a complete stranger for the evening. But if she had to be a princess tonight, then she might as well meet it head-on.

~Chapter Three~

Nightmares

"Carey dear, I'd like to introduce Lord Acheron," Jenny Lee said happily as they came to where Carey and Seramina stood.

Lord Acheron was a rather handsome gentleman, and although he would have been older than her parents, his face was smooth, and his light brown eyes twinkled merrily in the candlelight. He was wearing a long, almost floor-length coat-jacket, its high collar turned up against his throat; a bright silver cravat was knotted there, tucked neatly into a dark vest. His bronze-brown hair was pulled back, neatly tied with a velvet ribbon, and his mouth was lit with a good-mannered smile.

Carey stepped forward to meet the man and Lord Acheron smiled graciously, sweeping into a deep bow, his voice as soft as velvet.

"Your Highness. It is a pleasure to finally meet you," he said cordially.

Trying to remember her lessons in court etiquette, Carey dipped her head slightly and replied, "And you, Lord Acheron."

"I believe I have the honour of sitting next to you at dinner this evening, Your Highness. I can only hope that my company will be satisfactory," Lord Acheron added, still smiling gently.

"I suppose we shall see soon enough," Carey answered obligingly.

There was something familiar in the way his smile reached his eyes, something she couldn't quite place, and she supposed he didn't seem the worst of dinner guests.

He bowed his head again before following the Empress for more introductions.

Carey's eyes followed the man as he made his way through the crowd, thinking on what her mother had told her about his past; another broken soul from the fight. She wondered what he had done for the Order in the past and whether he would be taking up his role again.

Lost in thought, it took her a moment to realise that dinner had been called. The Kitchen Head was standing regally by the door, gesturing for the crowd. There was a general shuffling and polite fuss as everyone took their seats at the long, decorated table in the middle of the room. Lord Acheron was already seated in the chair by hers, his bright eyes surveying the room about him. He smiled warmly as she took her place beside him, but they were distracted from any conversation as doors swung open at the side of the hall. Platter after platter of mouth-watering food flowed through from the kitchens. With a single sweeping movement, the waiters placed the gleaming trays on the table. Racks of meat steamed on silver platters, garnished with vegetables of every colour. Freshly baked seeded rolls, and tureens of gravies were spread amongst them, their delicious aromas wafting through the air. Elaborately cut cheeses and fruits were displayed alongside, all of which made Carey's mouth water. Once the waiters had retreated back into the kitchen, Carey's father, Robert Lee, pushed back his chair and rose to his feet, a glass in his hand. His bright brown eyes glittered with happiness as he spoke:

"Ladies and gentlemen of the Council. Tonight, we welcome back a dear friend and valued ally. In the months since the Empire's defeat we have sought to rebuild the Council as we knew it before the dark rule. It has not been an easy task — we ask much of you all, many of you have already suffered terribly at the hands of the Empire. We are forever grateful that you are willing to place yourselves, once more, in the way of danger, forsaking your own freedom for the greater ideal.

"Lord Acheron, a former advisor to her ladyship, Fianna Parnell, has returned to us. He was an invaluable member of the original Order, and we are glad to have his service once more. As part of the council, he will be instated as our High Chancellor, our most trusted advisory position of which we are truly grateful. His expertise and knowledge will serve us well.

"What's more, we are joined by Seramina Jessup, a young lady to whom we are indebted to for her courage and bravery in the face of Imperial oppression. Miss Jessup is now a permanent guest of the Council's; a courtesy we hope she will take full advantage of."

Carey glanced down at where Seramina was sitting between Kat and another Council member, and saw tears glistening in her bright eyes, her face alight with joy.

"Now, I would like you all to charge your glasses in honour of these two wonderful people. You have our gratitude." Robert Lee lifted his glass. "To Lord Acheron and Seramina."

"Lord Acheron and Seramina," the room echoed as glasses were lifted into the air, Carey joining in.

"Now," her father continued, "I am sure you are all sorely tempted by this wonderful feast so I shall not keep you from it any longer. Please, enjoy."

At his invitation, the table was suddenly alive with a flurry of movement as people reached for the heavily laden platters of delicious food. Carey was busy filling her plate, when Lord Acheron's voice came from her left.

"It has been quite some time since I've seen a banquet such as this," he said, admiring the food as he filled his own platter.

"Oh?" Carey replied, taking up a fork. "Where were you before this?"

Lord Acheron looked at her for a moment, gently placing his plate back down in front of him. "I was in one of the hidden cities to the north, Your Highness."

She knew of these cities, hidden throughout this realm and the Common one. They were the homes of witches and wizards seeking to escape the tyranny of the Empire during Malevolence's rule.

"I've heard of the cities. Will you be staying here in the castle, then, now that you're here?"

She wasn't sure what the protocol was for a High Chancellor, but she supposed being her parent's advisor meant he was required to stay close. He nodded, taking a bite of food. Swallowing, he said, "I have been given quarters here, yes. It was most generous of your parents and the Council to allow me to return to the Order, given my time away."

"My mother said you served under my grandmother. Is that true?" Carey asked, after thinking how young he looked to have served so long ago.

"I did, Your Highness," he said, picking up a bun and tearing it in half. "I knew your grandmother for a time."

Carey took a bite of a vegetable and chewed it slowly. "Sorry, but you don't exactly look old enough to have served with her," she said, hoping she didn't sound rude.

Acheron laughed. "Thank you, Your Highness. I shall take that as a compliment." He took another mouthful of food. "No, I suppose I don't, do I?"

Watching him with slightly narrowed eyes, Carey didn't say anything, and he carried on. "It is a kind of power I have, ageing slowly."

This was not what she'd been expecting, and Carey choked a little on the drink she'd been sipping at. "Well… that seems quite the power," was all she could say, feeling a flush rise in her cheeks as he smiled jovially.

"Yes, I suppose it is."

Carey and Lord Acheron conversed easily for the rest of the meal; the ice now thoroughly broken with that revelation. She found him easy to speak with; quiet and unassuming as he shared stories of his life within the confines of a hidden city. He didn't speak of his family, but Carey noticed a sadness at times, as though the memory came too close to something raw.

Taking advantage of a lull in their conversation to try a particularly delectable cheese in front of her, she saw Lord Acheron's gaze shift to her throat.

"That's a curious pendant you have there, Your Highness. Quite unique."

Carey looked down at the red stone around her neck. "Really?"

"Indeed. I've never seen one quite so unusual," Acheron answered, looking hard at the gem. "Can I ask where you got it from?"

"Oh, I…" Carey's hand clenched the stone. "I found it, here in the castle."

His eyebrows pinched in the centre. "Do you know what it is?" he said, looking up now, and Carey shook her head.

"No. I've not been able to find that out."

His lips rose at the edges, and Carey knew that look — excitement at the challenge. It was one of Kat's more familiar emotions. "I have some books that might shed some light on it, if you wanted to take a look?" he suggested.

Before Carey could answer, her father interjected from where he sat at the head of the table. "Lord Acheron! How are you faring this evening? I see you two are getting along famously."

"Yes, Princess Carey has been wonderful company, Your Majesty. I could not have asked for a more wonderful host," Lord Acheron replied genuinely, flashing Carey a warm smile. "I was hoping she would escort me after dinner, so we could talk some more?"

Robert looked to his daughter. "Carey?"

She turned to Lord Acheron and smiled back. "Of course I will."

As the members of the Council began to rise from the table, the Kitchen Head reappeared, and with a sweeping gesture, the remaining food and the large round platters vanished from the table in a haze of magic. Carey glanced over at Kat and Ji, but they had already risen from the table. She could see them across the room, standing against a polished wooden sideboard, listening as Seramina chatted animatedly. Lord Acheron was already on his feet; he held out his hand for Carey to take.

Leading her out to the balcony beyond the hall, Lord Acheron came to stand at the edge, the countryside beyond the city bathed in light from the star strewn indigo sky. He released Carey's hand and leant against the balustrade, gazing out into the night.

"It truly is wonderful to be back here again," he said, his voice low. "I didn't think I'd ever see the Centre City restored." His gaze flickered back to Carey. "I hear you're largely to thank for that."

Carey pursed her lips, turning her gaze from his. "It wasn't just me. If I hadn't had my friends with me…"

Lord Acheron clicked his tongue with a smile. "Oh, but you're being too modest. Your parents told me all about what happened. You have some magic."

She wasn't sure she wanted to talk with Lord Acheron regarding what happened with Malevolence. He appeared genuinely interested, but despite the ease in which they seemed to get along, she still didn't really know him.

What had happened that night, and the magic she had commanded, was still a mystery even to her, so it was unlikely she'd be willing to tell it all to someone she had only just met.

Carey looked back at Lord Acheron, who was waiting patiently for her to answer. "Honestly, I don't really know what happened that night," she said finally. "All I know is that I have some kind of special power, though don't ask me what it is exactly. I don't have the answer to that."

It wasn't exactly a lie; the magic she spoke of was indeed something unusual, but more than that, she knew it wasn't hers. It was foreign, like she was simply a carrier for whatever lay within her. She could wield it — oh yes, she could definitely wield it — but there were times where it almost wielded her in return. There were those moments where she felt it surface, reacting of its own volition to whatever threat she was faced with. The idea of a sentient power that she could not completely control terrified her, and if it scared her so, then how would others react? No. She would not reveal that particular piece of information to someone she barely knew.

Lord Acheron considered her with those brown eyes of his, the light from castle windows dancing in them.

"Well, whatever it is, I am most certainly glad you have it," he said, turning back to look out from the castle. "I have some knowledge in the realm of unusual magics. If, one day, you feel like talking about it in earnest, my door is always open."

Carey wasn't sure how to take this, but she nodded regardless. Lord Acheron seemed genuine in his concern, and perhaps she would take him up on his offer.

If she wanted to talk about it.

~Chapter Four~

Translated

C arey peered through the darkness; she was lying in bed, having gone to sleep weary from the banquet earlier that evening.

But something had woken her, something that was moving just beyond her field of vision. She blinked, willing her eyes to adjust.

"Good evening, Your Highness."

The sound of that voice sent a wave of shivers up her spine and Carey sat bolt upright in her bed. She stared into the darkness, the shadows that gathered beyond the moonlight, her chest constricting with each breath she took. She had not heard that voice in months, yet it haunted her each time she closed her eyes.

"No..." she breathed, hoping it was just her imagination, but a sneering voice answered her unspoken fear.

"Yes."

Carey leapt from her bed as Saar emerged from the dark into the pale light, robed in a deep, blood-red coat that ended at the top of shining black boots. His hair fell in loose dark waves, framing his face, and his eyes gleamed silver through the gloom.

"It's been some time, Princess," he purred, eyes fixed on her face.

Fists balled, Carey lifted her chin, refusing to be intimidated by him, despite her heart flying against her ribs. "Not long enough, clearly."

Saar's lips lifted at the corners, the familiar smirk rising on his face. "Come now. That's no way to greet an old friend."

Carey spluttered with outrage. "Friend? You're nothing more than a murderer clinging to the past."

Her words flew at him with venom, but Saar merely raised an eyebrow, clearly

34

enjoying the effect he was having on her. "Of course I am," he said, inclining his head to one side. "But at least I accept it."

"And what is that supposed to mean?" Carey snapped, but her pulse stuttered at the implication.

He knew she had magic; power that had made her the Liberator, but surely, he did not know how she loathed it, refused to recognise it as her own. But there was something in his eyes, those terrible, unnatural eyes that had her doubting his ignorance...

Mouth slanting into a knowing leer, Saar brought his hands together, fingertips steepled in thought as they pressed against his lips.

"You really have no idea what you can do," he said slyly.

Carey bristled, her teeth grit together as she hissed, "I know well enough."

"But you won't believe me when I say that you can do so much more. You think I'm lying, when really, that couldn't be farther from the truth," Saar said, a little more emphatically than usual, his hands flying out, gesturing about them as though to encompass their surroundings in his point.

A derisive laugh left Carey's mouth before she could stop it. "As though I would ever believe a word you say."

"Really?" Saar replied, his tone quieter now. "What if I spoke it like this?"

Eyes widening, Carey watched as he ran his hands over his face. As they passed over his features, he wiped away his own, revealing large eyes and dark lashes. His fingers raked at his black hair, lengthening it until it rippled down his back in soft waves. His waist thinned and hips widened until Carey no longer saw Saar before him, but Kat. He had shapeshifted into her best friend, only not. His steel-grey eyes still shone through where Kat's green ones should have been.

She felt bile rise in her throat. She knew what shapeshifters were capable of — her whole life has been affected by one — but she still found it profoundly unsettling, seeing someone she absolutely loathed steal the form of one of her beloved friends.

Kat's lip peeled back into a sneer, an expression Carey had never seen on her face.

"Would you believe me now?" Saar's voice came through in Kat's soft tones. "Believe me if it was Miss Lawrence speaking those words?

35

"Or... perhaps you would believe me more if I looked like this...?"

Again, he covered his face with Kat's long, thin fingers, and this time as they dragged down towards his chin, his jaw widened, and cheekbones grew sharper. The black waves shrank back into his head and lightened to a ruffled brown. His shoulders grew broader and his hips narrowed, and Carey staggered back, heat prickling her neck and cheeks as Ji appeared before her. He took a few steps in her direction, slow and confident, and it was all Carey could do to stop herself crying out for him to stop.

"I knew you'd appreciate this one," came Ji's voice, the one she adored, now spiked with malice.

He stared down at her with those eyes of molten steel. "Oh, but perhaps this wouldn't be the most trustworthy... I must say, young Master Schultz did a spectacular job, wouldn't you agree, Princess?"

Those last sibilant sounds sent tremors down her spine and she spat back, "Stop it. Stop it right now."

But he was clearly having too much fun tormenting her, stepping closer as he continued: "Terrible end, I must say. You must have been devastated, given your... history."

Carey's breath caught in her throat at his words. "How do you know what happened to Jeremy?" she choked.

Jeremy's fate had not been made known to anyone outside the castle. Magical restraints had been made in that respect, so how could he know? How could he have this knowledge without knowing someone within the castle?

He didn't answer, but his eyes said it all.

Blood on the walls. Last words. They hadn't been Jeremy's. They'd been his.

"You had him killed," Carey managed to say, the words cutting like razor blades.

His eyebrow twitched, his eyes gleamed. "Such an accusation. But who's to know what truly happened to the young master," he said silkily in a way that conveyed he knew exactly what happened.

Carey stared him in the eyes, refusing to withdraw from his icy gaze. Nausea, which had so far been contained to her stomach, was creeping up her throat now, and she clutched at the front of her night dress as it swirled into her head. Her legs felt weak and with a sudden jerk, she slipped and fell to her knees.

He had killed Jeremy, whether by his own hand or that of another, there was no doubt. It was written in those merciless eyes — blood, and pain, and death. How had she not considered this before? Worse than that, how did he do it?. Had an assassin entered the castle, unnoticed, to murder Jeremy? Or had he himself shapeshifted in order to gain entry? Both were equally horrific possibilities, and the thought sent a wave of dizziness rolling about inside her.

Forcing herself to look up into the false face of Ji, Carey grit her teeth and fought back against the vertigo threatening to drag her down. Saar changed back into himself, a long finger tracing his bottom lip in thought. Slowly, he crouched down in front of her, drawing level with her face. Carey resisted the urge to pull back farther, her breath ragged as she tried to regain control over herself.

"You waste your time, Princess," he said finally, his burnished eyes trained greedily upon her. "All of this nonsense, it's such a waste."

Frowning at this, Carey took a deep breath before answering: "I'm afraid you've lost me."

He paused, continuing to run his finger along his lip pensively.

"You have a rare gift, Princess," he said quietly, dangerously. "Such... raw power. But you squander it, waste it learning tricks with a sword and learning the dominions under your reign. You sit in that castle, holed away with your little friends when you could be so much more. You should be out in the world, using your powers the way they were meant to be used, not stuck in some city acting lapdog to your parents. You could be great, greater than Benjamin Merilius, maybe even greater than the Empress herself, yet..."

He trailed off but his eyes never left hers.

"What are you saying?" whispered Carey, sure she knew the answer.

"I am giving you the same chance I gave you before. Forget this city. Forget being a Seeker — all you're ever going to achieve as one is a life of death. Come with me and discover everything you were meant for. I offer an alliance, and in return, I am offering you everything you ever wanted."

Carey's pulse quickened. She stumbled back to her feet, drawing herself up to her full height. "You don't know what I want," she choked, anger mixing with something less defined yet equally as limiting on her ability to breathe. "You have no idea."

Saar stood up to meet her, his eyes narrowed, and his thin lips pressed together in a menacing sneer. He stepped closer, leaning inwards as he did so, but Carey held her ground. "Oh, but I do. I know your deepest, darkest desires. I've been inside your mind and I know what you crave," he whispered, circling her now until he stood right behind her.

He placed a cold hand on her shoulder and Carey took a deep steadying breath, reminding herself that he could not hurt her here.

"You want your sisters back for one," he murmured, his breath raising goose bumps on her skin. "You want your past, your memories, your childhood.

"And you want Ji back, or at least, what you thought you had with him."

The sardonic emphasis of those last few words struck a chord and Carey turned sharply, breaking away from him.

"You dare mention that. You could never bring back anything I have lost, never, and I will not ally myself with dark forces in order to better my chances. You were mistaken if you believed you could persuade me otherwise. I do not care about what power I may possess; my answer remains the same as before, Saar. I am a Seeker, and I remain loyal to the Order. I will continue to fight you and people just like you. I will not join you as a traitor, ever," Carey said forcefully and finally.

Saar's expression darkened now. "Then you are a fool. Squander your gifts on frivolous endeavours then... but know this — I gave you a chance," he said venomously, drawing back away from her now.

He crossed his arms in front of him and drew them sharply back down to his sides. Carey gasped as the surroundings faded to black, blown away like smoke on the wind.

Carey woke staring at the underside of her bed's dark green canopy. She was back in her room, back in her own bed, the soft down of her night clothes bunched up around her. The moonlight sifted through the gossamer curtains fluttering gently in the warm night breeze, and she lay there, listening to her heart thud frantically against her ribs. Her mind was racing, a million thoughts and emotions jostling for attention, but as her breathing slowed and her heart settled back into place, there was one thing that troubled her above all.

Saar had given her a chance to join him, but a chance to do what exactly?

*

"Let me get this straight," Kat said, her voice throbbing with restrained anger. "You have had an Imperial loyalist — and not any loyalist, mind you, a *madman* — in your head, and you're only *now* deciding to say anything?"

Carey was sitting in an armchair by Ji's fireplace, her elbows propped on her knees and her head in her hands. She had not slept at all after Saar's intrusion, and spent the remainder of the night trying hard to imagine what he might be planning. Exhausted, she had decided that she needed to tell her friends about the Imperial. She could no longer justify keeping it to herself, especially if he was having assassins sneak into the castle.

Having found her two friends in Ji's room, she sat them down and narrated each of her encounters with Saar. As she spoke, Kat's face paled, her brow darkening. Ji sat in silence, frown deepening with every word. When she had finished, there was a full minute where none of them spoke. Kat seemed livid, furious that she had kept something like this from them for so long, though it was Ji's reaction Carey minded most. As Kat raged, he remained quiet, his hazed stare fixed just over her shoulder.

"I am sorry," Carey repeated, drawing her gaze back up to meet Kat's. "I thought, since I hadn't heard anything from him in so long, there wasn't anything to say. But now—"

"Now there's the possibility that he's actually been in the castle," Kat cut across her, leaning on the mantel of the fireplace, rubbing her eyes.

Carey nodded disconsolately and Kat sighed heavily. "Fine. Fine." She seemed unable to say anything else at that moment and Carey turned to Ji. "Ji?"

He sat for a moment, still staring over her shoulder, then leant forward, running his hands slowly through his hair. "You say he's a shapeshifter."

The word pierced Carey's heart like a cold steel blade. "Yes," she managed to whisper.

"Like Jeremy."

It was a simple statement, but now that steel blade was twisting inside her. "Almost."

"Almost?"

"His eyes… they're silver. They were silver when he was that priest in Burtonport. They were silver last night when he shifted into you…" Carey's voice faded away.

Ji's brow pinched in the centre. "So, when he shapeshifts, his eyes don't change? That seems like an unfortunate trait for a shapeshifter."

"Yes, well, at least it gives us something to catch him with if he does attempt to get inside the castle disguised," Kat said heavily, still frowning. "You need to let your parents know, Carey, so our guards can be put on alert."

Carey had been afraid she'd suggest this, though in all honesty, it made perfect sense. If Saar was planning something, she couldn't just assume that he was far away doing so. There was every possibility he was inside the city walls. But his attacks against her, his summonings, they had all seemed so personal. Perhaps that was why she had not said anything before. She didn't want Saar thinking her weak by seeking out help in catching him, she wanted to do it herself. Or maybe it was exactly what he had wanted her to do; hide his intrusions from her family and friends to face him alone. After all, one target was easier to destroy than many.

Carey now realised how ridiculous that had been; Saar was clearly much stronger than her magically and given her inability to even resist his night-time summonings, she should have known she wouldn't be able to overpower him. She thought of what he'd said the night before, about her being stronger than even Malevolence… she shook her head in disbelief at her naivety.

"Of course. Let me tell them. I'll need to explain everything to them anyway," she sighed as Kat strode to the door and opened it.

"Ji," she said brusquely. "I'm going to get ready for training. I'll be back soon, and we can go down together."

As the door swung closed with a dull THUD, Carey turned back to face Ji and wilted. She expected him to berate her like Kat, tell her that she'd been a fool, but he merely rested his elbows on his knees and stared in her direction. His face was softer, sympathetic.

"Are you all right?"

His question startled her, and she swallowed. "I…" She didn't know what to say. How could she convey the fear she felt each time Saar came to her? The terror at being unable to break free from his hold?

He gave her a small smile, and she could feel the ice that had lodged itself in her chest slip slightly. "I wouldn't worry about Kat. I think it's more of a shock than anything. I just want to make sure you're all right, given everything."

His voice was soft, and undercurrents of warmth made her pulse race. But as she looked back at him, all she could see was silver eyes and smirking lips. Slowly, she got to her feet.

"I'll be fine," she lied. "I should really go speak to my parents before the day gets away from me. I'll find you and Kat after."

Pulling her gaze from Ji's, she turned and left, feeling much like she was fleeing his presence as she did.

*

Her parents had reacted much as Carey had expected them to — surprised and concerned, but ultimately understanding, far more so than Kat. They had understood her compulsion to keep it personal, though recognising the guilt she already felt, they refrained from admonishing her further. They set about organising a meeting with Oliver and Lord Acheron to see what needed to be done, asking Carey to provide any detail she could remember that she hadn't already recounted that might prove important. She combed through every conversation and every encounter she'd had with Saar, and when she'd finally exhausted her memory, her parents had given her leave with a caution to tell them immediately should Saar attempt to speak with her again.

She now found herself striding away from their quarters feeling lighter than she had felt in a long while. Until that moment, Carey hadn't realised how isolated Saar had made her, how he'd used her abilities against her to intimidate and coerce her. Now that everyone knew about him, though, she felt she'd been brought into the light, away from the darkness he'd created. She would not allow him to drag her back there again.

Looking out a window as she passed, she supposed Kat and Ji would still be in the training hall, but not wanting to sully her surprisingly good mood with Kat's surly one, she went searching for Rupert instead. The door to the healer's ward was propped open, and Carey entered quietly, looking around for their head healer. Bright sunlight filtered in through the stained-glass windows, casting bright shades upon the stone floors. The beds of the ward were unoccupied save for one, which was inhabited by Ji's older brother, Zacharia. He still hadn't awoken from whatever horrors had been inflicted upon him by the Empire, and Carey felt a pang of sorrow at the sight of his sleeping profile so like his brother's.

Rupert was standing by Zacharia's bedside, his back to the door, unaware of Carey's presence. His hair was a sickly shade of yellow this morning and it flopped over his brow as he scribbled something on the side of a bottle filled with a menacing ruby red liquid.

"I hope you're not going to make someone drink that," Carey smirked as she sidled up beside him, laughing as he jumped in surprise.

"Carey!" Rupert cried as he managed to catch the bottle, preventing it from smashing on the stone floor. "Fer the life o' me, girl, you'll gimme a heart attack one o' these days, an' then I'll be the one needin' healin.'"

Carey chuckled at his exaggeration as she looked back down at Zacharia. "How is he doing?"

"Abou' th' same really," he replied with a sigh. "Jus' when I think I might be on ter somethin'…"

Carey placed a consolatory hand on Rupert's shoulder. "You'll work something out. Aren't you supposed to be good at this kind of thing?" she said, and he snorted at her jibe.

"Oh, well, I try. By th' way, you should probably know tha' the Council's got a meeting planned fer tomorrow. Apparently, they're looking to send out more o' those groups to find renegade Imperials. I say that's probably exactly what those darned Imperials want," Rupert said as he finished his label on the bottle of red medicine.

"Now how is it you know about this and yet I, an *actual* member of the Council, am yet to be told of it?" Carey asked with feigned incredulity.

Rupert rolled his eyes. "Well, I do keep sayin' that they need to tighten their security."

Carey snorted. "Sure you do."

"Tha' said, if yer not doing anythin' right now I'll be joinin' Kyna and Seramina on a jaunt outside the walls. I think Kyna is gettin' a little stir crazy and needs some fresh air. Yer more than welcome to come," Rupert said as he stored the bottle in the medicine cupboard.

Rupert's invitation was extremely tempting. It had been a while since Carey had gone beyond the walls of the Centre City and the sunshine streaming through the stained-glass windows called to her.

"All right, I'll come. I could use some fresh air as well."

The sky above them was clear, a periwinkle blue without a hint of cloud as they stepped out into the courtyard. The sun shone so brightly that at first Carey had to squint to allow her eyes to adjust. Its warmth sank into her clothes and the cold that inhabited the castle vanished instantly. They set forth, and within no time they had passed the city gates and were met by the rolling green hills and wide fields of the shire. Carey perched herself atop a small knoll and watched as Rupert and Kyna teased each other; Kyna trying in vain to tackle her older brother to the ground. Despite his constantly shifting hair colour, and Kyna with her own long dark tresses, the siblings were remarkably similar, both with bright dark eyes and heart-shaped faces. A smattering of freckles dashed across the bridges of their noses, highlighted against their fair skin.

Seramina sat by her side, playing with a flower she had picked on the way. She twirled it between her fingers, the petals changing colour from pink to white to yellow. Carey couldn't help noticing the ease with which she wielded her magic; it was almost accidental.

With a flick of her wrist, Seramina sent the petals flying into the air, transforming them into tiny fluttering butterflies. She caught Carey

43

watching her and grinned.

"Aren't they pretty? I was always so terrible at controlling my magic; Alexander used to tease me so badly. You never would've guessed that I was the older one. But now, it's so easy!" she exclaimed, following her creations with her eyes. "Maybe it has something to do with being in this realm, but it just feels so simple now." Seramina looked up into Carey's eyes. "You're surprised."

Carey smiled, knowing it was not her expression that had given her away. "Could you do that before?" she asked, nodding at the butterflies as they drifted away on the breeze.

Seramina shook her head. "No. I was only really just starting to learn how to control it. Father was my teacher. He always said I was too easily distracted." She smiled sadly. "My mother used to make pretty things for me though. I always wanted to be able to do things like that."

Carey reached over and squeezed Seramina's hand in comfort. "I think you're doing fine."

Seramina beamed at Carey's compliment. "You really think so?"

Carey nodded, picking another flower and handing it to her. "Definitely."

"What's goin' on here?" Kyna asked as she plopped herself down on Seramina's other side, brushing her long black hair back from her face. "Are you doin' that trick again? You have ter show me how you do tha'!" she demanded as Seramina twirled the flower, the petals changing once more.

Rupert sat beside Carey, breathless from chasing his sister, and lightly punched Carey on the arm. "So, fancy a game?" he teased.

Carey raised her eyebrows. "Um, no, thank you. I think I might pass. Besides, what would the Council say if they knew I'd been rolling about with one of the castle's healers?"

Rupert laughed. "I think it'd be good fer you, an' bollocks to the Council!"

Carey laughed along with him, the sensation feeling quite alien to her body. She was glad she had come along with them; she found the sun and fresh air to be exactly what she needed.

"Oh, look at that!" Seramina exclaimed as a herd of great white horse-like creatures galloped into view. They were easily twice the size of an ordinary horse and their manes were long and silver, glinting in the sun.

"They're Sleipnir," Rupert told her as the two young girls gasped in excitement. "See how they have eight legs?"

Carey gazed in wonder at the magnificent creatures. As they watched, the Sleipnir turned in a great arc, their bodies moving in perfect unison as they thundered across the green planes. Their strange forms felt so unfamiliar to Carey, so surreal. Since coming to this realm, she had tried learning all she could about it; she spoke to those who had lived here their entire lives; she'd read books and taken lessons with Lady Marksis. This realm was her birthright, but there was so much of it that still felt so foreign.

"Carey?"

Carey blinked, pulling her gaze away from the spectacle of the great white beasts. "Yes?"

Rupert was watching her, a small pout on his lips.

"What is it?" she asked, concerned by the intensity of his gaze.

"You feelin' all right?" he said, scrutinising her closely.

Carey was slightly taken aback. "Yes. I feel fine. Why?" she added as Rupert continued to look at her with his bright green eyes.

"Hmm. Nothin'. Just fer a moment there you looked a 'lil... lost," he said slowly. "Are yer sure there's nothin' wrong?"

Carey hesitated before shaking her head and rubbing her eyes. "Nothing at all. Just tired. I didn't get much sleep last night is all."

He squinted at her, as though he knew that was not all it was, but eventually he smiled. "All right then. I was jus' wonderin'. I mean, what kind o' healer would I be if I didna ask when someone was lookin' sickly?"

"You'd be rubbish, that's fer sure," Kyna interrupted, throwing her arms around her brother's neck and resting on his back. She ruffled his hair, and as her fingers ran through the thick strands, they changed to a violent shade of purple.

"Why thank you fer that vote o' confidence, missy," Rupert laughed, dragging his sister down to the ground and tickling her until she was gasping for air.

"Rupert! Stop — stop it!" she squealed as Seramina rolled on the ground in fits of laughter at the spectacle.

"Hey, Carey! What's that?" Kyna asked, looking at her upside down from the ground. She was pointing at the blood-red gem still hanging from Carey's neck.

Carey looked down to see the red-stone pendant she'd worn the night before; she had forgotten she was still wearing it. "This?" she asked, lifting it up to the sunlight. "It's just something I found. Nothing special."

"It's pretty," Seramina commented, looking at it closely. "Can I hold it?"

Carey glanced down at the necklace. "Sure. Why not," she said as she slipped it over her head and handed it to Seramina.

Seramina and Kyna examined it with many *oohs* and *aahs*.

"Is this th' same one Kat an' Ji are always on about?" Rupert asked, leaning over to see it as well.

"What? Have they been carrying on about it to you as well?" Carey cried, flushing in annoyance. "You have got to be kidding me."

Rupert shook his head with a small smile. "Not really. Kat's not particularly happy about it, but yer know how she is once she gets started."

Carey grunted, folding her arms across her chest and cursing her friend quietly.

"Do yer know what it says?" Kyna asked, squinting to read the minute writing on the clasp.

Carey shook her head. "No. I think it might be in Gadælic."

"It says, *Men dela fia, Fianna. Kali men afiri, Elara.* My dearest sister, Fianna. All my heart, Elara," Seramina said suddenly.

Stunned silence followed her words, causing Seramina to look up from the stone with surprise. "What?"

"Ah, where did that come from?" Carey asked, stunned.

Seramina squirmed self-consciously as the others continued to stare at her in disbelief. "I, uh, I can read it," was all the explanation she gave. She repeated the translation, looking up at Carey for approval. "Have I done something wrong?"

At her words, Rupert was shaken from his stupor. "Oh, no, of course not! It was just a surprise, is all."

Relief flickered across her face, but Carey could tell she had been affected by their reactions.

"Hold on," Carey said as she took back the necklace, Seramina's words only just sinking in. "You said *Fianna*. That was my grandmother's name."

Rupert nodded slowly, "Aye, it was too. Fianna Parnell."

Carey turned the stone over in her hands, the Gadælic glinting in the sunlight. "And you said *sister...*" she said to Seramina. "Did you know my grandmother had a sister?"

The others shook their heads. Carey frowned at the stone. Her grandmother had lived in the castle as a young girl so it could be hers, but Carey had never heard anyone speak of a sister. She had never heard her parents speak of one, that's for certain, and surely Kat and Ji would have said something.

"Perhaps this Elara wasn't her real sister. You know, like a close friend or somethin'," Rupert suggested.

Carey nodded slowly, but something was telling her that wasn't the case. "Perhaps. Or perhaps my grandmother really did have a sister, and something happened to her."

Turning the stone over in her hands, Carey frowned in consternation. Sister... *sister...*

A memory came rushing back to her. Silver eyes and a venomous tongue.

"Stubbornness killed your grandmother and it destroyed her sister because they both failed to accept the inevitable."

Saars words echoed back to her, half-forgotten in the back of her mind. He had spoken them to her after the Empire's defeat, after she'd fought against Malevolence, after she'd turned down his offer to join him again. Her hand shook, her pulse quickening as she stared down at the stone now. He knew. She closed her fingers around the pendant, tightly. Saar knew of Elara's fate. But how?

~Chapter Five~

Found

Walking back to the castle, Carey was quiet as she thought of the crystal that once again hung around her neck and the memory it had brought forth. She had imagined what the scrawl across the stone had said, pondered upon it at length. She had guessed a spell or even a family motto, but nothing could have prepared her for the truth.

It was not just the fact she had never heard of Elara, but that Saar had. What was more, he seemed to know what had become of her. Had she been an Imperial like him, or just one of their many unfortunate victims? The thought sent a chill through her and her hand drifted to where the stone sat at her throat.

"I need to find my parents," she said without further explanation as Carey left the group at the front hall and sprinted up the stairs. Perhaps they could shed some light on who Elara Parnell had been.

She headed for the Council meeting hall. Her parents could generally be found in one of the main chambers, conducting business important to the realm. She would just wait until they were done and then ask them outright who Elara had been and whether they knew anything about her.

Carey pushed opened the heavy door to the meeting hall. The Council was assembled but they were not seated at the table in their usual manner. The room was quieter than usual, and the bright sunlight drifting through the high-set windows was met with a far sombre atmosphere than she expected.

Something was wrong.

She spotted her mother sitting at the head of the table; her head was in her hands and her body shuddered. She was crying. Her father was trying to comfort her, although he seemed to be struggling himself, a grave expression across his taut face. The other Council members spoke quietly amongst themselves. A few looked up as she entered, and any thought of the necklace and Elara Parnell flew from her mind.

Kat and Ji were leaning against the wall to her right, talking in low voices with Kat's father. Carey drifted slowly over to them, her eyes on her parents.

"Ji," she whispered, unable to tear her gaze from her mother. "What's happened? Why is my mother crying?"

"A search party has just returned," Ji told her in a low voice. "They found something."

Dread rippled through her body and settled deep within her stomach.

"What? What did they find?" Carey asked slowly, watching as her mother broke down audibly. She was holding something in her hand that Carey couldn't quite see.

Ji paused for a moment and she noticed his hesitation. "What is it?" Carey asked again more urgently.

"You might want to sit down," Ji suggested but Carey shook her head. The dread was growing now, threatening to overwhelm her.

"No, Ji. Just tell me what they found," Carey demanded.

Ji nodded, hearing the distress in her voice. "They... found your sisters," he said without any further preamble.

"What?" Carey asked, confusion dipping her brow. "They *found* them. What do you mean? If they found them..."

And then she understood. She understood why her mother was crying and why her father looked close to breaking down himself.

"They were found in a mass grave, just on the border to the Darklands," Ji whispered, his hand finding hers and squeezing it.

Carey gripped it tightly without even thinking; her mind was reeling, tipping her sideways like the storm-washed deck of a ship. She struggled to comprehend his words; the sheer gravity of them and what they meant to her.

"How... how did they know it was them?" she asked Ji in barely a whisper.

"Their Seeker necklaces. They were found with their bodies," Ji answered simply.

Carey whipped her head around, this small detail bringing her crashing back. "Their necklaces? But... Jody and Laurel betrayed us, turned their backs on the Order. Why would they have their necklaces on them? Were they wearing them?"

Ji shook his head. "No. They were holding them, and the grave was filled with bodies of other rebels, others who had tried to fight the Empire. They were all wearing those metal clasps around their necks, probably to prevent them from escaping."

Carey looked over at her mother. She did not know how to react. She thought her sisters had been close to Malevolence. Why then had they been found in such a state, executed alongside enemies of the Empire? She had barely any memory of her sisters, and any she did were tainted. However, something stirred within her, something beyond the grief and pain of this discovery.

Until now everything had been so clear-cut, so black and white with regards to her older siblings, but now... her perception was shifting. This discovery did not fit. To be killed with the remnants of their former lives begged the question — had they been murdered as punishment, or was it something far more meaningful?

Carey stared as her mother dropped the two Seekers' necklaces she had been clutching, overcome by her grief. As her father stooped to pick them up, Carey saw silent tears running down his face. He made no move to wipe them away.

This was too much. Her parents, the news of her sisters, the sheer gravity of the situation threatened to overwhelm her. Carey tore her hand from Ji's and ran from the room, ignoring Kat's cries for her to stop. She sprinted down the hallway, her feet pounding the stone hard and her head full of the scene in the Council room when she almost ran headlong into Rupert.

"Carey! What's wrong?" he cried out, but she did not stop. She could not. Her feet were intent on running as far as they could, and she wasn't about to stop.

She flew down the front steps, past a concerned-looking Jensen and Faren and out to the stables. She wanted to feel the devastation rip her apart but all she felt was confusion. Confusion, and something that might have been indifference. She had not known them the way everyone else had, she could not remember them as her parents did, and again she felt that great disconnect between her and everyone else.

To her, they were two girls of whom she had only the vaguest memory. The only time she had encountered them in person was when they had tried to attack her and her friends in Irvinestown. That last memory was negligible at best — she had been trapped inside their old home during their attack, and she had not even seen them. She had no good memories, no past reminiscences of Jody and Laurel that she could cherish, and this thought only made her feel worse. They had been her sisters, part of her family, and yet that very idea felt foreign to her.

The sun was still high in the sky, its bright rays a stark comparison to the mood within the castle. She needed to escape. There was no logic behind her need, simply a blatant urge to get away from the death and the grief. The grief she did not feel.

Firefly stood in the farthest stall from the front of the stable, and she tossed her head fretfully as Carey came sprinting up to her. She leapt onto Firefly's back in one swift movement and nudged her sides with her heels; the pegasus reared before tearing out of the stables at full speed. As they sped past the stable doors, Carey saw that Kat had followed her. Firefly's wings narrowly missed her as she spread them in preparation to take off. She stumbled backwards, calling to Carey, but she ignored her as she coaxed Firefly onwards. She needed to be alone.

Her hair whipped at her face as they left the castle behind. The cool autumn air stung her eyes as they flew higher and farther, but Carey did not give heed to it. Ignoring it, she urged Firefly on, gripping the pegasus's mane tighter as they sped through the sky.

They landed not far from the city borders, atop a cliff overlooking the vast capital. Carey did a quick sweep of the area to make sure they were alone. She knew what she had done was reckless, but at that very moment she just didn't care.

Dismounting from Firefly's back, Carey sat down upon the grass and stared out at the sprawling landscape as the pegasus wandered away to sniff at some nearby bushes. Far below in the Centre City, its streets were bustling, the People wending their way through tight cobbled streets and packed markets. Houses leaned against each other so close that not even a breeze could get through, and colourful silks and fluttering flags hung about their dwellings. The People had proven themselves to be stronger than the horrors of their past and had built a thriving society within the city. Any other day this would have been a source of great pride and joy, but right now, Carey barely even saw it.

She closed her eyes and breathed in the cool air floating past her. Slowly, the beating of her heart returned to normal, but the shock and pain still weighed heavily on her chest. She fisted the grass beneath her, tearing it from its roots and crushing it within her hands. Wilted and broken, she let it fall back to the ground, dark green stains marking her palms like blood.

She knew that running away had probably not been the best reaction — the heat of the moment fading the longer she sat on the outcrop — but now she was there she felt a tiny touch of freedom. Everyone in the castle carried their own pain, and Carey could not help but be affected by it. This discovery was but one in a long line of many. Every week brought more news and it was becoming painfully obvious to Carey and the others just how much devastation the Empire had managed to wreak during its time. It was difficult to focus on a better future, to build a new world free of Malevolence's taint, when the past kept coming back to haunt them.

She sat there in silent contemplation as the afternoon dwindled and the sun sank towards the horizon. Carey watched as people came and went through the city gates, noticed the lamps in the streets as they burst to life on dusk, observed as the night sky presented itself. The stars winked at her elusively as she sat huddled against Firefly's side. She let her mind wander, not really coming to rest on anything in particular, but instead drinking in her calm surroundings. It was only when she heard the thundering of hooves behind her that she broke from her reverie.

In an instant, Carey was on her feet. She could hear them getting closer and Firefly whinnied nervously. A great black stallion burst into the clearing, but before Carey could let fly any curses, a voice cried into the night.

"Carey? Is that you?"

She gasped in relief. It was Ji.

"How did you find me?" she said as he slowed to where she was standing. He dismounted, sliding down carefully from his mount.

"It wasn't hard. I had Seramina track you," he said with the faint hint of a smile, his eyes not quite meeting her face. "You really shouldn't run off like that, you know. You gave us all a heart attack."

Carey waved off his chastisement. "I couldn't be there anymore. It was too much."

She sat back down on the grass where Ji joined her a moment later. His fingers brushed cautiously over the ground before sitting down at her side.

"I'm sorry about your sisters," he said quietly.

Carey grunted in acknowledgment. There was nothing she really wanted to say. When she didn't reply, Ji spoke again. "Your parents want to have a memorial for Jody and Laurel. At the end of the week. Nothing big…"

He trailed off and Carey knew he was waiting to see how she'd react. The idea of a memorial was sure to bring mixed emotions considering what her sisters had done, yet Carey wasn't sure how she felt. Unwilling to talk, she flopped back onto the grass to stare up at the sky. She was grateful when Ji said nothing more on the subject but laid back to join her.

They lay in silence for some time. Carey listened to the wind rustle at the leaves, the snuffling of the horse and the pegasus, the slow deliberate breathing of her friend. She wished she could bottle this kind of tranquillity, to call upon it again when times proved difficult. She wanted to stay forever in this suspended state, where there was nothing to confront and no one demanding anything of her.

Carey rolled her head to the side, her eyes finding Ji. His dark brown hair was mussed from lying in the grass, the ends curling slightly around his ears. His head was resting in his hands, and he looked serene, his profile lit only by moonlight.

His lips moved and words cut across her musings.

"Hmm, what?"

"I said, I was wondering if the stars were out tonight. It seems like the kind of weather that would be perfect for star-gazing," he repeated, indicating the heavens above.

Carey gazed back up at the sky and the majesty that spread before them. It was indeed a perfect night for viewing them, not a whisper of a cloud, still and clear.

"I never pegged you as one for star-gazing," she said, looking over at his faded blue eyes.

"Well, it was something I used to do with Zacharia, but that was a long time ago," he added unnecessarily. "I just remember thinking how absolutely wonderful they seemed, burning out in the black, lighting the way for traveller and dreamer alike... They are one of the only things I feel I'll never truly forget the sight of..." he said with a touch of sadness.

As his words trailed away again, Carey was gripped suddenly with an odd sense of longing. "I wish I was a star."

It was certainly an odd thing to say, but she didn't back down from it. Ji turned his head, his face questioning. "Why would you wish that?"

Carey paused, considering her answer. "I suppose... because everyone admires them and yet they've never done much to deserve that kind of acknowledgement. Yet me..." her thoughts ran back to how she had killed that man in Burtonport and wondered what people would really think if they knew what lurked inside her.

Ji nodded as she spoke. "That may be true, but I don't think that's right."

Carey turned now to look back at Ji, not sure where he was going with this.

"Look at the stars and what do you see?" he asked, gesturing towards the sky. "Everyone may admire them, but there is nothing special that defines any one of them. They are simply stars, and nothing more. But you, Carey — you did something worthy of admiration. Wouldn't it be better to be admired for something true? We're all reluctant heroes in this situation, you must know that, but you are unique, Carey. And that is what defines

FOUND

you, makes you different to all those stars. At least you are your own and are someone worthy of that adoration."

Carey stared at him as she felt heat rise in her cheeks. It was not the same confusion and awkwardness that usually invoked such a reaction. It was the undercurrent in Ji's voice, the absolute certainty and faith he held in her that was painful to hear. She wanted to tell him that it wasn't so, that who she really was was not the person everyone made her out to be. She wasn't a hero. She didn't want to be admired for something she felt wasn't even a true part of her. Carey continued to struggle with the idea of something dark living within her, for surely something that only brought about death was not something to be revered.

She said nothing. She didn't look back at him, afraid that he might be expecting her to answer. Instead, she sat up, hugged her knees and resigned herself to the fact that she would have to go back. Closing her eyes, Carey took a deep steadying breath and stood up.

"My parents have been through enough already today. Perhaps this wasn't the best idea," she said, fetching Ji's mount for him.

Carey couldn't help but notice Ji's disappointment as he nodded in agreement, standing up and taking the reins she placed in his hands. "You're right. We should go."

The ride back was quiet, and Carey wished now that Ji hadn't been the one to follow her. She didn't enjoy the unease that came between them, which seemed even more profound when they were alone. As soon as they reached the castle grounds, Carey dismounted and left Firefly to find her own way back to the stables.

"Thank you for coming to find me," was all she could manage to say before turning to leave.

Ji simply nodded and as she entered the castle, Carey struggled not to look back, for she knew that if she did, she would not be able to bear the look on his face. And for that she hated herself.

~Chapter Six~

Mastering Unreality

Carey woke suddenly to a loud thumping at her door. She blinked, bemused; she had slept badly, and her brain was sluggish and unresponsive as the pounding continued. She'd lain awake, not for the first time that week, turning the blood-red stone over in her hands and thinking about its former owners. Endless possibilities tumbled over each other, keeping her from rest; Elara's fate enthralling her. And despite the late nights and little sleep, she appreciated the distraction, for at the edge of her mind lurked Saar. The odds that he might one night summon her again made her edgy and unwilling to sleep, so the stone provided the perfect excuse not to.

There came a shout followed by more banging and Carey rolled off her bed with a groan. She opened the door to find Kat standing there with her hands on her hips.

"Nice to see you're ready," she remarked, and when Carey looked at her quizzically, she said: "Your sisters' memorial?"

Of course. How could she have forgotten? The memorial was set for that morning, small and to include only the families from the Order. She raced to get ready and five minutes later was making her way down to the castle courtyard with Kat, who was straight-faced and silent. Even though the others had never forgiven the betrayal of Carey's sisters, their respect for their oldest friends was too great for them not to attend.

Half an hour later, Carey found herself at her mother's side, staring as two small bronze spheres containing the remains of her sisters were placed in the ground at the foot of the great rose monument. The day was still and overcast, grey clouds hanging low over the city, mirroring the mood of those gathered. Carey and her parents stood at the front, her parents clothed in long, dark cloaks. Kat and her father stood behind to her right, Peter with his arm protectively about Kat's shoulders, and to the left was Ji and his family, Oliver's face straight and stoic whilst Meela's was drawn and weary. Carey could only imagine the type of thoughts this ceremony was invoking for her, especially given Zacharia's uncertain future.

There were no speeches, no final words, just silence. The funerary attendants stepped back from the statue and motioned for the family to approach. Jenny and Robert each lay a necklace down into their daughters' final resting place; Jody and Laurel's pendants from the Order. They then each took a handful of blood-red rose petals and scattered them over the top, each petal a reminder of death, that they would all fall one day. Their silence was painful, and Carey knew what they were thinking—what, if anything, *could* they say? What could they say about their daughters who had betrayed them? What could they say, given the state in which they had been found? As it was, it must be painful enough to say goodbye even without so many questions left unanswered.

As the attendants began shifting dirt over the plot, Carey's mother broke down into heavy sobbing, the choked sounds punctuating the still air. Robert Lee wrapped an arm around her shoulders and slowly they made their way back into the castle. Carey stayed though, watching as the two bronze urns slowly disappeared . She tried hard not to imagine how many others were found with them, and whether they would ever be laid to rest by those who had loved them.

*

"How are you feeling after this morning?" Ji asked, his hand on Kat's arm as they strode down the hall towards the training hall.

It was the afternoon following her sisters' service and outside the clouds had finally relieved themselves upon the countryside, thick sheets of rain hammering the windowpanes. Carey had spent the better part of the day in her room, contemplating what her sisters' deaths meant and what had led them to that unmarked grave. Their discovery had affected her parents in such a way that was both devastating and unnerving, for until that week, Carey had never seen them express the kind of emotion they had upon the discovery of her sisters' bodies. Before that, they had been so steadfast and unwavering in the face of all the devastation that had been wreaked by Malevolence's Empire. Perhaps this had been the tragedy to break them, as so many around them had already done.

Carey had always known Malevolence had loathed her family and the Order, but until that week she had never fully appreciated how very much. Even if Jody and Laurel had believed in the Empire and its absolute power, there was every possibility that Malevolence had always planned to kill them once their purpose had been fulfilled. What better way to demonstrate her total dominance than to accept into her circle those who had once been foes, only to execute them once they were no longer useful? Jody and Laurel had been the perfect pawns in a greater game and they, along with so many, had been played to the advantage of the Queen.

So consumed had Carey been with these thoughts that it had taken Kat and Ji several minutes of knocking to bring her out of her reverie.

"I'm... fine," Carey answered, haltingly.

She didn't elaborate and they didn't push for more. Wanting to change the subject, she said: "Have either of you had a chance to speak with Lord Acheron since he arrived?"

Carey had not seen much of the new advisor since the banquet, but his presence intrigued her, nonetheless. There was still something familiar about him that she'd been unable to place.

Kat nodded. "I spoke with him a day or two ago."

"Why do you ask?" Ji enquired.

"I was just wondering what your thoughts on him were, is all."

Kat raised a single eyebrow. "Why? Have you noticed something suspicious?"

Carey waved away the notion. "No, nothing like that. He just seems... familiar to me, like I know him from somewhere but can't place his face."

Lips pursed in thought, Ji said, "Well, you have met him before now, when you were younger. Perhaps it's that?"

Grunting softly in frustration, Carey rubbed her forehead as though to wipe away the fog obscuring the memory of Lord Acheron that seemed always just out of sight. "I don't know. Maybe? Yes? I just feel like there's more..."

They turned a corner to the hall leading up from the dungeons where they trained, and a short way down the corridor stood Seramina talking animatedly to Lord Acheron. Seramina turned as the three approached, her grin widening as she saw them.

"Carey! Kat, Ji! Are you heading down to train?" she asked happily. "I was just on my way down to meet Kyna there when I ran into Lord Acheron."

Seramina's bubbly attitude filled the corridor, at stark contrast with the weather beating the window beside her.

"Yes, we were just heading down there," Ji said with a smile. "Would you like to join us?"

Carey caught Lord Acheron watching her as Seramina spoke enthusiastically of the weapons she wanted to try that day. As she turned to face him, he approached her with hands clasped reverently, his handsome features sombre.

"Your Highness," he said solemnly, his brown eyes lowering in respect. "I would like to convey my condolences for the loss of your sisters. This must be a terrible time for your family."

"Oh," Carey replied, his words unexpected. "Thank you, Lord Acheron."

"I hope you know that we are doing everything we can to try and find out what happened to them. We will not rest until we uncover the truth."

He gave Carey a small, reassuring smile which she returned. "Your words are appreciated. I'm sure my mother and father appreciate them even more."

Lord Acheron bowed before excusing himself from the group, the flame from a nearby torch rippling down his bronzed locks. "I shall see you again soon, Miss Jessup," he said, turning back to Seramina, who beamed up at him.

"I certainly hope so, Lord Acheron," she said, bopping a small curtsy his way.

Acheron gave Kat and Ji each a word of farewell before striding past them the way they had come. Carey watched his retreating back as he turned the corner, that familiar feeling tugging at her once more.

"Well, he seems pleasant," Kat said, cocking her head to the side. "I hadn't really seen him up close. Young."

Ji smirked. "Oh really, Kat?" he said with a nudge, which she slapped away.

"Oh, stop it."

"He's not actually as young as he looks. A special ability, apparently," Carey explained, turning her gaze away from where Acheron has disappeared.

Kat tsked jealously.

"I think he's nice," Seramina chimed in, eager to join the conversation.

"What were you talking about before we came barging in?" Carey asked.

Seramina twisted her lips, thinking back. "We were talking about what it's like to live here in the castle and how different it is to the hidden cities we've lived in. Then, we talked a little about what I've been doing since I arrived, my studies, and training. I don't know if he was that interested, but I think he was just happy to talk to someone. He's very sad, and a bit lonely," she added, with a small frown.

"Really?" Kat said, her eyebrows rising slightly.

Concerned, Carey frowned. "You felt that in him?" she asked, referring to Seramina's empathy.

She nodded sadly. "His family."

Of course. But he wasn't alone in that fact, Carey thought as they continued walking to the training hall. This castle was filled with ghosts, and the people who had loved them.

*

The following few weeks passed by quietly and Carey continued to think on Elara and the stone. She had finally asked her parents about her grandmother and whether she'd had any siblings.

"No, none that I'm aware of," her father had answered. "Why do you ask?"

She hadn't told them of the stone. She didn't think it terribly important in the face of the grief they were still enduring. If it did end up proving of some significance then she would say something, but until then, she was more interested in Elara.

That left only one person.

Saar had made no attempt to summon Carey again since she had denied him the night of the banquet, and although at first it had been a source of great anxiety and sleepless nights, she suddenly found herself hoping he would. Questions burned within her, mysteries that begged answers, and it now seemed that only Saar and Saar alone could answer them.

Yet as the days carried on, it seemed less and less likely that he would visit her again. Carey had not yet been able to master her ability to Twilight Travel; each experience as random and unexpected as the next. The likelihood that she would be able to summon Saar as he did her was not encouraging, and her frustration was undoubtedly not helping the situation.

Her shortcomings, however, were not shared by others within the castle, most notably Seramina. In the short time she had been in the castle, Seramina had taken to her training and studies with impressive ease. Carey watched with keen interest as the young girl's powers grew, her abilities outstripping any expectations and flying far beyond those of simple telepathy and empathy. Kyna would often remark upon them with awe and wonder, but strangely enough, Seramina herself did not seem truly aware of the amazing speed at which they were expanding. At one point, Rupert commented on how her powers now encompassed a range more fitting to someone at least twice her age, an amazing feat, given the short time period. This simple observation served to deepen Carey's intrigue; she felt the magic that surrounded Seramina, that faint hum of power. And it was growing.

"You've noticed it too, then? Personally, I find it intriguing, this transformation of hers," Kat said as she leaned against Carey's bedpost one afternoon. "And not only her magic. You should have seen her today during training."

A tray of breads and cheeses sat half-eaten on the table by the fireplace. Carey was perched on the windowsill, the shutters flung open to the gathering grey beyond. The clouds rumbled overhead, the smell of rain in the air. Carey frowned in contemplation.

"I wonder what caused it, this sudden augmentation of her abilities… Have you ever heard of this happening, beyond the course of special abilities, that is?"

Kat pursed her lips and shook her head, her dark waves of hair fluttering about her face. "Not to this extent. Singular abilities, yes, like your Twilight Travelling and such magic, but an overall surge in one's magical abilities? I can't say I have. Why? What are you thinking?"

Carey twisted her Seeker necklace between her fingers, her lips pursed in thought. "Do you think it might be dangerous, her abilities acting as they are?"

Moving around to sit on the bed, Kat shrugged. "Who can say? At least she's in the best place in case something does happen. Perhaps Rupert can find something in that library of his."

"You think it might be an illness?"

"Well, if we are to believe what Seramina says, and that it all began after what happened to her family, then perhaps it's a trauma of sorts. That said, I have experienced many who have suffered as she has, some even more so, and I have not known anyone to exhibit such powers," Kat said as she rubbed her brow pensively.

"So, this could be rare, possibly even unique," Carey suggested.

"It certainly looks that way," Kat said, flicking her shoes off and tucking her legs up under her. "It's beyond anything I can comprehend, that's for sure.

"Speaking of special abilities, what about your Twilight Travelling?"

Carey sighed heavily, putting her head in her hands and rubbing her eyes wearily. "I want to say that I've figured out how to control it, but I just haven't had any luck. And what with my sisters and everything, I just can't seem to concentrate on it. I would like to, though. It would certainly make sleep a more enticing option and it would definitely limit Saar's ability to summon me whenever he so pleases."

She didn't dare say how she truly felt, that she would invite the idea of facing Saar again. Carey had a feeling Kat wouldn't approve of such notions.

An optimistic smile split Kat's face and Carey raised a reluctant eyebrow at her. "What?"

"Well, we're here now. How about we have a crack at it?"

Momentarily taken aback, Carey said, "*Crack at it*? What, right now?"

Kat cocked her head to the side as if to say, *"Why not?"*. "You have to sleep some time, Carey, and if this gives you some peace, then I'm all for lending a hand."

Carey bit her lip; the offer was certainly enticing since she was certainly not having any luck on her own. She shrugged and moved over next to Kat. Secretly, she was glad not to be the one to ask for help. "Sure, why not."

Gleefully clapping her hands at the challenge, Kat cleared her throat. "Right. So, what exactly do you want to do with it, this ability of yours?"

"I just want to be able to control where I go," Carey said simply, and it was the truth — if she could control where she wanted to go, then she should also be able to control where she *didn't* want to go.

"How does it work, exactly? Didn't you say it's like you're travelling but you're not actually going anywhere?" Kat asked.

Carey considered it for a moment. "I'm not really sure, it's all kind of accidental. I mean, one moment I'm falling asleep or dreaming, the next I'm somewhere that's a real place, not some dream plane. I can talk and hear what's happening, but my senses are different. I can only feel what I want to feel."

Kat folded her arms. "Perhaps it's how your mind is when you fall asleep. What about when you saw Ji in the dungeon? What were you thinking of when you fell asleep?"

It wasn't difficult to recall the memory of that night and the thought made Carey's stomach lurch unpleasantly. "I had been thinking of, well, Ji actually," she said awkwardly, not looking at Kat directly but staring down at her hands. "It was after that conversation we had, remember?"

There was a moment of silence in which Carey forced herself to look up.

63

Kat was peering at her with an expression that looked dangerously close to pity.

"It's because of Jeremy, isn't it? The reason why everything is so strange with Ji?"

"What? Nothing's strange with me and… What makes you think…" Carey began lamely, but she could see that Kat wasn't having any of it.

"Look, Carey," she said matter-of-factly, "I can see how it is with you two. Any time you're in the same room with each other I swear I could cut the tension with a knife. You're not how you used to be with him, and it's because of that good-for-nothing traitor, isn't it?"

Carey sat in silence, her insides squirming. Kat reached over to her; her arm outstretched as though to placate her. "Please, don't shut me out. I won't say anything, especially to Ji."

There was a moment where Carey considered not saying anything but then she nodded. "I… I want so badly for everything to be all right, with Ji, with us, but it just… isn't," she said, flopping back onto her pillow and covering her face with her hands. She felt embarrassed, weak even, to be saying this out loud, but at the same time she felt relieved. She had spent so much energy trying to keep these feelings at bay that by finally speaking it aloud she was freed from the great weight that had been resting on her chest. She took a deep breath and let her hands fall from her face.

"I don't even know what I want anymore. Right now, I'd settle for just friends again. I mean, we're friends, but it's always seems to turn… awkward. Sometimes I think we're almost there and then… I know it's Ji, I do, but at the same time I don't. *He* really messed things up," she said in small voice. She still couldn't bring herself to say Jeremy's name. Speaking it aloud seemed impossible, dangerous even. "And you know what I really hate about this whole thing is that Ji knows this. He knows that the reason I can't be around him half the time is because of that man. And I know it's hurting him…"

Carey closed her eyes again. She felt Kat take her hand and squeeze it. "It will work itself out. It has to," she heard her say.

"How do you know that though?" Carey asked almost desperately. She sat up and looked Kat in the eyes. "How?"

With a small smile, Kat said, "Because the universe has a balance. It may take some cataclysmic event, or you may just awake one day to realise the absolute truth of it all. Either way, it will happen eventually. You just have to believe it will."

Kat's words were full of hope, and yet Carey found it hard to believe that faith was all it would take. There may be some balance, but what if it wasn't Ji… What if it was Jeremy she was meant to share it with? The idea made her cringe and Kat noticed her hesitation. She pulled Carey into a hug. "Try not to worry, and don't keep everything to yourself all the time. I know you hold back, but I'm here if you need to talk about anything, anything at all."

Carey broke from the hug and tried for a more optimistic expression. Kat gave her a playful nudge to the shoulder.

"So," she said, bringing them back to Carey's Twilight Travelling. "That night you dreamt of Ji in the dungeons, you were thinking of him when you fell asleep, no?"

"Except falling asleep is usually how I end up in these situations. I'm not sure about you, but I find it a bit difficult to fall asleep on command," she said.

Kat crossed her arms in contemplation. "I think we need to find out more about Twilight Travelling. Perhaps there's a trick to it."

"A trick?" Carey repeated sceptically.

"Oh, you know what I mean," Kat said with a wave of her hand. "It might be a stretch but perhaps there's something in the Archives about it."

"The Archives? But wasn't a lot of that destroyed by the Empire?" Carey wondered as they got to their feet.

Kat nodded. "They built quite a few bonfires in their day with the contents of the Archives, but it can't hurt to try, can it?"

Kat held open the door expectantly.

"No, I suppose not," Carey answered, leading the way.

A half hour later, Carey and Kat stood at one of the doorways to the castle's Archives. They had traipsed down past the ground level of the castle to reach them; the bright sunlit spaces replaced by windowless, torch-lit hallways that were profoundly cold despite the seasonal warmth outside. They pushed open the heavy wooden doors and gaped in awe at what lay before them. They stood on a balcony that hung around the inner wall of an endless hall, disappearing down into the darkness to their right and curving around to their left. The vaulted ceiling rose to dizzying heights, the very highest parts hidden in shadow. Spire after spire of honeycomb-like shelves grew down from the great arches like stalactites and were overflowing with a vast collection of books, scrolls and artefacts. A shimmering white light that seemed to emanate from nowhere in particular illuminated the seemingly never-ending vault. Carey couldn't see the far wall it was so enormous. If the Archives had indeed incurred the fiery wrath of the Empire, she could only imagine how much more there had been once upon a time.

Carey and Kat took one of the spiral staircases curving down to the main floor of the Archives. As they descended, they passed at least three more balcony floors, these with their own entrances but also inlaid with rows of dusty bookshelves. As they reached the main floor, quick, sharp footsteps sounded to their right and Carey and Kat turned to find Lady Marksis walking briskly towards them.

"Princess Carey, Lady Kat," she greeted them with a bow. "I was not expecting you, was I?"

Surprised to see Lady Marksis down there, Carey said, "Expecting us?"

Lady Marksis chuckled. "I am a chronicler of the Archives, as well as a tutor," she said in her rapid-fire manner, referring to the lessons she'd been providing Carey. "I work here, along with my brother of course. Is there something I can help you with?"

Carey hesitated for a moment. Not many people knew about her ability as a Twilight Traveller — she somehow felt the need to keep it a secret from anyone but those closest to her. But as she looked at the immense collection of the Archives, she couldn't help but feel that it would be impossible to find anything in there without Lady Marksis's help.

"Yes, there is. We're looking for some information, if it exists, about a particular type of magic," she said.

"Oh, yes?" Lady Marksis replied, her interest piqued. "Well, as you can see, we have quite the collection here, even after the Empire's efforts. What is the information you seek?"

"We want to know if you have anything on Twilight Travellers," Carey supplied, making sure to remain as vague as possible..

"Well, the Empire had much destroyed during their time, mostly that which was transcribed in Gadælic, but in the grand scheme of things, especially with regards to the Archives, it was relatively limited damage," Lady Marksis prattled as she led them down a small set of steps onto the main floor of the Archives. "Most of what they destroyed was deemed dangerous to their rule, or in other words, anything that could be used against them."

They made a turn and headed left down a seemingly endless row of towering shelves.

"Now, you said Twilight Travellers… do you know if they are known by any other name?"

Kat shook her head, but an unpleasant memory stirred in Carey's mind as she remembered the first time she had heard the term *Twilight Traveller.*

"Wait… what about *Fiorilusa?*" Carey said slowly, hoping she had remembered it correctly.

Lady Marksis raised her eyebrows. "Indeed! That makes things much easier. This way, if you please."

As Lady Marksis led them on, Kat tugged at Carey's sleeve with wide, questioning eyes.

"The time I saw Ji tortured," Carey said in a whisper, trying hard not to let the rest of that memory fill her mind. "The man, Liseau, called me a Fiorilusa."

"Yes, Fiorilusa is the Gadælic term," came Lady Marksis's voice and Carey jumped at how loud it was in the echoing space. "Despite the Empire's feelings towards the language and its proliferators, the keepers of the Archives at that time managed to convince them to keep the original system of using Gadælic to order the Archives. Makes it much easier to find anything, especially amongst all of this."

"Convince them?" Kat said, turning her attention to Lady Marksis in earnest.

"Yes," she said as she stopped and reached for a bunch of scrolls. "The chroniclers at the time were not Imperial loyalists but Order sympathisers, and the Empire knew that. However, they told the Empire that no one else, in this realm or any other, had the knowledge required to keep the Archives, and so they kept them here as custodians and their prisoners."

Impressed by this daring tale, Carey said, "They convinced the Empire to let them live so they could continue being the Archive's custodians?"

"Which gave them the perfect opportunity to save some of the works the Empire sought to burn. Ah! Here it is," she said, extracting one of the scrolls from the pile and handing it to Carey so she could replace the others.

Carey unrolled the parchment and tried to read it, but found it covered in the same script as the blood-red stone.

"It's in Gadælic," she exclaimed as Kat leaned in to have a look.

"One of the works the custodians managed to save," Lady Marksis smiled, taking it from her. "This section of the Archives was heavily targeted — special powers were something the Empire was particularly afraid of. The custodians had to use all the magic they possessed to ensure they didn't get everything. Now, let's see..." and with her brow furrowed in concentration, she began to read:

"*A Fiorilusa, so named for Marielle Fiorilusa, who first exhibited the power in the third year following the Gion War, is a being who possesses the unique ability to transport one's consciousness to a physical location outside their body. This is commonly known as Twilight Travelling...* does this sound like what you are searching for?" Lady Marksis asked after she read the first part of the scroll.

"Yes, but... you can read Gadælic?" Carey said in surprise.

"Of course," Lady Marksis said matter-of-factly. "Both me and my brother can. Our parents made sure of that. I am, however, a touch rusty. I didn't get to practice much under the Empire's rule so forgive me if my translating abilities aren't up to scratch."

"Well, no, it sounds about right," said Kat, who seemed just as surprised as Carey.

68

"And yes, that's what we're looking for," Carey added, eager to know what the rest of the document said. "However, we want to know more specifically how to control it, if you can find anything."

Lady Marksis scanned the parchment, muttering to herself. Carey glanced over at Kat, who raised her eyebrows.

"There might be something here…" Lady Marksis said finally, pointing to the last paragraph on the page. Carey and Kat leaned in as she began to read.

"The Fiorilusa enters a sleep or a trance-like state in order to transport their consciousness. They focus on their desired destination with absolute deliberation, which in turn separates the body from the mind. This practice can also be used to block other Fiorilusa from summoning them, a practice which is highly invasive."

"A trance-like state…" Carey murmured pensively, staring, unseeing, down at the scroll. She beckoned Kat over to one side, away from Lady Marksis. "So, I wouldn't even have to sleep… What do you think?" she said in hushed tones.

"If a trance is all you need to be able to Twilight Travel, then we could induce one. I mean, I could help place you in a trance. You wouldn't have to wait to fall asleep," Kat whispered back, and Carey felt almost hopeful at these words. Finally, they were getting somewhere.

Lady Marksis cleared her throat. "Is that all, Princess?" she asked Carey with the scroll still in hand.

"Yes," she nodded fervently. "Yes, I think we have enough to work with. Thank you. Thank you so much."

As Kat turned to leave and Lady Marksis began rolling up the parchment, Carey approached her in a low voice. "Lady Marksis, can I trust you to keep this conversation to yourself?"

Lady Marksis's sharp, dark eyes met Carey's own, and the older woman nodded. "Of course. You can trust me with this. I shall tell no one."

Nodding gratefully, Carey jogged away to catch up with Kat. They had reached the bottom of the twisting stairs when a thought occurred to her and she turned to Kat.

"Wait a moment. I just need to check something with Lady Marksis. No need to come," Carey cut across Kat as she opened her mouth to speak. "I'll be quick."

Luckily, Lady Marksis had not gone far. She looked up at Carey with surprised interest as she approached.

"Something else, Princess?" she asked as Carey came up beside her.

"Just one more, but not to do with Twilight Travelling. I'd like you to have a look at this," she said, pulling out the red stone necklace that she had taken to carrying around in her pocket. "It has an inscription in Gadælic on the setting here."

She pointed out the minute script and Lady Marksis squinted as she read it by the dim shimmering light.

"Hmm, hmm," she murmured, as she took the stone and looked over the inscription. "It seems simple enough. This here says *My dearest sister, Fianna,* and this part here is *All my heart, Elara.* Wait, your grandmother, Fianna?"

"I think so. Did you know she had a sister? I know you were friends with my grandmother," Carey asked hopefully, but to her disappointment, Lady Marksis shook her head.

"No, I'm sorry. I came to know your grandmother later in her life. I'm afraid I never heard her speak of a sister," she said, handing the stone back with a saddened expression.

Carey placed the necklace back in her pocket with a nod. As much as Carey believed in Seramina's abilities, she had half-hoped that she had been wrong in her translation. As her heart sank, it seemed the young witch had indeed been correct; there was a secret sister of Fianna's that either no one knew or spoke of. Carey thanked Lady Marksis before catching up with Kat, unable to shake the feeling that this stone, as her friends had implied many times before, was much more than it appeared.

*

"All right then. Did you want to try without any help first?"

They were back in Carey's room; Carey sitting on her bed cross-legged and Kat leaning against the wall by the head of her bed.

"Mmm, let me have a try by myself first since you won't always be there to help me out. If that fails, which I have a feeling it probably will…"

"Don't be like that," Kat said sternly. "If you don't believe in yourself it'll never work. Just as with weapons training, it's all about confidence."

"All right, all right, fine," Carey said, feeling slightly chided. "Confidence then."

Carey lay back on her pillow and tried clearing her mind of everything save for a single thought. Closing her eyes, she cast about for something to concentrate on, a singular place, and landed upon the castle courtyard. She concentrated on it with all her might, imagining the trees, the cobblestones, and the statue at its centre. She pictured the tiny yellow birds that were always fluttering about. Then she thought of the feeling Twilight Travelling had always brought her — a feeling of non-existence, yet firm reality at the same time, dreamlike yet real. She felt a slight tug, and for a moment Carey smelt the wildflowers that grew at the gates and the warm breeze that heralded the return of summer. But there was nothing but darkness. It pressed against her eyes, as though it was pushing her back, and she flinched. She tried pushing back but the darkness remained immovable, sealing her eyes shut against the light. The smell of the blossoms began to fade, and she tried to hold on to it, picturing them once more in her mind, but she was panicking now, confusion seeping in. There was a loud chirp from a bird nearby and it startled Carey out of her trance with a jerk. Her eyes flew open and she found Kat staring at her. She was back in her bedroom, the breeze and the smell of wildflowers gone.

"So?" she asked expectantly.

Carey smiled uncertainly. "I thought of the courtyard. I could smell the flowers and feel the breeze."

"That's fantastic!" Kat cried, but Carey shook her head in disappointment.

"I couldn't see anything though. It was just the smell, the feel of the wind. It was like I couldn't open my eyes."

"Come on, Carey. It was only your first real try at doing it," Kat said bracingly. "I'm sure if you keep trying, you'll get there."

Carey grunted in assent as she closed her eyes. She tried clearing her mind again, pushing everything out, but a small seed of doubt was starting to take hold.

"All right," she heard Kat say near her head. "Try and concentrate."

Again, Carey focused on the feeling of mixed reality and non-reality and felt the familiar pull, only this time it was not as strong. The smell of flowers, the wind on her skin, it was there, only it was vague, coming and going and not growing stronger. Carey tried desperately to hold on to it but she felt it slipping. She opened her eyes again to find herself still lying on her bed, Kat staring down at her expectantly. She shook her head disconsolately.

"It was even worse that time," she sighed as she sat up. "The smells, the wind, they were both weaker and it was still dark. I couldn't see anything..."

"Try again," Kat encouraged.

It continued this way for the next hour or so, Carey drifting off, seeking to awake in a place other than her room, imagining the courtyard, the Council chambers, the kitchens... However, try as she might, she was unable to progress past hearing and smelling her surrounds, the darkness still holding her back.

She was missing something, she knew it. Her inability to transport herself properly as had happened before was starting to infuriate her. She knew she shouldn't let it get to her and that Kat was right, she just needed to practice, but still... she had done this before, so why was it so hard now?

"I'm thinking too hard about it," she said finally, looking down at her hands. "Every time I've ever done it, I've been relaxed, asleep. But I can't wait for myself to fall asleep every time I want to do it, and I can't seem to clear my mind..."

"How about," Kat suggested, "you try something else."

Carey pouted at this rather unhelpful tip. "Such as...?"

"How about your magic?"

Carey wasn't quite sure what Kat meant. "But this is my magic."

Exasperated, Kat sighed, as though Carey was being frustratingly dim. "I don't mean that. I mean your magic. The one you summoned to protect Seramina, the one you used to defeat Malevolence. It's powerful. Perhaps what you need is to give your ability to Twilight Travel a sort of ... boost."

"A boost?" Carey echoed, considering the idea. She had never been fond of the strange magic that dwelled inside of her. Its nature seemed inherently sinister and yet it had helped her before, not to mention Seramina. Perhaps there was some merit to the idea.

"I'm not sure if it will work..." Carey started.

"But you'll give it a try?" Kat said with a hint of anticipation, and Carey nodded.

Lying her head back down on the pillow, Carey closed her eyes once more and thought again of the courtyard, only this time she summoned just the tiniest trickle of the magic within her. Surely only a little magic would give her the boost she needed, and she was right. She felt it tingle at her fingertips and as it spread, Carey thought of that pull towards the unreal. In an instant, she was transported. She could feel the sun's warmth on her face and the air tickling her skin. The smell offlowers and the warm summer breeze was strong in her nostrils. The darkness seemed to have dissipated, light pressing in through her eyelids. Slowly, she opened her eyes.

Blinking dazedly in the brightness of the day, she looked across the yard. Carey could see the guards, Jensen and Faren, standing by the front door. Slowly, she raised a hand and waved experimentally. Jensen noticed the motion and waved back, only to be instantly chastised by Faren. Carey grinned with elation, it had worked! She spun around, taking it all in; the warmth, the smells. Tiny petals fell from a nearby tree, tossed about by the currents in the air. Carey held out her hand to grab one, unsure of whether she would be able to hold onto it, and in that tiny fraction of a moment as doubt entered her mind, she was pulled back to her body where she woke, feeling exhausted but filled with hope. The joy at finally being able to do it, even if it had only been for the briefest of moments, felt amazing. She grinned at Kat who smiled expectantly back at her. "It worked?"

Carey sat up, grinning. For the first time ever, the ability to Twilight Travel made her feel exhilarated instead of terrified. She threw her arms around Kat. "It worked. It was fantastic, Kat! If only you could feel what it's like... Kat?"

Kat felt strange in her arms; she was suddenly rigid and as Carey pulled away, she began shaking, convulsing. She screamed as Kat slipped from her hands to the floor. Her eyes rolled back into her head so that only the whites showed, and her head flopped from side to side as her body thrashed about on the stone floor. Carey tried to grab hold of her distraught friend but was knocked aside by one of Kat's flailing arms.

"Help! Someone help me! Rupert!" Carey screamed, hoping desperately that someone was nearby. She managed to scramble back to Kat's side and for one agonisingly long minute, she hovered at Kat's head, watching her jerk and shudder upon the floor. She screamed out for help again, a sob escaping her as she did so, and finally, thankfully, Ji and Rupert came bursting into her room. Rupert was instantly by her side and with his palms facing Kat, he began muttering beneath his breath while Ji helped Carey up from the floor. She clutched at his arms, unable to tear her eyes away from Kat as she continued to thrash about on the floor.

"Carey. Carey, what happened?" Ji asked her, his arms around her, but Carey just shook her head, unable to call on words.

She wanted to help Kat, but it was like she was frozen with shock, her brain failing to call her to action. All she could do was watch on helplessly, her heart racing as Rupert worked his healer's magic. She pleaded silently for it to work, for Kat to be all right, and finally, after a few tense moments, Kat began to calm; she still twitched but her eyes were now closed, and her breathing was beginning to slow. Carey leaned over her, and as she did so, noticed that she too was shaking. A heady mix of fear and adrenalin coursed through her body and Carey shook back the dizziness that had accompanied her moment of panic.

"What did you do to her?" she asked Rupert, who was now moving his hands down Kat's body, she noticed, making absolutely sure not to touch her as he assessed her condition.

"Jus' calmed her. I used an incantation t' calm her mind which in turn relaxed her body. The more important question is wha' did *you* do t' her?" Rupert said, looking up at Carey.

She shook her head fervently. "Nothing! We were just trying to work out how to control my Twilight Travelling. I had finally managed it, just for a moment, and when I woke up, we were so excited that I gave Kat a hug. But that's it. Next thing she went all stiff and started shaking, and then she collapsed. I didn't—" Carey gasped, her hand to her mouth. "You don't think it was something I did? But I wasn't even using any magic!"

Rupert shrugged. "Can' be sure at the moment. It could be any number o' things. I need ter get her back to the Healer's Ward. Ji, can yer help me? Just take care not t' touch her."

Ji nodded. He turned to Carey and squeezed her shoulders. "I'm sure it was nothing you did. Don't worry, we'll figure this out. You know how good Rupert is. Kat will be fine."

And as she followed Ji and Rupert to the Healer's Ward with Kat suspended between them, Carey couldn't help but pray with all her might for Ji to be right.

~Chapter Seven~

Visions of the Past

"Where is she? Where's Katrina?" Ji had sent immediately for Kat's father, Peter, sending a servant flying through the castle in search of him. Rupert had only managed to complete a set of preliminary checks when he came bursting into the Healer's Ward, casting about wildly in search for his daughter. As his eyes found her, he let out a low moan.

"What happened?" he whispered as he took to her bedside.

The anguish upon Peter Lawrence's face was palpable, so much so that Carey just couldn't bring herself to tell him how Kat came to be in that hospital bed. She was still unconscious but at least now she seemed peaceful. Rupert began examining her more thoroughly, his eyes closed in concentration. Peter stood in silence, watching as the healer completed his investigation. Ji moved away and he and Carey hung back, leaving Kat's father by her side.

"Rupert, please tell me she'll be all right," Peter said quietly as he looked down upon Kat.

Rupert shook his head with an expression of consternation. "I can' seem t' find anythin' wrong with her. Whatever it was that made her collapse, it's not there anymore. She's perfectly fine," he said with a slight tone of annoyance.

"But she is still unconscious," Peter said as he sat on the edge of the chair by the bed.

"Tha' was me. It helps in recovery with these kinds of episodes. She will wake in a short while," Rupert assured Peter.

Despite Rupert's words, Carey couldn't feel any relief. The room was thick with tension, and she had her doubts that Kat would be perfectly fine. They still didn't know what had caused Kat's episode, and she couldn't dispel the gnawing feeling in her gut that she had something to do with it. She wanted Kat to wake so that she could tell them what had happened, or at the very least tell Carey that it wasn't her fault.

Peter let out a long sigh as he held his hands in his face. With a shaking hand, he reached across to take Kat's in his own. Yet no sooner had his fingers touched her skin did Kat's chest heave, lifting her body off the bed. Her eyes flew open this time and she began to scream, the sound echoing off the stone walls of the ward. Carey and Ji jumped back in alarm as their friend's screams cut through the air, the terror they carried so incredibly real that they felt as though Kat's fear was their own. Her eyes were unfocused, rolling around as she struck out at some unknown assailant, clawing at the air frantically. Rupert yelled at Peter to let go of Kat's hand and no sooner had he released her; Kat's screaming stopped. She flopped back onto the bed, her chest still heaving with laboured breaths, her hair splayed about on the snowy white pillow beneath her. Her face, taut with agony only a moment before, had smoothed once again. The sudden transformation was shocking, and Carey stood back, hand in hand with Ji, the tightness of his grip mirrored in her own. She hadn't even realised she'd grabbed his hand, but her fear and astonishment overrode any other feelings at that very moment. Peter had backed away quickly from his daughter's bedside, his eyes wide in alarm.

"I just touched her... It was nothing..." he muttered, leaning against the wall by Kat's bed and gazing fretfully at his daughter.

Once Rupert had worked his magic and Kat had resettled, he came over to join them. "I guess we can all assume tha' whatever it is, it responds to touch. I will ge' Seramina in here to see if she can see into Kat's mind and determine wha' is causin' this. I won't wake her 'til I know it's safe to do so," Rupert told Peter in a quiet voice. "But 'til then, I need everyone to stay clear of her. Hopefully once Kat's awake, she'll be able to enlighten us."

Peter dropped onto the end of the bed next to Kat's and buried his head in his hands once more. There was no doubt that this was dredging up horrific memories for him, and Carey knew he was thinking of his wife, Jiani. She refused to consider that something so horrible would happen to Kat, that Peter might lose them both — Kat was too strong, too stubborn to succumb to this, surely. She just couldn't accept that.

Carey turned to Rupert. "I'll summon Seramina. She's still in the castle, so she should be able to Hear me."

Rupert nodded gratefully. Ji squeezed gently on her hand before releasing it; she acknowledged the mark of solidarity with a whispered "Thank you" before leaving the room.

Once outside the ward, Carey leaned against the stone wall and closed her eyes. Concentrating singularly on Seramina, she called out to her.

"Seramina, can you hear me?"

A few moments of silence passed before Carey heard the young girl's voice in her head.

"Carey?"

Carey smiled. *"Yes, it's me. Could you come to the Healer's Ward straight away? We need your help."*

"Of course! Is everything all right?"

"I'll tell you when you get here. Just come as soon as you can."

Seramina acquiesced and Carey returned to Ji and Rupert.

"Seramina's on her way, she'll be here in a moment," she told them quietly.

Peter had returned to Kat's bedside where he sat watching her intently. The rest of them stood a short distance away and were quiet as they bore witness to a father's darkest moments.

"Do you really think having Seramina go into Kat's mind will work?" Ji murmured to Rupert.

"Well, like I said, Kat seems ter be reactin' to touch so it seems the logical thing ter try," Rupert answered, his eyes on Kat and his arms folded in front of him.

"I wouldn't worry about Seramina," Carey added. "Her mind-reading has really excelled since she first arrived. I'm sure she'll be careful. Just… try not to alarm her. She's already been through enough already."

"Yes, I have. But that doesn't mean I won't be able to help," a small voice came from behind them.

Carey, Ji and Rupert whipped around to find Seramina standing in the doorway, staring at Kat in her hospital bed. Carey felt embarrassment redden her cheeks when she realised Seramina had overheard her.

"Seramina, I meant nothing by it—" she started in apology but Seramina shook her head in dismissal.

"It's all right, Carey. I know you were only saying that because you want to protect me," she said, looking up at her. "But I really don't need it."

Feeling abashed, Carey watched as the young telepath walked to where Kat lay. Rupert followed her, muttering suggestions and theories to Seramina. Ji came up beside Carey and whispered, "Oops."

Carey nudged him back, the embarrassment still hot in her cheeks. She shook it off though and joined the others — she would apologise to Seramina properly later.

Seramina was listening intently to Rupert as he spoke, her brows puckered ever so slightly. She was calm despite his words, nodding in comprehension, and Carey saw that the young telepath she had met in Burtonport was gone. She was no longer the scared, meek child they had saved from burning; she had transformed, perhaps not in appearance, but there was that inexplicable feeling which, at that very moment, Seramina seemed to be radiating. What had changed her? How had she suddenly become this confident and powerful being that so differed from the young girl in her diary?

There was a short pause following Rupert's speech, in which Seramina looked down upon Kat in silence. Peter stood up from his chair and placed a hand on her shoulder.

"I know we're asking a lot of you right now, Seramina, but I would greatly appreciate it if you could try," he said softly, though it was difficult not to hear the strain of desperation in his voice.

With a nod Seramina said, "Of course I'll try. What's the use of being able to read minds if I can't help?"

"Jus' don't touch her," Rupert reminded her as she made her way around to the top of Kat's bed.

With the four of them watching on, Seramina closed her eyes and took a deep breath. She held her hands in front of her chest, her palms facing down towards Kat. The room was suddenly so quiet that Carey swore she could hear the thudding of her own heart. She felt Ji move closer to her, but he didn't take her hand again. They stood in absolute silence as the young telepath investigated Kat's mind.

Seramina's eyes flew open and she looked up at her four spectators.

"She's fine but… something's different now. She has all these memories in her head that aren't hers," she frowned.

"How can you tell?" Ji asked.

"The mind is like a puzzle. I can tell if something is there that shouldn't be, and now, Kat's memories are mixed up with someone else's. I'm not sure what it is," Seramina said uncertainly. "But it wasn't there before."

"She is all right, though?" Peter asked with wide eyes.

Seramina nodded. "I don't sense any damage. Just… extra memories."

"Can we wake her then, Rupert?" Carey enquired, relieved to hear that there was no immediate danger.

Rupert let out a sigh through his nose. "I'll release her from the spell I've set over her so she can wake, but I won't rouse her yet. I would rather she come back on her own."

Peter seemed to struggle with this for a moment before giving a terse nod and resuming watch over his daughter.

"Do you need anything else?" Seramina asked quietly, still looking down over Kat.

Carey shook her head. "No, I think that's all for now. We'll call if we need you." And with a small nod and a tight-lipped grimace, Seramina left the ward.

Peter remained at Kat's side as she slept, and Rupert went about his duties as healer, leaving Carey and Ji sitting a few beds over to wait. Carey sat cross legged on the white sheets, her back to the wall; Ji sat opposite her, his smoky blue eyes downcast. They sat in silence as time moved slowly, each agonising minute that passed piercing Carey's heart. She wound a loose thread from the sheet around her fingertip until it was blue, the cotton digging into her skin so she might feel something other than what she felt in that moment.

Ji's hand crept across the bed between them, stopping as his fingertips met her hands. Carey didn't pull away, so numb was she that any feelings she may have felt otherwise were dimmed in comparison.

"It's not your fault," she heard him whisper. "You heard what Seramina said. Kat's fine, Carey. She's going to be fine."

Carey swallowed the bile rising in her throat. It burned.

"No, it's not," she rasped. "There's something wrong, I know it. She has memories in her head that weren't there before. How can that be?"

When Ji didn't answer, she pushed on. "I know it's something I did. It has to be. I'd been using that magic of mine right before it happened, the one I…" she trailed off and Ji reached a little farther and took her hand in earnest.

"Listen to me. You did nothing wrong. It's not you. Peter had the same effect when he touched her, you saw it too. You can't blame yourself. Kat's going to be fine. She's tough," he said in pleading tones, and Carey blinked back hot tears that were forming in her eyes.

They fell into silence once more, Ji's hand in hers, and they remained this way until a groan sounded from Kat's bed. They pulled apart, immediately alert. She was stirring, and Carey and Ji moved swiftly to her bedside, along with Rupert. Slowly, Kat's eyes fluttered open. At first, she simply stared up at the ceiling, everyone waiting for her to say something. Then, without moving, she looked around until her eyes fell on Carey.

"I saw the dungeon," she said.

Rupert and Peter turned to look at her as Carey said, confusedly, "The dungeon?"

Kat nodded slowly. "The dungeon. The one where they kept Ji when he was being held captive."

Carey's insides froze, ice dropping into the pit of her stomach. "W-what?"

"I saw it all — Ji and what they did to him. But I wasn't me. I was you, Carey," Kat said, her eyes round and her complexion pale.

It took a moment for them all to absorb what she'd just said. It was Ji who spoke first.

"They're not your memories, the extra ones Seramina spoke of. They must be Carey's."

"It was because Carey touched her, isn't it?" Peter addressed Rupert. "She has Carey's memories somehow because they touched. And if that's true, then…" he added, his eyes slightly unfocused as though seeing something the others could not. "Oh Kat… what did you see…?"

He went to grab Kat's hand without thinking but stopped himself when she pulled away.

"I saw Mother… the day before she died. She knew something wasn't right…" Kat whispered painfully, and the colour from her father's face drained away. She looked from her father's face to Rupert. "What's happening to me?"

For a moment Rupert seemed lost for words, but then with a shake of his head he said, "I'm not sure, Kat. Ter me, everythin' seems fine. You're not sick or injured — you seem perfectly normal."

"Except that all of a sudden I can see other people's memories when I touch them. Rupert, that's not what I would call normal!" she cut across, pushing herself up to sit and tapping her head a little manically. "Where is that coming from?"

"A special power, perhaps?" Ji suggested before Rupert could answer. "If everything else is normal then perhaps you've suddenly developed a special power."

Kat stared at him, considering his words. "A special power?" she said in a small voice, and Ji nodded cautiously. She looked down at her lap, wringing the edge of her blanket. "A special power…"

She was silent for a moment, lost in thought, but when she lifted her head again, her voice was filled with a supressed anger. "No. This isn't a *special* power. This isn't something new and wonderful. *This* is some cosmic joke! I… *touch* someone and suddenly I'm on the floor. Memories… horrible, terrifying memories play out in my head and I see everything! I *feel* everything! It's as though I'm there, *right there*, and I can't stop it! I can't…" Her voice was now loud and forceful. *"How* exactly is that supposed to be *special?"*

Kat's outburst was so aggressive that it forced them to retreat a few steps from her bed.

"I'm sure Ji didn't mean it like that, darling," Peter Lawrence said, trying to console his daughter. "If it's a new power though, it could be that you need to learn to control it."

"Yer father's right, Kat. If it is a new power then perhaps yer mind is in shock an' tha' is what is causin' these fits," Rupert offered in a soothing tone.

Kat shut her eyes; her fists balled up in her lap.

"Can everyone just go, please?" she said finally through grit teeth.

When no one moved she barked, "Please! Just… go."

Carey tugged at Ji's sleeve and reluctantly they made to leave. Carey glanced back momentarily to see Kat flop back on the bed, her arm lying across her eyes. Rupert had taken Peter to the Healer's quarters at the other end of the room, so they carefully closed the ward's doors behind them as they left.

"Have you heard of this before?" Carey said, turning to Ji.

He shook his head dismally. "I've known Seers who can See a person's future with a single touch, but they're born that way, their powers don't develop at some later point in life. What's more, Kat is seeing the past, not the future. This isn't Seeing. This is something else."

They continued walking in silence until they reached the top of the stairs leading down to the front hall. Carey thought about the implication of Kat's newfound ability, if that's indeed what it was. She shuddered at the idea of Kat being able to see into her past; she was honestly glad that the dungeon memory was the worst of what she'd seen. Kat and Ji were her best friends, there was no doubt of that, but even then, there were memories she'd rather not share. The people she had killed with that power of hers, for example…

She followed Ji to his room, and they took seats on the balcony. Ji lay back in his and threw his legs up, boots resting on the balcony railing. His hair rippled gently in the light breeze and his blank gaze settled somewhere far in the distance as they sat for a time, silent in their companionship. He had taken his Seeker necklace from around his neck and was turning it over and over in his palms.

"I sometimes wonder about us Carey," he said, continuing to turn the pendant over in his hands.

For a heart-jerking moment she thought he was referring to the two of them, until she realised, he was talking about them as a whole — Kat included.

"What do you mean?" she asked warily.

He stared unseeing down at his necklace. Then he shook his head and placed it back around his neck. "Nothing. Forget I said anything."

Briefly, Carey wondered whether she should ask him what the matter was but stopped, knowing that if it were her, she wouldn't want to be pressed. He would talk when he was ready.

"So, do you really think Kat might have a new power?" she said, changing the subject.

Ji folded his arms behind his head, his face scrunched up in thought. "That's the thing, isn't it? I have a theory as to why she saw those particular memories. What were you thinking of before she collapsed?"

Carey could see where Ji was going with this. "Of course! I had just managed to Twilight Travel properly and it was so wonderful... it wasn't horrible or terrifying, like that time I saw you in the dungeon being tortured..." her eyes flit to Ji's but he made no acknowledgement of the fact. "I was thinking of it, so therefore... that would explain why she saw that memory. But what about her father?"

"Well, it makes sense. Peter had just heard that something had happened to his daughter. The only thing he would be thinking about would be losing Kat like he lost Jiani. What if they had been Kat's last moments? Of course, he would be thinking of his wife," Ji reasoned, and all Carey could do was nod; she could not argue with that.

"But just imagine," Ji continued, "If Kat can get this power under control, if that is what it is, imagine what that would mean. No one could lie to her. She'd be able to see the truth in anyone..."

"Poor Kat, though," Carey said softly. "To have those memories forced on her."

"Which is why I'm hoping it's an ability she can master," Ji answered her concern. "She might be able to control what she sees, or even *if* she sees."

Carey grunted. "You saw how she reacted earlier. I'm not sure she wants to see any of it, to be honest. To not be able to touch anyone without seeing their memories…"

Running a hand over his face, Ji sighed. "Kat's resilient. She may have reacted like that, but I think once she's calmed down, she'll find a way of dealing with it. She always does. Perhaps she'll finally be able to find out how Rupert knows so much about Council meetings."

Carey gave a small chuckle and Ji winked, a sly grin stretching across his face. "Oh, I don't know if anything would be able to prise that secret from him."

"That said, if Kat did manage to control it and was willing to use it, it would be an advantage, strategically speaking that is. Hypothetically, we could find out the truth from anyone, especially any loyalists we catch," Ji thought out loud.

"In any case," Carey carried on, "if she does choose to wield it, she won't have any issues grasping it, unlike me…"

Ji noticed the bitterness in her voice and gave her a pitying look. "Ah, Carey. Everyone is different. Everyone's powers are different. Give it time — you'll get there."

Carey snorted. "And yet, you can bet Kat will probably have this under control by tomorrow morning. You know how she is."

"Ha. Very true," he concurred, rocking back in his chair. "I'm not particularly sure I would want her seeing *my* past, though. It was bad enough for me, let alone for anyone else."

Carey said nothing to this; she wasn't sure what to say even if she could. They sat for a while longer, each deep in their own thoughts, contemplating the events of the day. Ji eventually sent for a plate of food to be brought up and they ate quietly, Carey only managing to eat a few bites before abandoning it.

"Do you think we should go see how Kat's doing?" she suggested as the orange glow from the setting sun began to creep across the balcony.

Ji finished the last of his cup and placed it back on the table between them. "As long as she doesn't try to throw us out again."

"Well, we just won't let her then."

Approaching the Healer's Ward, they ran into Peter Lawrence. He seemed happier than when they last saw him, a smile upon his face. They asked how Kat was faring.

"She's better now, much calmer," he said. "I think she feels embarrassed with how she reacted before but it's understandable. Knowing Kat, she'll be back on her feet in no time."

Carey sighed with relief. "That's good to hear."

"Now if you will excuse me, you two, I need to go and meet with your parents," and Peter patted Carey and Ji on the shoulders and strode away.

Ji listened as his footsteps retreated, a deep sadness etched across his face. Carey put a hand on his shoulder. "Ji?"

Ji turned to her, his face suddenly smooth and a small smile playing on his lips. "Come. Let's see if we can't cheer Kat up."

They walked in to find Kat sitting up in her bed, eating. She had changed into a loose white top and her hair was pulled back into a knot on the top of her head. When she saw them, she placed the chicken wing she'd been working on back on her plate and eyed them awkwardly.

"Evening," Ji greeted her cheerfully.

"Evening," she returned, not quite meeting their eyes.

There was a moment where Kat picked at her chicken before blurting out, "I'm really sorry about before. I know you were only trying to help, and I was being ridiculous, and this isn't your fault or anything but I just... I just..."

She couldn't quite finish; Carey stepped forward and sat by her side. "You have nothing to apologise for. Don't think on it for another moment."

Kat smiled in relief. "Thank you."

She picked up the chicken and started eating again. "I am so hungry. I feel like I haven't eaten in ages."

"Well I'm glad it hasn't affected your appetite then," Ji quipped as he joined

Carey on the end of Kat's bed.

Kat brandished a chicken leg at him. "Oh, shut up."

"Always one for a witty comeback," he said with a smirk.

With narrowed eyes, Kat said, "Indeed. Just count your blessings that I can't thump you one right now."

"How are you doing with that, by the way?" Carey asked, cutting across what was sure to be a smart comment on Ji's part.

Kat shrugged. "It does seem to be what Ji and Rupert said — a new power, although right now it doesn't feel particularly fantastic. My regular powers seem to be fine..."

"We have an idea as to why you saw those visions before, when you touched Carey and your Father," Ji told her, all playfulness gone from his voice now. "Here's what we think..."

With deep interest, Kat listened as Ji explained his and Carey's theory.

"Well, it certainly makes sense, at least," she said as she placed her plate on the bedside table. "The question now is how to control it. It's going to be a nightmare trying to walk around the castle without bumping into anyone. I can't keep collapsing all over the place — that would get tired very quickly."

Carey looked down at Kat's hands and a sudden thought sprung to mind. "Do you have to touch someone with your bare hands to see their memories?"

"What do you mean?" Kat asked.

"Do you have to touch skin? Or can you still draw memories from someone say, through clothes?" Carey explained.

"I don't know. Maybe," Kat said as she held out her hands in front of her. Tentatively, she reached out towards Carey, but then she pulled back, hesitating. She looked down at her palms, fingers splayed out on her lap. Her breathing was heavy, and Carey could feel the apprehension radiating off her in waves.

"Should we get Rupert?" Carey suggested, gently.

Kat pressed her lips together, working her bottom lip between her teeth. She gave a small nod. "Yes. Just in case."

Ji stood up and strode across to the Healer's quarters, returning a moment later with Rupert. "Kat's going to try something, and we need you here in case she has another fit," he said in explanation to Rupert's look of consternation.

"Ah, do you mind if Kat tries on you, Ji?" Carey said. Kat looked at her questioningly but did not press her.

"All right," Rupert directed. "Ji, come a bit closer t' Kat. That way, if she has another seizure, she will at least fall onto her bed an' not sideways an' out onto the floor."

Ji shuffled over and sat on the chair by her bed, leaning over to her. Cautiously, Kat reached out. Carey looked on tensely as Kat paused for a second, her finger hovering barely an inch from Ji's shirt before extending it and making contact with the fabric.

There was a collective gasp in which Kat sat there with her finger stuck to Ji's chest. Nothing happened and a grin stretched across Kat's face.

"Nothing!" she said triumphantly as she lowered her hand.

"Then I guess a good pair of gloves is your answer for now," Ji said with an equally wide grin.

Rupert sighed audibly in relief. "Thank heavens fer that," he said as he wiped his brow. "I'm gonna go lie down. I've had enough excitement fer one day."

"*You've* had enough excitement?" Kat said incredulously as Ji sniggered and Carey rolled her eyes.

"Yes! Curse the day I stumbled across ye lot!" Rupert said in mock seriousness and the four of them laughed, although Carey couldn't help thinking that perhaps there was just the smallest bit of truth in that.

~Chapter Eight~

Sighting Responsibility

Carey sat in the chair by her fireplace, watching with unseeing eyes as the embers glowed and crumbled within. Night had well and truly fallen hours before and the castle was still, quiet as a graveyard. The light from the coals illuminated a blood-red stone in her hands, its contents ever swirling as she ran her fingers over its surface. All their focus on Kat's new ability had thrown her own into sharp relief — she finally felt a flicker of confidence in the way she had managed to Travel the day before, even if it had only been momentary.

She glanced down at the pendant in her hands and wondered… Could she risk it? She hadn't forgotten her desire to know about Elara Parnell, hadn't forgotten Saar's words. Kat's predicament had served only as a short-lived distraction, yet now Carey knew she was in no danger, her mind had wandered back to the stone and her grandmother's sister. She needed to know now, and the mystery surrounding her only grew more enticing the longer Carey waited.

Gripping the stone tightly, she leaned back in the chair and closed her eyes, reaching for just a glimmer of that magic within. She concentrated on Saar's face, allowing his voice to fill her head for the first time, willing him to appear, summoning him like he had summoned her…

"Well, isn't this a surprise."

Carey's eyes flew open. She was still sitting in the chair by the fire; the blackened wood still glowing softly within, and the night air still fluttering in through her open window, but the edges of her room were soft, almost blurred. And sitting across from her, legs crossed, a finger tracing his bottom lip, was Saar. His dark hair was tied back, and his bright silver eyes were watching Carey with amusement.

"Why, summoning people now, are we? I didn't realise you had advanced so far," Saar said, lip curling.

Carey said nothing, waiting for him to ask. Finally, after another long minute of watching her with a wolfish expression, he said, "Why have you summoned me? I'm guessing it's not to let me know you have changed your mind."

She scoffed. "What if I had?" she challenged him.

"You'll never know now, will you," Saar answered cleverly. "Like I said, you had your chance."

"Chance to do what, exactly?"

She was trying to catch him off guard, hoping he would reveal something, anything, about his plans, but he only smiled, white teeth glittering.

"Trying to catch me out, Princess?" he said silkily, leaning forward in his chair and resting his elbows on his knees. "Nice try, but it will take much more than a bit of summoning and a few well-placed questions for me to tell you anything."

Carey swallowed, trying not to let any disappointment show on her face. It had been a long shot, but still...

"I wonder," he continued, fingers steepled under his chin, "What is it you will tell your dear parents once you wake?"

She narrowed her eyes. "What do you mean?"

"Well, you have sworn to tell them any time you have contact with me, haven't you?"

Carey stopped. How on earth could he know that? She had made that promise only to her parents. Who else had they told that it had made its way back to Saar? Her heart fluttered uncomfortably in her chest.

"I wasn't planning on saying anything," she managed, lifting her chin and squaring her shoulders.

Saar's eyebrows lifted towards his hairline. "Really now? How interesting. Clearly there is something you wish to speak with me about, then. Well, what if I refused? Simply left...?"

Carey grit her teeth. "I summoned you here—"

"Oh yes, very good," Saar cut across her, waving a hand about the room. "But I'm

afraid that is all you have done. Keeping me here..." he fixed her with narrowed eyes. "That, I must say, is much more than you can handle."

Slowly, he reached out in front of him, palm facing downwards, then curled his fingers into a fist. The room about her shuddered and Carey felt a tremor shiver through her body.

"You may have summoned me here, but I now have control," he snarled, the corner of his mouth curling viciously. "So, I suggest you tell me what it is you summoned me here for, Princess, or you will find my patience starting to wane."

Carey stared hard at him for another moment, pushing back the terror now trying to surface, before glancing down at her closed fist. She felt the difference now. Where a moment a go she had felt the magic flowing about her, creating this illusion as her own, now she felt stuck, like she had fallen into a mud pit and the sludge was holding her down. This was not how she had imagined this going...

"Just after I defeated Malevolence, you visited me," she said, willing her voice to be calm and smooth. It wavered only slightly. "You spoke of my grandmother... and her sister."

She looked back up at Saar to find him watching her still with those cold eyes. Her words had brought about a look of smugness upon his face and he smiled wickedly.

"You speak of Elara."

Carey sat up a little straighter, trying not to seem too eager, the terror subsiding a little at his words. "You knew her, then?"

His lips parted ever so slightly, and he ran his tongue along the edge of his teeth, pausing as he considered his answer. "You could say that."

"Well did you, or didn't you?"

She hadn't meant to speak so sharply, but Carey knew that Saar was familiar with Elara's story and that he was deliberately toying with her. He could sense her desperation and he was enjoying it.

"Elara's story is... complicated," he said, still smiling as though enjoying a private joke. "Let's just say that your grandmother took one path, and Elara took a very different one."

"She became an Imperial?" Carey said in hushed tones, eyes widening.

"Mmm," Saar hummed, "In a matter of speaking."

So that was why she had never heard of Elara — if people knew Fianna Parnell's own sister had been an Imperial, it would cast doubt upon the entire Order. She had been the blackest of black sheep, and this was surely how Saar had known her.

Saar was watching Carey closely now, an eyebrow raised as he sat back, languid against the dark upholstery. He was observing her with hawk-like intensity, and Carey set her jaw. She knew he would tell her no more, but he had the upper hand now, this plane under his control once more, and somehow, she knew he was not done.

"How did you come by her name? I don't believe I had mentioned her before," he asked, his voice smooth and low.

Carey didn't answer, but she clenched her fist even harder, only just realising that even though they were not really in her room, the stone was still set firmly between her fingers. She held it as she had summoned him, and inadvertently brought it with her; she had imagined herself in her room just as it was, when she should have thought to hide it.

Saar's bright eyes flickered down to her hands, then back to her face, his lips curving knowingly.

"You have something of hers..." he said, mouth stretching into a proper grin now. *"A token... or a trinket..."*

Carey couldn't deny it; she was clearly hiding something within her fist, but she wasn't about to reveal it to him. He couldn't force her to open her hands here, she knew that, but she still shuddered with silent panic. She closed her eyes, trying to draw back into herself, away from this dreamscape, but it was no use — Saar held her firmly in place, and she heard him laugh softly at her efforts.

He waited for her to open her eyes, nodding at her fisted hands.

"I am guessing you have not shown this object to your parents then?" Saar continued, mirth dancing in his eyes now.

She didn't say a thing. Saar's gaze flickered towards the fire; a log shifted heavily in the fireplace, and the light flared in the hearth. Carey threw up her hand as it bounced sparks into the room, and in that moment, her hand slipped on the stone; it flashed in the firelight, its red gleam dancing in Saar's eyes. He had managed to glimpse the ruby-coloured jewel before Carey could tuck it away, and his expression was hungry now. Slowly, he got to his feet, looking down at Carey as she tried to hold her wits about her. He bowed low, his face nearing hers as he did so.

"Until next time, my dear Princess," he hissed quietly, his voice wavering with suppressed glee.

He made the same movement he had done before, crossing his arms before bringing them down at his sides, and the room dissolved. Carey heard his laughter fade with the light before her eyes fluttered open and she found herself alone once more, the embers glowing low in the fire by her feet, Elara's stone clutched tightly to her chest.

*

"Carey! Wait up!"

Kat's voice rang through the castle foyer. Carey stopped midway up the main stairs and turned to see Kat bounding up to meet her. She was smiling wildly, her mess of wavy hair framing her jubilant face.

"You look happy," Carey observed. "What's going on?"

As they continued up the stairwell, Kat said, "I've just been to see Master Henlow."

Master Henlow was the wizard helping Ji to manipulate his magic in order to sense his surroundings. He had once told Carey that it was as close as he would get to seeing again. After Kat had been reluctantly discharged from the Healer's Ward by Rupert, she and Ji had gone to Master Henlow. He had agreed to help, and Kat had taken to these sessions with the same kind of fervour she generally applied to her weapons training. It had barely been two weeks and already it seemed she was making some real progress.

"How did it go this time?"

Kat was ecstatic. "Fantastic. You have no idea. I didn't collapse at all this time. I'm finally managing to slow the memories as I receive them, too. Apparently, that's what was causing me to seize up — the memories were just too much for me to handle and it would just knock me out cold."

"What, so you've mastered this already?" Carey asked, although not entirely surprised.

Kat chuckled. "No! I might not be collapsing like I was, but I still faint from time to time. I can hold on without completely losing it for about thirty seconds but if I don't pull back before then..."

She mimed passing out. Carey laughed.

"I told Ji that I knew you'd have no problem with this. If only I was having as much luck with my own magic," Carey added irritably.

"Why don't you ask Master Henlow for help?" Kat suggested as they turned right down a corridor.

"Do you think he'd be able to?" Carey asked, wondering if Master Henlow had any experience with Twilight Travellers.

Kat shrugged. "It's worth a try. He's been able to help Ji and me so why not?"

Carey considered it for a moment. After her disastrous summoning of Saar, she had been reluctant to try again. Clearly, despite any success she had made with Kat, she still needed help.

"I'll go see him tomorrow — the worst he can say is no."

"Good idea. You're still not sleeping because of it either, are you?" Kat observed, gazing into Carey's face.

Carey tugged a piece of hair behind her ear. It was true — Saar's interest in Elara's stone had made her uneasy, and she hadn't forgotten his parting words. Of course, Kat knew nothing of this. Carey knew Kat's aversion to the stone and she did not feel like getting berated for what she realised now had been an incredibly stupid thing to do. After all, Saar had not threatened her, nor had he revealed anything of importance, so Carey felt quite uncompelled to tell Kat, or anyone else for that matter, anything about it. "He hasn't shown his face once since that night all those weeks ago and I still can't sleep. When I do, I have such nightmares..." she lied, speaking only partial truths.

Kat placed a sympathetic hand on her arm. "I think going to see Master Henlow is a good idea, then. You can't keep going on like this."

Throwing her head back, Carey closed her eyes. "Oh, the plight of a Seeker."

Kat gave a small titter. "By the way, do you know where Rupert is? I feel like I should tell him about my progress. He's been ridiculously worried about me," Kat said.

"I think he, Kyna and Seramina are in the garden. Have you seen Ji?"

Kat started walking again. "I saw him briefly outside Master Henlow's quarters. He was going in to see him when I left. I'm sure we'll see him later."

They found the others in the garden, lazing beneath a large tree whose branches spread wide before drooping to the ground. Its tendrils were thick with bright flowers that Seramina and Kyna were examining.

"Kat! Carey! We've been expectin' you!" Rupert called out as he spotted them crossing the lawn. His younger sibling had gifted him with a mop of red hair today and he looked more like Seramina's older brother than Kyna's.

"Expecting us?" Carey repeated.

Kyna laughed, her bright dark eyes crinkling at the edges. "Wha' he means is tha' he wants ter know all about Kat's session."

Rupert waved a hand at his sister. "Wha' yer talkin' about, Kyna. I already know it went well."

Kat put her hands on her hips and pursed her lips. "Oh? And how is it that you know that?"

Rupert winked mischievously. "Ye know better than ter ask me tha', Kat."

Narrowing her eyes, Kat flopped down next to him, careful not to touch him. "One day, Rupert, I'll find out how you know all these things," she threatened.

He snorted. "I'd like ter see you try."

Carey seated herself across from the two and stretched out her legs. The grass was soft and cool beneath the shade of the large tree.

"So? Tell me how it went?" Rupert coaxed Kat, and she relayed everything she had just told Carey. When she was done, Rupert grinned.

"So, in other words, I don't have ter keep a spare bed ready for ye anymore."

Kat glared back haughtily.

Kyna and Seramina came over to join them and Kyna said, "Can ye show us now, then?"

After a moment's consideration, Kat nodded. "Yes, I think I can try."

"Ooh! Then do Rupert!"

Carey and Seramina laughed as Rupert slunk away from Kat a little. "Come now, Kyna, I was only jokin' before. Besides, I don't want ter put Kat under any more stress, if she's only jus' come back from a session of doin' it," he said nervously.

"Ye don't have ter let her see how yer know everythin', dear brother. Think of somethin' only I know, tha' Kat won't know about," she sniggered.

He turned his head towards Kat. "Yer don't have to, if yer not feelin' up to it."

Kat fixed him with a steely eye, one eyebrow raised playfully. "I'm feeling quite all right, Mister Tagore. You have absolutely nothing to worry about. Now stop playing healer and hold out your hand."

Rupert hesitated, then held out his hand to Kat, who grinned wickedly. "Ready?" she teased, removing one of her gloves.

"Just take it, would ye?" he said, and Kat reached out.

As Kat grasped Rupert's hand, Carey could see her eyes flickering beneath her eyelids, as though she were dreaming. Her brow was creased in concentration as she took possession of Rupert's memories. Carey counted the seconds and smiled as Kat managed to hold on for the longest time yet without fainting or letting go. Seramina and Kyna held their breaths in anticipation. After almost a minute of holding on, Kat returned and, swaying slightly, she leaned back, releasing Rupert's hand. Her eyes were set upon Rupert's, searching.

"So?" Kyna interrupted. "What did ye see?"

Kat hesitated but Rupert gave her a consenting nod. She took a deep breath; her voice was no longer playful, but steady and low. She turned her gaze to Kyna. "I saw… a garden, overgrown but filled with beautiful flowers of every type. It was like a maze with an endless number of places to hide and trees to climb. A large stone house stood alongside it where you lived. You would play in the garden for hours — you even had a sort of playhouse where anything seemed possible and the troubles of the world would just disappear. It was your sanctuary.

"Your home was in the mountains, so you managed to stay hidden for a long time, but then the Empire found you. They burnt everything, your village, your house... your garden..."

"You were brought to live here in the shanty town with the other slaves. The city was grey and dark, and your parents soon fell ill. They passed away not long after you arrived.

"But Rupert..." she now turned back to him. "You never let the darkness, or the Empire get you down. You would spend hours recounting your adventures in that garden, helping Kyna to remember what it was like — the green of the leaves, the colours of each of the flowers, the blue of the sky... You helped her to escape..."

Kat faltered; she couldn't carry on. She was looking at Rupert with a mixture of admiration and sadness, but he didn't notice, he was watching his little sister, whose eyes were glistening with tears. He reached over to her, and she buried her head in his chest.

"Tha' wasn't fair," she mumbled into his shirt. "This was a game..."

"I know," Rupert said gruffly. "I'm sorry..."

Seramina looked on, a tear streaking down her cheek, and Carey could only guess at what she was thinking. Perhaps she was remembering her own brother with whom she must've played with and shared happy memories. Carey thought of her own sisters — had she possibly shared similar times, playing in gardens and sharing in happiness? How many joyful memories had been forfeited for her siblings and herself? They had each lost much in the way of their childhoods; innocent times erased by the war that consumed their families.

Kat heaved a deep sigh as she ran a hand through her hair.

"I think I need to go see my father," she said pointedly. "I really should let him know how it went today. Seramina, Carey."

Kat nodded towards the siblings, and Carey motioned for Seramina to follow. The three of them left the garden in silence, leaving the brother and sister alone.

"Did you know that about Rupert?" Carey asked Kat once they were out of earshot.

"No," Kat said heavily. "I knew his parents had passed away a while back, but he never told me how. I guess I don't really know that much about Rupert that's actually personal."

Seramina began quietly sobbing and Carey wrapped an arm around her shoulders in comfort.

"Do you think that's why he is the way he is? Always joking around, I mean," Carey wondered.

"Possibly," Kat said with a shrug. "I suppose everyone has their own ways of coping."

They walked on in silence, each lost in their own thoughts. Carey had never asked Rupert about his past, possibly because she herself was not one for divulging much of her own. She had never realised how incredibly selfish that was until now.

"I had a feeling there was more," Seramina said in a hushed voice, tears wet on her face. "I always have. I always felt a kind of sadness…"

The poignancy of this lay heavily on the two Seekers. Carey knew that Kat was experiencing the same guilt as she was.

"You did well, though. Those sessions really are paying off," Carey said, desperately wanting to move the conversation away from Rupert. "How do you feel?"

"I have a bit of a headache, actually," Kat said, rubbing her forehead, "but it's nothing terrible. I really stretched it with Rupert — I could feel myself losing it again at the end there. I'll need a lot more practice if I'm going to be able to hold on longer without fainting."

"Seriously, Kat? It's been, what, two weeks since you first experienced this power? I think you're doing extremely well," Carey added in consolation.

"And you're more relaxed too, I can feel it," Seramina said. "That's good, isn't it?"

"I'm more relaxed when I'm concentrating, when I'm expecting it. If I forget my gloves or my sleeves aren't quite long enough… I'm always so worried that I'll end up touching somebody by accident," Kat said with a grimace.

"Well there goes your pastime of randomly rubbing up against passers-by," Carey said with a smirk and Seramina giggled nervously.

Kat laughed sarcastically. "Yes, well, laugh all you like."

"I wasn't making light of it, Kat," Carey said apologetically, and Kat gave a small smile.

"I know," she said before falling back into thought and leaving Carey and Seramina to walk silently beside her.

It was just on sunset, which was customarily dinner time for their three families and Seramina, so the three girls made their way to the dining hall. Carey hoped that it would provide some distraction from what had transpired that afternoon.

Generally, it was unusual for everyone to be present at mealtimes — one or more of their parents were usually engaged elsewhere — so it came as a surprise when they entered to find all five of their parents seated at the table chatting away quietly. Ji was deep in conversation with his father when they opened the door. As Kat, Seramina and Carey entered, the four men in the room stood respectfully and didn't sit until the girls had taken their seats. Carey and Kat looked about the room warily, both wondering what occasion warranted a full dinner attendance. They were, it seemed, not to know until after dinner had been served though.

As they ate, Carey noticed that her parents were more reserved than their normal talkative selves, which immediately made her wary. She was only vaguely aware of Kat's conversation with Ji as butterflies were mounting in her stomach. She managed only a few mouthfuls of food as she watched her parents. It was difficult not to notice the meaningful glances, the reassuring squeeze of a hand. What was going on?

Once the dinner plates had been cleared, Robert Lee cleared his throat and the room fell silent.

"Jenny and I have an announcement we wish to make," he said as he took to his feet. "I know that you are all well aware of the circumstances in which Jody and Laurel's remains were found a few weeks back. Since then, we have been unable to uncover any further information regarding their final movements, especially those that lead to their deaths."

This came as a surprise to Carey. She wasn't aware that her parents had been investigating her sisters' deaths, although now she thought about it, it really should not have come as much of a surprise.

"What we wish to do now is take a small team and head out to where they were found in the hope that we may find more clues as to what exactly happened," Robert said, looking down at Jenny who gazed back at him determinedly. "We are hoping to leave in the next few days."

"Do you wish for any of us to join you?" Ji's father Oliver asked. "For you have my services, should you wish it."

Robert shook his head. "No, my dear friend, we are not asking any of you to join us this time. Besides, it is still early days, and there is many an Imperial who would salivate at the idea of the last Seekers all heading out from the Centre City at once."

Carey spoke up now. "But wouldn't the royal family be more of a target?" she asked, thinking that she, too, would be joining them.

Jenny reached across and took her hand; she didn't even have to speak for Carey to reach full understanding. "I'm not going with you," she said quietly.

"We need you here, darling. We need one of the royal family to be here to oversee our affairs whilst we're gone. We know it's such short notice," Jenny said apologetically, "but we know you'll be able to handle it. If you have any problems, Meela, Oliver and Peter will be here to help you, and of course, Lord Acheron."

Carey stared at them, struggling with the notion that her parents would be leaving for a place that was renowned for its high concentration of Imperial loyalists.

"Can't you send someone else to investigate?" she asked with slight desperation.

Jenny squeezed her hand. "We wish to see the burial site for ourselves, and perhaps... find some closure there."

"Don't worry, Carey," Ji's mother Meela said softly. "Your parents are stronger together and we will be here to help in any way possible."

Regardless of their reassurances, Carey felt a twinge of unease. She stayed behind once dinner had finished and waited for everyone else to leave before approaching her parents.

"Is there no other way you can find out more about Jody and Laurel without travelling to the Darklands?" she asked in a low voice. "Is there no one else you can send?" She tried to hide her anxiety but failed miserably.

"Sweetheart," her mother said gently. "Why are you so worried? We have gone out of the city before. What is troubling you about this time?"

Carey swallowed hard; Saar was troubling her. He hadn't so much as hinted at a plan during their recent encounters, and she could deal with his threats and intrusions easily enough on a plane where she knew he could not hurt her. But if he knew her parents were heading for the Darklands, she was sure that would prove too great a temptation for him not to act on.

She said as much to her parents, knowing that they would believe her, but they shook their heads, and tried again to put her at ease.

"We'll have others with us," Robert said reassuringly. "Master Henlow will be joining us. He has travelled the Darklands before, so we won't be wandering in blindly."

Carey felt her stomach drop a little further at this; if she had hoped to find some wisdom in Master Henlow regarding her Twilight Travelling, it seemed it would have to wait now.

"How… how long do you think you'll be gone for?" Carey finally asked.

"We hope to be no longer than two weeks," Jenny stated bracingly.

"But aren't there some foreign dignitaries coming soon?" Carey asked, vaguely remembering a conversation that had happened during a recent Council sitting. "You will be back for that, won't you?"

"We hope to be, yes, but if we are unable to make it, then you will represent us," her father answered. "Again, you have nothing to worry about there. They are visiting to merely meet with our Council for the first time since the liberation. They will deliver information on their present situations, but that is all. You won't be called upon to make any decisions, only to discuss our current standings. Oliver will help you with that as the General of our armies."

"Oh," was all Carey could say, as the thought of having to meet these foreign ambassadors gave rise to a small thrill of anxiety in the pit of her stomach. The most she had ever done with regards to the Council was to sit in on their meetings in silence. She had been given tutelage in the geography and politics of the realm, so she supposed it wasn't a great surprise; the time would come when she would have been required to live up to her title, however much she detested it.

"All right," she nodded. "Just… just be careful."

Her mother pulled her into her arms and gave her a long hug. "We'll be back before you know it, darling."

~Chapter Nine~

Powers and Plans

Carey spent the two days before her parents' departure practicing her Twilight Travelling incessantly, determined to master it. She had to assume that Saar would know of her parents' plans so she needed a way to contact them swiftly, should the need arise. Master Henlow was distracted with preparations so was unable to help her, but perhaps there was someone else who could. Lord Acheron had said he was familiar with unusual magic; perhaps he knew something about Twilight Travelling…

In the meantime, Carey took to her room and spent every spare moment she had attempting to Travel. Since her last conversation with Saar, she found that her ability to hold her location had begun to slip; she was soon unable to hold on for more than a minute, which was barely enough time for a greeting let alone a proper conversation. Carey quickly discovered that the more frustrated she became, the less hold she had on her power, which then gave way to a desperate sense of panic.

She was lying on her bed following yet another failed attempt to Travel successfully when there came a quiet knock at the door. Carey lifted her head from the pillow. "Yes?"

It opened a crack and Seramina poked her head around the corner. Carey smiled. The young redhead entered, and Carey saw she was wearing an ankle length dress of emerald green with long chiffon sleeves that gathered at her wrists. Her hair was loose about her shoulders in its customary wild style.

"Seramina," Carey gave her a welcoming hug. "What brings you to my neck of the woods?"

Seramina sat on the edge of Carey's bed without a word; she was fidgeting nervously and wasn't quite meeting Carey's eye. Carey sat down beside her and took one of her hands in her own. "Seramina? What's the matter? Is everything all right?" she asked seriously.

The young telepath looked at her uncertainly. "Carey, I..." she stopped, biting her lip. "I don't know. I'm not sure, that is. This thing... I don't really know where to start," she rambled.

Carey said nothing, just gave her a moment to try and collect her thoughts. Seramina took a deep breath.

"I think something's happening."

Carey's heart leapt in her chest. "Happening? What do you mean?" she asked, trying to keep the anxiety from her voice, but Seramina felt it, flinching and pulling away. Carey cursed inwardly, regretting her momentary loss of control. "I'm sorry, I didn't mean for you to feel that. Please, tell me what's bothering you. Perhaps I can help."

Slowly, Seramina nodded. "I think you can. At least, that's why I came to you. You might know..."

Looking down at her hands, Seramina spoke softly; her voice shaking with nerves. "It started the day Kat collapsed and you called me to the Healer's Ward. It was nothing much at first. It was like a bit of a twinge, something annoying that I couldn't quite grasp, but then this morning I was at breakfast and your mother and father walked past me and... and I... I felt... it was..." she struggled to convey what had happened, shaking her head as words failed her.

"Just say what you felt, Seramina. Perhaps if you tell me that then we can work it out together," Carey said gently.

Seramina lifted her head. "But that's just it, Carey, I already know what it is."

"What?" Carey said, confused. "You know what it is? But I thought you didn't know."

Seramina shook her head. "It's like when I was first able to Hear when others were thinking of me. I knew straight away that's what it was. It was

104

a kind of magnification of what I could already do. At first, I could only speak with other telepaths, and then it was with others, like you. And then it was my Empathy. But this thing..." she trailed off.

"Is it different? Different to what you can do already?"

Seramina gave a small nod.

"You said you felt it as my parents walked by you. What did you feel?" Carey pressed, feeling a sense of growing alarm. She needed to know if it was something important, something that might affect them during their travels. She had to warn them.

Seramina's eyes widened. "No, no! It's nothing to do with your parents, Carey, it's most certainly me," she said, quickly reassuring her. It took Carey a moment to realise Seramina had heard exactly what she had been thinking.

"Let me think for a moment. How can I explain it? I can..." Seramina screwed her face up, searching for the right words. "I can sense other people's powers; how strong they are. But not just that... I can tell if they have any special powers, something they can do that others can't."

Her answer was not what Carey had been expecting, and for a moment she was at a loss for words. First Kat, now Seramina...

"So, you can sense the strength of a person's magic and if they can do something unique," she repeated slowly. "Is that right?"

"Yes!" Seramina said, her face lightening. "Yes, exactly. But that's not even the strangest part of it all."

"Oh?" Carey said curiously.

"No. That day Kat collapsed, all I wanted was to know what was happening to her. I wanted so badly to know if it was a new ability or if she really was unwell."

"We all did. We all wanted to know that," Carey said.

"But that's when it started, after I wished for it. I *wished* to be able to know her powers, to know if it was something special, different, and then suddenly, I could."

Carey was starting to see what Seramina was eluding to. "You think that just because you wished for it, you now have that ability?"

105

"It's the only thing I can think of," Seramina said wildly. "I wished to be able to and then I suddenly could! It sounds crazy. Do you think it's crazy? Is that even possible?"

"I... I can't say," Carey murmured. "I suppose anything is when it comes to magic."

Seramina pondered her words, pulling absent-mindedly at the hem of her sleeve. "You must really hate not being able to remember your past," she said suddenly. "I keep forgetting, and then I go and ask you things like this..."

Carey grimaced. "It's not so much not being able to remember that's frustrating," she paused, "It's feeling as though I'm missing something, as though I'm always one step behind."

"I get it," Seramina said consolingly. "That seems to be how I've felt every day since the Empire took my family."

Carey wondered whether Seramina knew exactly how she felt or whether she was just being empathetic, but she appreciated it, nonetheless.

"Oh, I don't know," she replied bracingly. "You seem to be doing an awful lot better than I am, if that's the case."

Seramina blushed before saying more seriously, "But really, what do you think? Do you think it's like my other abilities and merely just an extension of my telepathy, or could it be something completely new?"

Carey couldn't help but notice the expectation in her voice and wished she could give her a more reassuring answer. "Well, it's certainly an amazing ability, knowing another's strengths. It's not painful or anything, is it?"

Seramina shook her head.

"Well, I suppose it could be an extension of your telepathy — you are able to sense powers like you are able to hear thoughts. It might just be that, considering how easily it seems to come to you. I really wish I had something a little better to say about it though, Seramina. I'm sorry," she said apologetically.

Shaking her head, Seramina's face broke into a proper smile for the first time since entering the room. "No, no need to apologise. I think you're right, though, it is sort of similar, isn't it?"

"So, you're not upset?" Carey asked tentatively.

Seramina laughed lightly, as though the idea was ridiculous. "No! No. It was just what I needed to hear. Honestly, it scared me, especially when I thought it was something completely new, like Kat's, but it doesn't feel that way, you know? I felt what it was like for Kat — it was painful and scary for her — but it's not like that for me. It's familiar, easy. I mean, how could it be new if it's so easy?" she asked, her voice quivering with nervous laughter.

Her observation was not lost on Carey, though. She was right. She and Kat struggled with their new abilities, yet Seramina had grasped this skill so easily, and all by herself no less. The young girl seemed to be mastering much lately — only a few weeks ago she had managed full control over what she Heard. Seramina now only responded if someone consciously called for her, and she would not intrude on someone else's thoughts unless they were aware. For Carey, this mastering of her abilities seemed to occur almost instinctively, which was nothing short of amazing. The rate at which Seramina learned was astounding, yet she herself seemed blissfully unaware of her progress. Carey bit her lower lip; perhaps this ability was like hers or Kat's, but because of her amazing knack for learning, it didn't cause her the same sort of trouble.

"Thank you, Carey, for listening," Seramina said, grinning widely, the worry gone from her face now. "I know you don't think you were very helpful, but it really did, you know... help."

"Not a problem. I'm glad you thought so," Carey replied. "Are you sure you're fine, though?"

With a nod, Seramina got to her feet to leave. "Yes, I think so. I guess I just needed someone to talk to about it."

As she made to leave, Carey asked her one more question. "Seramina? Why me? Why did you come to me about this?"

Seramina looked back pensively. "Because I thought you of all people would understand. You're always so afraid of your power," she said as though this was the most obvious answer.

Carey was taken aback slightly. "I'm not afraid of my Twilight Travel-ling—"

"No, not that power, your other one," Seramina stopped her. "You always seem so afraid of it. But don't worry, Carey, I won't tell anyone."

And with that she closed the door, leaving a stunned Carey behind her.

*

"Carey?"

It was the afternoon following Carey's parents' departure and she had been sitting in the castle gardens, staring into nothingness when Kat and Ji found her. Until that moment she had been thinking of Saar, imagining what he was doing, what his plans were. Surely, he would have something waiting for her parents and their party.

She had warned them, hadn't she? Carey had made her fears known, yet still they had gone. As much as she admired their courage and strength, she couldn't help but feel afraid as she'd watched them leave.

"Oh... nothing. Actually no, not really nothing. I'm worried about my parents," she stammered as her friends joined her.

Kat reached across a gloved hand and placed it on her arm.

"Try not to worry too much, Carey. Remember, this is your parents we're talking about. I am most definitely sure they can weather anything that comes their way."

Carey nodded, unconvinced. "I know but... I can't help but feel like something bad will happen. I feel it in my gut..."

Ji sat on her other side, the dappled light through the branches above falling across his face.

"Is there anything we can do?"

Carey shrugged despondently. "I just wish I was there with them. I'm just so worried that Saar..."

"Look, Carey," Kat said seriously, giving her arm a light squeeze. "Your parents are strong, as are those that went with them. They know of Saar, and I don't doubt for a second that they won't be taking every precaution necessary. So, stop worrying."

Carey tried to laugh but it came out more like a hiccup. "Easier said than done. If I could get a grip on my Twilight Travelling once and for all, that would be swell. I'd be able to check in with them, make sure they're all right." She chewed her lip. "I was thinking of asking Lord Acheron for help."

"Lord Acheron?" Ji said in mild surprise. "Does he know about Twilight Travelling?"

"I don't know, but he told me once that he has some experience with unusual magic," Carey replied. "Perhaps he knows about Fiorilusa."

Kat frowned in thought, tipping her head to the side. "Perhaps."

"Well I know for a fact that Lord Acheron is in meetings with my father at the moment," Ji said, standing up. "How about we head down to the training room to spar in the meantime. Help take your mind off things," he said as Kat nodded in agreement.

She hadn't trained in a few weeks and Carey was glad for the distraction. Perhaps a good session of sparring was what she needed.

"Lead the way," she smiled.

Down in the training room, Ji, Kat and Carey found Kyna and Seramina amid their own training session. Not wanting to disrupt their practice, the three of them sat along the wall behind Sir Garrow and watched the two girls. Seramina was easily the better of the two, wielding her two short swords so effortlessly and with such grace that Carey thought she looked more like a dancer than a warrior, a comparison exaggerated by the sight of her skirts twirling about her knees as she moved. Her reflexes were sharp and Kyna's swords barely came close to finding their mark. Seramina deflected her efforts with such precision that there was no loud crashing of metal against metal that was typical of Carey, Kat or Ji's sessions, but rather a slight metallic pinging sound each time their swords connected, and within the space of a few short minutes, Seramina had pinned her opponent down no less than eight times.

"She's impressive, isn't she?" Ji leaned sideways to whisper to Carey. "I've observed Seramina, followed her movements a few times now, and I can hardly believe the improvement she's made in such a short time. I could only imagine what might happen should we put her in the arena with Kat,"

109

he mused with a smirk.

Kat, sitting on his other side, said nothing to this; she seemed too focused on the match in front of her to reply.

"This is the first I've seen her, actually," Carey admitted as she watched Seramina deftly flip Kyna onto her back and hold a sword to her throat.

"Did you know she's developed a new ability?" she continued in a hushed voice, hoping Seramina was so distracted with her spar not to notice the conversation.

With a frown, Ji shook his head. "No, I did not. What is it?"

"She said she can feel other peoples' powers, sense their abilities. Apparently, it started the day Kat's new magic presented itself. She said she *wished* for it, and the next thing she knew, she could do exactly that."

Ji's eyebrows stretched upwards. "Well that's certainly something I've never heard before," he said with a tone of surprise. "Wishing for an ability. So, she sought help from you, then? To master it?"

With a shake of her head, Carey answered, "That's the thing, she doesn't need help with it because it would seem she's already mastered it. What's more, she's already mastered it to the point where she's just wondering now whether it is part of her telepathy or something completely new."

Ji seemed momentarily awestruck. "And what did you say?"

"Well, I'm hardly an expert, but I said it sounded like it could be an extension of her telepathy, being able to know a person's powers like she can their thoughts, but I can't be sure. The real reason she came to see me was merely to tell me about it."

Carey left out the part where Seramina mentioned the fear she had of her own power. Kat and Ji knew only that she had a special power that had helped her in her defeat of Malevolence, but that was all. She still hadn't divulged the exact nature of that power to them and wasn't sure she ever would. Carey barely understood it herself.

Ji nodded in agreement. "I think you're right. It does seem an extension of her powers, although... have you noticed how rapidly Seramina has progressed since arriving here?"

Carey nodded silently, eyes following Seramina as she and Kyna began again.

"Then have you not noticed how much more confident she is compared to when she first arrived? She's almost a completely different person."

"Not to mention the strength and incredible precision of her powers," Kat said suddenly, her eyes still on the match. She had been listening after all.

"Who else has noticed Seramina?" Carey said, suppressing the tone of worry that shook her voice ever so slightly. A disturbing thought had just occurred to her. Saar had ways of knowing exactly what was going on within the castle. He had also shown interest in Carey's power, tried to persuade her to join him because of it. If he found out about Seramina, would he be enticed by her abilities as he had been with Carey?

"Mostly just our parents. We're really the only ones that spend any real time with her. The other Council members merely perceive her to be talented, but nothing beyond anything they've seen before," Ji whispered as Kyna almost landed a blow, only to have it deflected at the last possible moment by Seramina. "What are you thinking?"

Carey swallowed. "The usual."

Ji's jaw clenched and Kat glanced at her sideways, understanding her meaning at a glance.

"We won't let anything happen to her," Ji growled in a low voice and Carey nodded, eyes hard now.

"I know."

"I would love to know what is driving her though," Kat said, her gaze still fixated on Seramina.

Ji snorted. "Of course you would, if only to have her skill with a blade," he teased.

Without looking away, Kat landed a punch on Ji's shoulder. He smirked as he rubbed his arm beneath the cloth of his shirt and Carey smiled, enjoying their banter.

The door to the training room opened and Carey turned to see the tall figure of Lord Acheron enter the room. He wore a long, dark green coat over a dark suit, looking more like a city gentleman from the Common realm than a wizard of the Council. His golden-brown hair was tied back neatly in a queue as usual, and he wore a pleasant smile upon his face as he looked about the training room.

"Is there something I can do for you, Lord Acheron?" Sir Garrow called from where he stood, his eyes never leaving the girls sparring in the centre.

Walking smoothly across to where the sword master stood, Lord Acheron said, "When you have a moment, Sir Garrow. I need to speak with you."

Seramina pirouetted gracefully, blades twirling as she went, forcing Kyna to stumble back away from her. Sir Garrow nodded curtly. "If you don't mind, we are almost done here. Kyna! Watch your footing!"

Lord Acheron gave Sir Garrow a nod before moving back against the wall. Carey watched him, pausing for a moment in thought, then got to her feet.

"I'll be back," she said to the others before walking over to her parents' adviser.

Lord Acheron spotted her approaching and gave her a bow. "Your Highness. I hope you're well."

Carey gave him a warm smile in reply. "Well enough. I was wondering if I could speak with you about something?" She motioned to the doorway, and with a politely bewildered look, he gave her a nod and followed her out into the hallway.

"Your Highness?"

Carey paused a moment, wondering how best to broach the subject. "You told me when you first arrived that you have some experience with unusual magic."

He gave a small nod. "I did say that, yes."

"Well, I was wondering if you had any experience with... Twilight Travelling? Or Fiorilusa?"

Lord Acheron's eyebrows pulled together slightly. "I have worked with some Twilight Travellers in the past. Why do you ask?"

Carey grinned, an eager thrill surging within her. "Do you mind if I ask you something?"

~Chapter Ten~

Travel No Further

Carey stood before the dark wooden door leading to Lord Acheron's study. Her heart was beating a little faster, her breath coming a little quicker as she raised her hand to knock. It was just on sunset, and the castle inhabitants were beginning to settle for the night. Her knock echoed down the quiet corridor.

"Come in," she heard a voice call, and with a steadying breath, she opened the door.

Lord Acheron's study sat within one of the castle's towers; it was a wide, circular room with high arched windows of stained glass. The red light from the sunset shone through the panes, casting red-tinged hues upon the floor. A great circular rug lined the centre of the floor depicting a great battle; hundreds of tiny soldiers on steeds embroidered with stiff wool. Bookshelves laden with heavy tomes lined the walls where there were no windows, and a low-burning fireplace stood just to the side of the door, flanked by two high-backed lounge chairs. Towards the farthest wall, silhouetted against the largest of the windows was a heavy wooden desk, chairs on either side.

Lord Acheron was seated behind the desk, facing Carey when she entered. He rose gracefully to his feet, approaching her before gifting her a low bow.

"Your Highness," he said as he straightened up. "Welcome. Please come in."

He motioned to one of the chairs by the fireplace and Carey sat, perched on the edge.

"Please, just Carey, if you don't mind," she insisted as he sat down opposite.

Acheron had changed into a set of simple black robes since she had seen him earlier in the training room. The neckline was buttoned high at his throat and the long sleeves widened at his wrists. The hems were embroidered with a gold thread that gleamed in the light cast by the fire.

"Of course," he said with a voice like velvet, a genial smile upon his lips. "I've been told you are less than fond of being addressed by your title." At the look on Carey's face, he added, "Your parents," by way of explanation.

"I just prefer Carey. *Princess* seems a far cry from the orphanage, and I'm not quite used to it," she replied, fidgeting in her chair.

He was watching her with those bright eyes, his handsome features soft in the low light.

She cleared her throat. "But I didn't come to talk about titles and my aversion to them," she said, straightening up. "You said you might be able to help me?"

Lord Acheron leaned forward, resting his elbows on his knees and looking at her intently. "I can, but you need to tell me what you are able to do already, so I know what we need to work on."

Carey clasped her hands in her lap and began to speak. She told him everything, from the first time she Travelled, to Saar's summonings, and finally to her attempts to Travel with Kat. Lord Acheron sat and listened closely, not saying anything until she had finished her speech.

"Well, it sounds as though you have the basics covered at least," he said with an encouraging smile. "What you need to do now is practice your focus. You are losing your grip because you lose focus. Think back to the times you have Travelled without meaning to — you were so focused on where you were, on what was happening, that you were able to maintain your grip. With your recent attempts, however, you've been so focused on slipping, and that's exactly what ends up happening. Understood?"

Carey nodded slowly; it made sense. She had noticed the more she became frustrated and anxious, the less likely she was able to stay where she had Travelled to.

"Do you think you could help me to focus, then?" she asked hopefully.

He nodded. "I think so. Here," he said, sitting on the edge of his chair as she did and reaching out his hands to her. "Take my hands and I will guide you."

Carey hesitated for a moment before placing her hands in his.

"You'll feel a sensation as you Travel, like something is pulling you in a certain direction," he said, his slender fingers tightening slightly over her own. "That will be me. Focus on that pull, and when you arrive, centre yourself around it, feel it ground you, anchor you to that place. If you can focus on that, you will be less likely to slip."

Carey swallowed then nodded. "All right. I'll try something close first. The courtyard."

She closed her eyes, her hands still in Acheron's, and she thought only of the castle courtyard. Carey felt the rush of her ability taking control, but for the first time, she felt a tug, pulling her onwards. She focused on it, allowing the darkness to swirl about her.

Her feet hit pavement. A soft, cool breeze brushed her cheeks, but she ignored it, instead feeling for that sensation at her feet holding her there. Slowly, Carey opened her eyes and saw that she was in the courtyard. The sun had almost fully set, only wisps of red weaving through the dark sky now. She looked around, not moving her feet but gathering her senses and centring herself as Lord Acheron had advised.

It held.

She allowed herself a momentary smile, a hint of elation as she lifted a foot and took a step towards the monument in the centre of the courtyard. She could feel it, now that she knew it was there; a drag at her heels, as though the souls of her boots were laden with stone. It was ever so slight, but now that she felt it, she wondered how she had never noticed it before.

Carey encircled the rose statue, looking about her as she savoured this moment, this small triumph. It was working. After a few more minutes, she closed her eyes again and willed herself back to Lord Acheron's study.

He was watching her expectantly and her face broke into an elated grin.

"It worked," she breathed, hardly willing to believe it. "It really worked. Thank you, Lord Acheron, thank you."

He shook his head sincerely. "It was nothing. I merely helped you to focus."

Carey let out a thin laugh. "It certainly isn't nothing. I've been trying to do that for weeks now and you were able to help me Travel properly with a few words and a handful of minutes. I give you credit, Lord Acheron. If I'd known this before I'd have come to you for help earlier."

Lord Acheron smiled graciously at her words. "Again, it was nothing. I am glad I can help. Would you like to try again?"

Carey bit her lip, gazing down at their hands still linked in front of her. She was feeling confident now with Lord Acheron's help, and there was one place she wanted to go more than any other at that moment.

"I wish to visit my parents," she said, looking back up at him. "I want to know that they are all right."

Lord Acheron took a deep breath, his face serious now, the twinkle gone from his eyes. "Yes, of course," he replied simply. "When you're ready."

With a steadying breath of her own, she closed her eyes and concentrated on her parents. She pushed aside her doubts and fear and felt herself sinking into the familiar darkness. She envisioned their faces and, as she summoned the tiniest bit of her magic, felt the familiar rush that took her where she wanted to go. Focusing on the pull, there was a whirl of colour, and the darkness exploded into scenery she had never seen before. Taking a moment to centre herself, to feel the anchor at her heels, she looked about her. Surrounding her on all sides were high rock walls; they burst from the earth in jagged spires that reached towards the heavens. Black streaks stained the stone face, the lines running from the rock in strange web-like patterns at her feet. There were no stars in the sky, no sign of the moon, and it was pitch black, except for a blazing fire that flickered brightly in the centre of a clearing.

A small group of people sat huddled and tense about the flames. Among them were two she recognised, and with a flutter of relief and excitement, she started for them.

Carey opened her mouth to call to them when a sharp, excruciating pain rippled across her forehead, beginning at her left temple and running across to her right. Crying out in anguish, Carey saw her parents look up before the scene cut to darkness.

She forced her eyes open; the pain burned all the way across her forehead, and dropping Lord Acheron's hands, she clamped her own to her head. She called out as she slipped from the armchair and fell to the floor at the hearth, clutching at her skull.

"Carey?" she heard Lord Acheron say in alarm, his voice muffled by the pain.

It was torture, unlike any pain she'd ever experienced. She balled herself up on the cold stone floor, as though by doing so she could shield herself from it. Something warm and wet ran across her cheek and Carey lifted her hand to find blood trickling from her right nostril. She was shaking uncontrollably, her hands so unsteady that she couldn't wipe the blood from her face properly.

She felt firm, gentle hands at her shoulders, and they rolled her onto her back; Lord Acheron was kneeling at her side, worry etched upon his face as he gazed down upon her.

"Carey?" he said again. "What happened?"

She took several, long deep breaths, and slowly she felt herself begin to calm. The searing pain in her head began to fade and soon enough it was nothing more than an unpleasant prickling along her brow. She didn't move though. Lord Acheron was silent as he waited for her to answer.

"I saw them," she breathed, her voice weak and thin. "They were somewhere wild and dark, so dark."

She saw the group by the fire in her mind's eye, her parents huddled against the omnipresent black surrounding them. She shivered.

"I centred myself. I was focused. I started walking towards them, made to call out... and then..."

She waved a hand about her head, trying to think of the words to say.

"Pain. Searing pain."

Lord Acheron took her by the elbow and slowly, he lifted her up from the ground and sat her back in the armchair. Slumping back against the dark upholstery, Carey accepted a handkerchief from him and dabbed at her nose. Cautiously, he sat too, leaning forward ever so slightly in case she pitched forward suddenly.

"Have you ever experienced anything like it before?" he asked gently, passing her a cup of water poured from a jug by his chair. "This pain?"

Accepting the cup gratefully, she shook her head, the movement sending a sharp spike of the same pain across her forehead. Carey winced.

"What happened?" she murmured, squeezing her eyes shut against it.

She heard Lord Acheron shift in his chair. "I can't be sure, but..."

Carey opened her eyes at his hesitation. "Yes?" she said, putting down the cup.

His mouth was set in a tight-lipped grimace. "A witch or wizard is only as strong as the power they possess. If they try to go beyond their limits, it can be dangerous—"

"But I've done this before, I've Travelled," Carey said through gritted teeth, flopping her head back against the chair and kneading her temples with her fingertips. "I've travelled much farther and for much longer. It can't be that."

Lord Acheron licked his lips as his eyes flitted around the room uncertainly before bringing his gaze back to Carey. "The Darklands... there is a high density of dark magic there and it tends to have an effect on one's abilities..." he said uncertainly. "Perhaps by travelling there it affected you too, even though you weren't physically present."

Carey closed her eyes again and groaned. That sudden pain had almost completely diminished now, but it was still fresh in her mind. Pin pricks moved under her skin, flickering and dying. It had been excruciating, almost beyond endurance. She felt unsure, disturbed, and Carey pressed the heels of her palms into her eyes, blocking out the light from the fireplace.

"Carey?"

She dropped her hands from her face to find Lord Acheron still watching her, eyebrows knit together and mouth downturned. She heaved a great sigh.

"Do you really think that's the case?" Carey asked heavily.

Lord Acheron glanced down at his clasped hands before looking back at her and nodding. "I have a feeling that it just might be, unfortunately. What you experienced — your magic — it rebelled against you, forced you back. I know that what I'm about to ask may seem impossible, but I would suggest that you do not try and contact your parents again while they traverse the Darklands. You could do yourself some serious damage."

Carey lifted her hand to her nose, which had finally stopped bleeding. She wanted desperately to ensure her parents were well, and that they were not in danger, but that pain... She could not imagine feeling that pain again, like her magic was fighting against her. She would just have to practice what she had learned here tonight, focus on what she could do and hope that her parents returned safely. It was, after all, only a week until their return, and they were strong, talented in their own right. They could take care of themselves, regardless of that feeling in her stomach.

*

The breeze was light and cool as it drifted in through the bedroom window. The dry smell of autumn leaves dying wafted upon it, and Carey leaned her head back against the side of her bed, her legs outstretched on the rug on the floor. She listened to her companions as Ji, seated by her fireplace, and Kat, reclined upon her bed clothes behind her, talked about the impending arrival of the delegates. It was still unclear whether Carey's parents would return in time to meet them, and given her inability to reach them, she had no way of finding out. Kat and Ji had been suitably sympathetic when she'd told them what had transpired in Lord Acheron's study the night before and were kind enough not to reiterate her fears regarding her mother and father.

Instead, they had taken to speculating about the two visiting envoys.

"Do you know who they are?" Ji asked, leaning back in his armchair and ruffling his hair with one hand.

Carey shook her head. "Not yet. You?"

"Apparently, they're two women, a Lady Sirona and a Princess Mizéi. Lady Sirona is from Russo, and the Princess is from the Near East," Ji replied, crossing his legs and resting his hands behind his head.

"Considering I've not even been told this yet, I'm guessing Rupert?" she asked with a raised eyebrow.

"Who else?" he replied with a grin.

Kat tut-tutted. "He's going to get himself in trouble one of these days," she said with a shake of her head. "The Council hasn't even announced this yet. Does he know anything else?"

"No, that's all," Ji answered. "Although I have heard that name before somewhere... Lady Sirona. I'm not sure where though."

"I can't remember if Lady Marksis told me about them during my studies," Carey frowned, trying to rack her brain for the tiniest bit of information.

Her mind flew to the maps and books she'd studied; she had marvelled at the world within this realm, cities and continents far beyond the Centre City, filled with people of different cultures and tongues of their own. She had studied geography in the Common Realm as a child and knew of the countries that curved the earth, but to see a whole new world laid out before her, countries and lands so different to what she had come to know... It was overwhelming and wondrous all at once. If she lay one map over the other, she would find the Near East somewhere near the Chinese Empire, though its territory was smaller and great lakes dotted its surface like pock marks. Russo stretched above it; a great land mass streaked with lakes that lined up closely with the Russian Empire. Even the names were similar, and Carey wondered if they had influenced each other, or whether it was simply coincidence.

"They're travelling a long way to be here," she said thoughtfully, gazing ahead as though she could see the map of the world spread before her.

Torarn, the Centre City, was part of a large island not too far from where Ireland sat on the maps in Lady Marksis's study. They were half a world away from Russo and the Near East, and Carey contemplated how they would travel. She had heard of witches and wizards who could transport themselves and others instantly from one place to another, a talent she thought would be most helpful over long distances.

"They'll have their ways," Ji replied, swinging his legs over the arm of the chair so that he was lying sideways in it. "No doubt we shall find out soon enough. They would have to announce it at the meeting tonight so that preparations can be made."

He was running his hands through his hair, mussing it with his long, slender fingers, and Carey turned away, a flush rising at her neck. She remembered those same fingers at her cheek, pushing her hair from her face, tracing her jawline... except they hadn't been Ji's at all. Those actions had not been his own, and that look she had seen had not come from him. They had been another's, a dead man's, a traitor's. Her stomach flipped over on itself and she forced herself not to think about it. No good could come of it.

"I'll be interested to hear what they have to say," Kat said, sitting up and crossing her legs on the bed. "We've not done too badly since the Empire fell. I wonder if they've had similar success."

"Well, we could always ask Rupert," Carey added with a wry smile. "I bet he already knows."

Later that evening, the three of them walked into the Council chambers just as the gong sounded, calling for the beginning of the session. Carey took her parents' place at the head of the table and Ji and Kat sat flanking her sides. She looked around to find Lord Acheron sitting halfway down the right side of the long, polished wood table. He gave Carey a warm smile and small nod, which she returned, glad that her parents had such a man to give counsel. She thought of the night before and the help he had given her; he exuded a quiet intelligence, and she considered visiting him again. She wasn't too keen on Travelling again anytime soon, but there was still the mystery of Elara and the stone after all...

Peter got to his feet and began the customary opening speech of the Council. After he had thanked Carey for joining them, to which Carey acknowledged with a small, awkward nod, he took his seat and began on the topics for the evening.

"First of all, I would like to assure the Council that the Emperor and Empress are well and have reached the Darklands," Peter said, to which Carey instantly perked up. "They sent word late last night to say that they had encountered only one group of Loyalists on their journey so far, of which they were able to avoid confrontation with. They expect to remain for at least the next three days — any longer and they risk being discovered. That said, they have taken longer to reach the site than first expected so, Your Highness, you will be called upon to meet with the delegates when they arrive later in the week."

Carey nodded in acknowledgement again, although this time it was with a lighter heart. Her parents were safe, for the time being. Although they would not be back in time to meet with the delegates, she didn't mind. She looked sideways to find Ji and Kat smiling, knowing that their emotions mirrored her own.

"With regards to the delegates, it has been confirmed that Lady Sirona of the Russo Peninsula of Mirovsk, and Princess Mizéi of Peichung in the Near East, will be arriving at the end of this week. We, as the Council, will receive them in the castle courtyard and they'll be expected sometime mid-morning. We will have two days of discussions wherein we will exchange what we know of the Imperial loyalist movements within our regions. If so, we will also discuss possibilities of assistance, should they require it. Once the conference has closed, we will be holding a ball in their honour on the same evening before they depart, and all Council members are expected to attend." Peter looked about the table. "Does anyone have any questions, or anything to add before we move on?"

When nobody answered, Peter's talk turned to the tracking of a certain group of Essedarian with Ji's father, and the meeting carried on from there. Carey's hand was in her pocket, curling around the stone which she had taken to carrying on her person, as though the proximity would allow for some sudden realisation. She watched Lord Acheron as he spoke, his gentle, calm and eloquent speech easing her fears and frustrations. She still felt that odd sensation that she knew him from somewhere, that they had crossed paths before, but it was not something she felt she needed to pursue. Carey was quite happy to leave that mystery alone.

As they stood to leave at the end of the meeting, Carey excused herself from Kat and Ji. She called to Lord Acheron as he made to leave the chambers, catching him by the door.

"Your Highness? I mean, Carey?" he said, catching himself with a smile. "Is there something I can help you with?"

Leading him away from the other Council members, Carey saw Kat give her a quizzical look as she and Ji passed on their way out. Lord Acheron's face was similarly set as they came to stand in the corner of the room.

"Is this about your Twilight Travelling?" he began softly. "Because I'm not sure I can help..."

"No, no," she said quickly with a shake of her head. "It's not that. I was going to ask you about something else, something I found in the castle. I can't find anything special about it, but it belonged to my grandmother."

Carey reached into her pocket and pulled out the pendant, its red stone gleaming in her palm.

"It was given to her by her sister, who no one seems to know anything about," she said, holding it in front of her by the long, thin chain. "And I thought... since you were part of my grandmother's Council before..."

Carey trailed off, watching Lord Acheron as he raised an upturned palm to the necklace. She let it fall into his hand, the chain curling about the stone, and gently, Acheron inspected it. He held it up to his face, squinting as he looked over the inscription. His face held a look of pure wonder, as though he had never seen anything so spectacular before.

"What did you say her name was? Your grandmother's sister?" he said, still looking at the stone, enraptured.

"It was Elara," Carey provided, wringing her hands as she waited on his reply.

"Hmm..." he hummed, brows creasing. "I'm sorry, but I don't think Fianna ever mentioned anything about a sister."

Carey's heart fell, wilting with disappointment. "How about the stone?"

Lord Acheron's mouth lifted now. "This," he said confidently, "is really something. I have an idea of what it might be, but I'll need to confirm something first, do some research. Do you mind if I hold onto it for now?"

She was a little hesitant at his request but agreed when he laughed and said, "I promise I will take very good care of it."

The promise of at least some answers buoyed her spirits, and although she was no closer to discovering what had happened to Elara, the stone was a good place to start.

"I trust you will," Carey said, watching as Lord Acheron wrapped it in a blue silk kerchief and placed it in his own pocket. "I just... want some answers. Anything you can find out, anything at all."

"I will let you know immediately," he said reassuringly, and Carey grinned.

~Chapter Eleven~

Noted

Carey rubbed her eyes in exhaustion. She was standing alongside the other members of the Council, awaiting the official arrival of Princess Mizéi and Lady Sirona. She tried to stifle a yawn but failed spectacularly, and Kat raised an eyebrow in her direction.

She'd awoken in the dark early hours of the morning, a strange dream fading fast from her mind. Many pairs of eyes had stared out at her from the darkness, watching her, their gaze malevolent. She'd tried hard to shake the image from her memory, but one set of eyes had stood out from the rest — a pair of piercing silver.

She had eventually given up on sleep as the sun began creeping over the edge of the horizon. As she joined the others for breakfast, her nerves were starting to jangle in her stomach. She knew the elder members of the Council would be taking the lead when the delegates arrived, but she was still her parents' representative and she didn't want to disappoint them.

Autumn was beginning to set in; orange and red leaves falling about their feet as they stood waiting in the courtyard a few hours later. The last warmth of summer was now tinged with a slight chill, and Carey stood with her hands clasped in front of her, trying not to let her nerves show. The delegates would be arriving soon, but the minutes seemed to be moving slower and slower as she stared out watchfully at the courtyard entrance. She felt a hand, a gentle touch at her elbow, and there was Ji, a small reassuring smile on his face.

"Kat said you looked nervous," he whispered in her ear so that only she could hear. "Don't worry. You'll do fine."

Something that had nothing to do with her nerves rippled through her and she swallowed.

"Thanks," she managed to murmur in reply, and he pulled back, his hand dropping from her arm.

Before she could think any more on it, she was distracted by a sudden flash of light. It pierced their vision and illuminated the courtyard with bright white light. As it faded from their sight, they found a single flame flickering on the ground before them. A few cried out in shock as the flames caught at the leaves about it, and Kat jumped forward to extinguish them, only to be stopped by Oliver.

"Just wait," he said in a quiet voice, and as they watched, the flames grew upwards.

They spiralled upwards in a way no flame would naturally. It wavered and twisted into a tall, willowy shape, spreading upwards instead of out. Gradually, a more distinct figure began to form within the tongues of flame. Carey squinted against the burning light, but then just as suddenly as it had appeared, the fire burned bright, then flickered and died.

Standing in front of them without a hint of smoke or flame was a woman who Carey could only assume was Princess Mizéi. She struck an impressive figure in a long red and gold gilded dress, the many folds of the beautiful silk draped elegantly over her slender shoulders. Upon her head sat an ornate circlet that wove its way through her silken black hair, pulling it back from sharp features and shrewd almond-shaped eyes. She surveyed her new surrounds, but only subtly. There was silence in the moments following her dramatic arrival and it wasn't until she felt Kat give her a slight jab in the back that Carey realised; she was supposed to be greeting their guest.

She stepped forward, trying to ignore the fact that everyone was watching. Princess Mizéi bowed her head as Carey approached.

"Princess Mizéi, Your Highness," Carey said with a slight warble in her voice. "On behalf of the Council, welcome to Torarn."

A small, accepting smile crept across the Princess's face. "Thank you, Your Highness. It has been many years since I was last here and under much less happy circumstances. Pray tell, am I the first to arrive?"

Carey nodded slightly. "Yes, indeed you are. I will have someone escort you inside, if you wish." At her words, two of the castle staff arrived at her side.

"My attendant should be arriving soon," Princess Mizéi informed as she turned towards the castle. "Unless you are further requiring my presence?"

Carey gestured to the castle obligingly. "I imagine Lady Sirona will understand your absence. Please, go ahead."

Peter came forward to accompany her, and the welcome party shifted as they made their way towards the castle. Knowing there would be time for more comprehensive introductions later, Carey turned her attention back to the courtyard, awaiting the arrival of their final guest.

They didn't have to wait long. Barely a few minutes had passed before Carey noticed something different.

There was a crackle in the air; the warm autumn sky prickled with magic. Sparks began to flicker about the courtyard, small at first, but then they began to grow. Carey stood completely still, feeling the magic build around her. It swirled throughout the courtyard, circling about them. Its path grew tighter and tighter until it came to focus on one singular point in front of the waiting Council. With both eyes narrowed against the glare, Carey watched as the magic faded to reveal their final guest.

With wide dark eyes, Lady Sirona cast her gaze about the company before her. She was tall and graceful, long auburn hair rippling down her back in waves. She wore a black dress with long fitted sleeves that reached all the way to the ground, a deep red corset cinched over her waist, and a number of delicate rings which glittered at her fingers. Her face was soft and heart-shaped, and as her eyes met Carey's, she smiled and walked forwards, her arms wide.

"Carey, my dear. How long it has been," she said as she embraced Carey, much to her surprise. "Oh, but of course!" Lady Sirona released her before bowing, a hand to her chest. "You are now the Princess here."

With slight confusion, Carey acknowledged her with a nod. "I'm sorry, but have we met before?"

Brushing her long hair from her face as she straightened up, Lady Sirona smiled enigmatically. "Once before, a long time ago. I assume your parents have not returned. A mere deduction," she added upon seeing the look of surprise on Carey's face. "I know it is customary for the next-in-line to take the place of the Emperor and Empress, should they be away from the city. I can only assume this is why you are greeting me and not them?"

"Um, yes… you are correct," was all Carey could say. She looked sideways to find Kat watching Lady Sirona with raised eyebrows. "Would you care to come inside? Princess Mizéi is already here and waiting."

What followed was an extensive round of introductions with the other Council members, a full banquet lunch where Carey was required to make a long and slightly nerve-wracking welcoming speech, followed by an afternoon of talks. Princess Mizéi led proceedings as the Council sat in rapt attention. She spoke of her city, Peichung, which was one of the great nobel cities of the Near East, and one of only a handful of cities to have never been occupied by Malevolence's Imperial forces. The citizens' abilities to tame and train dragons had afforded them the strength to resist, but it had also garnered them much unwanted attention. Malevolence had fought hard to acquire the city, and therefore its people and their dragons, but never managed to succeed. Carey shivered at the imagined terror the Empire could have inflicted had they been able to acquire dragons for their cause.

The Russo Peninsula had not been so lucky. Once Princess Mizéi had finished her speech, Lady Sirona took to the floor. She represented a small yet important peninsula that had been a major port for trade before Malevolence's rise to power. Being a particularly cold and barren land, the Russo Peninsula had sourced most of its food provisions and supplies through the trade route. As much of the realm had done in the beginning, they fought the imposed rule of the Empire until all trade and imports to the area had been halted by Imperial forces. The inhabitants of the Russo Peninsula had been on the brink of starvation when they finally surrendered, only to be enslaved by the Empire and used as a port for the Essedarian. She gave detailed accounts of what her people had endured, and by the end of Lady Sirona's speech, Carey felt physically ill. She thought she had heard it all, but what the people of the Russo Peninsula had suffered was a different kind of cruelty. She almost wished she hadn't heard it, but Carey knew that to defeat their enemy they had to know everything they were capable of.

"I should be used to hearing this kind of thing by now," Carey confessed, rubbing her temples.

It was late in the evening and she was sitting on Ji's balcony with Kat and Ji, discussing the day's events.

"I'd be more surprised if you weren't affected by it," Ji said, stretching in his seat. "Once you feel nothing, you know something's wrong."

Kat grunted in agreement. "Well I definitely feel something, like I want to go out and find some rogue Imperials to try out my new sai on," she said, holding her arms the way she did in weapons training.

Ji gave a short snort of laughter.

"I only wish there was more we could do," Carey said with a sigh. "I wish we could actually fight."

Ji hummed but didn't answer, drumming his fingers absent-mindedly on the table.

Kat fell into a chair beside her. "Don't we all," she huffed.

For all the training and studying they had done since Malevolence's fall, they were yet to do anything of consequence with it. Carey felt as though they were being kept back, hidden within the castle for safe keeping. They were given glimpses of the struggle beyond their walls through the Council meetings and the like, but never given a chance to ride out and engage.

Carey couldn't imagine how much Kat and Ji were struggling with these limitations — she had tasted the freedom of being in charge of their own fate for only a short time and she was already restless. Of course, they had never been as safe as they were now, but she felt so far removed from the conflicts that raged beyond the Centre City that she may as well have been on another world.

A shooting star streaked through the dark as they gazed out over the sprawling city, the flickering candlelight of the houses below mirrored in the twinkling of the night sky.

"Speaking of doing something," Ji said, breaking through Carey's reverie,

"Have you heard anything new from Jenny and Robert?"

Carey shook her head. "Nothing today. I was hoping..." she trailed off.

"I'm sure they're fine, Carey," said Kat in comfort. "If anything bad happened, we would know about it, one way or the other."

Carey knew what Kat meant by that, yet none of them were eager to voice it. Imperials were never shy when it came to taking credit for their handy work.

After a few moments of silence, Ji stretched and yawned loudly, signalling their cue to leave. Kat murmured a goodnight as she exited, muttering something about an early training session. As Carey went to leave, Ji took her gently by the wrist.

"Ji?"

Carey could see the concern on his face. "They'll be all right, you know that, don't you?" he said softly and for a moment Carey wasn't sure if he was talking to her or merely saying it out loud for his own benefit.

With a small, uneasy smile, Carey put her free hand over his and squeezed. "Goodnight, Ji."

*

Imperials were everywhere. They had come during the night, their curses mixing with the screams of the People. They were in the castle, hundreds of them, gathering up the Council members and forcing them into the courtyard. Carey looked down and found herself in a ball gown, though its sheen was gone, and it was tattered and frayed. Heavy manacles enclosed her wrists and she looked back up to find a band of Imperials striking a slow waltz on battered instruments. Slowly, the Council members around her began to dance, their chains clinking in time to the music...

Carey woke with a start. Someone had knocked on her door, tearing her away from the bizarre dream. What in the heavens had that been about?

Shaking her head of the strange vision, Carey lifted herself up and said, "Who is it?" in a cracking voice. There was no answer; instead, a folded piece of paper slipped in under the door. Still groggy with sleep, Carey squinted at it. It was barely dawn, judging by the greying sky beyond her

130

window. It was an odd sort of wake-up call, Carey thought as she made her way across the cold stone floor to pick up the note. As she went to open it, her middle finger slipped clumsily on the paper's edge.

"Ouch!" Carey exclaimed as a droplet of blood trickled from the cut. "Damn it."

Sucking on her finger to stem the bleeding, Carey opened the paper to find a message written in elegant script.

Carey,

I am terribly sorry for this, but I feel mistrust for some members of your Council and there is a matter of great importance of which I need to speak with you alone. As I understand, your Council chambers are empty unless it is in session. Please meet me in the main Council room at nine o'clock this evening. Speak of this to no one — this is a matter for the royal family only and tonight is the one time I will have to speak with you in private.

Yours in confidence,

Lady Sirona

Carey scratched her head sleepily. What could be so secretive that Lady Sirona needed to see her alone? She could have just waited for her to answer the door if the matter was so urgent. Re-reading the note, Carey couldn't help but feel how very strange it was for her to not simply ask of this in person — surely there had been many a moment where such a conversation would not have been overheard. Was it that much of a secret to not even risk doing that?

Note in hand, Carey sat back down on her bed, mulling it over. The sun was straining to make an appearance through some dark clouds sitting on the horizon. Carey yawned. Perhaps she could get a little bit more sleep in and think on Lady Sirona's cryptic note later...

*

Carey rubbed her eyes resolutely. She had barely gotten back to sleep when

Kat came banging on her door. Now, sitting in her place at the head of the Council table, she was struggling to keep her attention from wandering. Her mind kept flitting back to Lady Sirona's unusual request that was now tucked away in her pocket. She looked over at Lady Sirona, intent on giving her some sort of acknowledgement that conveyed she had received the note, but Lady Sirona seemed too enthralled by a conversation she was having with one of the Council members to notice Carey's attempt. Princess Mizéi, on the other hand, was watching her most keenly, nodding slightly as Carey looked her way. Unsure, Carey nodded back, not wanting to seem impolite, before returning her attention to Oliver Binx as he took to his feet.

For much of the morning, Oliver and the two delegates discussed what each region required with regards to military reinforcements and what aid could be afforded. Carey listened intently as they spoke of rogue militants that were taking hold of the Dead Plains, using the magical dead spots to their advantage. Some were Imperial loyalists, but most in these small armies were dark creatures that had thrived under the Imperial rule. Their skills required little to no magic and they were vicious in their attacks. It appeared that their threat was not necessarily immediate, as they seemed to prefer the limbo of the Dead Plains and were therefore unlikely to venture forth from there.

"I have been assured by Captain Tutari of the Vuletian garrison that their army is still capable of holding the Northern borders that run by the Dead Plains. As long as they're able to hold that front then we need not worry. Pirates keep no allegiance but are less likely to ally themselves with Imperials. Many of them were persecuted under Malevolence's rule so there is no real threat there."

"We have also seen no danger from Pirates in our region," Princess Mizéi interjected in her lilting accent. "Besides, they prefer sea warfare to land."

Carey listened intently, trying to keep up with the talks as they flitted from one geographic location to another, and she was glad for the hours she'd spent with Lady Marksis. If she was unable to fight on the ground, she would make sure she knew what was happening behind the scenes instead.

At the end of the day, Ji's father stepped down, weary but seemingly pleased with their negotiations. With a nod, Carey stood to make the customary closing statement on her parents' behalf.

"Thank you, Oliver. My parents, despite not being able to be here, will be delighted with the outcome of the past two days. These rogue elements cannot hope to succeed in their attempts as long as we continue to strengthen our ties and help in each other's defences. Freedom is hard won, but we have the will and now the power to garner it for our people. I thank you, Lady Sirona, Princess Mizéi," she said, dipping her head in gratitude at the two delegates, "for travelling here. I hope that what has transpired here over the past few days will give you the tools to bring about peace in your regions."

As Carey sat back down, the Council members and delegates clapped politely. Lord Acheron caught her eye and gave her an approving nod and a smile. Again, she tried catching Lady Sirona's attention, but she was deep in conversation with the Councilman who had been sitting beside her. Feeling it a lost cause, Carey slipped from the room and went to find Kat and Ji.

Down in the dungeons, she found the two of them sparring under the watchful gaze of Sir Garrow. Their presence hadn't been required at the talks that day, and they had clearly made good use of their time. They were both sweating with exertion, Kat's hair loosing from its plait, and Ji's slicked back from his face.

Sir Garrow gave her a perfunctory greeting without taking his eyes off his students, following their progress with a critical eye. He gave a clap. "Excellent foot work, Ji. Take care not to let Kat get you on the back step."

Kat lifted her sai over her head and with a delicate pirouette, swooped down on one knee and caught Ji by surprise. She caught him behind his leg with her weapon and Ji crashed to the floor. With a sidestep, Kat brought the tip of her sai to his neck and Ji dropped his spear, conceding.

"Very nice work, Katrina," Sir Garrow applauded as Kat helped Ji to his feet.

Despite his loss, Ji smiled and clapped Kat on the shoulder. "Fair go. You definitely had me on that one."

Trying to suppress a grin of superiority, Kat punched him playfully in the arm. "Well you didn't make it easy, at least."

The two of them placed their weapons back on the training wall, and after a quick word with Sir Garrow, left the dungeon with Carey. They headed out to the courtyard where the preparations for the ball were being completed. As they wandered through the garden beyond the draped silk dance floor, Carey gave them a quick overview of what had transpired during the Council session.

"I'm so very glad your father was the one to head the talks, Ji. Even with all my study there is still so much I need to learn if I'm going to be able to hold my own like he did."

"Well at least it's all over now," Ji said. "It's just the ball now and that's it."

Thinking of the ball, Carey debated whether to tell Kat and Ji of Lady Sirona's strange note. Surely neither of them was the basis for her mistrust, but Sirona had made it very clear that it was a matter for the royal family only. If she was so desperate to speak only to Carey, then that's what she would do. It's not as though she was asking Carey to do something dangerous — they were meeting in the Council Chambers after all. Carey reasoned that once she knew what it was about, she would tell Kat and Ji, but until then, she would say nothing. She couldn't see the point in speculating about it anyway, not until she knew what Sirona wanted.

Content with this compromise, Carey turned her thoughts to the ball itself.

"I'm guessing they'll be expecting us to dance," she said aloud.

"Why? Not excited for a bit of dancing?" Kat asked, leaning back with one leg up on the bench, kicking Carey teasingly with her toe.

Ji laughed. "Ah, at least you won't have to dance with any of the delegates."

"Who says I won't?" Carey said, and she and Kat laughed as Ji struggled to find a comeback.

*

Later that evening, Carey walked down to the courtyard with Kat, dressed in a soft cream-coloured gown with a pale gold corset. The sleeves billowed out from her shoulders before tapering in at her wrists, and her light brown hair fell delicately about her shoulders, her crown perched atop her brow. She had her ceremonial dagger once more at her hip, hanging from a soft leather belt. Kat was wearing a spectacularly bold gown of ruby red, this time studded with crimson and emerald crystals along the sweetheart neckline, the green mirroring her bright eyes. Black tendrils of hair curled down the back of her neck, the rest of her raven locks swept elegantly onto the top of her head. She had her hand on her own dagger, its dark obsidian hilt protruding from its sheath.

Carey could hear the revelry before she saw it, and despite her misgivings, was astounded with the general splendour of it all. The castle's servants had outdone themselves yet again with the decorations surpassing anything they had done before. Brilliant silk tapestries were draped about the banisters, and glittering decorations hung from the trees overhead, gently trickling gold over the attendants. The kitchen had arranged a feast for the ball from which wafted the most mouth-watering aromas, and for a moment Carey felt a twinge of excitement. Kat, who was never one to shy away from a party, was grinning from ear to ear at the sight.

"Her Royal Highness, Princess Carey Lee, and her ladyship, Miss Katrina Lawrence," cried the Herald as they passed through the doors.

"Beautiful," Kat breathed as they descended the stairs.

Ji and Rupert were waiting at the bottom for them, dressed in their very best. They both wore long dark jackets that were cut longer at the back than the front; Rupert with a blue vest beneath, Ji with a silver embroidered one. Their fitted trousers were tucked into the tops of high leather boots, and they reminded Carey ever so slightly of French gentlemen she had seen in pictures from the Common realm. Despite herself, she couldn't help but appreciate how handsome Ji looked, and she was both hoping and dreading that he would ask her to dance.

"As always, ye two don' scrub up too badly," Rupert said with a twinkle in his eye, his hair a slightly subdued hue of forest green this evening.

With a click of her tongue, Kat addressed Rupert as she looked around. "Just because we're at a ball, Rupert, do not think for a moment that I won't take you on," she said with a lofty air.

Rupert grinned widely and took her hand. "I accept yer invitation. Lead the way to th' dance floor, milady."

As she watched Kat and Rupert carve their way across the dance floor, Carey felt Ji move to her side. He held out his hand, palm facing up in invitation.

"Care to dance?" he said, hopefully.

Carey glanced up at him, her heart trembling at the request. She glanced about the room at the Council members and castle peers flitting about the dance floor, talking at the edges. Conversation and music mingled together, and she thought that perhaps she could get away with this just being a dance and nothing more. She lifted her hand to his.

His lips broke into a brilliant smile and he led Carey out to where the other dancers were swaying and twirling. A grand waltz was playing, and as Ji placed his arm around her, she couldn't help but allow herself to be swept away by it. They began to turn, Ji sure-footed from all his training, graceful and elegant as they wended their way around the floor. Carey's heart swelled at the way Ji's hand felt in hers, his firm but gentle grip at her waist, and the mischievous glint in his eye. He spun her out under his arm, then back in, catching her and turning, their bodies pressed together with the music. Carey's breath hitched in her throat as he looked down at her, their faces little more than a hand's-breadth apart now, dancing all the while. His faded blue eyes were fixed on her, a soft, earnest smile upon his lips.

"You're quite good at this," he said as they continued to glide about the dance floor.

Carey took a shuddering breath; they were so close that she was sure Ji would feel her heart thudding against his chest.

"You're not so bad yourself," she managed to say, her throat suddenly dry.

Carey didn't know what else to say, dancing this close to Ji, his hand at her waist, his face turned down to hers. What could she say? She hardly knew where to begin, if there was even a beginning to be had. Unease began creeping into her mind and she clenched her jaw tight against it.

They continued to twirl and spin, their steps in time with each other's as though it was the simplest thing in the world, as though it was meant to be. The music grew about them and the rest faded, until it was just her and him, moving as one.

She looked up into Ji's face and for a moment she noticed him hesitate, as though he was on the verge of saying something. His smile twitched and then faded a notch. A familiar trickle of dread slid down her back and she suddenly pulled away, stumbling out of step. The world came back about her in sharp relief as she realised what she was doing. What was she doing?

"I'm sorry," she muttered distractedly. "I need to..."

She didn't know what she meant to say there, but she couldn't do it. She couldn't bear to have his hand in hers, have him look at her like that, like *Jeremy* used to...

For a moment she felt his grip tighten on hers, like he wanted to pull her back in, but then it slackened, and she turned, not wanting to see the look on his face.

Carey pushed her way to the far side of the courtyard and sat amongst the shadows on a low bench. She watched as Ji stood still amongst the dancers, his hand now at his side. His face was inscrutable and Carey looked away before she could see any more.

Taking a deep breath, she willed her heart to still, but it was beating a violent tattoo against her ribcage and no matter what she did, it would not calm. Carey closed her eyes and leaned her head against the stone wall behind her, trying not to think about it, about any of it, but she soon realised that was impossible. Instead, her mind rebelled, dredging up memories from when she had thought Jeremy to be Ji, his smile, his touch, his laughter... How his face had turned, revealing the traitor beneath. And then it was Saar pretending to be Ji, that night he had summoned her, his taunting words in Ji's voice. Those silver eyes...

Carey clapped a hand to her mouth, stifling a traitorous sob. The sound seemed to break through some invisible barrier, scattering the notions that had long threatened to overwhelm her. Slowly, she pulled her hand away from her mouth, her fingers shaking with anger now. She could not allow this to be what defined her; fear at a touch, hatred at a look. These thoughts and memories that taunted and mocked her were indeed still hers, and she had allowed them to run rampant long enough. Her hand moved to the dagger at her side, the magic in her fingertips. She was stronger than what they had done — Saar and Jeremy were nothing but Imperial loyalists who wanted to see the world burn around her. But these were her friends, the ones who stood by her no matter what, and she would be damned if she let those pieces of scum drive a wedge between them.

Carey looked back over to where Ji had stood, furious at herself for the thoughts that threatened to drive them apart, but he was nowhere to be seen. Kat was still dancing with Rupert but Ji...

"Carey!"

Seramina appeared at her side, flopping down onto the bench and flattening the pale pink skirts of her dress with her palms. "Isn't this so absolutely wonderful? I love dances!"

"Oh," Carey stuttered, tearing her gaze from the dance floor and her mind from Ji. "Seramina... how... how are you this evening?"

She painted on a smile and released the dagger at her side, clasping her hands in front of her to still the shaking. "I haven't seen you much the past week. What have you been up to?" she asked, trying to close her mind to the thoughts of a moment ago. Seramina didn't need to know, sensitive empath that she was.

"Oh, I've been practicing my new powers with Kyna. She's so much fun to practice with. She acts as though what I'm doing is so amazing, but I know she's just teasing," Seramina laughed, the sound tinkling and joyous.

With anyone else, Carey would have looked upon such self-deprecation as a bid for attention, but not Seramina. As ever, she was oblivious to how powerful she truly was.

She turned her eyes back to the floor and found her gaze drawn to the tall, striking figure of Princess Mizéi. She was dancing with a member of the Council, her graceful movements outdoing any of the others on the dance floor.

"That's one of the delegates, isn't it?" she heard Seramina ask.

"Yes. Princess Mizéi from Peichung in the Near East," Carey said as she continued to watch.

"Her power…" Seramina started before trailing off.

"What about it?" Carey asked immediately.

Seramina was watching the Princess closely with a furrowed brow. "Do you know what she can do?"

Carey, who was now officially curious, shook her head. "I wasn't aware she had any special abilities. What do you know, Seramina?"

Seramina looked back at Carey then down at her knees. She closed her eyes as though she was listening intently to something. "She… she can sense the energy of those around her, their magical energy," she said quietly. "And she can use it."

"Use it?" Carey asked, confused. "Use it how?"

Scrunching up her face, Seramina paused. "She can use it many ways. She can influence how people feel… their actions…" She bit her lip. "There's also something dark there… I can't really say though…"

"Hmm," Carey said as she watched the Princess.

In all her dealings with the Princess since she'd arrived, she had seemed a genuine person; caring and passionate. She wondered for a moment what that darkness was before she remembered that she herself held darkness within and was therefore in no place to judge. One did not choose the powers gifted to them.

"What about Lady Sirona?" Carey asked, clearing her throat.

This time Seramina was quiet for much longer, so much so that Carey wondered if she had even heard her. "Seramina?"

"I don't know," she said finally with a grimace. "There's power there but it's strange. Something… ancient?" She said this as a question, more to herself than Carey. "Something much more than anything I've felt yet. I'm sorry, Carey. There's something there that just doesn't make sense to me."

Carey didn't say anything to this, but simply looked out across the room to where Lady Sirona stood talking animatedly with Oliver and Meela, wearing a long-beaded ball gown with a fur shawl wrapped about her shoulders. She was young, not much older than Carey by the looks, and yet she spoke with the wisdom and knowledge of someone far beyond her years. Over the past few days, Sirona had stood before the Council with all the authority and intelligence of an elder speaking for her people, and Carey hadn't realised how unusual that seemed until now. Sirona reminded her of Lord Acheron. Perhaps that was her ability — youth beyond age.

Before Carey could say any of this, though, the clock began to chime. Nine o'clock.

Carey's heart jumped as she remembered the meeting with Lady Sirona. The woman had disappeared from the floor and Carey didn't want to be late for whatever she wanted to tell her. Not wanting to appear anxious or suspicious, she stood up slowly, patting her dress down as she did. "I need to speak with Ji about something, Seramina. Do you mind?" she said calmly.

Seramina shook her head in silence, her face still a mask of consternation as she undoubtedly continued to contemplate Lady Sirona.

"I'll be back soon."

Walking straight past the banquet, Carey slipped through a door beneath the balcony that led back into the castle. Once inside she broke into a run, cursing herself for not taking more care with the time. Up the main staircase she ran, taking two steps at a time, and turned down the hallway to where the main Council room was. She slowed down on approach, gulping in air and smoothing back her hair. She pushed open the door and stepped inside.

Lady Sirona was standing by the table, her figure silhouetted against the dark wood by the moonlight streaming in through the windows opposite. She turned as she heard Carey walk in but frowned when she saw who it was.

"Princess Carey, I was not expecting you," she said as she walked over to her.

Confused, Carey stopped. "Not expecting me?"

"No. I was waiting for Princess Mizéi," Lady Sirona replied. "Were you needing me for something?"

Carey shook her head, forehead creased at her words. "Wait. I'm confused.

If I'm not the one you're waiting for, then why did you send me that message?" she said, her mind racing. Something wasn't right here.

"Message?" Lady Sirona repeated, her frown deepening. "I received a message. I did not send one..."

At that moment, the door opened and Princess Mizéi appeared, looking around. "Princess Carey, I am so sorry I'm late—" Her voice died in her throat when she saw that Carey was not alone. "Lady Sirona. What are you doing here?"

At her puzzled tone, Lady Sirona stepped backwards, her face suddenly smooth. She seemed to have realised something. "You were not expecting me..."

Princess Mizéi shook her head as she looked from Carey to Lady Sirona. "What is going on here? I received your summons, Princess Carey. Is that not why you are here?"

Something shifted into place and Carey saw it in a moment of sickening realisation. They had been lured here, summoned, but not by each other. Suddenly she understood, just as Sirona had.

It was a trap.

She turned for the door only to see it close with a snap, and the tall figure of Lord Acheron appeared from within the shadows.

~Chapter Twelve~

Taken

The three women stopped in their tracks. Carey stared at him, confused by his appearance. The others shifted uncertainly and out of the corner of her eye she saw Princess Mizéi glance surreptitiously in her direction. After a moment of silence, Lady Sirona spoke up.

"Lord Acheron, what is the meaning of this? Are you the one who has brought us all here tonight?"

Lord Acheron was staring at Carey, his eyes fixed on hers as he spoke. "Yes, Lady Sirona, I was the one who summoned you here tonight. I assure you, though, the reason is more than sufficient to make up for the deception."

Carey blinked, but didn't say anything. There was something different about his voice, something horribly familiar. His gaze was hard too, his usual warmth nowhere to be seen.

As he walked over to the table and took a seat on the opposite side, Carey saw the glint of something dangling from his hand. She couldn't think of what it might be; in fact, she was having difficulty thinking at all. Lord Acheron's sudden appearance, the way he had gathered the three of them there — it didn't make sense, and that troubled her greatly.

"I'm afraid I don't understand what's happening here, Lord Acheron," Carey said, her tone carefully mute of any emotion. "Why did you not ask us to meet you yourself? Why the deception?"

His face slowly broke into a wide smile; again, it was a look she found strangely familiar, yet not one she'd seen on Lord Acheron's features before.

"If I had asked to see you, you would have thought it odd that I request a clandestine meeting during the ball. I am, after all, part of the Council, and could reasonably talk to you in private any time," he answered, drumming his fingers casually upon the surface of the table. "It would have seemed suspicious and I'm well aware of your penchant for telling your friends everything. But, have a foreign delegate request an urgent meeting, especially since they are due to leave so soon, well... that wouldn't arouse too much suspicion, I wouldn't think. Besides," he spread his arms wide, "I do enjoy a little deception."

His words washed over Carey in nauseating waves, trickling down her spine and paralysing her to the spot. His manner, his tone — it gripped her by the heart and was slowly wrenching it from her chest. She knew him now; she knew why he felt so familiar...

Lord Acheron was staring at her absolutely, Princess Mizéi and Lady Sirona forgotten as he held her trapped in his gaze. His raised a single eyebrow and blinked.

Silver.

The ground dropped from beneath her, Carey's head spinning with absolute petrifying dread. She watched as Lord Acheron, with his handsome features and bronze hair, morphed and shifted into the dark, terrifying figure of her nightmares.

Saar.

"No," she heard herself whimper as he stood to meet her, dark hair, sharp features, and burning silver eyes.

His mouth lifted into his customary leer.

"I'm afraid *Yes*'," he purred, sauntering over to where she stood, standing right before her. "Yes indeed."

Carey's mouth had gone dry. Her body refused to act, frozen in shock and pure panic. To her right she saw someone move. Lady Sirona spoke.

"Who are you, and what do you want from us?" she asked, voice like cold steel.

"My name is Saar. I am an Imperial Loyalist, but more importantly, I am the Dark Empress's most faithful servant," he said before finally moving his gaze from Carey's face. "I have something terribly important to ask of you all."

At his words, Princess Mizéi and Lady Sirona threw up their hands.

"Imperial Loyalist?" Princess Mizéi cried. "You dog!"

"Is this true, Carey? Do you know this man?" Lady Sirona demanded. "Is he truly an Imperial?"

Carey's throat felt blocked, obscured by her heart which seemed to be trying to force its way out through her mouth. Lord Acheron was Saar. Saar had been in the castle all this time. She had asked him to help, had his hands in hers…

She flexed her fingers and clenched her jaw tight.

"He is an Imperial, like he says," she said, her voice hoarse and shaking. "He… is a Shapeshifter, and before this night, I had only encountered him once in the Common Realm, and then only as a Twilight Traveller."

He was watching her with gleaming eyes, a wide, triumphant smile upon his thin, mocking lips.

"He has threatened me before, asked me to join him, but I refused," she said, her voice growing stronger. "He is nothing but a murderer and a wretched excuse for a wizard."

She didn't know why she said it, but Carey saw a flicker of anger ripple across Saar's features at her words. Clenching her fists, she stood her ground, lifting her chin defiantly.

Princess Mizéi was furious. "I expect nothing less from an Imperial," she growled. "Clearly you have something planned for us otherwise you would not have lured us here tonight. Well, you have us here now, so what is your design?"

"Indeed. If you are who you say you are then you haven't brought us here for a mere chat," Lady Sirona added, her hand still extended.

Watching this exchange with apparent relish, Saar grinned. "You're so very correct, Lady Sirona. I have indeed come here with a purpose. Before me stand three of the most powerful witches of the alliance. Power, which in my opinion, has been squandered until now."

"I would hardly call protecting our people squandering our powers," Lady Sirona replied almost conversationally. "Of course, to an Imperial, such selfless acts are generally considered second rate compared to the pursuit of power."

Saar gave Lady Sirona an appraising glance. "Perhaps. But we are not here to trade differences of opinion." He moved to the end of the table.

Carey stared after him, her heart still racing, her mind still spinning. He would know everything the Council was doing; all their plans and actions. She still could not believe he had been there this entire time.

"How did you fool Seramina?" she blurted out, unable to stop herself. It hardly seemed the most important thing at that moment, but she had to know. She had to know how he had fooled her again...

Saar tipped his head nonchalantly to the side. "I knew what she was able to do before I even met her — your parents," he added in explanation. "It was simple enough to block her, feed her false sentiments."

"But your eyes," Carey gestured at his face. "You've never been able to change them. You've always had silver eyes regardless of your form."

He almost rolled his eyes at her, making her feel even more ridiculous. "Clearly, I can."

Frustration and fury boiled within her; he had played her for a complete fool. He had infiltrated the Council, befriended her, and all this time she had suspected nothing.

"Aside from the Princess's ineptitudes," he continued nastily, "I have brought you all here because I have an obligation to fulfil that requires your particular abilities. There is something I need help with and your combination of unique... *skills*... will allow me to do so. I speak, of course, of the Third World."

"The Third World? As in, the unknown realm?" Princess Mizéi spat. "What kind of ridiculousness is this?"

"The lost realm is practically a myth. No one has ever succeeded in finding it," Lady Sirona said with a tone of incredulity.

Carey looked from the delegates to Saar. "Third World. Jeremy's note..." she breathed, thinking back on that traitor's last message. Or perhaps it had been Saar's message all along...

"Ah. That is where you're wrong. Though hidden by ancient magic, the

Dark Empress found it. She had planned on opening it once she was rid of your rebel Order, therefore allowing her to lead her conquest without challenge. However, as you well know, it did not go to plan. And so, it falls to me to finish what she began," Saar said as he started pacing slowly. The two delegates kept their hands trained toward him, but Carey was yet to raise hers. Something told her that Saar was building to something and it was whispering caution in her ear.

"You are delusional. The Empire has fallen. You have no power anymore," Lady Sirona argued. "Your armies—"

"Lie in wait," he interrupted. "Waiting for us to rise again."

Princess Mizéi let out a derisive snort. "Even if you had your armies, there is no way we would lend our powers to do your bidding, regardless of what you may threaten."

A dangerous gleam glinted from the corner of Saar's eye. "What makes you think that I need your consent?" And he held out his hand to reveal what he'd been hiding.

The blood-red stone that had been Carey's grandmothers.

It dangled from his fingers, its contents shimmering in the moonlight.

"I must thank the Princess for lending me this fantastic piece," he said, tilting his head mockingly in Carey's direction. "And I must tell you, Your Highness, I do indeed know what it is."

Before Carey could say or do anything, Princess Mizéi stumbled backwards as though the necklace had lashed out at her physically.

"Where did you get that?" she gasped, clearly terrified.

Saar said nothing but grinned as he looked back at Carey. "It's mine," she said in a small voice. "I found it in the castle. It... it belonged to my grandmother. I wasn't sure what it was, so I asked Lord Acheron to study it for me... I gave it to Saar unknowingly..."

Princess Mizéi and Lady Sirona's expressions made Carey's stomach clench with fear. They knew what the stone was, and they had also lowered their hands. Surely, they were not surrendering...

"Like I said," Saar purred dangerously, "What makes you think that I would need your consent?"

Carey's heart was pounding against her ribcage now. She could practically feel the others' panic at the sight of the blood-red pendant. Her magic was stirring within her, but it was holding back, as though it too was aware of something Carey wasn't. As she stared at the necklace dangling from Saar's grip, the whirlwind contained within began to grow, spinning faster, its contents emitting a glow Carey had never seen before. She saw the others stiffen as Saar took a step towards them.

"Now, if you don't mind," he said, and with a sudden sharp movement, like he was brandishing a whip, he threw his hand out towards the three women.

There was a shout and Carey was shoved aside as a blinding light engulfed them. She was thrown backwards as the room dissolved around her. Someone was beside her, but she could not tell who it was. They were speeding backwards, light and colour flashing. Carey grappled for a hold, but she couldn't find purchase on anything. There was another shout; Princess Mizéi's voice came echoing all around them, strong and powerful.

"Stop!" Carey heard her command, and with a force that knocked the air from her lungs, Carey hit something hard. She had landed roughly, rolling over and over until she finally came to an agonising halt. She was lying on ground that prickled and smelt of pine and dirt. She coughed the dust from her mouth, gasping at the pain radiating all over her body. She blinked as the world around her solidified again, and she found herself surrounded by the trunks of a dense forest.

One thing was for certain, they weren't in the Centre City anymore. There weren't any forests this thick and there was a chill in the air. Before Carey could begin to wonder where she was, she was pulled hurriedly to her feet by Lady Sirona. The other woman was looking about in a harried way and rubbing her index finger distractedly.

"We need to get away from here," she said shortly, and started off into the darkness.

Taken by surprise, Carey stumbled along in her wake. "Wait! What just happened? Where are we? Where's Princess Mizéi?"

"That Lord Acheron, or whoever he is, has Wayfaring abilities. He just tried Guiding us somewhere. I'm guessing the gateway to the lost realm," Lady Sirona said quickly as she walked onwards. "But Princess Mizéi managed to stop him. As for where, I'd say we're in the Northern Alpines."

Carey shook her head, confused. "Princess Mizéi stopped him? But how? Is that why she isn't here? And what is Wayfaring?"

Lady Sirona came to a sudden halt, causing Carey to almost run into her. She turned around and addressed Carey directly. "Look, Carey, I know you must have many questions, but right now we are in great danger and we need to move. He will follow us if we don't. There is a hidden city in those mountains," she said as she pointed to a peak to their right. "It is abandoned now but at least it's a better hiding spot than out in the open. Once we get there, I will answer all your questions."

Carey considered this for a moment before nodding. How Saar could trace them, she could only imagine, but she didn't doubt for a second that it was possible. So she swallowed her curiosity and kept up with Lady Sirona as she strode off through the trees again.

Lady Sirona kept up a strong pace as they marched towards the mountain, all the while looking over her shoulder constantly. The silence was unnerving for Carey. Her head was still reeling from whatever Saar had done to get them there, pounding painfully as she struggled on through the brush. It was getting thicker as they reached the base of the mountain and she wondered why Lady Sirona wasn't using her magic. Feeling she could at least help in this regard, Carey caught up to her.

"Here, let me help," she said as she raised her hand, but Lady Sirona grabbed her by the wrist.

"No, you mustn't!" she cried, forcing Carey's hand back down. Upon seeing Carey's look of confusion, she added, "You really have no idea about that stone, do you?"

"Stone?" Carey repeated. "You mean the necklace? Why? What does it have to do with any of this?"

"It has *everything* to do with this, Carey," Lady Sirona said as she turned back to the thick brush and continued fighting her way through it. "We are nearly there. I'll tell you when we get there but for now, don't use any magic."

Biting back the questions she longed to ask, Carey followed. Her face burnt with humiliation — she was a Seeker, not just some clueless Commoner, and yet she felt as green as the day she'd discovered she was a witch, stumbling along with no idea about anything. Coupled with Saar's deception, Carey couldn't help but feel like she wasn't living up to who she was meant to be. She balled her fists, refusing to acknowledge the burning pricks at the corners of her eyes. She was better than this, better than the fool she felt.

They came to a sudden stop. Carey looked up to see a stretch of flat stone before them and found herself instantly hoping that they wouldn't have to climb it. In her long ball gown, she was hardly dressed for it.

Lady Sirona stretched out her hand and laid it flat on the stone, murmuring, "It is here... somewhere..."

She walked a short way to the left as Carey watched on, bemused. There was a low crackling sound and she looked back up at the wall before her. She stumbled back a little in surprise. A large arched opening had appeared before her where not a moment before there had been nothing but stone.

"Um, Lady Sirona? I believe I've found the way in," Carey said, trying to sound as nonchalant as possible.

Lady Sirona returned to her side, a grin spreading across her face as she spotted the archway. "It is enchanted," she said, patting the stone appreciatively. "It will not reveal itself to Imperials."

Her words triggered a sudden memory in Carey. An inn that was never meant to be seen by Imperials, and how Jeremy had attacked her to gain entrance. "Yes, but that's certainly not infallible," she said as she gripped her wrist, the faded imprint of the Imperial brand tingling at the thought.

Lady Sirona's smile faded, and she gave a small nod. "Ay, that it is not."

Gathering up the skirt of her dress, she stepped over the threshold and led the way into the dark cavern beyond. Carey followed and looked back just in time to see the archway disappear, shrinking until the light from outside was extinguished. For a moment they were plunged into complete darkness. Then, as Carey's eyes adjusted, she noticed a dim glow emanating from the walls and ceiling of the stone cavern.

"Lichen?" she asked, reaching out to it.

Lady Sirona nodded. "Thank goodness too. I had no means to light the way otherwise. Just down here," she said, turning right.

"So, you've been here before, then?"

"Long ago, before it was used to hide from the Empire. I was a guest here, when it was the residence of a rather eccentric and reclusive Lord," she answered cryptically.

Carey would have asked more if she hadn't had to concentrate on where they were going; Lady Sirona led them through a veritable maze of dark passageways and tunnels. Off to the sides of the passages were large halls, many filled with old and broken tables and chairs, a kitchen with a large cobwebbed fireplace, and some smaller quarters that appeared to be sitting rooms and studies. They finally arrived at a small room that appeared to have once been a bedroom. Lady Sirona gave it a quick inspection, searching a set of overturned drawers, but to no avail.

"Oh well. I didn't really expect to find much anyway," she said as she took a seat on a dust-filled bed and slipped off her shoes.

Carey walked about, slowly taking it all in. Lichen gleamed from the roughly carved walls and ceiling; it highlighted the cracks and lines of marble that ran within the depths of the mountain. There were three beds crammed into the small cavern. Their iron frames were rusted from the indiscernible damp that pervaded the space, and mould had long since taken over the sheets that lay crumpled across their hay-stuffed mattresses. There was a single cupboard and small bedside table, both of which gave the distinct air of being emptied in a great hurry. Or perhaps they'd been searched.

Either way, they lay bare, the bedside table on its side and the cupboard with its doors wide open, one barely clinging to its hinges. The whole scene was thoroughly depressing, and Carey could only imagine what it had been like shut up in here, unable to leave for fear of being caught.

Lady Sirona was now removing the delicate hairpiece from her hair. Their elegant ball gowns and jewellery glittered through the gloom, their colourful hues bright and garish amongst the mouldering surrounds. Carey ran her hand over the gilded hilt of her dagger, which still hung miraculously at her side, and she wished she'd had the mind to pull it on Saar back in the Council chambers.

"I owe you an apology, Carey," Lady Sirona said. "I'm sorry for snapping before, but we needed to get away from there. We should be safe for the time being — we can rest here, gather ourselves before we decide what our next move should be."

"You said this had something to do with my grandmother's necklace," Carey answered, taking a seat opposite her on one of the mouldy beds. "What is it? You're afraid of it, you and Princess Mizéi, so you must know what it does."

"Yes," Lady Sirona said darkly. "I do. And it doesn't just have something to do with that stone. It has *everything* to do with it."

~Chapter Thirteen~

The Dragon's Heart

"Everything?" Carey said hesitantly.

Lady Sirona nodded. "I had thought that stone was a legend, mere myth. Until today I had only ever seen a picture of one, and coming from me, that's saying something." She gave a small laugh, acknowledgement of some private joke. "It is called the Dragon's Heart. The story is steeped in dragon lore, which I imagine is how Princess Mizéi knew of it."

"Story?" Carey repeated, raising an eyebrow in interest. "Do you know it?"

Lady Sirona tilted her head. "There are not many I don't know," she answered with a wry smile. "Would you care to hear it?"

Carey nodded. The stone had intrigued her for so long; its mysteries taunting her, eluding her. Her desire for answers had grown so deep that she *needed* them now.

Lady Sirona cleared her throat. "You must excuse me, it has been some time since I last heard it.

"The story tells of a small village surrounded by mountains that was terrorised by a great dragon. Unlike most dragons, he did not seek food, but attacked the village with what could only be described in stories as an unfounded vengeance. He was a monster of a beast, with a fearsome roar that would echo across the mountain range. It had only one eye, the other lost years before, and it burned a fierce red. Some say that to look into its eye was to see into the heart of the dragon itself, and the fire within its soul.

"One day the dragon came down from the mountains. The villagers ran for cover, but in the confusion, a young girl was left behind in the fields. The dragon swooped down on her, landing right before the girl in all its magnificence. The girl, however, did not move. Instead, she looked calmly upon the beast. Confused, the dragon held back the fire in his chest and lowered its head. With his one eye, he looked at the child and she in turn looked back. For a moment they were still, and then the girl reached out her hand and lay it upon the dragon's snout. The dragon closed its eye and then simply disappeared. In its place stood a bush of glittering green, the very same colour of the dragon's hide, and at its heart a brilliant red gem — the stone. The child had taken the dragon's power with a simple touch.

"For centuries the stone was passed on, stolen and murdered over until it was lost," Lady Sirona added. "It was lost for so long that it passed into legend, known only as the stone of inconceivable power, for the one who holds it has the ability to steal the magic of another and wield it as his own, just as the child had done with the dragon."

"*Steal* their powers? What, like a Tear Globe?" Carey asked fearfully.

"Almost, but a Tear Globe removes one's magic as well as their soul. This act renders one catatonic, for they cannot survive without their soul. No, the Dragon's Heart extracts your magic but leaves your soul intact. You essentially become a Commoner," explained Lady Sirona. "But with the Dragon's Heart you have the ability to use the magic of those you take as though it is your own. Unlike a Tear Globe, where magic and soul are simply separated from the host."

"That's what he meant by not needing our consent, isn't it? He was going to use the stone to take our powers, and then use them to open the gateway to the Third World," Carey said in quiet horror.

"Exactly."

"Then how do we still have our powers? He had the stone the whole time he was in the room with us. What was stopping him?" Carey asked.

"We didn't use our powers. He can't take them unless we use them in his presence."

Carey thought of how Sirona and Mizéi had both lowered their hands the moment they'd seen the stone.

"But we're not in his presence now," Carey said. "Surely we can use our magic now that he's not here."

"Yes, except there is this," Sirona said as she lifted her hand and showed Carey a thin, almost invisible black line encircling her middle finger where a ring would have been placed. It was the same finger, Carey noticed, that she had been rubbing just after they had landed in the woods.

"What is that?" Carey asked as Sirona lowered her hand.

"It's called a Token. It's a way of tracking a person."

"But…" Carey didn't understand. Then she looked down at her own hands, fingers splayed upon the silk of her dress.

There, exactly where Sirona's was, on her middle finger of her right hand was a thin black line.

"What? But how?" Carey exclaimed, frantically running her hand over the mark. It was smooth and did not move or smudge.

"I noticed it just after we arrived in the forest. I felt it."

"Felt it?" Carey said incredulously, still rubbing at the line on her finger. "How? If you hadn't pointed it out, I probably wouldn't have noticed it."

"I'm… *sensitive* to magic that isn't my own," Sirona explained, though Carey knew from her tone that this wasn't the whole truth.

"If it can track us though, should we be stopping?" Carey asked, glancing at the doorway nervously. She imagined Saar creeping through the passageways outside, searching for them.

Sirona's gaze flickered towards the door as well before shaking her head.

"It's fine, for now. Tokens only ever work if magic is used. Magic triggers them, if you like. He cannot find us using the Tokens unless we do magic."

Carey shifted uncomfortably at the idea of not using magic. "How did he manage to do this, though? How does this work?" she said, now staring down at her finger. "How did he get these on us?"

Sirona was quiet for a moment in which she examined her own hand with a slight furrow in her brow. She seemed to be examining the very tip of her finger rather than the thin black band.

"The letter," she murmured, holding her finger up to the dim glow of the lichen.

"The letter?" Carey repeated quizzically. "Saar's letter, you mean?" and Sirona nodded.

"There must have been an enchantment on the letter. When I opened it—"

"Papercut!" Carey remembered suddenly. "I received a papercut to the very same finger."

"As did I," said Sirona, showing Carey her hand. "A Token is not an easy enchantment and requires the blood of the intended."

"And he got it," Carey said ferociously.

"It would seem that this was his contingency plan, in case any of us managed to get away," Sirona continued darkly. "Which means he might have other measures in place to bring us back to him."

"Measures? Such as what?" Carey said, trying to keep the anger in her voice under control.

"I don't know, but whatever he has planned, it will not be good. These Tokens show that he's not about to underestimate us, nor leave anything to chance."

"He'll send everything he's got," Carey said, knowing that Saar would do no less. He needed them in order to open the gateway and he wouldn't stop until he had hunted them down. He would never allow them to reach the Centre City. Somehow, he would try to stop them, catch them before they alerted the Council.

"No magic though..." Carey muttered, a thrill of terror racing through her.

Back in the Common realm it wouldn't have been such an issue, but in this realm, where almost everyone and everything relied upon it, it was a disturbing prospect.

"You know this region, though? Is there somewhere we can go to send a message?"

Lady Sirona nodded. "There is a village about a day's travel from here. We will wait for morning to start out though — it's too dangerous right now."

Carey ran her fingers though her hair, thinking of everyone back at the castle. "They'll have noticed by now that we're not there. We can always hope that they will send out search parties as soon as possible."

"They can't know that we were sent away by a Wayfarer. It could take them days to come this way and by then it could be too late."

"Wayfarer... that's what you said Saar was, didn't you? That he 'Guided' us here," Carey said slowly. "I've heard of wizards who can travel from one place to another instantly. Is that what that was?"

Lady Sirona pursed her lips. "Yes, that is indeed a Wayfarer. However, the more skilled Wayfarers can temporarily transfer their powers and *Guide* other people, just as Saar tried to do with us," Sirona explained. "It's not a unique or special power. Work hard enough and almost anyone can develop the ability of Wayfaring."

"Fantastic," Carey muttered sarcastically. She frowned. "But Princess Mizéi was able to stop him. How was she able to do that?"

"Mizéi has the power to influence those around her," Sirona answered in hushed tones. "That said, Mizéi can also use a person's powers against them, reverse anything that is being directed at her back at her attacker. I can only assume that she tried reversing Saar's powers long enough to stop him Guiding us where he intended. It would have taken everything she had to hold herself there and attempt what she did."

"But he has her powers now, doesn't he? With that stone," Carey said, feeling guilty for allowing it to ever get this far. "This should never have happened."

Lady Sirona frowned. "You knew this was going to happen?"

"No, but I gave him that stone." She hid her face in her hands. "You saw what he is, a Shapeshifter. He used his abilities to take the form of Lord Acheron, but I've known Saar since before the Empire fell. The first time I encountered him he was disguised as a Commoner priest. When I saw him again, it was in a dream state. He knows that I'm a Twilight Traveller and he has summoned me on several occasions in attempts to form an alliance. I knew he was planning something, knew what he was capable of, and yet he wore the mask of Lord Acheron every day within the castle and I didn't even realise it," Carey said heavily. "I should've known it was him."

Lady Sirona shook her head sympathetically. "You could not have known, Carey. By what I observed during my time within the castle, he was well liked. You were hardly the only one he fooled. There is no point in lamenting what is past. All we can do now is to try and stop him before he can progress any further with his plans."

Carey nodded in silence, but despite Sirona's kind words, the shame of Saar's deception burned within her.

"So, he is a Shapeshifter and you are a Twilight Traveller," Lady Sirona stated simply. "Well, that is very interesting."

Carey sniffed. "I've not yet been able to get a handle on my power." She rubbed an eyebrow in thought. "Saar has been able to summon me in the past. Could he take my magic that way?"

"No," Lady Sirona said simply. "No, he must be in the same place as you to take your powers. If he were to summon you, it would be in a dream state where only your mind is present. But tell me, being a Shapeshifter.... does he have any tells?"

"Tells?" Carey repeated. "Like in cards?"

"Sort of. Many Shapeshifters have a trait they find hard to conceal. It's not impossible for them but many just leave it rather than overexert their powers by hiding it unless they have reason to. Does Saar have anything like that?"

Carey didn't even have to think. She knew exactly what his tell was. "His eyes. Even as the priest his eyes were that silver colour. Until today, he had never bothered to hide them."

Lady Sirona nodded. "I thought so. It was the first thing to change before anything else. Keep that in mind."

"In other words, we can't trust anyone," Carey said heavily, the gravity of their situation settling squarely across her shoulders. This was certainly a mess they'd found themselves in. No magic, unable to trust anyone, and being hunted. Dawn could not come quicker. The sooner they started for the Centre City the better, and perhaps they could get to the Council before Saar got to them.

"Can I ask you something, Carey? Where did you get that stone?" Sirona asked.

Carey hesitated for a moment. "I found it in the castle. It was in a strange little hiding place beneath my bed. If I had realised what it could do, I would have left it there."

"So, you have no idea who put it there?"

Carey bit her lip in contemplation. "There is a small inscription. It's in Gadælic."

"Gadælic?" Sirona said, her brows creasing at the centre. "And I don't suppose you found anyone who could read it?"

"On the contrary, Seramina could," Carey said, feeling a surge of pride for her young friend.

"Seramina? But she couldn't be more than twelve-years-old, no?" Sirona said in surprise.

Carey nodded. "She's very talented, more so than most."

"And she could read it, then? The inscription?"

"Yes. It said, *My dearest sister, Fianna. All my heart, Elara,*" Carey recited.

"Fianna? As in, your Grandmother, Fianna Parnell? And it was from Elara?" Sirona repeated with raised eyebrows.

"You know who Elara is?" Carey asked with a touch of excitement.

Was it too much to hope that Sirona also knew who Elara was?

With a slight frown, Sirona said, "You don't know who she was?"

"I figured from the inscription that Elara was my grandmother's sister, but no one seems to know anything about her," Carey said, her face souring. "No one except for Saar, that is. He alluded to knowing the truth about her, but never revealed more."

"For an Imperial to know of her is, unfortunately, not a surprise given the path she chose," Sirona said solemnly. "I am, however, surprised that no one else knows of her. She was a big part of Fianna's life when she was younger. A lot of what happened to her family is because of Elara."

"Then you do know her?" Carey asked, curiosity and excitement building within her.

Finally, some answers.

"I did," she nodded. "I was a friend of your Grandmother's family for a long time. I watched them grow up together."

Given that Lady Sirona seemed little older than her, Carey found this statement to be incredibly confusing, yet she said nothing. She was about to find out who the mysterious Elara was, and she didn't want to get side-tracked. One mystery at a time.

"Fianna was the oldest of the two and clearly the more talented," Sirona continued. "Elara was a sensitive, kind soul, but I could tell that she felt caught in Fianna's shadow. She was always trying to prove herself but could never seem to surpass Fianna's standing. It was not a fault of their parents, they loved their daughters the same, but to be a young lady of the castle — as your Great Grandparents were part of Emperor Merilius's Council — there were more than just family expectations, and Fianna seemed to meet them more easily than Elara.

"I watched the two girls as they grew into young ladies, and I became troubled by the friendship that had blossomed between Elara and her tutor. He had taken a shine to Elara and always seemed to be whispering in her ear. But your Great Grandparents saw no problem with him and believed he was simply giving her advice and help in her education. I did not want to lose their friendship, so I didn't pursue the matter further despite my misgivings.

"From then on, Elara became more and more withdrawn. She assured her parents that she was just focusing on her lessons, but it soon came to pass that she was in fact studying much more than that which they expected of her. The tutor had been teaching her the ways of Dark magic. He took advantage of her and her position, something none of us realised until it was too late."

"What happened?" Carey asked, her eyes wide.

"One night, her father was guarding the Orb. The Orb was a relic which contained the balance of Light and Dark magic. It's difficult to explain, but there is always a balance. Disrupt that balance and there is chaos. The Council had long guarded the Orb against any that might use it for dark purposes, for such power only brings out the worst in wizards. They dared not use it for themselves. As long as they guarded it, the balance of light and dark within the realms held fast.

"That night, Elara came to the tower, killed her father, and attempted to steal the Orb. Apparently, she had grown tired of living in her sister's shadow and this was her way of breaking free of it. She was banished, much to her mother's despair, and she and her tutor were never seen or heard from again."

There was silence in which Carey sat staring at Sirona, her hands covering her mouth in shock. "She killed her own father for this Orb?"

"Yes. He was a great man but like I said, poor Elara had been corrupted, although in the trial that followed, she denied anyone else's involvement in her scheme. She said that she had seen the light and realised that the Council was weak. That they should use the Orb rather than just guard it. At the time they dismissed her fanatical ranting and banished her. Sadly, they did not do it a second time when Malevolence was part of the Council and suggested the very same thing."

"Malevolence did what?"

"Oh yes. It was a popular idea amongst those who sought to revolt against the Council — take the Orb and use its powers. Unfortunately, no one realised that was what Malevolence sought to do, what with her clever persuasion. How do you think Malevolence became so very powerful? Instead of using the Orb for the betterment of the People, she took it for herself."

Carey looked up at the cavern roof, not quite seeing it. For her Great Grandfather to die at the hands of his own daughter... Carey had imagined something horrible ever since Saar had hinted at a darker past, and that is why Fianna had never told anyone about her. The truth, however, was a different kind of horrible. It became abundantly clear now that Elara would have joined Malevolence's Empire — how else would Saar know of her? She could still be alive for all Carey knew; many Imperials had escaped following Malevolence's downfall.

"Carey?" Sirona's voice cut across her thoughts.

Carey blinked. "Do you know what happened to her?"

Sirona leaned back against the rock wall. "We knew for a time, but then she disappeared into the Darklands and was never heard from again."

Carey's heart felt heavy in her chest. "She became an Imperial?"

"I hate to say it but yes. That is where they originated from after all. She was such a lovely girl too, it's a pity to think about what became of her."

"Lady Sirona—" Carey started.

"Sirona," she cut across with a small smile.

"Sirona. Can I say something?"

"I would say you just did," Sirona said, with a playful lilt to her voice. "But I suppose there is more?"

Carey smiled, appreciating her attempt to lighten the mood.

"I've noticed you say some rather strange things. You talk as though you're so much older, as though you've done or seen things that happened a long time ago, yet you cannot be much older than I am. Am I missing something?" Carey said, hoping she wasn't insulting her only ally.

Sirona smiled mysteriously. "I'll take that as a compliment."

"So, you are older, then?" Carey asked.

Sirona considered Carey for a moment, deciding silently upon something before taking a deep breath. "I can't quite remember my exact age, it's been so very long, but I would say I'm roughly about sixteen hundred years old. Or something thereabout."

Carey's mouth fell open. "I'm… I'm sorry, but did you just say *sixteen hundred* years old?" As Sirona nodded, Carey blinked in disbelief. "But how is that possible? I didn't think witches and wizards could be immortal."

"They can't. But that's not what I would say I am, although it would certainly seem that way."

When Carey said nothing in return, Sirona carried on. "My family were nomads. We travelled from village to village with our troupe. That was, until we fell ill with a crippling illness. It had been sweeping through the countryside, an epidemic of the likes we'd never seen before. My mother and father succumbed to it almost straight away. My little brother and I weren't far behind. I was a little older than you are at the time; Jachim was barely fifteen. I knew death was coming for us — I had seen it take most of our troupe in the days before, and by seen, I mean that quite literally.

Ever since I was young, I could see death when it came for someone, a dark shadow lurking, always over their left shoulder. Very few people knew of my power back then, as I would've been strung up for something as ridiculous as 'consulting with dæmons' or some other such nonsense. So, when this illness took over our lands, many believed it was some kind of black spirit roaming the lands. For me the black spirit was death, and he was doing a roaring trade."

Carey noticed how Sirona's eyes glazed over as she recalled what had happened all those years ago.

"It was early in the morning, long before the sun was due to break the horizon when I felt it. He had come for me, and even though I had seen him many times before, I was petrified. As he grew closer, I closed my eyes, and with all my being I wished him to pass me by, to leave me be."

Sirona paused and Carey gulped back the suspense. "What happened?"

Sirona looked straight at Carey. "He did."

"He did?" Carey repeated quietly.

"Yes, but the thing with death is that when it comes for a soul, it must have one, and even though he had passed me by, he still required a soul. That is when my baby brother died."

Carey's breath caught in her throat, a painful jolt of sympathy. "I'm so sorry, Sirona."

She shook her head dismissively. "It was a long time ago," she said shortly, but Carey could see that it was still something that would forever haunt her.

"What happened then?"

"I got better. People saw it as a kind of miracle, but I had a feeling it was something much worse. I could no longer see death, which troubled me greatly. It was as though he was invisible to me. What I soon found out was that it was I who was invisible to him. I have never been able to work out exactly what had caused death to dismiss me that night, but what I do know is that with that act, my soul no longer existed on the same plane as everyone else's. No matter what happens to me, I cannot die. I do not age, I do not scar. I simply exist."

"Do you think that is your power now?" Carey asked, utterly enthralled by this impossible story.

Sirona shook her head. "No, it's not a power, more a state of existence. However, the years have strengthened my magic beyond what many are able to achieve within their lifetimes, so I suppose that is my ability, my magic. That can be the only reason Saar is interested in me."

"Why does he need all of us, though? Can he not open the gateway to the Third World by himself?"

"The opening of any of the gateways requires an extreme amount of power if they are to be opened from one side. If he had an accomplice on the other side, then this wouldn't be the case, but as this gateway has never been opened…"

"It's *never* been opened?" Carey said in disbelief.

"Not that gateway, no. Even in all my years," Sirona confirmed. "The one leading to the commoner's realm has been opened and closed a number of times, but this is the first time that anyone has actually known where the opening to the Third World is. All I know is that I'm not looking forward to what happens when it is opened."

Carey frowned. "Why? What will happen?"

Sirona sighed heavily and rubbed her brow. "The balance of our worlds depends on whether a gateway is opened or closed. In the past, when the current gateway was closed, it caused havoc. Seasons go awry, the weather is unpredictable, birds and beasts are thrown into disarray. However, once the gateway is opened again, everything corrects itself and balance is restored. A common theory has been that, with consideration given to the Third World, an odd number of gateways need to be open in order to maintain the balance of our worlds."

"So, if Saar does succeed, then that balance will be thrown out," Carey concluded, the idea of Saar opening that gateway now seeming even less desirable than it had before.

"That, however, is not our main concern right now," Sirona said as she stood and stretched. "First we need to get back to Torarn. I imagine it is exceedingly late. You get some rest. I will take the first watch. This may

163

be a hidden city, but there are more than just wizards out there, and many of those things pay no heed to magical enchantments. I will wake you in a while. Carey, please," she said, cutting across Carey who had opened her mouth to protest, "you will need it."

Still fully clothed, Carey curled up on top of the musty bed blankets and stared up at the glow of the lichen on the roof. Her head spun with everything Sirona had told her and her mind fell upon the story of Elara and the Orb. To have a sister join that which you were trying to destroy… Carey sighed and turned over. It seemed to be a common theme within her family. Had Elara met her fate within the Empire like her sisters, though? So much had happened in such a short amount of time, and she felt as though there was more yet to come. It was going to be a long hard road back to the Centre City.

~Chapter Fourteen~

Within the Shadows

Something lurked in the darkness; Carey sensed it moving, searching. Unable to stop herself, she cried out and they stopped. Two silver eyes emerged.

"Got you..."

Carey woke to a hand clasped over her mouth and Sirona's face swam into view. She raised her finger to her lips then touched her ear. *Listen.*

Carey sat up slowly. She could hear it outside somewhere — high pitched keening, like a blade dragging along glass, an animal being dragged to slaughter, echoing through the passages beyond. Her blood ran cold at the sound. As she listened, the screams grew louder and louder.

"We need to get out of here," Sirona whispered, and together they moved to the door. Carey kept close as Sirona led them down the hallway.

As they rounded a corner, the screeching grew more insistent, and Carey felt Sirona grab her by the hand.

"RUN!"

Heart pounding in her ears, Carey stumbled as they hurtled down a corridor, the sound of their disembodied pursuers rebounding off the walls. The screeching raised the hairs on the back of Carey's neck and a deep sense of dread spurred her on faster as the noise continued to grow.

"It's catching up!" she cried in a wild panic as they raced across a cavernous hall, its carved grandeur wasted on the two.

Sirona came to a halt momentarily, with Carey almost slamming into her as she considered which way to go, then took off again, dragging Carey behind her.

"This way!"

The corridor was steeper, and Carey could feel a stitch begin to form in her chest, but the clamour of their pursuant was enough to keep her going. The walls around them began to lighten and as they rounded a bend, she saw the faint light of dawn peeking through an opening. Sirona's pace picked up when she saw it and with what breath she had left, gasped, "Almost... there..."

Hazarding a glance, Carey looked back to see the light disappearing behind them; great black tendrils were rushing up the passageway towards them, smoke and shadow lashing out. She screamed, and just as they reached out for her, their shrieking piercing her eardrums, she found herself flung out into the open air and into the glow of the rising sun. Backing away from the entrance, Carey and Sirona watched as the coils of darkness shrunk away from the opening, beat back by the sunlight.

"Come on," Sirona said, pulling Carey down the side of the mountain away from the entrance. "They'll soon find a way to follow us. We need to try and put as much distance between us and the city as we can."

"What are those things?" Carey puffed, trying not to trip as they skidded down the slope.

"Daeva," Sirona answered, her eyes darting about. "Dæmons that live within the shadows. They cannot live within the light, so as long as we stay within the sunlight..."

"Could Saar have sent them?"

"Most definitely. Only a wizard can summon a Daeva. Come. We need to get going."

"Wait," Carey said as she stumbled over a large fallen tree branch. "We need a plan. Those things are fast — surely we can't outrun them."

"Right now, the plan is to find an open space, lots of light. The dæmons will be after us, they always find a way. And you're right, we can't outrun them. Since we can't use magic to get out of here, getting out of this forest is really the only thing we can do right now," Sirona said as she stopped to try and garner their position. She pointed to the right. "This way."

They soon found the foot of the mountain, something Carey was very grateful for. She wished she wasn't wearing such ridiculous clothing as it kept snagging on the low hanging branches and shrubbery.

It was at that moment that they heard it again. Distant screeching. Sirona didn't need to tell Carey anything this time, Without a second's hesitation they took off through the trees. Carey paid no heed to the branches and hidden logs that scratched her face and threatened to trip her up; she was running so fast that she felt nothing but the panic pulsing through her body, and the blood pounding in her head as she forced herself onwards. She could hear the dæmons gaining on them — their keening wails growing louder — and Carey couldn't help but feel as though their efforts were all in vain. The forest was as dark as ever, despite the rising sun, and it would only be a matter of moments before the dæmons caught up with them. She was gasping for air now and the stitch was back, wrapping itself around her chest like a vengeful serpent.

"Sirona!" she gasped, stumbling on a hidden log. She reached out and felt Sirona's hand close around her outstretched palm.

"Come on, Carey, you can do it," she heard her say encouragingly.

Out of the corner of her eye, Carey saw the shadows lash out at her, tendrils reaching through the trees, and a wave of dread washed over her. "No!"

The darkness was all around them now, closing in at an alarming rate. Their shrieks were so loud now that Carey could hear nothing else, and the darkness reached out, searching, hungry.

Just as it reached a pitch set to split her in two, Carey burst from the trees and into the blinding morning sun, Sirona alongside her. The light burned their eyes, blinding them, but they stumbled onwards, away from the tree line. The blue of the horizon came into focus; a sharp, clear line of ocean ahead, and a sudden steep cliff. Skidding to a halt, Carey and Sirona found themselves overlooking an immense drop. Before them stretched an ocean, murky and rough, yet infinitely more inviting than what was behind them. With a single glance, Sirona took Carey's hand and they jumped.

Behind them, the dark tendrils of the Daeva reached for them, missing by barely an inch as their quarry disappeared over the edge of the cliff.

Flickering and shrieking, it shrunk back into the shade of the trees.

Falling through the air, Carey flailed about, the only thought in her head being the hope that she would miss any rocks looming below in the dark waters. As the water rushed up to meet her, she tucked her arms and head into her chest, curling up her legs and squeezing her eyes closed.

The pain of her body hitting the water was unlike anything she had ever experienced. The air was pushed from her lungs, the water set her skin aflame, and the pull of the water threatened to separate her head from her shoulders. She was momentarily dazed, blinded by the pain encompassing her body. She twitched, lungs screaming for air, and Carey realised she was no longer holding Sirona's hand. She struck out and kicked as hard as her abused body would allow, and finally, lungs fit to burst, found the surface.

Gasping for air, she looked about for Sirona; the ocean was churning, great waves swirling about her. Something caught her eye and Carey spotted the dark-haired form of her companion breaking the surface, just out of reach. She opened her mouth to call out, but a dark curling wave pushed her back under, dragging her beneath the surface. Carey let out a panicked scream, releasing a stream of bubbles into the swirling black. She kicked for the surface, but the ocean churned furiously about her, tossing her about like a ragdoll. Her lungs were screaming for air and black spots began to appear at the edge of her vision. Once more she reached out for the surface, feeling nothing but the sea water ripple through her fingers.

"This is it," she thought as the darkness closed in around her and the last of her strength left her body…

*

Cold wind bit at her exposed skin. Something harsh rubbed against her arm, rough and tight against her body. She felt strangely weightless. Her lungs ached and slowly her mind brought her back. An intense aching thrummed throughout her body where it had hit the water. Sunlight burned at her eyelids, shadows swinging back and forth beyond them. The creaking of wood met her ears above the swill of the ocean, and then suddenly she was dropped down onto something hard.

There were voices all around. Shouts and murmurs washed over each other in a garble of sound. Heavy footfalls beat close to her head and their owners called out in urgency. With great effort, Carey forced open her eyes.

She was lying on a wood planking surrounded by a mess of thick rope net. Something else lay beside her — no, not something. Some*one*.

Sirona lay not far from her and was deathly pale. She had a deep cut across one cheek and red was running from it in thin rivulets, blood mixed with sea water. She wasn't breathing. Carey's panic at their current situation was doused with a greater fear, and a dizzying wave engulfed her.

"No," she managed to croak, staring at Sirona's waxen skin, the look of a newly made corpse.

Bile rose in her throat. Carey reached out to her, her arms shaking, but then someone leaned over and picked her up, and Sirona slipped from view.

"No. Sirona," Carey gasped, her head lolling about on her shoulders. She looked up at the person carrying her and found a great black beard obscuring her view. She blinked the salt from her eyes, and straining her neck, found herself looking out over the deck of a great ship. Dark wood-carved banisters and blood-red sails. Before she could glean anything else, Carey was dropped roughly back on to the deck with a thud; a moment later Sirona was placed beside her in a similarly unceremonious fashion. Carey tried to scurry over to her, but someone held her roughly back by the arms.

"Please," Carey moaned, not taking her eyes of her companion. "She needs help. I have to help her—"

A cough. Carey stopped pleading, staring at Sirona as she heaved a great wracking breath and spluttered sea water all over the deck. Colour spread through her limbs rapidly, the waxy look disappearing before Carey's eyes. A few of the pirates around her muttered in surprise and took a step back as Sirona propped herself up with her hands flat on the deck, expelling the last of the water from her body. She looked over at Carey with a feeble smile on ashen features.

"Dying," she whispered, wiping her face and sitting back, exhausted, onto the deck. "Don't think I'll ever quite get used to it."

Before Carey could shake herself from her shocked silence, one of the men called out.

"Captain!" it cried, accompanied by three loud, wooden knocks. "Captain! You might want to come and see this!"

There was a moment of silence in which Carey discerned the distant thud of footsteps coming from within the cabin. Then, a door opened to her right and a pair of worn, brown leather boots preceded a tall, broad-shouldered man as he crossed over the threshold. A wide, tanned face stared down at her; the skin was pock-marked and leathery, and the eyes were round and dark, like two small black marbles. A mat of dirty blonde hair fell over the man's shoulders and a wide-brimmed red hat sat upon his brow. Without a single word, he appraised Carey before moving on to Sirona. It was only then that the man spoke.

"Get her to her feet!" he snapped in a deep voice. He then let out a bark of laughter, as though something about this was greatly amusing.

The man was now blocking Carey's view. She didn't know what they were planning on doing with Sirona, but she couldn't just sit there on the deck. Shaking herself from her stupor, Carey scrambled to her knees. Before she could do anything else, though, she felt a strong arm grab her around the waist and haul her upright. She was surrounded by a strange ragtag group of men, all weather-beaten and battle worn. Their skin was the same sun-lashed brown as the man who had stood over her, and every one of them had at least one noticeable scar. Carey cried out, kicking with her legs and straining against the hold of her captor when she heard Sirona's voice.

"Parlay! I demand a parlay!"

Carey stilled for a moment, watching as Sirona came into view, her eyes steely as she stared down the man in the red hat.

"I am Sirona, Lady of the Grey Seas and Huntress of the Southern Isles," she said in a loud, commanding voice. Any sign of her apparent death moments before was gone as she stared down the captain of the ship. "This is a pirate ship of the northern seas and I demand a parlay."

Pirate ship? Carey's breath caught in her throat. A rustle of murmuring shivered through the gathered crowd, and the man Sirona spoke to considered her intently. As Carey watched, heart frantic in her chest, the captain frowned a little.

"Sirona?" he growled, and Carey heard a vein of recognition run through that single word.

Sirona's jaw tightened at this. "Do I know you?" she said in a low, hard voice.

The captain swept his hat from his head, a small smile lifting one side of his mouth. "Perhaps the years have not been as kind to me as they have clearly been to you, but I doubt I will ever forget the passage of the Finean Reef under the fearful Huntress."

There was a moment in which Sirona stared hard at the captain's face.

"Marcus? Marcus Vordeaux?"

A wide grin spread across the broad man's face as he swept into a deep bow.

"Aye. And that's *Captain* now, milady," he said, replacing the great red hat back upon his head. "And this is my ship, the Siren. Welcome aboard."

~Chapter Fifteen~

Unlikely Allies

"Come. To my quarters. And back to work with the rest of yer!" The pirate crew scuttled back to their stations at the command of their captain, some chancing a glance back at Sirona and Carey as they turned. The two women followed Captain Vordeaux as they climbed the stairs up to his quarters, the pirate striding confidently along the deck. Carey glanced sideways at Sirona, observing her now blushed cheeks, life having returned completely to her skin. Blood and sea water still mingled upon her cheek, but the gash that had been there was gone; not a blemish remained upon her youthful face. So, it was true, then — Sirona was indeed touched by the immortal. The sight made Carey's stomach turn unpleasantly — what would it be like to die, only to be brought back again and again. She winced at her own pain, and almost wished for the smallest bit of that ability. With every part of her body aching, cut and bruised, she lamented not being able to use her own magic. She was nowhere near as skilled as Rupert when it came to healing, but she'd learnt the basics.

Through a heavily carved wooden door, they found themselves standing in a large and lavishly decorated room. Boldly dyed silks hung from the ceiling, covering the dark beams overhead, and colour was thrown about the room by the jewel-bright glass of hanging lanterns, dancing over every surface as the ship swayed upon the sea. Ornate pieces of jewellery were hung in display about the room, and a great painted vase stood by the stained-glass window at the far end. The furniture within was as elaborately carved as the door, heavy wooden pieces with dark velvet cushioning and gold gilding. Sirona and Carey were led to a wide lounge chair propped against the wall, and they sat amongst the piled cushions that lined it. Carey winced as she sat, the bruises covering her tender, even against the silken material of the lounge. She noticed the captain was watching them with a glint of curiosity in his eye.

"How do you know pirates?" Carey whispered once they were seated.

"I've had many lives, Carey," she said with a small smile, and Carey was left wondering what else Sirona had done in her exceedingly long lifetime.

"Indeed, she has," the captain laughed, sitting opposite them in a wide armchair and crossing his legs. "I honestly never thought I'd see you again, Sirona, considering the last time I saw you; you were fighting off a fearsome water beast all on your lonesome," he smiled, nostalgically. "Never have I ever seen such sword work, thought it was slightly marred by the fact that you were then promptly eaten by said water beast."

Carey coughed a little in surprise, but Sirona simply raised an eyebrow and said, "They didn't call me the Huntress of the Southern Isles for nothing, Marcus. I'm more astounded by the fact that you now have your own ship and crew. Who did you have to maroon for that piece of fortune?"

The captain leant back in his chair, rubbing his hands over his ring-adorned knuckles as he considered Sirona a moment.

"Who's to say I didn't come by the ship by honourable means?" he replied with a smirk.

Sirona pursed her lips, eyes narrowed. "Marcus Vordeaux, formerly the first mate of the Capricorn, was part of a crew I sailed with many years ago," she said to Carey, crossing her arms and continuing to stare at the captain. "I wonder, *Captain*, are you willing to parlay?"

Captain Vordeaux placed a hand over his heart in mock offense. "My dear lady, you wound me," he said dramatically. "Come now, my dear Sirona. You are clearly in need of aid, and who would I be to turn my back on the fearsome Lady of the Grey Seas?"

Sirona continued to survey him through narrowed eyes. "Hmm. Would you be willing to grant us passage to the nearest port? As you have undoubtedly noticed, we're woefully short of any transport."

The captain leaned forward, his broad tanned face split in a toothy grin, several gold teeth glinting in the low light. He held out an upturned palm.

Without another word, Sirona began removing her jewellery, her gaze one of quiet elation.

"Um, what are you doing?" Carey asked, perplexed.

"Payment, lass," Captain Vordeaux said, taking Sirona's necklace and earrings.

"What? I thought you were old friends," Carey said with rising indignation. What kind of person required payment for helping a friend?

Realising Carey's misunderstanding, Sirona shook her head. "Oh, no. Carey, it is not what you think."

"Your friend has not sailed before," the captain stated with a curl of his lip.

Carey looked at him. "I've sailed before. It's not my favourite way to travel," she said coldly.

"I'd say because you made no sacrifice," he answered unperturbed. "The sea is a demanding mistress. You sail upon her; you offer sacrifice to appease her. If you take your chances, well… you'll be sailing rough seas and holding tight to your helm."

"Sacrifice?" Carey repeated incredulously. "What do you do? Throw it overboard?"

"I can see you're sceptical, but to us, there is no greater sacrifice. Why else do pirates hunt treasure?" Captain Vordeaux said, indicating his cabin without a sideways glance. "So please, I know it must be of great inconvenience to you, but we must offer something for our new guests."

The idea of a vengeful sea seemed ludicrous to Carey but seeing as Sirona so readily believed him, there had to be something to it. Her crown had survived their swim somehow, and she handed it over along with her earrings.

"And the necklace," Captain Vordeaux said with a nod.

Carey grasped her Seeker's pendant. "No, not this one."

The captain leaned forward, brow creasing, and Carey opened her hand to show the man. His eyebrows rose upon seeing the golden triangle. "Seeker, hey?"

Sirona eyed the captain sharply. "This won't be a problem, will it, Marcus?"

"Not at all," he answered smoothly. "I only wonder how one comes to be so far from the Centre City."

Before Carey could think up a suitable lie, Sirona spoke: "We are being hunted. An Imperial."

Stunned that she would entrust this information to a pirate, Carey scoffed. Hadn't Sirona said not so long ago to not trust anyone?

The captain considered her explanation for a moment. "Aye, you speak the truth. Though I cannot say it be the entire story."

"That's a strange thing to assume," Carey said before she could stop herself.

Sirona let out a low chuckle. "One thing you should know about Marcus Vordeaux here is that he has the uncanny ability to know when someone is lying. A formidable ability amongst pirates, where truth is such a rare commodity."

"Ah flattery. You always did know your way around a pirate's ego," Captain Vordeaux said with a smile.

"Is that a special ability, then?" Carey asked, to which he barked with laughter.

"You, young lass, really do not know much about pirates, do you? The day a pirate does magic is the day this ship sails among the clouds instead of the waves. Magic indeed..." he laughed, gathering up their jewels.

"Pirates aren't witches or wizards. They have no magic. At least none they care to use," Sirona said quietly.

"Aye, less magic, less trouble," the captain said much louder and with a smirk. "Seeker, Imperial, it makes no difference. You are a witch and the sooner we make port, the sooner you can leave my ship. Don't be getting me wrong, my dear, Sirona is an old friend and I am happy to help, but magic draws trouble, and that," he said, pointing to Carey's necklace, "is trouble."

*

Carey sat quietly in the corner of her cabin, staring with tired brown eyes into a small, cracked looking glass that hung on the wall. There was a small, round bruise on her left jaw that was already beginning to turn purple, and a slight cut over her right eye. She had changed from her bedraggled ball gown to a pair of slacks and a loose-fitting shirt with a vest that the captain's first mate had procured for her. She was dry and clean, yet no real comfort came to her.

She could feel each small bump as the ship tapped the waves, and the creaking of the ship's bow as it swayed filled her with unease. Of all the places she would rather be right now, a pirate ship was not among them. She wanted to be doing something — sitting on this ship with nothing to do but wait was harrowing. Saar was undoubtedly searching for them, as would her family and friends. What was happening back at the Centre City? Would Saar have resumed his guise as Lord Acheron, using his skills at deception to learn more of her whereabouts? Carey shuddered as she imagined his false concern at her disappearance, his honeyed tones masking his true intent. She wanted to warn Kat and Ji, but without her magic, she was lost.

She did not trust this Captain Vordeaux. There was something about him that set her teeth on edge, though he seemed amiable enough. If Lord Acheron had taught her anything, it was that a genial disposition was not a promise of truth.

"Don't trust anyone," Sirona had reminded her quietly after their audience with the captain. "I may have sailed with this man before, but it's been a long time. He isn't likely to ally himself with wizards, Imperial or not, but that doesn't mean he isn't still out for himself. He is, after all, a pirate."

There came a knock at her door.

"Yes?"

"It's me, Carey," came Sirona's voice.

Carey crossed the room and unlocked the door, letting Sirona in. She had also changed into pirate garb, though somehow it suited her more than Carey. Her dark auburn hair fell loose and wild about her shoulders and there was not one bruise in sight.

"Are you all right?" she asked, searching Carey's face. When Carey didn't answer, Sirona nodded to the door. "Come. Let's get some fresh air."

Carey looked about her cabin tentatively, then with a deep breath, followed Sirona out onto the deck. Sirona leaned on the ship's balustrade, looking over into the waves. Carey looked up at the helm and found Captain Vordeaux watching over his ship, the wind flicking at the feather in his hat. The other crew members were busy and were generally ignoring them for the most part.

Carey joined Sirona, taking care not to lean too far over the railing. This was the first time she had been near the ocean since their disastrous crossing to the Aran Islands and she had still not conquered her fear of open water.

"Not a fan of the ocean?"

Carey turned her head away from the water to face Sirona. "How did you know?" she grimaced.

Sirona was watching her closely. "I heard of your crossing. Well, when I say *heard,* I mean I heard the rumours."

"Rumours?" Carey repeated, startled.

"Of course, Carey. You cannot possibly think that your defeat of the Empire wouldn't be talked about, would you?" Sirona said with a small smile. "There are wild rumours, several more outlandish than others, but there are some, like how you got here, that are a little more believable. Also, your body language gave you away."

Carey sniffed in disbelief and ran a hand through her hair. "I guess I never really thought about it, to tell you the truth, but yes, I'm not too fond of sailing."

"You endured much, you and Kat," Sirona stated, looking out at the ocean.

"And Ji," Carey added, affronted by her omission. "He endured much more than any of us."

"I'm sorry, of course Ji as well," Sirona said apologetically. "Like I said, I've heard only rumours and stories. As far as I was aware, Jeremy Shultz was with you for the most part—"

"While Ji was being tortured," Carey said, cutting her short.

She wasn't particularly keen to talk about either subject; Jeremy or Ji's ordeal. She had barely spoken of either to anyone else — she felt it was Ji's story to tell, not hers, and she was less than eager to speak of Jeremy.

"He's your Other," Carey heard her whisper with sudden understanding.

Carey's pulse quickened, and she bit down hard on her tongue. The implication of those words... how often she had contemplated them herself during the darkest hours of the night. She could feel Sirona's eyes on her, but she avoided their gaze, staring resolutely down into the waves.

Sirona, however, did not take her hint. "When did you first realise?"

Carey took a deep breath and let it out slowly with a small hiss. "I... I don't even really know if he is," she said, giving in to Sirona's unrelenting stare.

"I think the fact that you are even considering him means that he is."

Her mouth dry, Carey frowned. "I don't think it means anything."

"Why would you say it otherwise?" Sirona asked softly..

Bowing her head to the railing, Carey put her head in her hands. "It's just... it's all so..."

Carey couldn't believe she was even considering telling Sirona about Ji and Jeremy, but there was something about her that was so compelling. Closing her eyes, she let out a long sigh. "When I first felt *something*, I thought it was for Ji, only it wasn't. It turned out it was Jeremy Shultz all along. Now I don't know whether it was Ji I was feeling something for or Jeremy, and to tell you the truth, I'm terrified," Carey said in a rush, afraid that she wouldn't get it all out if she stopped to think about it.

Sirona was silent for a moment and Carey was scared that she was about to tell her exactly what she had been fearing for so long.

"How did you feel when you found out it was Jeremy and not really Ji?" Sirona asked simply.

Carey looked up, unsure of where she was going with this, but she racked her mind regardless. "Shock... hatred... betrayal..."

Sirona gestured as if to suggest the answer was obvious. "There's your answer then."

When Carey didn't say anything, she smiled sympathetically. "When you saw Jeremy, you felt none of what you feel for Ji. Regardless of any deception, when you discovered his identity, that was it. If you felt anything real for Jeremy, any favourable emotion at all, then you would not feel hatred or any of what you just said. Jeremy is not your Other, Carey."

Carey's knuckles were white from gripping the ship's banister. Her breath had caught in her chest and her mind was racing in a manic, excited sort of way. Was that it? Had she been worrying about nothing all this time?

"But how had Jeremy even known? When I first realised, it was Jeremy acting as Ji. He had acted so... intimate..."

Carey was reminded of the moments that had followed their close encounter with the Chimera at the falls. Jeremy had to have known that Ji had feelings for her to act so confidently.

"Could Jeremy have had those feelings also?" she asked, panicked, as she recounted this memory to Sirona.

Sirona shook her head. "It is most likely that Ji said something during the course of his internment."

Carey shook her head vehemently. "No, no way. Ji would never have told them something like that."

"He didn't necessarily have to. They could have found it out any number of ways. The heart can betray us too easily, unfortunately," Sirona said softly in comfort. "I'm sure he never meant for them to discover those feelings."

Carey stared out at the water, unseeing. If they had known, if Ji had unintentionally divulged his true intentions, then it was indeed as simple as Sirona suggested. She looked down at the frothing waves carved by the ship's prow. A wonderful warmth was spreading through her limbs, wiping away her long-harboured insecurities. Her chest seemed to be expanding, the weight of a thousand sleepless nights drifting away on the sea breeze. The more she thought about it the more she realised how ridiculous she had been. Ji knew it, Carey was sure of that, and yet not even that had convinced her. A creeping sense of shame was tingling about her ears and she gripped them with sudden dread.

"Is it too late?" she whispered, afraid. She looked around at Sirona who shook her head with a smile.

"If I have learnt anything in my many, many years, it is that it is *never* too late," she whispered.

Those words could have been magic for the effect they had on Carey. All the anxiety and doubt she had been hoarding the past few months suddenly dissipated, borne away on the waves below. They held an unspoken promise, unexpected hope that lifted the weight from her chest and breathed new life into her.

Despite their situation and the danger hunting them, Carey felt renewed. A spark of optimism had replaced everything that had been holding her back, and she felt as though she could do anything, take on any challenge. Face anyone. But most of all, Carey now had the confidence she needed to do what she should have long ago — tell Ji that he was not alone in how he felt. If only she wasn't stuck on this boat.

She heard a soft chuckle and turned to see Sirona watching her with an unmistakeable twinkle in her eye. "I've seen that look before and no, no amount of desire will get you to shore should you be thinking of jumping ship."

"You do realise you may be asking a bit much," Carey said jokingly, although she managed a last wistful glance at the water before turning her back to it resolutely. "And you know this look how?"

"How do you think?" Sirona said with a smile, but Carey could see a sadness in her eyes.

"You found yours?"

She nodded. "Long ago. For the longest time I vowed that should I ever find my Other I would run hard and fast in the other direction. Harsh," she admitted, seeing Carey's reaction, "but how could I ever stay? For them, they would spend their whole life with me, but I could never spend my whole life with them. They would grow old, wither and die, and I would live on, forever young. How could I possibly endure that?"

"But you did find them, didn't you?" Carey said, hopefully.

"I did, and in an instant my resolve crumbled." Sirona sighed as she leant over the side of the ship and reached out, allowing the ocean spray to lick at her fingertips. "I should've run, though…"

"Tomas saw my… situation… not as a curse, as I had seen it for so long, but as a gift. He made me realise that I could help others. He helped me see the good in what I was and showed me a new way of living."

Sirona paused, her eyes unfocused and her hand dropping back to lie against the side of the ship. Carey didn't speak — there was something Sirona was struggling to say and she didn't want to interrupt.

"They found out about me, some of the villagers," she said in a low voice, "And they came for me. They thought I was possessed, dark magic or some such thing. I should have told Tomas to run, to leave me. I would have escaped eventually, healed eventually. But he wouldn't. He tried to stop them. He couldn't see me hurt, even though he knew what would happen. The villagers, however, didn't appreciate his efforts..."

Her voice broke and Carey knew exactly what had happened even before she said it.

"Tomas was the one thing in my life that was finally good, and in a heartbeat, he was gone. Yet here I am, enduring... forever enduring."

She looked over at Carey, her face smooth with the kind of forced composure that only years of practice could have ensured.

"But do you know what, Carey? Despite my selfishness, despite everything telling me I should have run, despite how it all ended, and despite the fact that it was barely a moment in comparison to it all, it was the most singular glorious moment of my entire existence. Now tell me, would you run, now that you know that feeling?"

~Chapter Sixteen~

Sword Play

Carey could barely sleep, what with the waves rocking her about to their own uneven beat, the wind whistling loudly through the tiniest crack in the porthole, and of course, everything Sirona had revealed to her. She couldn't help but think of Ji now and wonder what he was doing, whether he was as disturbed in his sleep as she was, wondering where she had disappeared to. She let her mind wander, remembering that which she'd never allowed herself to think of before. She thought of the way Ji rumpled his hair when he talked, his brown tresses falling about his face in messy waves. She smiled for the mischievous twinkle in his eyes whenever he laughed. Then there was the curve of his mouth each time he smiled at her voice…

If only she could contact him; Twilight Travelling was out, which was unfortunate as Carey felt she could have done so without any trouble. Of course, she wouldn't risk it, but she wanted to. Truly wanted to.

She shifted her memory back to the last time she had tried to Travel — the pain that had erupted in her head — and she knew intrinsically that it had been Saar stopping her all along. He wouldn't have wanted Carey to contact her parents, wouldn't have wanted her to be able to stop him summoning her. Of course, it had been him who had stopped her from developing her power, and the thought made her seethe…

Unable to rest any longer, Carey waited until the sun had cleared the horizon before dressing and making her way to the deck. There, she found several crew members sparring on deck, their swords glinting in the new light.

Carey hadn't seen much sword fighting beyond the dungeons of the castle, and as she watched, she marvelled at their lightness of foot and unconventional style. There was much play with their swords; dropping and twirling that may have seemed unnecessary to the casual observer, but Carey could tell that they were clever devices used to trick their opponent. She leaned against the banister and watched eagerly as a tall and rather handsome pirate danced about his opponent, his movements graceful and his blows precise. He had long dark locks that were tied back in a messy queue, and a small curled goatee that gave him a distinctly roguish look.

As he turned, lifting his sword to deflect his opponent's, he noticed Carey watching and with a slight grin of arrogance, he quickened in his attack, all the while keeping her gaze. Carey could tell that he was showing off, but even his arrogance couldn't persuade her to turn away. With a speed that was almost impossible, the pirate wore down his opponent; then suddenly, he dropped his sword. It bounced at his feet with a resounding clang against the sea deck, and with a triumphant cry, the other pirate lunged at him. With impeccable timing, the pirate spun to his right, his opponent's sword barely missing his arm before he dropped to one knee, swept up his sword, twisted back to face his bewildered partner and thrust his weapon upwards, its tip coming to rest on the other pirate's ribs. There was a roar of approval from the onlookers and with a grunt of disappointment, the defeated pirate dropped his sword and held out his hands in surrender.

With a great laugh of self-satisfaction, the victor stood up, and with his eyes on Carey, patted his partner on the shoulder before walking over to join her. Leaning casually against the banister and inspecting his blade, the pirate said, "See anything you like?"

Carey answered, "That was a pretty impressive display. You seem to know what you're doing..."

"Gerard," the pirate said obligingly with a cheeky wink.

"Gerard," Carey repeated with a raised brow. "Would you care for a different sparring partner? I could use the practice, and I'm sure you wouldn't mind showing me that move you did at the end there."

Gerard flicked his sword so that it flipped over in the air before catching it right way up and tapping the tip to his brow in a strange sort of salute. "Not at all, love. You sure you can keep up?"

Carey took a sword offered to her by one of the other pirates who was watching and weighed it in her palm. "We shall see, won't we?"

The blade in her hand was slightly lighter than her training sword, and she swung it across her body, testing it. The rest of the crew drew in around them, intrigued by what was about to take place. Gerard turned to face her, twirling his blade confidently.

"Ready?" he asked with a gleam in his eye.

Carey smiled, suddenly reminded of her training sessions with Ji. Shifting her weight to centre, she raised her sword. "When you are."

As Gerard swung his sword upwards, Carey brought hers over her shoulder. With the crash of metal on metal, their swords connected. Gerard grinned widely and took a step forward, drawing his sword back around and striking out again. Over and over he brought his sword around, and over and over Carey blocked it. It was exhilarating, and Gerard was proving a challenge, much more than Kat or Ji had ever been. She was finding it difficult to get the upper hand — Gerard was skilled at keeping her on the defensive and he was so relentless that she was soon breathless. With a sweeping motion, he caught her off guard, and within a moment, his sword was at her throat.

"Give up?" he asked with another wink.

Carey narrowed her eyes and shook her head. Gerard backed off, giving her some breathing space before bringing his sword up at the ready. Rubbing her throat, Carey took a few steps to the side and adjusted her grip on her blade. Before Gerard could say anything else however, she struck out, determined to get the advantage. There was a touch of surprise on his face as he stumbled slightly, matching Carey's blows.

"Ho ho!" he cried, laughing as he caught his footing.

It didn't take long, however, for Gerard to best Carey again. With a quick duck under one of her swings, he caught her off-side and before she knew it, Carey found Gerard's sword at her throat again.

"Still don't give up?" he grinned.

Tapping his sword away with the tip of her own, Carey smiled back. "Not just yet," she quipped, making her way back to the centre of the deck.

"You're not bad," Gerard commented, following her. "But might I make a suggestion?"

With a raised eyebrow, Carey nodded.

"Your style, is too 'palace soldier'. Don't watch your strikes, follow mine instead. It's all about…" he raised his sword again, "anticipation."

There was a round of sniggers from the crew and Carey, choosing to ignore his suggestive tone, readied her sword with an emphatic, "Thanks."

"My pleasure," Gerard said before taking his sword and swinging it over his head and down to meet Carey's.

Watching for Gerard's next move was a lot more difficult than he made it sound and Carey, unable to keep her footing, soon found her back against the hard, wooden deck with her opponent looking over her.

"You think too hard!" he said as he helped Carey to her feet.

Her cheeks smarting with humiliation, Carey dusted herself off. She hadn't felt this incompetent since her first day with Sir Garrow.

"Watch me…" Gerard said, pointing to his eye before gesturing to her.

She took a moment, closed her eyes and drew in a deep breath. She concentrated on the position of her feet and the slightly uneven slope of the deck. She focused on the leather of the hilt in her hand and the way it rubbed slightly against her palms, sticky from the salty sea air. She could hear the crew murmuring, wondering, and then the slight whistling of the air.

Carey's eyes flew open just as she raised her weapon to block Gerard's. He'd clearly thought he'd had the advantage of this attack and was therefore surprised when Carey pushed him back and landed a few quick blows before he'd had a chance to recover. With the advantage, Carey struck out with all her might, deflecting Gerard's attempts at regaining his stance and forcing him back. She could hear the crew urging him on and she knew that each one of them were just as surprised as Gerard by Carey's sudden show of strength. He ducked and she knew he was trying to catch her off balance again; she used the momentum from the missed strike to tuck herself into a roll, missing Gerard's retaliatory swing and putting a few feet between them.

Keeping herself low, Carey watched as Gerard chased her with a great arc of his sword. She turned, dodging to the side, and he stumbled as his sword missed its mark. Taking advantage of this moment of weakness, Carey raised her sword and as Gerard turned, its tip found his throat. With a look of surprise, he stopped short, his sword barely raised. Dropping his blade in defeat, a great grin broke across his face.

"See?" he said, placing a finger on her sword and slowly pushing it away from his neck. "Anticipation."

Clapping sounded from the upper deck and Carey turned to see Captain Vordeaux applauding, with Sirona watching by his side. She was just beginning to wonder what Sirona was doing with the captain when Gerard spoke across her thoughts.

"Care for another go at it, love?" he asked as he stooped to pick up his sword.

Grasping her weapon by the blade, Carey passed it back to Gerard with a smile. "Perhaps another time. Thanks for the…. lesson," she said, not entirely sure that that was the word for what had just happened.

"Besides," came the booming voice of the captain, "you bunch of mangy seadogs have work to do. Off with yer!"

With that, the crew were sent scuttling off to their various stations. Gerard swaggered past Carey, nudging her with his elbow and giving her a wink before leaping onto a rope ladder that took him to the top of the mainsail.

Carey joined Sirona and the captain at the helm; Sirona was talking in a low voice to Captain Vordeaux, her voice covered by the wind. As Carey approached, Sirona pulled away and smiled, beckoning to her.

"That was an impressive display, Carey. Excuse me, but I would never have guessed you to be such the swordfighter," she said with an air of surprise.

"Well you've never seen Kat and Ji at it. I don't really have a choice with those two," Carey said smiling back. "Besides, it's a requirement of all Council members to be proficient in some kind of weaponry nowadays."

Sirona nodded. "Ah yes, of course. There are those armies that still heed the Imperial call and the Dead Plains are a favourite battle ground for them, that's for sure."

"You've been there before?" Carey asked curiously.

"Yes, many years ago. I fought there in the Great Battle that created them," she shivered at the thought. "It's dark and desolate, and I hope you never find yourself there, Carey."

"And if those armies you speak of decide to try and reclaim the Centre City?" Carey said, the hairs on the back of her neck prickling.

Sirona shook her head, her lips a thin line. "We can only hope that Captain Tutari and the Vuletian army can hold them back."

Carey was about to ask about this Captain Tutari when an urgent shout sounded from the crow's nest.

"Captain!" came Gerard's voice. "Starboard side! You better take a look at this!"

Sirona and Carey rushed to the starboard side along with the rest of the crew on deck. Looking over the side, Carey gasped in horror at the sight that lay before her.

"What in the stars…" Sirona whispered.

Floating on the surface, glittering innocently in the sunlight, were the bodies of hundreds of mermaids. They were borne along by the ebbing of the sea, their lifeless forms drifting forlornly by the side of the ship. One of the bodies floated up just below where Carey stood; its long hair stark white and swirling about its expressionless face. All colour seemed to have been sapped from its form. Even the mermaid's tail lacked its usual brilliance.

"What happened here?" she managed to ask, her voice shaking.

"This is the Filisee Clan," said the captain, his face a mask of deep concern. "This has to be the entire clan."

Gerard swung down from his perch, landing deftly at his captain's side. "There'd been rumours, Captain. Last port. Some'd been saying they hadn't seen the Queen in a few moons. Perhaps another clan?"

Captain Vordeaux shook his head. "This is not the work of a rival clan," he said, looking down at a corpse as it floated by. "These are unscathed."

"Rival clan?" Carey said quietly to Sirona.

"Mermaids are fiercely territorial. If this had been a clan war, there would be signs of it."

"Not mermaids," Carey murmured, drawing her gaze from the bodies in the water. "If not mermaids..."

"Wizards," Captain Vordeaux said with a sneer. "The Queen is dead and now so is her clan. No other race is so sneaky or cunning in its dealing with others as a wizard. To destroy an entire clan by killing the Queen... Mark my words, *Princess*," he spat, pointing his finger in Carey's face, "at least pirates be taking you on face to face!"

The captain stormed off, leaving Carey shocked by his sudden outburst. Sirona placed an arm around her shoulders. "Don't let his words worry you, Carey. He's been burned in his dealings with wizards too many times to have a decent opinion of us."

"Could a wizard have done this though?" she asked shakily. "Perhaps it wasn't wizards. Perhaps it was an accident. That's possible, isn't it?"

"It could have been an accident but it's not very likely. The Queen is very rarely away from her clan, so it certainly suggests foul play. The continued survival of a mermaid clan rests on the Queen naming an heir before she passes on. If she hadn't named an heir, well then... this is all very worrying," Sirona said, looking out over the scene.

"Worrying?"

"Yes. If someone killed the Queen, you have to wonder what for."

Carey thought of the mermaids who had saved her from the storm, and their prophecy.

"Do all mermaids possess the gift of prophecy?" she asked Sirona, staring down unseeing at the mermaids below.

"Generally, the queens are the Seers of the clan," she answered with a hint of curiosity. "They speak prophecy for their clan. Why do you ask?"

"The mermaids that saved me... they spoke of a prophecy, about a Liberator."

Sirona nodded. "Yes. I've heard of this. I did not realise it was a Mermaid prophecy though. Wait... are you suggesting that has something to do with this?"

Carey bit at her thumb in contemplation. "Maybe, maybe not. But the ability to See into the future could be a motivation. Someone could have captured the Queen for her ability to See."

"That would make sense if they were like ordinary Seers in that they could See the ordinary. But mermaid prophecies are extraordinary. They relate only to that which affects us all; pivotal events in history. Their prophecies are few and far between, so for someone to kidnap one of them for their Seeing abilities would—"

"Would be useless unless they were taken regarding a certain prophecy," Carey surmised, feeling as though she knew exactly where this was going and yet hoping vehemently that she was wrong.

"Listen, Carey," Sirona said, placing a hand on her shoulder. "This is all merely speculation. There could be a million explanations for what happened here, and Saar is not the only one whose choices have led to death and destruction. This might not have been about a prophecy at all. Besides, you have already defeated Malevolence — isn't that what the prophecy was about?"

"It told of a Liberator who would defeat Malevolence. They believed that person was me," Carey said quietly, remembering the mermaid's proclamation.

"Then the subject of the prophecy, was you?" Sirona said slowly as though something was suddenly becoming clear to her.

"What? What is it?" Carey asked.

Sirona seemed to consider for a moment before answering. "Nothing. It's as they said. You defeated the Dark Empress," she said in a slightly evasive manner, which gave Carey the distinct impression that she knew more that she was letting on.

"So, this might not even be related?" Carey enquired, watching Sirona closely, but whatever it was that had crossed her mind seemed to have been waylaid by the reiteration of Carey's triumph over Malevolence.

"There is no doubt that Saar is dangerous, but there is no rule saying only one dangerous wizard may exist at any one time," Sirona said reassuringly.

189

"And yet, if he did have some part in this…"

Carey stared out at the hundreds of glittering tails floating just below the surface; the mermaids wraithlike and ethereal even in death. The morbid display of beauty cleaved at her chest and Carey closed her eyes against it.

"All the more reason to get word to the Council," she said, turning from the waters. "Who knows what kind of havoc he'll wreak in the time it takes for us to get back."

"What would you say, though?" Sirona said with a frown. "We still can't use our magic and even if there were some way to get to them, you can't be sure Saar won't be keeping an eye out. Men like him never work alone. He may very well have spies within the Council, willing or not."

"Are you sure there's no other way to get to them?" Carey asked, unable to hide her desperation.

"If you're needing to send a message, I may have a way for you," came a voice behind them.

The two witches whipped around to find Gerard leaning against the helm.

"How long have you been there?" Carey asked a little sharply.

"Long enough to know a witch is not a witch without her magic," he said nonchalantly. "You've nothing to worry 'bout, love. I've no opinion of you. I can help, if you're needing a way of sending a message."

Carey looked over at Sirona, who was considering Gerard with narrowed eyes.

"If it doesn't use magic…" Carey started hopefully.

It was a moment before Sirona nodded. "Lead the way, Gerard."

With a cautionary peek over his shoulder, Gerard reached over and, clasping Carey's hand, led them to the far end of the lower deck where they came upon a door. With a quick glance behind him, he slipped through the doorway, leading Carey and Sirona down a set of rickety stairs and into the dimly lit belly of the ship. They were in a hold; none of the other pirates were down here and the space was largely taken up by stacked barrels and wooden chests. Wending their way past the cargo, Gerard pushed a heavy case from against the wall to reveal a narrow door. Gerard pulled on a chain around his neck, drawing a large and old-looking key from within his shirt, and with a heavy *clunk*, the door swung open.

Within was a small room with barely enough space for all three of them to stand. The walls were covered in pigeonholes, deep rectangular cavities stacked from floor to ceiling. Some were the size of a saddlebag, whereas others had barely enough room to fit a mouse. It was from one of these smaller holes that Gerard pulled a long, thin wooden box covered in ornate carvings. It seemed ancient and brittle; a spiderweb of cracks covered the casing and the carvings were worn smooth in places. Handling it with immense care, Gerard held it out for the two witches to see.

"What is it?" Carey asked, unable to read the inscription on the lid. "It's beautiful."

Sirona, however, said, "It's what's inside that intrigues me more. The box is merely a vessel for what lies within... where did you get this?"

Her voice was filled with awe as she gazed upon the box in obvious disbelief.

"An old wizard at the port of San Eves. The Captain uses it to arrange meetings."

"He uses it?" she said, unease creeping into her voice.

"He likes it because it's untraceable," Gerard said, holding it up to the light of a small lantern bobbing overheard.

"What is it?" Carey said, thoroughly intrigued now.

"It's called a Sídhe," Sirona said, reaching out for the box, but she hesitated. "Since when did the captain become so comfortable with magic?"

"I believe because it's what you call *ancient magic?*" said Gerard as he opened the box. "It is different, no?"

"Ancient magic," Carey repeated.

"The magic of the Ancients is not like that which we use nowadays. If we were to send a message, we would use our own magic that we possess within us," Sirona said as she stared, entranced by the contents of the box. "But this... ancient magic is elemental. It uses the magic which surrounds us. Therefore, anyone can use it."

"How does it work?" Carey asked as Gerard reached in to pull out what looked like a piece of translucent ribbon. It fluttered gently in a non-existent draft.

"Hold it, think, and it will go. It will ride the wind to that which you seek," he said. "Like I said, the captain uses it to arrange meetings. A place, a time, and no more. It is completely untraceable."

"Don't think of anything too complex, though. A few words at most," Sirona warned.

"A few words?" Carey repeated incredulously. How was she supposed to convey anything in just a few words?

"Perhaps don't mention Saar — we can't be sure what he has planned or how he'll react to being cornered. There's every possibility he'll use that stone against anyone who tries."

Carey nodded. Since there was no way of letting them know the full story this way, it was best she didn't coax them into doing anything potentially disastrous. If he was still under the guise of Acheron, Saar wouldn't dare try use the stone. He had the perfect hiding place; one he wouldn't give up easily. Exposing him could force his hand, and who knew what destruction he would wreak if it came to that.

Gerard handed her the long wispy Sídhe, and instead of slipping within her grasp as she half expected it to, it wrapped itself around her fingers. Carey looked up at Gerard. "Do I need to say anything?"

"Not out loud. You just need to think. Think of what you want to send," he answered simply.

Taking a deep breath, Carey closed her eyes as she settled on four words to send to Ji and Kat.

Alive. Trust nobody. Carey.

There was a sudden rush of wind and the three of them were knocked back against the cupboards. Carey's head bounced painfully against a large knob, and it was as she went to grab her affected temple that she realised the Sídhe was no longer wrapped around her fingers.

"It's gone," she gasped.

"Sorry. I should have warned you about that part," Gerard apologised, still clutching the box protectively. "And yes, it's gone. It will return to its place once it has delivered its message. We will not need to watch for it.

Don't be telling the captain though. I feel it is best he knows nothing of this."

"Yes, for someone so against magic, he seems perfectly content to use it himself," Sirona remarked under her breath. She watched Gerard turn and leave before saying quietly, "I have a feeling that my dear old friend the captain is hiding something. The Marcus I knew would never have even touched a Sídhe. We were correct in not trusting him. The faster we make port, the better. Say nothing to the rest of the crew."

Hoping that Gerard could be trusted not to turn on them, Carey nodded. They headed back towards the stairs, Gerard already reaching them in front. As he started to climb, Carey and Sirona heard the doors to the deck open and sunlight flooded the lower deck.

"Gerard!" came the captain's voice and Carey stumbled sideways as Sirona grabbed her by the arm and dragged her behind a stack of barrels. From there, Carey could see Gerard's back and the captain as he came slowly down the stairs.

"Stay down," she heard Sirona whisper and Carey ducked lower behind the barrels.

"What are you doing, lad?" came the captain's voice.

"Just been in the supplies cupboard, Captain," Gerard answered casually, and Carey felt Sirona tense up beside her. She suddenly remembered the captain's penchant for knowing when someone was lying, and her stomach did a panicked flip.

"Counting for when we reach port, I suppose?" Captain Vordeaux surmised, but when Gerard didn't answer, his voice changed. "Not hiding anything, are we, lad?"

"Sorry Captain, but I need to find the Princess. She was wanting a re-match," Gerard deflected, and when the captain didn't respond, he made his way quickly up onto the main deck.

Peeking through a crack, Carey could see Captain Vordeaux surveying the cabin suspiciously. A few long moments passed before he turned from the hold and let out a gruff "*humph*," before following Gerard upstairs.

As the door closed, Sirona stood up, staring hard at where the captain had stood.

"I have a feeling Gerard isn't the one hiding something."

~Chapter Seventeen~

The Captain

"That's it! Bravo, love!"

Carey was on her knee, her sword at Gerard's side. She smiled, having just pulled off the move she'd seen Gerard exhibit two days before.

"Well, you would think after almost two days of practice I would be getting some results," she said as he helped her up.

"At least now you fight more like a pirate and less like a soldier," Gerard commented cheekily.

With a smile, Carey glanced over to where Sirona stood watching. She grimaced, acknowledging Carey's searching gaze before moving her eyes back to the captain. Captain Vordeaux stood proudly at the helm, the sea air lifting the tails of his royal blue coat and ruffling the feather in his hat. He grinned down at Sirona, who forced a smile in return. For the past two nights they had dined with the captain, his booming laugh and extravagant storytelling providing little evidence of any deception he might have planned. Other than his outburst over the mermaids, he had played the gracious host impeccably, though there was a glint in his eye that did nothing to put Carey at ease. Gerard had remained quiet about their foray into the storage room and so far, the captain seemed none the wiser. Nervously, Carey hoped it would remain that way.

"One more time, perhaps?" came Gerard's voice.

Carey turned back to him, quickly covering her concern with a laugh. "We have time. Why not?"

As Carey deflected Gerard's sword, there came a loud whistle and Captain

Vordeaux's voice announced, "All hands on deck! We make port within the hour!"

"Ah well, love, it's been a pleasure," Gerard said with a bow as she passed her sword back to him.

"The pleasure's been all mine," Carey said politely to which Gerard winked.

"I'm sure it has."

Scoffing at his cheek, Carey watched as he ran off to join his fellow crew mates and she moved to join Sirona. The other woman was looking out at the approaching coast pensively.

"Keep an eye out, Carey," she said quietly without turning her gaze. "Until we are clear of this ship…"

She didn't finish her sentence, but her meaning hung heavily over them. *We are not safe.*

A low level of anxiety had hummed just beneath the surface since the mermaid discovery, and Carey felt it kick up a notch as she stared out beyond the ship's prow. Her dreams of silver eyes had been replaced by shimmering tails and the shrouded stares of the dead, and she'd woken more than once drenched in sweat, her heart racing. She longed to get away from this ship and the sense of foreboding it instilled in her.

Heavy footfalls sounded upon the deck behind them and they turned to see the captain approaching.

"Well, ladies, you'll be on your way soon enough. We'll be making port at Ebora — you should have a pretty straight shot through the mountains from there," he said jovially, though Carey noticed his smile did not reach his eyes.

"You don't have to act so heartbroken, Marcus," Sirona said, expertly masking her suspicion.

"Don't you worry, Sirona dear, I won't just be throwing you overboard as we pass. I'll be escorting you both into town, just to be sure of your safe arrival."

Sirona's eyes flashed at his words. "You? Set foot on land?" she said, sharply.

"It's the least I could do for such an old friend," he simpered in what he must have thought was a sincere manner.

Sirona recovered from her outburst. "Of course. Thank you, Marcus."

Captain Vordeaux nodded and then started back to the helm.

"What is it?" Carey asked as they watched him begin to whistle happily.

"Everything," Sirona muttered. "The Marcus I knew would never have stepped foot upon land. Whatever is drawing him from this ship must be very great indeed."

The two witches leaned on the ship's railing, watching the port of Ebora grow closer in silence. Carey wondered if she could ask Gerard for a sword to take with her. She felt incredibly vulnerable without her magic as her defence, and a sword might allow her some semblance of control. If the captain was to try something, she'd at least have that.

Carey stared out over the blue-grey swirl of the ocean; Sirona silent at her side. They made no attempt to speak, and Carey felt a rumble of nerves shiver through her body. Her heart beat harder as the ship ploughed through the waves, a dark roiling cloud of pitted grey chasing them from behind. A cool breeze flitted about the deck, whipping Carey's unbound hair about her face and seeping through the thin cotton of her shirt. Sirona shifted her hand on the balustrade and gripped Carey's tightly, her knuckles white as she squeezed.

Captain Vordeaux and his crew brought the ship into port and docked at the far end of the harbour. The crew leaned on the ship's rail, calling out goodbyes and waving as Sirona and Carey disembarked with the captain and Gerard. Sirona shook Gerard's hand cordially before moving to speak with the captain. Gerard took Carey's hand and pulled her into a warm embrace. A round of shouting and whistling rained down from the ship which Gerard ignored.

"You take care, love," he said in a low voice.

Pulling back, she felt him press something into her hand and she looked down to see the sword she'd been practicing with.

"Just in case," he murmured, and Carey gave him a swift kiss on the cheek.

"Thank you, for everything," she replied with a small nod, and she strapped the sword to her hip before setting off after the other two.

Glancing backwards, she saw Gerard watching them with a look of deep concern.

"Keep up, Carey! We must get you into town and on your way!" called the captain, and she sped up. The ship and Gerard were soon out of sight.

The port of Ebora was buzzing with activity. Horses and carts jostled for room on the strip that ran alongside the water and crews were calling out to one another as they pulled cargo on and off the ships moored there. Carey ducked as a net full of barrels was hauled overhead, their contents sloshing audibly. Street urchins crouched by the wayside, watching for any chance to snatch from an unsupervised load. The captain led them to an open square filled with market stalls and townsfolk. The stall owners' voices mixed over the general rumble of the crowd as the three made their way through.

Carey caught up to the other two just as a loud *BANG* sounded from across the market. The two witches jumped; Carey grasped at the sword on her hip and Sirona threw up her hands reflexively as laughter followed the sound. It seemed part of a street performance hidden by the crowd, and Carey straightened up, releasing her grip on the sword's hilt. Sirona followed suit, dropping her hand. It was then that Carey felt a sharp point dig painfully into her back and heard a voice in her ear. "No sudden movements, Princess... M'lady... Just keep moving."

It was Captain Vordeaux. He had used the commotion to his advantage and now there was a blade to each of their backs. Carey made to draw her sword, but the captain pushed the dagger in harder, and with a wince she felt it draw blood. She dropped her hands grudgingly.

"That's it, Your Highness," he growled. "Now, if you don't mind..."

Carey felt Sirona take her hand.

"Just do as he says, Carey. There are innocent people here."

"That's right," the captain said, moving them forward with another painful jab to the back. "You don't want to cause a scene now. Besides, this is not where we're meeting."

The captain steered the two down the main street. He kept close, making it look as though they were just three friends out for a walk; none of the passers-by gave them a second glance. With a sharp turn, the captain forced them down a much smaller fairway; balconies jutted from the buildings and clothes lines crisscrossed overhead, blocking the sunlight so that it fell in broken rays.

They came to an intersection with another alleyway that was bathed in mottled light. There, the captain dropped the knives, and before Carey could move against him, he had spun them around to face him. With a surprising amount of strength, he picked them up by the fronts of their shirts and slammed them against the wall opposite. Carey smacked her head hard against the brick and stars popped across her field of vision. She fell to the ground, unable to keep her balance. She grasped at the hilt of the sword still strapped to her hip, but as she brought it out from its hilt with a *schick*, it was knocked from her grasp. Before she could move to where it had fallen, Carey felt another blow land hard against her jaw, knocking her sideways onto the flagstone and out of reach of the blade. Pain shot through her skull and her eyes smarted with unwanted tears. Trying to catch her breath, she felt her hands being pulled together; the pinching of rope as it was wrapped around her wrists. As her head stopped spinning, her jaw still throbbing from the blow, Carey looked over at Sirona to see that she too had her hands bound. The captain pulled Sirona roughly to her feet, kicking Carey's fallen sword across the alley as he did so.

"Now, my darling Sirona, we shall see how much you're truly worth," said the captain ominously.

"What have you done, Marcus?" Sirona asked, stumbling slightly.

"You seem to have forgotten what I am, Sirona. I'm a pirate, and I'll be a pirate till the seas run dry. And as a pirate, there is one thing we value above anything else."

"And here I was thinking my past exploits had earned at least a modicum of respect," Sirona said as she regained her balance. "A true pirate would've respected the terms of our parlay. A true pirate wouldn't have gone near a magical item like a Sídhe. Seems to me, Marcus, that you're not a pirate after all — you're nothing but a thief and a liar."

199

Captain Vordeaux's hand moved with a flash of rings, landing a cracking blow across Sirona's face. She cried out in pain.

"You'll be watching your mouth, Sirona, or I won't wait for our guest," Captain Vordeaux threatened. He then reached down and grabbed Carey by the shoulders, hauling her to her feet. "You're wrong, though. Our parlay was to see you safely to port — there was nothing agreed beyond that. I hold true to a parlay, lass, and I'll hear nothing against my honour otherwise. As for the Sídhe…" he leered at her. "Times change, my dear. You should know that better than anyone. Besides, had I not had it; I'd never have received such a wonderful offer for your *return*."

"What did he promise you, Captain?" Carey asked, swallowing the fear that was rising rapidly within her. She twisted against her bonds, but they held tight, rubbing her wrists raw.

"Why? Think you can top it?" he said with a sneer.

Carey shook her head. "You don't know him. He won't pay. He'll take us and nothing and no one will stand in his way."

Captain Vordeaux laughed. "Oh, you'll see, lovey. No one crosses me and gets away with it," he answered confidently. "But we'll see soon enough. Not long now."

Carey couldn't believe how arrogant he was being. She knew Saar and his sadistic nature; he would destroy this entire town if it meant getting his hands on them. Captain Vordeaux was nothing but a pirate; no magic and only his weapons at his disposal.

"You need to let us go. You don't understand this man. He will—"

"Quiet!" the captain bellowed, and Carey reluctantly fell silent. She glanced over at Sirona who lifted her hands slightly and gave a minute nod. *Only me,* she mouthed, and Carey stared back.

No, she worded noiselessly back, not daring to move. Sirona was planning on using magic to get them out of this. But the thin black token still wrapped itself around their fingers — Saar would instantly know where they were. She wanted to shake her head, demand that Sirona think of something else, but the steely look on Sirona's face told Carey she was beyond reasoning.

Sirona closed her eyes and Carey held her breath. The ropes around her wrists dissolved in a golden haze, whispers of light illuminating the alley around them. Before Captain Vordeaux knew what was happening, Sirona had raised her hands and flung him across the narrow courtyard in a shower of red sparks.

"Carey! Run!" Sirona yelled, waving a hand at Carey and releasing her from her bonds.

Unfamiliar with this city, Carey made a dash back the way they had come, but the captain wasn't about to have his meal ticket escape, and he lunged at her as she passed. Sirona hit him again with another curse and he cried out, doubling over. His hand managed to clip Carey's ankle and she tumbled painfully to the flagstone. As she struggled to get up, she felt a strong hand grip her arm, pulling her to her feet.

"Come on, love, up you get."

It was Gerard.

"What are you doing here?" Carey gasped as she shakily got to her feet.

"No time for that, love. We need to get away from here. M'lady!" he shouted back at Sirona. She jumped over Captain Vordeaux, who was still gripping his stomach in agony, and joined them as they sprinted back towards the main street. They could hear the captain roar in pain and fury as his quarry ran from the alleyway.

"I came for you. The Captain hasn't been himself lately. I knew something was amiss," Gerard said simply as they ran out into the main street. "I just had a feeling."

"Thank you, Gerard," Sirona said as she looked up the main street, away from the markets. "Right now, we need to get away from here. Not the markets, though."

The dark grey clouds that had followed them into the harbour blanketed the sky now, dousing the bright sunlight and throwing the city into a premature twilight. The street they had turned onto was cast with long dark shadows thanks to the tall buildings on either side, and Carey felt a sickly dread creep into her stomach.

Gerard nodded, glancing up the street and away from the town centre.

"This way," he said, but as he made to grab Carey's hand, they noticed something rushing up from the harbour. Flitting between the shadows brought on by the low storm clouds, Carey heard terrifying screeches.

"Shadow Dæmons!" she screamed as she saw their dark forms swell within the shade thrown by the buildings around them.

Pulling on Gerard's hand, she ran in the opposite direction, knowing that it would be moments before the Dæmons caught up to them.

"We must fight them!" Gerard shouted to her.

She shook her head manically. "You cannot win against them! You have to run!"

Carey felt Gerard come to an abrupt halt as her arm jerked her backwards. He placed a hand bracingly on her shoulder, pushing her back. "Then I will fight them. Perhaps I can give you some time," and with that, he drew his sword and strode back towards the oncoming darkness.

Carey watched him for a moment before turning and taking off again, Sirona at her side. The screams and screeches of the Daeva were growing and Carey chanced a look back. Gerard stood, sword glinting in his hand as the Dæmons rushed up to meet him; he roared a challenge and Carey thought for a moment she saw the Daeva falter. But then, with a great swirling of smoke and shadow, it whipped about Gerard, swallowing him from view. Holding back a sob of terror, Carey kept running, heart pounding and panic clouding her.

Villagers were crying out in fear, darting into the alleyways and scurrying out of the path of the Dæmons as Carey and Sirona sped past. Carey's legs burned and her chest was aflame as she ran onwards, but she did not falter. The street was growing darker and the clouds overhead rumbled ominously, adding to the waves of sound now rushing about her.

Screams mingled with animalistic screeching and terror ripped at her; Carey shook the darkness from her eyes as her lungs grappled for air. They were almost at what looked like a town square when Carey noticed Sirona was no longer with her. She skidded to a stop, turning to see the dark shapes of the Daeva almost on top of them.

"What are you doing!" Carey screamed over the top of the Dmons.

"I'll hold them off!" Sirona cried back. "Just run!"

A blazing blue glow of magic was building around Sirona, and as the Daeva rushed towards her, she threw out her arms and a great blast of light erupted towards them. Lightning crackled about her, illuminating Sirona against the gathering darkness. Carey gaped as the shadows beat against the magic, echoing shrieks and screams rising and falling around them. Sirona's face was slick with sweat, her teeth grit and her eyes searing as her arms shook with the effort. Carey took a step towards her, hands over her ears now as the shrieks grew deafening. Sirona's gaze snapped to her; her chest was heaving, and her eyes were wide with fear. Carey knew that look — it was the look of someone steeling themselves to do something crazy. Something dangerous.

"Sirona!"

Sirona clenched her jaw in resolve. She withdrew a hand from repelling the Shadow Dmons and flung it toward Carey. It felt like a punch to the chest. Carey was flung backwards and with a familiar blast, everything began rushing past her, pulling her away from the Dæmons. In the moment before everything blurred from view, she watched in horror as Sirona's magic flickered and died, and she was swallowed up by the darkness.

"No!" Carey called out, but her voice was drowned out by the sound of the world rushing by. Everything flashed past in a blur of colour and light, and Carey cried out in alarm when it suddenly stopped and she fell, rolling onto something hard and cold. She tumbled down a short incline, her elbows and knees banging on rock and gravel before coming to rest at the bottom. The abrupt halt knocked the wind from her lungs, and she gasped for air. She tried to fathom what had just happened, but her mind was a confused mess: Gerard drawing his sword, the oncoming darkness, Sirona pushing her away... No. She hadn't pushed her. Sirona hadn't even touched her. She had Guided her to this place, just as Saar had tried. She was a Wayfarer too. But where was she? Where had Sirona Guided her to?

Carey pushed herself up to a sitting position, and it was only then that she realised how cold it was. The ground was icy and a sharp breeze bit at her exposed skin. Looking around, she saw that she was in a desert — rolling hills of pale, yellow sand, spread far beyond the horizon. The storm clouds were gone, replaced by a burning yellow sun, yet it gave no heat. Carey shivered, rubbing her hands together as she felt the cold beginning to cling to her fingers. She tried to remember her geography lessons with Lady Marksis and vaguely recalled a desert to the north, but no more. She had never known a desert to be so cold and void of heat. Her breath was rising before her in white puffs and she shuddered involuntarily. Carey couldn't imagine Sirona trying to Guide her to this desolate landscape on purpose. She would have thought Sirona would attempt the Centre City at least. Or perhaps she had tried to, but something had stopped her...

The Dæmons. They had stopped Sirona from Guiding Carey to where she had intended her to go. It was the only explanation.

Carey shivered, although this time the cold had nothing to do with it. No magic would explain her sudden release from Sirona's enchantment, and she felt an intense rush of urgency. If Saar had gained Sirona's powers, then she was the only one left to capture; the final piece of his plan. The only good Carey could see in her current position was that at least there was nowhere for a Daeva to hide amid the stark landscape.

In fact, as Carey turned to look around, she realised there was nothing but a distant ridge of mountains to her right, and even those were so far away that they were barely higher than the rolling dunes that surrounded her. She could see no other choice but to try for them and hope that civilisation existed between here and there.

Carey stumbled to her feet, her body battered and bruised. Her legs were beleaguered from running but she forced herself to move. No sooner had she taken a handful of steps did she find herself gasping for air. Black spots sprung up in front of her eyes and her head reeled. The air was incredibly thin, like that at the top of a mountain, and yet they were anywhere but. She gasped for air again, but her lungs could not seem to fill. Dropping to her hands and knees, she was overcome by a wave of panic. Her heart was racing, her chest clenching as it rolled over her, sending tingling through her extremities. Carey lifted her head, but everything swirled and dipped, the ground swaying beneath her hands. Gripping the cold sand, Carey tried to take a single deep breath. It did not help. Her hold on reality was slipping and she couldn't seem to stop it. Perhaps she needed to stand up; kneeling on the ground didn't seem to be helping and it seemed to be her only option. With every ounce of strength she could muster, she made to pull herself up, hoping it would right the spiralling sensation. She realised her mistake instantly. She staggered as the world tipped on its side and Carey fell sideways into darkness.

*

She was floating. At least that's what it felt like. The sun burned through her eyelids, but the dizziness that had caused her to faint still lingered there, and she was unwilling to open her eyes. But how was she moving? Her body was still buzzing and slowly she began to feel a little more than a dull heaviness. Something was holding her up. No, not something. *Someone.*

Carey forced her eyes open but then immediately regretted it; the sun, instead of a strong round orb, stretched and shook dangerously. She couldn't make out the person carrying her, but she was lucid enough to see that whatever was affecting her seemed to have no effect on them; their strides were sure and steady and the arms that held her were strong. She tried to say something, but her words were garbled and sounded like nonsense. The person carrying her made no sound in response and Carey slipped into unconsciousness.

*

There was someone searching, a low voice calling her name in the darkness, sending shivers up her spine. She pushed it away, blocking it out with thoughts of Ji and Kat. The voice receded then disappeared completely, the shuffling in the dark gone. She opened her eyes.

Carey was looking up at a high ceiling with great thick beams. As her eyes focused, she noticed words and pictures carved ornately into the wood that crisscrossed overhead. Slowly, not wanting to induce any more fits of dizziness, Carey turned her head. She was lying on a large bed; a dense fur lay beneath her, warm and comfortable, and a large embroidered quilt covered her. The bed was in the middle of an expansive room. A basin stood to her right, and a chaise lounge with a carved wooden back rest was at the far end of the room. It was draped with more furs and pillows, and as Carey's eyes moved along it, she noticed someone sitting on the end farthest from her. He was lounging with his arm along the back of the chair, but Carey could tell he was far from relaxed. His eyes were watching her intently and as she pulled herself up to sit, he also straightened before leaning forward. A strange tattoo wound itself around his right eye.

"Who are you?" he said in a low voice. It wasn't a threat or a demand; his question was laced with genuine curiosity.

Carey blinked, unsure of what to say. She was filled with the dull sense of confusion she often felt when she was dreaming. She considered the man more closely. It was then that she noticed his hair: his head was covered in tight curls. It reminded her so suddenly of Torena Patroni and her family that she gasped in shock. The man frowned.

"You're Vuleta... a Vuletian," Carey corrected herself, catching her breath. The man nodded.

"Yes, I am," he said simply, watching her closely.

"I... I knew a family once, in the Centre City. They helped me escape Imperials when Malevolence was still in power. The family head was a Seer. Alois Patroni," she said, her voice shaking slightly. She was caught unawares by the sudden emotion that rose within her, tears pricking at the corners of her eyes, but this was not the time to appear weak. She knew nothing of this man or whether he would be as hospitable or sympathetic as the Patronis. She averted her eyes to hide the sudden glaze of tears.

"You are Carey Lee," the man stated, unperturbed by this sudden show of emotion.

It was not a question. Carey looked back at him sharply, the tears gone, but instead of hostility, he gave her a slight, benign smile. It was so small but that smile, that tiny gesture, filled Carey with a surge of inexplicable warmth.

"You needn't worry, Your Highness. You are safe within these walls."

When Carey didn't say anything, the man sat back against the lounge. "I knew Alois and his family. I also knew what they did for you. Don't blame yourself for their fate. I can assure you that anyone within this city would do the same in an instant."

Confused by his supposition, Carey could say nothing but, "Who *are* you?"

The man stood up and Carey's eyes widened in surprise. He stood almost seven-foot-tall, with olive skin and broad shoulders. His chest was bare except for the wide leather strap that held a fur-lined cloak across his shoulders, and he wore dark slacks that fell just short of the floor. Looking down, Carey saw that he wore no shoes despite the obvious chill that permeated the room.

"My name is Marjen Tutari, and I am the captain of the Vuletian army."

~Chapter Eighteen~

The Vuletian and the Madman

"Tutari?" Carey repeated, sitting up straighter. "You're Captain Tutari?"

Captain Tutari narrowed his eyes. "That is what I just said."

Carey ran her hands through her hair as thoughts raced through her mind; first he was mentioned in the Council meetings, and then by Sirona. A week ago, she hadn't even heard of him, and yet now...

"Who are you exactly?" she asked, unable to keep a note of disbelief from showing in her voice.

He considered her for a moment. He then strode across the room and pulled back one of the curtains by the bedside. Beyond the glass, the jagged summit of a great mountain range surrounded them, their white snow caps visible from where Carey sat. Eyes travelling down from the icy peaks, Carey found herself looking down upon a handsome city. It was carved from the very side of the mountain below, the buildings built along the steep incline. The sun shone down upon it, its glow illuminating a shimmer in the grey stone of the range. The narrow streets were teeming with busy townsfolk and children played happily about them, all dressed in bright colours that were mirrored in the flags and silks fluttering from poles and lines.

Surrounding the city was an astoundingly high wall with watch towers positioned every so often along the ramparts. There Carey could see people standing guard, hidden in the shadows of the towers. Beyond the city was a valley; its basin wide and filled with luscious greenery, but the mountains on either side were incredibly steep, the rock bare and slick.

"This is the City of Hilarus. For thousands of years the Vuleta have lived here and defended this valley. We are an autonomous entity — we do not recognise the sovereignty of the Centre City," he said with a hint of pride.

"I've heard of you," Carey said, thinking back on her studies. "You are essentially a different country, separate from Torarn. If that is the case, why are you so keen to die for me, as it were, if you don't recognise my sovereignty?"

Captain Tutari looked over at her again, his eyes searching. "You are right. We don't, but we will protect you, regardless of the cost."

Bemused, Carey said, "But why?"

"Many millennia ago, the Centre City was not the ruling entity in these lands. We were a divided nation. Wars between rival clans were common. The woman who governed the Centre City at the time, who would later become the very first Empress, sought to unite us. She built a formidable army and one by one, the clans fell under her rule.

"But the Vuleta were not so keen to relinquish their lands, and so we fought. The Empress saw the power and might of the Vuletian army and offered a truce. She would not attack or try to take our lands as long as we defended this valley against those who would bring harm to the Centre City and the royal family within its castle."

"So, you protect the city," Carey confirmed. "But right now, I'm nowhere near there. Does your protection extend beyond the walls of Torarn, then?"

A small smile lilted at the corner of his lips. "Indeed, you are not. It is usually not our responsibility to watch over the royals outside of the city. Can I suppose that you are aware of the foretelling of your future? That which names you Liberator?"

Carey blinked. She hadn't expected this. She supposed it wouldn't be unusual for him to know about the prophecy... but what it had to do with anything perplexed her.

"I've defeated Malevolence though. That prophecy has been fulfilled," Carey said, observing the captain shrewdly.

Captain Tutari looked at Carey discerningly for a moment before turning away his gaze. "Perhaps," he said offhandedly.

"Perhaps?" Carey said with a frown. "You don't believe I succeeded?"

"Oh, you succeeded in way-laying Malevolence, that much is true," the captain said, retaking his seat on the lounge and leaning back against the furs, arms outstretched along the back of the seat. "Whether you succeeded in fulfilling the prophecy is another thing entirely. Regardless, the fact remains that you are foretold to destroy her. Your success in this endeavour affects not only the lives of the People, but everyone in this realm. Alois and his family knew of your value and purpose and accepted the risk that came with aiding you. Yes, we protect your city, but our protection of you as a singular person is based purely on the fact that should we not, we risk inviting a greater evil. Besides, I couldn't very well just leave you out there, unless that is what you preferred?"

Carey was flabbergasted. She didn't know how to respond to any of this, much less consider the idea that she hadn't fulfilled the prophecy.

As for whether she bemoaned his actions in helping her…

Carey looked up to find Captain Tutari smiling in a way that clearly told her he was not being serious. She huffed at his audacity.

"Fine," she said. "Even if you do believe all that, I still don't want people risking their lives for mine. Enough people have been hurt because of me."

This seemed to sober the captain as the smile disappeared at her words. "You are a very strange royal," he said without humour.

Carey grimaced. "Perhaps," she replied in the same off-handed manner he had used, and she found herself smiling.

The captain returned the sentiment.

"Where was I when you found me anyway?" she asked, steering the conversation away from prophecies and unexpected fits of heroism.

"To the north." Captain Tutari pointed out the window to the right of where the valley disappeared between mountains, "The Crystal Fields. That is where I found you. Clearly you had passed out from their effects. They are extremely dangerous to cross if you are unprepared or you are without the proper training."

Carey rubbed her forehead, recalling the troubling effects the desert had caused her. "What was that? I could barely stay conscious," she muttered.

"The crystals that make up the Fields have their own magic. The Vuletian Army trains out there so their influence doesn't affect us. It will drain your energy if you're not prepared. That said," Captain Tutari said with a quizzical brow, "if you were so affected by the Fields, how is it you made it so far?"

Carey hesitated. Despite the captain's manner, she still wasn't sure she could trust him with the truth just yet.

"I'm just grateful you found me," she deflected.

Something flickered behind the captain's eyes at her words, but he recovered almost instantly. "I couldn't very well just leave you there now, could I?" he said, and she was glad he didn't press her for the truth. "The Crystal Fields provide fair protection from the north," he continued, pointing in that direction. "This valley is the only passage between the Crystal Fields and the Dead Plains. Beyond the Dead Plains, the Centre City is barely one day's ride."

"The Dead Plains?" Carey repeated, the words catching her attention.

"Yes," the captain said, raising an eyebrow. "It is the only place in this world where magic cannot be used, unless you are Malevolence, that is."

"What? She was able to use magic there?" Carey said, and as the captain nodded, she wondered why she had never heard of this before. She thought it would have been something worth telling.

"She was rarely seen in battle — I myself only ever saw her once — but the one time she crossed the Dead Plains, it held no hindrance for her powers."

"None whatsoever?"

Captain Tutari shook his head grimly. "None. We may well have been ants beneath her boot for all the difference we made. We had nothing but our swords and our wit." The captain's face darkened. "It is not something I will easily forget."

Carey listened intently, his words sending shivers down her spine. For all she had heard about the Dead Plains and their desolate nature, the fact they had held no obstacle for Malevolence suddenly had her questioning everything. As far as Carey knew, not one Council member, not even her parents, could boast that kind of magic. As she had done many times before, she wondered how she had ever managed to defeat Malevolence at all. Maybe she hadn't really, if what Captain Tutari had said was true. Her so-called defeat could really be nothing more than a momentary setback for Malevolence; the outcome of pure luck. The mere thought sent Carey's heart into a panicked frenzy. She had barely survived stopping the Empress last time. If she really wasn't gone, then what magic was Carey supposed to perform in order to truly defeat her?

Casting about desperately for something to distract her, she got up cautiously from her bed and walked over to the window with its drawn back curtains. As she approached the glass, she looked down upon the city. The mountains blocked any view of the Dead Plains, but that didn't stop Carey from imagining what lay there.

"How long have I been here?" she asked, looking out at the sun in the sky, casting the Dead Plains from her mind.

"Less than a day. The Crystal Fields certainly knocked you out," Captain Tutari said from the lounge. "But it could have been much worse."

"And you were the one who found me?" Carey asked, and the captain bowed his head slightly in affirmation. Carey nodded graciously.

"You may still need some rest, however. For the uninitiated, the Fields can pack quite a punch." He stood up. "Please, rest. However, if you'll excuse me, Your Highness—"

"Carey," she interrupted out of habit.

"Marjen," Captain Tutari answered with a small smile. "I need to go and speak with the Elders and let them know you are awake. You are perfectly safe within this city, but perhaps just stay here until I return. I'll have something to eat brought up to you."

Marjen swept from the room, closing the door behind him. Carey stared after him. A strange feeling accompanied his presence and now that he was gone, she felt his absence quite profoundly. A shiver of panic ran down her spine; a reaction she thought was rather delayed despite having been awake and aware of her surroundings for minutes. Carey looked out of the window at the tall mountain range surrounding them, her gaze unfocused. She was less than willing to trust the captain, given everything that had just happened. Ally of the Council or not, Sirona's warning to not trust anyone weighed heavily upon her. Carey bit her bottom lip, letting a slow, shuddering breath escape through her nose. She desperately needed someone to trust at this very moment, though...

Carey tried to imagine what Kat, Ji and Rupert were doing, whether they would be out searching for her and whether her note had reached them safely. Saar would be there, no doubt, wrapped in his guise of Lord Acheron. She gripped the curtains tightly, her knuckles whitening. Whatever Saar's plan was, she couldn't see his endgame. Opening the gate to the Third World was surely only the beginning; there had to be more to it than that. If he was doing it as part of some enduring loyalty he felt towards Malevolence, then what had the Empress planned for when it was finally opened? Saar was powerful in his own right, and Carey wondered if he planned to take up Malevolence's mantle once he'd succeeded.

There came a knock at the door, and Carey jumped in surprise, the sound jolting her out of her reverie.

"Ah, who is it?" she said, turning from the window.

The door opened a crack and a woman with long, frizzy hair pulled back into a plait stuck her head through. "My name's Versi. Marjen said you might be hungry."

Carey walked over and held the door as Versi carried in a small tray of food. She wore a tight corseted top of dark fitted material that sat high on her neck and ran all the way down to her wrists. Her fitted black pants tucked neatly into a pair of dark leather boots that laced at the back, and a tattoo, not dissimilar to Marjen's, curved along her right cheekbone, glistening like wet ink.

Versi set the tray down on a small table by the lounge and turned, surveying Carey in a way that made her feel that she was no castle servant.

"Um, thank you?" Carey said uncertainly.

Versi nodded. "You're welcome," she said, not moving.

Carey frowned, confused. "Can I... help you?"

"You're the Royal, then?" Versi stated without a moment's hesitation.

Slightly taken aback by her bluntness, Carey nodded. "Yes."

Versi continued to stare at her as she moved to lean against the windowsill. "Marjen found you in the Crystal Fields," she said. "How did you end up there?"

Her manner was very direct, and her body language was not particularly friendly. Her eyes continued to scrutinise Carey and Versi pursed her lips, her eyebrows raised expectantly.

"I'm sorry, but who are you exactly?" Carey asked, unwilling to divulge the details of her ventures to this stranger who seemed so very eager to judge her for some unknown reason.

"My name is Versi Padu. I am a friend of Marjen's," she said, as though this was all that needed saying.

"All right," Carey said, still unsure of what this woman wanted.

"He's very intrigued by you, you know," she continued without hesitation, her arms crossed in front of her. Versi did not take her eyes off Carey the entire time, which Carey found incredibly unnerving, not to mention the direction of this conversation.

"Look," she said firmly. "I'm not sure—"

At that moment, there came another knock on the door and Marjen's voice called through. Carey strode past Versi, frowning at her with narrowed eyes, and pulled open the door.

"Versi?" he said quizzically when he saw the woman, but she brushed past him and was gone before he could say anything else. He turned to Carey. "I'm sorry. She's rather used to just inviting herself in. Is everything all right?"

"I'm not sure," Carey answered slowly, taking a seat by the food Versi had brought in. She picked up a piece of bread that was slathered in some sort of spiced oil. "She brought this in and then wanted to know why I was in the Crystal Fields. Does she have something against me? It seemed a little like she was judging me."

Marjen chuckled, seating himself on the edge of her bed. "Versi can be a little rough around the edges, especially with people she doesn't know, but you'll not find a more loyal friend."

Carey grimaced. "I don't think I came across very... She did tell me she

214

was a friend of yours," she confessed, but Marjen waved it away.

"I don't blame you. She doesn't make it easy to be friendly when you first meet her. Besides, it really wasn't her place to ask questions of you in the first place. She just likes to look out for me."

Unsure of how Versi was doing that exactly, Carey took a bite of the bread. She hadn't eaten properly since the night of the banquet; the ship's food being largely comprised of hard biscuits, rum and water. So, as the bread hit her tongue, a strange combination of sweet and spicy exploded in her mouth and she had to stop herself from groaning with delight. It was unlike anything she had tasted before and rivalled anything she'd eaten at the castle. The spicy-sweet bread was accompanied by a bunch of overly bright berries and several bulbous fruits that tapered into a teardrop shape. She savoured each, the flavours exquisite and intense, and it was not long before Carey had made her way through the entire plate.

"Hungry, then?" Marjen said with slight amusement as he watched her eat.

Carey blushed as she placed the pit of the last piece of fruit on the plate. "Sorry. Just a touch. It's been a long few days."

"Well, the Elders will be glad to hear that you are well at least. They will, however, want to know how you ended up in this part of the land. To have found a missing royal so close to our borders, you must know that they are understandably concerned."

Carey played with the edge of the water goblet she now held in her hands. "I don't think I could do that, Marjen. I'm not confident, regardless of who they are, that my trust will not be betrayed again."

She looked up and found Marjen watching her silently, but it was not like when Versi had done so. Instead of mistrust and judgement, Carey felt a strange sense of ease in his presence, as though she knew she could confide in him and no harm would come to her. She had no explanation for this feeling — the closest she could think of was how she felt when she was with Kat and Ji.

"If I tell *you* what happened, would that be enough?" she asked, hoping he would say yes.

He looked at her for another moment before nodding. "Yes, it would be enough."

Carey gazed at him for another long moment, and that feeling deepened. Marjen's intense brown eyes held her own as she took a deep breath and began to tell him her story. Marjen sat quietly, his eyes never leaving hers, his brow growing darker.

"This man you call Lord Acheron, the Shapeshifter," Marjen said slowly once she had finished, "Is he still in Torarn?"

Carey shrugged. "My guess is yes — no one else knows his true identity except for me, Lady Sirona, and Princess Mizèi. Also, he'll want to find me first, so he'll stay close to those who are looking for me."

Marjen sat, contemplating her situation, running a finger along his bottom lip.

"A madman within the Council," he murmured, more to himself than to Carey.

"That's... putting it lightly," Carey said with a wan smile.

"In the Council..."

Marjen's hand stilled and he looked up at Carey with wide eyes.

"What is it?" Carey said in alarm.

"The Elders. It is their duty to report your presence here to the Centre City," he said, his voice hard.

Carey jumped to her feet, realising immediately what Marjen meant. "When?"

"Not long after I brought you here and they were alerted to your presence," Marjen said getting to his feet also as Carey made for the door.

With her hand on the doorknob she felt her heart plummet in her chest. "Then he already knows."

~Chapter Nineteen~

Cruel Intent

Carey followed Marjen quickly down a long hallway with high ceilings and came to a halt in front of a pair of ornate double doors inlaid with gold and tiny glittering jewels. If they hadn't been in such a hurry, Carey would've been able to appreciate the workmanship a little more, but Marjen placed a hand on the door and pushed it open. Carey followed and found herself in the most unusual room.

The space was like no other she'd ever been in. The walls were hidden by darkness and the ceiling was either so high she couldn't see it, or they were not there at all. It gave Carey the strangest feeling of floating, given that the only solid structure visible was the grey stone floor upon which she stood. The room, which was almost completely dark, was lit not by a flame but by a great number of tiny droplets that were slowly rising towards the ceiling. They emerged from the floor, creating an eerie glow as they slowly crawled up through the air and out of sight. Upon entering, Carey had thought it silent, but now she discerned something barely audible; a distant hum. Just as she began to wonder what it was, a soft voice echoed from within the shadows.

"What is the meaning of this interruption, Captain Tutari?" it said as a tall willowy figure dressed in silver robes emerged from the surrounding darkness. She was raven-haired, her locks twisting and curling down towards her lower back.

Marjen bowed low and Carey watched as three other figures appeared alongside the first. One was a woman, the other two men, and they all wore long, sweeping robes and were decidedly pale compared to Marjen and

Versi. Their ethereal presence radiated from them, compelling Carey to bow along with Marjen.

"Please excuse our intrusion, Elder Nevaeh. This is Her Highness, Princess Carey—"

"We know who she is, Captain Tutari. We are wondering why you are here," one of the men interrupted. His long, flowing red hair framed a thin, pallid face with faded blue eyes, and he was clothed in a long set of pale blue robes. Marjen bowed his head slightly at his words.

"Of course, Elder Ezra. We would like to know; have you notified the Centre City of the Princess's presence here yet?" Marjen asked without any further introductions.

"Of course," Elder Navaeh said, raising a brow slightly.

Carey felt her stomach drop and Marjen glanced over at her briefly.

"Is there a problem, Captain Tutari?" asked the other man, his grey eyes calm and aloof. His hair was also long and unbound, but a bright white-blonde that made him appear sickly.

"Elder Marak. Princess Carey has informed me that there is a traitor in the Council. A man who has tricked her parents and is the reason for her disappearance from the Centre City. He pursues her now and Princess Carey fears what he will do if he discovers her location."

Carey stepped forward and added, "If you have alerted my parents to my whereabouts then he will most certainly know by now. This man is dangerous and there is nothing he won't do in his pursuit of me. I thank you for your hospitality, but I must leave at once. I could not forgive myself if something were to happen to the people of your city because of my presence here."

Elder Marak held up a pale hand. "Princess. It has long been our duty to protect the Centre City and the royal family that inhabits it. Your presence here is not one of inconvenience, but if you feel you must leave then we will help you reach the Centre City safely."

Elder Ezra nodded in agreement. "Captain Tutari will escort you, but we must ask that you at least wait until morning. The lands that surround our city are treacherous enough during the day."

Feeling this was as good a compromise as any, Carey accepted with a nod. "Thank you."

Marjen bowed again. "Elders Marak, Ezra, Seris and Navaeh, thank you. Please accept my apologies once more for our intrusion."

"Please return to us once you have escorted the Princess back to her chambers, Captain Tutari," said the other woman, who Carey took to be Elder Seris. Her dark features stood out stark against her white skin, and her gaze fell upon Carey as she spoke. "We have much to discuss."

Marjen and Carey bowed again.

"As you wish," Marjen said in a low voice.

As Carey followed Marjen from the room, she looked back over her shoulder; the Elders were fading back into the shadows, the sight sending a shiver down her spine. What a strange and sudden experience.

"So... tomorrow..." Carey said, letting out a long, wavering breath as they entered the hallway beyond the strange dark room. "I am... so sorry about this, Marjen."

Marjen *tsked*, shaking his head at her. "You have nothing to apologise for. I will be honoured to escort you back to the City."

Carey chewed on her tongue, not wanting to contradict him. They continued down the hall towards Carey's room, passing more of those large wooden doors, though none were as spectacularly adorned as the one leading into the Elders' quarters.

"Carey, what does this man look like?" Marjen said as they passed through a high stone archway. "I need to warn my army of this Saar in case he decides to try and enter the city."

"Well that's the thing," Carey said with a grimace. "He's a Shapeshifter so if he did try to enter the city he would not do so in his original form."

"But most Shapeshifters have a feature they struggle to hide, isn't that correct?"

Carey sniffed. "Yes, you're right, though, if Saar really wants to, he can hide it. He wouldn't have been able to fool me as Lord Acheron if he hadn't..." She scowled. "That said, if he doesn't hide it, it's easily spotted. It's his eyes."

Marjen came to an abrupt halt. "Eyes?"

"Yes," Carey said. "Silver. His eyes are silver."

An unexpected look of dread came over Marjen's face.

"Is something the matter?" Carey asked in alarm but Marjen shook his head and continued to walk.

"No, nothing. For a moment I thought you were about to say something else. Here," he said, opening the door to her room. "I must return to the Elders, Carey. I will send Lieutenant Therow. He is a dear friend and can be trusted. I will return as soon as I am able."

Marjen turned and walked back towards the Elders' chamber, leaving Carey to wonder what it was that had stopped him so suddenly. She opened her door and immediately flopped onto her bed. Staring up at the ornate ceiling, she couldn't get the look on Marjen's face out of her head. It was a dread that made her stomach twist and she knew instinctively that he knew more about Saar than he was letting on. The only explanation Carey could think of was that he knew him. But how? She looked sideways out of the window and wished the sun would hurry up and set. With every moment that passed Saar was getting closer, preparing whatever means he had for retrieving her. There was no doubt in her mind that she would not sleep that night and that waiting was a waste of precious time, but she had to take the Elders' advice into consideration. It was true — she didn't know anything about the surrounding areas and it would be foolish for her to set out unprepared. She could find herself in trouble and then what? Wait for Saar to find her? If she got into strife there was no way she wouldn't use her magic if it meant saving herself, and with a sigh, Carey resigned herself to the fact that tomorrow morning would have to do.

As the sun drifted lazily towards the ridge of the mountain range, Carey started to feel edgy. She had no idea how long Marjen would be and her room was beginning to feel stifling. She got up from the bed and walked over to the door to let herself out. There was no one else in the hallway and Carey looked around for somewhere to get some fresh air. She walked the opposite way to the Elders' room and found herself walking onto a foot bridge connecting two towers. A slight wind fluttered about and Carey leaned on the balcony, taking in the sweet smell that accompanied it. She could see the city better from this point and the people within it. She could hear their voices, chatting and laughing, drifting up on the breeze to where she stood. A kite darted up from the rooves below, accompanied by the excited shouts of children. The colourful figure of a dragon flitted about before her, reminding her of Sirona's story of the Dragon's Heart. Why hadn't she listened to Kat when she had the chance? She had known something was amiss with that necklace, yet Carey had not heeded her advice and now look what had happened. Attempted kidnapping, pirates, Dmons, and a psychopath on her trail. Carey cursed herself and vowed that when she returned to the Centre City and everything was set right, she'd apologise to Kat for not listening to her. She'd certainly be listening to her in the future.

The sounds of footsteps alerted Carey to someone approaching, and she looked up to find a man equally as tall as Marjen, though much older in years; grey streaked his curls and lines stretched out from the corners of his eyes. He wore similar attire to his Captain although, he at least, wore boots and a light shirt. It made her wonder if Marjen's lack of clothes and footwear was a symbol of status or whether he just chose to freeze.

"Princess Carey?" the man said as he came closer.

"Lieutenant?" Carey answered, and she smiled when he nodded.

"Efren Therow, My Lady. But you may call me Efren."

"In that case, it's Carey," she said, holding out a hand for him to shake. He took it in his hands warmly and bowed his head ever so slightly.

"Marjen said you might be in need of some company," Efren said, turning to look over the city as she had been.

Carey looked at him for a moment, considering the lieutenant. Despite the betrayal of the pirate captain and Saar's deception of the past week, she felt an overwhelming sense of benevolence in this city. Sure, the Elders had been a little unnerving, but Carey couldn't find it in her to be distrustful of the captain. This Lieutenant Efren seemed equally as effable, and she decided to lower her guard, just a little.

"Thank you. I'm grateful for the hospitality you have all shown me," Carey said as she turned and leaned back against the railing. "You have a beautiful city here."

"It is a shame, then, that you will be leaving us so soon," Efren commented, looking sideway at her.

Crossing her arms, Carey said, "I must. It will be too dangerous if I stay any longer."

"Oh, but what is life without a touch of danger?" Efren said with a twinkle in his eye. "Do not worry, Carey. Whatever the danger, be sure, we have faced much worse in our time. Marjen would say the same."

"You are friends, then? You and Marjen?" Carey asked, noticing the jovial tone with which Efren used when mentioning him.

"He may be my Captain, but he is also one of my dearest friends, yes," Efren answered. "Why do you ask?"

"The way you speak of him," Carey said, and Efren narrowed his eyes suspiciously. "Well no... there is something else," she confessed under his gaze.

"Oh?"

"Is it normal for him to be so... mindful towards someone he's just met?" It was the best she could do without sounding crazy by admitting her sudden inexplicable trust in Marjen. He was, after all, a stranger.

Efren laughed. "You'd rather him be cold and indifferent?" he asked.

"No, no, I didn't mean that," Carey said shaking her head. "I guess the only people who have ever been so attentive to me are people I've known a long time."

Efren nodded knowingly. "I think I know what you mean. He does seem a touch protective of you but do keep in mind that you are no ordinary guest."

"Yes, he said something to that effect," Carey mumbled, although this didn't explain how she felt.

There was a moment where neither said anything. Efren gazed watchfully over his city and Carey pondered asking what was on his mind.

"If you don't mind," she said, clearing her throat. "How long have you served with Marjen?"

Without withdrawing his gaze, he answered, "Quite some time now, although I undoubtedly show it more than he." Efren drew himself up to his full considerable height. "Though, let it be known, there is no man more honourable than Marjen Tutari."

Although his voice was calm and measured, Carey couldn't help but feel as though Efren was being slightly defensive.

"I meant no disrespect," she said softly. "It's just…" she wasn't sure she should say anything now, but she also couldn't ignore her suspicions, "I only asked because I think he might know something about the man pursuing me."

Efren hesitated. "He did mention him. The man with the silver eyes," he said in a strangely controlled voice, which saw Carey's curiosity intensify even further.

"Please. This man is dangerous. I need to know what Marjen knows of him."

Carey saw Efren's knuckles whiten as he gripped the stone banister. He shook his head. "I'm sorry, Carey. You may be the Princess, but I do not know you well enough to divulge the circumstances of that particular acquaintance."

"He knows him, then?" she said in an urgent whisper. "Efren please, if there is anything… this man, what he might do—"

"Please, Princess," Efren cut across her, and she noticed his return to using her formal title. "This is not a matter of knowledge. We are very much aware of what this man is capable of. It is a matter of loyalty to a friend. What you ask is something I have no right to tell so please, do not ask me to."

This wasn't what Carey had expected. What made Efren so reluctant to tell her what had happened between Marjen and Saar?

"I understand. I'm sorry," she said softly. "However, is there anything that you *can* tell me about that man? Anything at all?"

Efren looked at Carey for a few moments, his brow slightly furrowed as he considered what to say. "If he is pursuing you…" He took a deep breath and let out a long sigh. "It all began with the Empire, as it so often has in recent times. When it first rose to power, Malevolence and her armies attacked our city in the hope of taking it, as they did with every other city. She came at us from all sides with armies of creatures and wizards — the likes of which we had never seen, and trust me, we have seen much," he said with a slight smile. "But her forces couldn't breach our walls. We may not have magic, but the Ancients imbued our walls with powerful protections so that none who weren't welcome could enter. Malevolence soon realised that our city would not fall, but she also did not want our army rising against her, so she stationed a sizeable army outside our walls, not to attack, but to prevent us from helping the Centre City and any who may oppose them. It was almost unbearable for us to be trapped within our city, unable to fulfil our duty.

"When Marjen became Captain, he vowed to strike back at the Empire and began to train some of his warriors in a more clandestine type of warfare. His plan was to sneak past the invading army, get into the Centre City, and try to undermine the Empire."

"Militia. But where does Saar come into this?" Carey asked, unsure of where this was going.

Efren held up a hand. "*That* is where Saar, as you call him, came in. Back then we came to know him as Caecus. He came through a back passage, one that was unknown to the army outside. He told us he had come from one of the outlying cities, having just escaped an Imperial attack. He was seeking refuge and we were only too happy to help one of our kin, for that is how he appeared to us. Vuletian. We took him into our care and in the weeks that followed, he became a friend."

Efren paused and Carey could see such pain in his eyes that she didn't dare ask him to carry on.

"He betrayed us, in the worst way possible. He attempted to destroy Marjen with his deception," Efren said darkly. "He tried to drive a stake through his heart."

Carey didn't push for details. This was undoubtedly what Efren was so reluctant to speak of.

"Did you confront him?" she asked gently.

"Confront him?" Efren scoffed. "The coward ran. We didn't get a chance, for if we had, he would surely not be alive today. No, he ran..." Efren's voice trailed off. He sniffed loudly and raised his chin proudly. "He failed, though. That man had hoped to break our Captain with his treachery, but Marjen is strong, far stronger than any Imperial, that's for sure."

"Is that why Saar came here? To try and break him?"

"We assume so," Efren said, lowering his gaze. "Perhaps they assumed that without him, we would not succeed with our plans or that without a leader we would be defenceless."

"And were you?" Carey asked.

Efren shook his head, his eyes gleaming with admiration. "It merely strengthened his resolve."

"And what of his plans?"

Efren gave Carey a small smile. "I'm afraid you may have beaten him to the punch, My Lady."

Carey turned back to see the sun setting in a blaze of glorious colour, yet its beauty held no wonder for her. She wanted to know the full story of what Saar had done, but at the same time, she was hesitant. Clearly Saar had hurt Marjen irreparably; tried to strike at the very heart of him. Carey could imagine the ways he'd have done so but wished with all her might that each and every one of them was wrong, for Saar's cruelty knew no bounds. Yet Marjen had not broken; perhaps she didn't need to know what had happened to him after all.

"He is a dangerous man," Efren concluded. "And yet we never thought we would encounter him again."

"Let us hope you don't," said Carey, a shiver running through her body that had nothing to do with the twilight chill. "Let us hope that when I leave tomorrow, it will only be once I reach the Centre City and with my parents by my side that I encounter him again."

"What do you think will happen to him?" Efren asked.

Carey thought for a moment then tilted her head in a shrug. "I can't be sure. I can only hope that he answers for the atrocities he has committed."

Efren was quiet but then stood up and gestured towards her chambers.

"It is getting cold and Marjen should be back soon. Perhaps we should retire inside where it is a bit more comfortable?"

"Do you mind if I stay here for a while?" Carey asked as she watched the last of the sun sink below the horizon. The lieutenant nodded.

"Of course. I'll be just down the corridor, should you need me," he said, gesturing towards her chambers. "Again, I am sorry I could not be more informative."

Carey watched as Efren walked away; his story still running through her mind. Whatever Saar had done, she wanted to feel angry, furious at him and his never-ending trail of destruction, and yet Efren's sorrow penetrated her, driving away her resentment. She sunk down onto the cold stone and gazed up at the stars as one-by-one they began to appear, the pink of the sunset slowly dissipating to reveal a clear night sky. *So calm compared to the worlds below*, Carey thought. She closed her eyes and let out a long sigh.

She had believed so naïvely that peace would follow their victory over the Empire, but as she sat there staring up at the heavens, she began to realise how very foolish she had been to hope for something as elusive as real peace. So many had suffered at the hands of the Empire, and Imperial Loyalists like Saar would never stop; they would always find someone to fight, something to cling to in the hope that the Empire would return. Perhaps the peace Carey had idealised for so long is not the peace they would finally achieve. Perhaps they were always going to be fighting for it...

Carey didn't know how long she'd been sitting there when Marjen finally came back from his meeting with the Elders. She had almost drifted off in her musings, and the cold stone had made her joints stiff and sore.

"I'm so sorry for the late return," he said as he helped her up off the ground. "I just saw Efren and he said you'd been sitting out here the whole time?"

Carey dusted off her clothes with the heel of her palm as she stood up. "I was just thinking," she said as they walked back inside, and Marjen asked no more.

"I took the liberty of having your dinner sent to your chambers," he said. "I hoped I might join you?"

Carey smiled a little, suddenly realising how very hungry she was. "Of course. In any case, we have much to discuss before we leave tomorrow."

They entered Carey's chambers to the most amazing aroma. A table for two had been brought in during her absence and was laden with a wonderful assortment of food. Her stomach grumbled loudly and Marjen chuckled.

"Just a little hungry?" he commented, pulling a chair out for her.

"I don't think I've ever felt so hungry in my life," Carey said as she looked over the many plates and bowls overflowing with strange and unusual foods. "This food looks amazing."

"Well don't let me stop you," Marjen winked as Carey made for a turret of colourful vegetables.

Carey tried a bit of everything; there were strange, brightly coloured root vegetables of every shape and size, steaming sauces and gravies, and pink meats that fell easily from the bone. There was the same sweet bread from before in great thick slices, and a strange red pickle that made her tongue tingle pleasantly. A tantalising pile of flaky sweets drizzled in a sweet sugary glaze stood waiting. As they ate, Carey watched Marjen out of the corner of her eye. If he was affected by the news of Saar, then he certainly wasn't showing it. Perhaps Efren had been exaggerating, yet she somehow doubted that.

She must've stopped eating because Marjen looked up and asked, "Is something the matter?"

Carey swallowed and placed her fork down on the table. "Efren told me some of what Saar did, the last time he was here."

The humour slipped from Marjen's face and his fork, though laden with food, did not move from his plate. "Did he, now?"

Carey nodded slowly.

"What did he tell you exactly?"

"Not much," Carey went on carefully, watching Marjen for a reaction. "He said that Saar betrayed you... That he tried to break you?"

Marjen gave a small, humourless laugh. "Efren was being kind. Do you really want to know what that man did?"

For a moment Carey almost said no, but she had started this. She couldn't very well back out now. Besides, she needed to know Marjen's motivations

— if they were to come face-to-face with Saar, she had to know what he would do. She gave a small nod. "Yes, I do."

Marjen gave a small sigh; he steepled his fingers in front of him, his elbows planted on the table. He rested his forehead against his fingertips for a moment, looking down at his plate, and Carey waited, her heart flitting nervously against her ribs. Finally, Marjen lifted his gaze to hers, his dark brown eyes determined.

"It was on a night I was out with my regiment, training. He took it upon himself to visit my family in my absence, as he had done so many times before."

Marjen clenched his jaw and he dropped his hands to the table, balling them into fists.

"They welcomed him as a friend and he *slaughtered* them like animals. My wife, Zafira, and my two sons…"

Carey's breath hitched and Marjen looked down again, away from her face. Carey wanted to reach out to him, to comfort him; the anguish in his voice was clear when he spoke.

"He was their friend. *I* was his friend…" He lifted his head, his eyes dulled with pain.

Carey swallowed thickly. "I'm so sorry, Marjen" she said, reaching across and laying a hand on his. "I'm so sorry that I have brought him here again." She took a deep breath. "Efren said you never got to confront him, after… after what he did. What would you do, if you ever saw him again?"

Marjen didn't answer immediately. "Honestly, Carey, I never even thought I would find out who he really was, let alone be given the possibility to face him again," he said finally. "I suppose most would want revenge, and for a brief moment, that was what I wanted too."

"But it's not anymore?" Carey asked, raising an eyebrow slightly.

"No," he said, straightening and lifting his chin. "My wife and sons deserve better. I will not stoop to the level of their murderer and sully myself in the process. Besides, such a man has no doubt bloodied his hands with more than that of my family's. Those people deserve justice too. It would only serve my own purpose to kill him myself. He needs to feel the full weight of what he has done, not just what he has done to me."

Marjen looked directly into Carey's eyes as he said this, and she suddenly understood why he was Captain of the Vuleta. Revenge would have satisfied a much lesser man. Marjen embodied a greater purpose, one of hope rather than bloodshed.

"Don't worry, Marjen. Once he is exposed, he will feel the full force of the Council," Carey said sincerely. "He won't escape what he's done."

Marjen nodded in gratitude. He stabbed a small red vegetable with his fork, toying with it pensively before popping it into his mouth. "I'm sorry. I'm not usually such a miserable host. Shall we talk of something else?" he suggested.

Carey hadn't been thinking this at all, but she got the distinct impression that Marjen was not eager to speak more on the topic of his family. She nodded permissively.

"About tomorrow," he said, continuing to eat. "I'll be accompanying you along with two other commanders."

"Efren won't be coming?" Carey asked.

"He has to stay here and lead in my stead," Marjen explained. "The other two, Commanders Ueran and Riist, are some of our finest though. You will be in good company."

Carey took a bite of a sweet, its centre oozing a pale-yellow liquid. "To tell you the truth, it's a bit of a relief."

"Oh? How so?"

"Not being able to use magic has made this entire ordeal a whole lot harder. Until you found me, I wasn't even sure I'd make it back without Saar catching up to me first. It was only a matter of time. But now, you've given me hope that I'll manage to get there first. I have a real chance now."

Marjen raised his goblet. "So glad to be of service," he said before taking a sip. "And we will do everything in our power to get you there safely."

*

The sky outside was an inky black, but slowly, one by one, the stars began to disappear. Sunrise was approaching and Carey sat quietly on the edge of her bed, having woken an hour earlier and finding herself unable to go back to sleep. Her mind was racing. She had slept fitfully with visions of Sirona and Princess Mizéi tormenting her subconscious. She had dreamed of Saar — he had been speaking to her, telling her how much he desired the power within her. She had wanted so badly to curse him, to make him feel pain, but the Dragon's Heart hung from his neck and Carey knew she was powerless to stop him, lest she lose her powers as Sirona and Mizéi had done. She woke to find her heart racing and her body drenched in sweat.

Carey slammed her fist against the wooden frame of the bed, frustration welling up inside. Power. He so badly wanted hers, but if she truly was so powerful then how was it that she felt so defenceless when it came to him? Why was she so afraid to face this man? If she did hold such enviable magic, then Saar shouldn't even pose a threat.

Carey knew the answer at once. It wasn't just magic that made her fearful of him. It was his influence, his connections, his cunning. He made her second-guess everything and filled her with doubt, which Carey now saw was his true power. He had reduced her to barely more than a Commoner for all the good she could do. Carey looked out the window at the vast mountain range surrounding Hilarus and imagined the Centre City beyond them. She thought of her mother and father and hoped they were safe, that nothing terrible had befallen them in the Darklands. She knew it had to have been Saar who waylaid them in his attempt to procure Carey's magic. Her parents were powerful, and he had eliminated their threat by keeping them far away from the castle. Kat and Seramina were really the only two left with the abilities to expose him. Carey hoped he would slip up, give them an opportunity to see the truth. Surely, he wouldn't be able to get past them for much longer…

And then there was Ji. Her insides ached at the very thought of him. She had imagined what she might say when she finally saw him again. Would it be easy to confess her feelings, or would she find herself plagued once more by the familiar awkwardness she had come to know around him?

No. No more awkwardness. Those days had passed, Carey was adamant in this. She no longer felt doubt or confusion, and she was determined to tell him as much. She wanted nothing more than to be with him, hear him speak, enjoy his laughter…

Carey shook her head, trying to push the melee of thoughts aside. She had a long and dangerous ride ahead and needed her head to be clear. She got up from her bed, washed and then changed into the new set of travelling clothes she'd been provided — dark fitted pants and a navy tunic. She had only just finishing lacing up the high leather boots when the sound of someone running down the corridor outside reached Carey's ears; she stood just as a loud banging shook her door.

"Carey! Carey, it's Marjen!"

Carey ran to the door as Marjen burst in.

"What is it?"

Without speaking, he grabbed her by the hand and pulled her from the room.

"Marjen!" Carey cried again but still he didn't reply. He was walking so fast that Carey found herself jogging to keep up. His face was hard and etched deep with concern. They passed the door that would have led them to the Elders and up a great sweeping staircase to a set of double doors with no handles.

"Keep holding my hand, Carey, otherwise the doors will not let you in," Marjen said cryptically as he laid a palm on the wood and pushed.

They opened wide and as they passed over the threshold, Carey felt something tug at her momentarily. She felt Marjen's hand tighten around hers and the feeling relented. They were in a round room that was completely devoid of windows. The beams that extended from the floor to the centre of the vaulted ceiling were carved with a script Carey had never seen before, and the floor was a slick onyx. In the middle of the room was a circular table that created a perfectly concentric feel to the space. A group of people were already there, and Carey released Marjen's hand as they drew close.

"Captain Tutari. What has drawn us from our beds so early in the morning?" It was one of the Elders — Marak, if Carey remembered correctly

— from the day before. The other three Elders stood alongside him and to their left was Efren and two others Carey did not know. One was a tall broad-shouldered man dressed similarly to Efren and the other was a woman with a haircut so short her curls were barely noticeable. They both wore armour and stood at attention when Marjen entered the chamber.

"The situation has changed," Marjen answered simply, and Carey's heart jumped into her throat.

"Changed?" Elder Seris repeated, echoing Carey's thoughts.

"Two envoys arrived not long ago with news of Imperial armies marching towards Hilarus," he added, cutting a glance over at Carey.

She knew why he had looked at her. No doubt the same thoughts were running through his head.

"It's Saar," she said, gripping the edge of the table in front of her. "It has to be. How far out is this army?"

"They will reach the city in three days," Efren interjected before Marjen could answer.

"Then we'll leave now. Send word to the Centre City of my departure. We will draw his attention away from here," Carey said immediately. She was not going to have Saar attack this city because of her.

"We would, My Lady, if it were just the one group of Imperials," Efren said apologetically.

His words filled Carey with dread. "How... how many are there?"

"The envoys were from two different cities, My Lady, on either side of Hilarus. They will intersect at the Dead Plains pass. The man you call Saar, the one we know as Caecus, is trying to cover his ground. If you ride out now, there is no guarantee that we will be able to avoid them. The armies consist not just of wizards; they are all manner of creatures. Raazut, Örd and Tenebrax to name but a few."

Carey stared down at the table before them. "I've come too close to the Centre City. He's desperate. He doesn't want me to escape this time..." she said fearfully. Saar was usually so subtle with his attacks but this... this was pure desperation.

"If that's the case then we have no choice but to stay here," Marjen said.

"We must protect the Princess the best we can. Our walls have never fallen to a siege before."

The others murmured in agreement, but Carey shook her head. "No. I will not put your city and your people at risk by staying here."

"Carey, how many times do we have to tell you that your protection is our duty?" Marjen said almost exasperatedly.

"Lieutenant Therow told me that you have enchantments protecting the walls of this city?" she asked, ignoring him.

"Yes, exactly."

"He also said that the last time Saar was here, he gained your confidence, got past those same enchantments?"

Marjen's eyes hardened at her words. "Yes, that is true," he admitted in a low voice.

"Then what's to say he can't get past them again?" she suggested, pushing on despite Marjen's unease.

Elder Seris spoke up. "The enchantments you speak of are strong, Princess. They were placed there by the Ancients and cannot be broken by any ordinary wizard."

Carey fell silent, her mind racing. "But he isn't any ordinary wizard," she muttered.

"What?" Marjen said.

"He isn't any ordinary wizard," she repeated, louder this time. "He is currently in possession of a stone that allows him to take the magic of those used against him, and right now he has the magic of two very powerful witches at his disposal. If anyone has a chance of breaking those enchantments, he does. He also wouldn't take big risks like this without a plan to get past your walls. What's more, last time he came to this city via the tunnels that apparently only the Vuleta know of. You have to wonder what other secrets he knows of this city, because he will exploit every one of them to get to me."

Marjen was quiet, taking in everything Carey was saying. He leaned over the table, both hands on its surface. "If what you say is true... Elders, what have you seen of this?"

"It is as before," Elder Ezra spoke up. "We cannot see him nor what is to come from this. Even we, with our Sight, were unable to see his armies approaching. I am sorry, Captain. There is something about this wizard… We cannot divine his intentions."

With a deep breath Marjen looked down at the table; Carey watched as he struggled with his decisions.

"Ready the garrison, Lieutenant. If what the Princess predicts comes to pass, then our people are at risk. We will ride out and meet this force on the Dead Plains the day after next where we will have equal footing. The Princess is to stay here, under the protection of the city."

"Marjen, no. I'm coming with you," Carey said, horrified at the thought of being left behind to wait.

"It will be too dangerous for you, Princess," Elder Ezra said softly, trying to placate her.

"It's not that," Carey shook her head. "If by some chance your army fails to defeat this force, they will come for the city. I need to be there; I need to be seen. Their quarrel is not with you. If you fail, I can at least lead them away from Hilarus."

She hoped this would convince Marjen as he stood watching her indecisively. Efren cleared his throat.

"The Princess makes a good point, Captain," he said, leaning across the table towards Marjen. "We are strong, but we have underestimated this man once before. If we do fail, who knows what he will do to our city if she remains behind. Besides, if she is with us, we need not come back here before setting out to the Centre City and it will save us a half day of riding."

Marjen contemplated Efren's reasoning before consenting with a single nod. "But she is to stay at the back. We cannot risk your safety in battle, My Lady."

Even though being held back from the fight was not something she was completely content with, it was a compromise she could live with. Carey was not going to risk the lives of Marjen's people by staying behind. She could not bear the thought of having their deaths on her conscience.

The Elders bowed their heads, signalling the end of the meeting.

"We will leave you to prepare, Captain Tutari. We are sorry that we cannot be of any more assistance and that you must face this danger without our foresight," Elder Nevaeh said apologetically.

"It cannot be helped," Marjen answered as they walked towards the door. "It seems this man, Saar, or whoever he may be, is doing all he can to keep this fight to his advantage."

Marjen took Carey's hand again as they stepped back through the doors, and although she knew this was not necessarily meant as a comfort, she couldn't help but feel it as exactly that. She would gladly find comfort where she could, knowing what was to come.

~Chapter Twenty~

The Oncoming Storm

"Was that your version of the Council?" Carey asked as they walked back the way they'd come.

"That was some of our High Council, yes," he answered, leading her down a staircase. "There are usually more, but for what has transpired, we only needed the Elders, Efren, the two Commanders and me."

"And the enchantment at the doorway? Was that the reason you had to hold my hand?" Carey surmised and Marjen grinned.

"You could feel it, then?" he said, nodding. "Yes, only members of the High Council can enter the Citadel. If you are not one of them, you must have the permission of a member to enter. It is similar magic to that which protects our walls."

"Huh. For a people without magic you certainly have a lot of it around here," she commented, to which Marjen shrugged.

"Well it is the realm we live in. We couldn't do what we do without a little magical help."

Carey stopped for a moment, biting her bottom lip. "Marjen, I'm so sorry about all of this. I should have left straight away; I shouldn't have stayed—"

Marjen fixed her with a hard look, the grin falling from him face. "No. Don't apologise. You are not to blame for anything that is happening."

"But your city—"

"Will be safe," he said, stepping towards her and placing his hands on her shoulders. He towered over her, impressive in his stature, and Carey felt comfort in the power that rippled through him. "First of all, this man

Saar is to blame, not you. And secondly, we will fight, like we have done for hundreds of years, and he will come to know what it is like to fight us head-on."

Carey looked up into Marjen's determined gaze and wondered at the strength of this man. She nodded and the corner of his mouth lifted.

"Come," he said gently, and they continued walking.

They crossed a wide, open entrance hall; a riot of colour fell across the floor in the soft morning light and Carey looked up to see a beautiful stained-glass window arching towards the high ceiling.

"Where are we going?" she asked as Marjen opened a door at the side of the hall and led her through.

"If you're going to be joining us, you need to have a weapon. You've had training, I assume?" he said as they made their way down a spiralling stone staircase.

"Under Sir Garrow, yes," Carey said with a note of elation. She would not be entirely useless, then. If it came to it, she would be able to fight.

"I've seen him fight. You've been privileged in your tutelage. Are you hungry?"

"What? Oh. No, not particularly," Carey rubbed her stomach. The news of Saar's army of Imperial misfits had filled it with knots. "Maybe later."

Marjen nodded in understanding and led her out of the stairwell. They crossed a wide corridor to a doorway that led out into an extraordinary outdoor arena. The ground where they stood was lush with green grass, although as Carey looked around, she found that it varied; patches of the training ground were covered in sand, whereas others were dotted with clusters of sharp rock formations. Platforms rose up from the ground and Carey watched in awe as two early trainers leaped with enviable ease from one to the other as they fought.

"This is impressive," she remarked, turning to Marjen. "We've got nothing like this back in the Centre City."

With a smile, Marjen motioned for her to follow. There was a small door to their right and upon entering, Carey found herself in a cavernous storage room filled with some of the most extraordinary weaponry she'd ever laid eyes upon. She grinned at the sight, excitement welling inside her. The walls were laden with gleaming curved scimitars and intricately carved shields. There were racks of spears, delicate in their appearance, and weapons so strange that Carey was unsure of how one would wield them. She walked past each of them, trailing her fingers along their surfaces, marvelling at the craftsmanship. One sword caught her eye as she wandered about the room, its curved blade gleaming in the dim light. It was a beautiful piece, the hilt a marbled mix of red and black with a carved guard that depicted a dragon curling its way around the base of the blade.

"Its name is Arach," came Marjen's voice from behind her. Carey jumped a little — she'd become so entranced by the room that she'd almost forgotten Marjen was with her.

"Arach?" she repeated.

"Dragon," Marjen translated, moving around her and lifting it from its mount.

"No. Really?"

Marjen looked at Carey with a quizzical brow, the surprise in her voice piquing his interest. "Yes. Why?"

"The stone Saar has; the one he is using to obtain our powers, its name is the Dragon's Heart," she said, her eyes drifting back towards the dragon carved into the sword.

Marjen looked down at the sword. "Hmm… that is quite the coincidence…" he said as he handed it to her. "Perhaps you were meant to find this sword."

As her fingers gripped the hilt, a thrill ran through Carey's body. It was flawless, balanced perfectly in her hands. It was light, but not so much that it felt flimsy, and it was extremely well made. She felt a rush of anticipation at the idea of trying it out in the training arena.

She looked over at Marjen who was grinning back at her. "Yes?" she asked, lowering the sword.

"I know that look, is all," Marjen said, grinning even more broadly.

"Oh? And what look is that?"

Marjen took another sword from the wall and lifted it to the light. "The look of a warrior as they take up their weapon."

Admiring Arach, Carey took the sheath from beside its stand and slid the weapon inside. "I know you want me away from the battle but at least know, just in case, that I can fight. I will not be some helpless princess."

Marjen chuckled at her words. "Oh Carey. Never for a second have I believed you to be helpless." He motioned back towards the door. "Shall we?"

Smiling at his response, Carey made her way out to the arena. More people had arrived now to commence their daily training sessions and as they emerged from the weapons room, Carey almost collided with someone. It was Versi.

"Oh, Versi! I'm so sorry!"

Versi, affronted by her appearance, looked from Carey to Marjen and then back again before turning around and leaving the arena in a flurry of frizzy hair. Carey stared after her.

"Did I do something to offend her?" Carey asked as she watched Versi disappear around the corner.

Marjen clicked his tongue. "Don't mind Versi, she has her own way. Like I said before, she's not fond of sudden change so your presence has really thrown her. I think I'll go and talk to her. Will you be fine here for a moment?"

Carey nodded and watched with pursed lips as Marjen went after his friend. Looking around, she saw a patch of grass not far from where she stood with a tall wooden pole wrapped in thick rope set at its centre. Placing her sword's sheath at the edge of the grass, she approached the pole, rolling her shoulders. Carey gripped the hilt of her sword with both hands, shifting her feet into an attack stance and eyeing the pole strategically. With a grunt, Carey swung Arach around her head and down at the pole with all her might. As she did so, however, a bright spark of brilliant blue illuminated the blade, and she promptly dropped it in surprise.

"Oh!"

Hitting the grass, the light faded instantly, and Carey bent down tentatively to inspect it. The hilt and blade were as they were before; there was no blue light or sparks, and she was beginning to wonder if she'd imagined it when she heard a voice behind her.

"First time wielding a Vuletian weapon?"

Carey jumped and spun around to find the woman who had accompanied Efren at the meeting earlier. She held out her hand.

"Commander Fiika Ueran. I will be riding with you to the Centre City," she said in introduction as she shook Carey's hand.

"Carey Lee," Carey replied and Commander Ueran dipped her head in acknowledgement. "I know who you are, Your Highness. Here."

She picked up Carey's sword and handed it back to her.

"What was that?" Carey asked as she took the sword and examined the blade.

"That would be the Blocker. It won't hurt you," Commander Ueran said as she unsheathed her own sword and swung it across her body. The same blue light lit her weapon.

"Blocker? Magic?" Carey said as she brought her own sword down by her side and watched as it did the same.

"Of sorts. It helps us to block magic used against us, otherwise how would we be able to fight against wizards?" she answered as she placed her sword back in its sheath.

Carey ran her finger along the edge of her sword. How indeed.

"So, you have experience with a blade, then?"

Carey grimaced. "Training? Yes. Practical experience? Not so much." She swung the sword at the pole and relieved it of some of its rope. "But I have been in combat before. I'm not afraid of what this might bring."

The commander was silent as she watched Carey swing her sword again at the pole. "I have heard of you and your exploits, Your Highness. I did not mean to cause offence by suggesting you could not handle the situation."

Carey lowered her weapon to face the commander. She hadn't meant for that to come across so defensively.

"Sorry. I didn't mean to sound so… I just meant that I can handle this, magic or no magic. But I could do with some practice with this sword. It's much lighter than what I am used to."

Commander Ueran nodded curtly and drew her weapon at the invitation. Carey moved away from the practice pole and raised Arach in response.

"This man, the one who has rallied this army… Is he really as powerful as you say he is?" the commander asked as she readied her footing.

"Unfortunately, yes," Carey said as she swung her sword. The blades clashed and the blue magic snaked its way around the tips. "He may even be more powerful than that, but I can't be sure. He is a master of deception and I doubt he has revealed his full potential to me yet."

The commander was quick with her blade and Carey only just managed to duck out of the way as she brought it around over her head. She blocked it as Ueran swung it around a second time.

"Then I'm glad we are meeting him and his army on the Dead Plains. He will be as powerless as the rest amongst those trees," Commander Ueran said with a grunt as Carey pushed her back.

"These Dead Plains… I've heard of them, but Marjen — I mean, Captain Tutari — said that Malevolence was able to use magic there," Carey said as she made a run at the commander. "Is that true?"

Commander Ueran blocked her attack with relative ease, bringing her sword around and forcing Carey back. "Yes, it's true. It was before our city was closed and an Imperial force placed on our doorstep. The end of the battle that had created the Dead Plains. She wielded her magic as though that place held no challenge for her."

Carey knocked aside Ueran's blade and ducked under her outstretched arm, managing to place the tip of her sword to the commander's back. The defeated woman dropped her sword and raised her arms in surrender.

"Looks like you got me," Commander Ueran said, turning to face her.

Carey lowered her blade. "And yet I doubt I did so fairly. For a commander in the Vuletian army, I thought you would be more of a challenge. Unless it was no challenge at all?" she mused with eyebrows raised.

A laugh came from behind them and they found Marjen nearby; he had been quietly observing them until now. "Come Commander. I believe the Princess has caught you out."

Commander Ueran picked up her sword and with a grimace, admitted her deception. "Well, you are the Princess."

"Please," Carey stopped her. "It's Carey, and I will regret the day when I am happy to receive special treatment from everyone simply because of some title."

"If that is what you wish," Commander Ueran said, shrugging as she shifted the grip on her sword, "Then I promise to be fair in how I conduct myself from here on out."

Carey smiled in appreciation but then shook her head. "I just need a moment, though. Marjen? Do you mind taking over from me?"

She moved aside, and as she watched the Vuletian Captain ready himself for Ueran's attack, Carey's mind wandered back to Malevolence. They had been told countless times that the Dead Plains were a magical void where not even the strongest witch or wizard could wield their powers. So how was it that she had never heard of Malevolence's ability to do what others could not? Carey couldn't help but wonder if perhaps she had possessed some special ability that placed her above the normal laws of magic. It would explain her dominating prowess and the fact that no one had been able to destroy her magic. Malevolence's magic had endured after Carey defeated her, whereas the same type of attack had been fatal for others. She couldn't be simply talented or strong in her magic — if it was simply a matter of intensity, then what was there to stop Saar from wielding his stolen magic within the Dead Plains? For the first time ever, Carey hoped this was the case and Malevolence had been one-of-a-kind. She needed Saar to be as powerless as she when they met upon that scorched earth in a few days' time.

"Carey!"

Marjen's voice interrupted her thoughts and she found him standing over the commander, who was down on one knee.

"Care to put your talents with a sword to the test in earnest this time?"

Pushing her concerns to the side for the time being, Carey picked up her sword.

*

By the end of the day, Carey was exhausted but exhilarated. Commander Ueran really had been modest with her sword skill; she was faster than anyone Carey had ever sparred with and watching her fight with Marjen was mesmerising. Their movements were so fluid and precise that it seemed effortless. They reminded her of Seramina. It was so far removed from the style she had been taught by Sir Garrow, and much more refined than that of the pirates. Even Kat would have a hard time keeping up with them, and this notion made Carey smile.

"You know, once this is all over, I'll introduce you to Kat," Carey said to Marjen as they placed their weapons back in the storage room. "You may just be the challenge she's been looking for."

Marjen chuckled. "No doubt it would be a pleasure. If her level of skill is anything like yours then I will welcome the chance to spar with one of the original Seekers."

"Honestly though, I can see now what makes you and your army so formidable."

"It all comes down to the fact that as Vuletians we are born with a talent; we are either a Seer or a warrior," Marjen said as he and Carey left the training arena.

"Oh? Can one be both?" Carey wondered.

"No one can be both a strong warrior and a perceptive Seer at the same time, but some have minute traces of their less dominant talent. My mother was a very perceptive Seer and at times I can feel that influence in myself," Marjen said enigmatically and with no further explanation.

"So, when did you find out you were of the warrior-persuasion?" Carey asked as they climbed a spiral staircase.

Marjen tilted his head in thought. "We are brought before the Elders at the age of six so that they might determine our calling. That's what these signify," he said, tapping gently at the tattoo below his eye. "Our marks are given to us then, indicating the path our lives will take. Where we are marked hints at our potential — around the eyes means clarity, the temple," he indicated, "intelligence. The cheek, strength. My son, Deshiel, inherited my mother's talent for Seeing. Even before he was two years old, we knew.

He would always find where we'd hidden the sweets. Zeefan, on the other hand, was destined to follow in mine and Zafira's footsteps. He'd only just begun his training..." Marjen trailed off. They were now in the middle of the wide lobby with the stained-glass window and they had come to a halt.

"You know, that is the first time I've said their names..." Marjen said in a quiet voice, and Carey could hear a tremor of pain. She was unsure of what to say and instead placed a soft hand on his arm. She felt him flinch slightly under her touch, but he didn't pull away. Marjen turned to look her in the eyes, brows pinched as though he was searching for something. Carey swallowed hard and was about to say something when she was interrupted by someone else suddenly entering the hall. It was Efren.

"Ah-ha! There you two are," he said, smiling widely at them.

Carey dropped her hand and Marjen called back, "Looking for us then, I suppose?" all traces of the previous moment vanishing. She frowned, wondering what Marjen had been thinking. The lieutenant approached them and gifted Carey a small bow.

"Versi and I have had a wonderful dinner prepared for all of us. I am determined that, despite this oncoming storm, you are to enjoy your time here. I am all too familiar with what is on offer when out on the battlefield and I intend to put off the moment where I am forced to eat such food until it is necessary. Carey, would you care to join us this evening?" Efren said with a twinkle in his eye.

Carey raised a slight eyebrow — the lieutenant seemed rather joyful given the impending armies. It was rather intriguing.

"I would be honoured, but I'm not sure Versi will be happy to see me," Carey said as she thought of her earlier reactions.

"No?" Efren said confusedly. "It was she who suggested this dinner."

Now it was Carey's turn to be confused. "Marjen?"

"Like I said before, what you must understand about Versi is that she doesn't like change. New people, sudden events, she just doesn't handle them like everyone else. The only thing that doesn't put her off is going into battle," Marjen explained.

"Oh, and you should see her fight," Efren said fondly. "It's almost as though she goes somewhere else, becomes a different person. It's really something."

"I believe this is her way of getting used to you," Marjen said, shaking his head at Efren in amusement.

"But I'll be gone soon. I'm sure I could have just stayed out of her way until then if it's so upsetting to her," Carey suggested as they started walking again.

"Ah, but Efren and I are her friends and so your being with us is just as much as a concern to her. Don't worry, it'll be fine, you'll see," Marjen said reassuringly.

When Carey arrived back at her room, she found that someone had laid out a long, dark green gown on her bed. It had long draping sleeves that hung from the shoulders and came back up at the wrists, leaving the length of her arms exposed. As she observed herself in the mirror, Carey rubbed at the faded goat's head mark on her arm where Jeremy had branded her. Normally it wouldn't worry her, but for some reason tonight it made her feel a touch self-conscious.

There came a soft knock at the door and Marjen called out her name.

"Come in," Carey called back as she smoothed out her dress.

Marjen stuck his head around the corner and smiled. "Ready then?" he asked, holding out his arm for Carey.

Carey linked her arm with his and grinned; Marjen's smile was proving infectious.

"Oh, and you look wonderful," he complimented, making the blood rise in Carey's cheeks.

He led her a short way down the hall, across the bridge from the night before and into a tower where the high ceiling was made completely of bevelled glass. Candles surrounded them and the flickering flames created a soft glow as their light refracted off the glass. There was a large, dark wooden table in the centre of the room and Versi, Efren and another woman, who Carey supposed was Efren's wife, stood waiting for the rest of their party to arrive.

"Carey, this is my wife, Leira," Efren gestured as she reached the table.

Leira bowed her head in reverence. "Your Highness."

Leira had similarly curly hair to the others, only hers had been knotted into tiny plaits and curled into intricate patterns upon her head. She, too, had a tattoo, only hers wound its way from her left temple down to her neck.

Carey nodded in return. "Please, just Carey," she corrected before motioning for them all to take a seat.

The dinner was just as spectacular as the other meals she had eaten whilst in Hilarus and she relished every mouthful. She soon discovered that Efren's wife, Leira, was just as vivacious as her husband was proving to be, keeping the party entertained as they ate. Marjen and Efren talked and laughed, reminiscing on old times for Carey's sake and toasting to her good health and success. As the night wore on, Carey felt more and more at ease with Marjen and his friends; it was something she hadn't felt in a very long time. They joked and fell into easy conversation, though she noticed not once did they speak of the Imperial armies or Saar. If it had been Kat and Ji at the table, they would have spent the night strategizing and predicting what Saar might do. Instead, the Vuletians steered their talk towards happier topics; light and enjoyable, and Carey understood why — they were warriors, bound to a violent and cruel fate. Marjen and Efren were happy to live in the moment and enjoy it for what it was rather than focus on the storm beyond right now; a night with friends. And while Carey appreciated this, she struggled with it, her mind shifting imperceptibly to Saar and his plans the instant she stopped talking. She wished she could join them in their momentary forgetfulness — she couldn't fault them for it — but it wasn't how it worked for her. She supposed that was what a lifetime as a dedicated warrior afforded them, and Carey sat back and listened to Marjen and Efren laugh, a small smile upon her lips.

As she sipped from her goblet, the warmth of the wine slipping down her throat, Carey noticed Versi watching her from the corner of her eye. She couldn't help noting that any time she would join the conversation, Versi would immediately stop talking; her expression would switch from happy and carefree to serious and almost sullen. Despite Marjen's reassurances, there was a critical air to the way Versi looked at Carey; she seemed to be holding back criticism, though of what, Carey didn't know.

"Well, this has been a most spectacular evening, thank you Efren, Versi," Marjen stretched as he stood up. "Leira, thank you for putting up with me once again."

"Oh Marjen, as though I have a choice with you two. I guess I'm just doomed to be stuck in the middle," she laughed. "Carey, it was lovely to finally meet you."

Carey shook hands with Leira as Efren beckoned for Versi to join them in leaving.

"You have wonderful friends," Carey remarked as she and Marjen watched them leave. The night had left her feeling painfully nostalgic. "They remind me of Kat and..." she let her sentence drop at the thought.

"You miss them," he replied gently, and Carey nodded, surprised by the sudden sting of tears in her eyes.

"More than I ever thought possible," she whispered in a strained voice.

She looked up at Marjen, his face soft and sympathetic. Carey tried to scrunch her eyes up against the tears, but they were being stubborn, burning hot at the corners. She felt Marjen take her hand, and as she opened her eyes again, he pulled her towards him and into in his arms. It was at once sudden and yet, not unwelcome. His warmth comforted her as he wrapped his arms about her, and Carey laid her head on his chest. She listened to the steady beat of his heart and let it soothe her as they stood in silence amongst the candlelight.

It was odd to feel so comforted by someone who was almost a stranger, but there was something about Marjen that pulled her towards him. It was not the same as with Ji, where her heart ached at the very thought of him, where she was drawn to him by something deep within her soul. No. With Marjen it was the simple need for him to be where she was, a comfort in a difficult situation, a light amongst the growing shadows. It was inexplicable trust, a deep-rooted knowledge that he was there to protect her and nothing more.

"I promised I would get you back to them, Carey, and I intend to keep that promise," he said quietly, and she had no doubt that he would.

~Chapter Twenty-One~

Finding Hope

Carey lay in bed gazing at the carved beams of the ceiling, wide awake despite the hour. The city below had long fallen into a sleepy tranquillity and the night air was so still that it felt as though she were the only one still awake. She had tried to relax her mind, but it seemed that her thoughts just would not allow it. She flitted from one encounter to the next and tried to decipher her feelings towards Marjen to no avail, before skipping to the armies and their slow approach. Her hours of training should have left her exhausted yet instead of making her want to sleep, it only proved that she was not ready for battle. She itched to get back to the training grounds but felt it would be useless to train on her own, not to mention unreasonable at such an hour.

Knowing she would not be sleeping any time soon, Carey slipped a robe over her bed clothes and set off towards the bridge where she had first met Efren. It was very late now, and the hallways were completely deserted. Her footsteps echoed eerily off the stone walls and the low burning torches accompanied them with dancing shadows. She was about to turn the corner when she heard voices coming from out on the bridge. Carey stopped and was about to turn around when she heard her name. Edging forwards, keeping within the shadows, Carey peered around the corner to find Marjen and Versi standing out in the middle of the bridge. Marjen stood with his back against the railing and his arms crossed; the moonlight caught on his dark curled hair and broad shoulders as he looked at Versi in confusion. Versi was facing him, her lips downturned and her eyes flashing.

"Don't lie, Marjen. I could see what was happening tonight. I can't believe you would do such a thing," Versi said, her voice shrill.

"I really don't know why you are so angry, Versi. We had a nice dinner with friends and nothing else. Carey does not deserve this hostility you seem to have towards her," Marjen said, his voice bewildered.

"Don't think I can't see what's happening here, Marjen," Versi said, pointing an accusatory finger at him. "You know how it is with them, witches and wizards. They're not the same as us, Marjen. How could you even consider this?"

"Consider *what*, Versi? What am I supposed to have done, exactly?" Marjen said, a little defensively now.

Versi huffed impatiently. "You know what, Marjen. Fall in love!"

Her words hung in the air. Marjen stared at her as stunned as Carey felt standing in the shadows. Surely not...

Then Marjen began to laugh. *"Fall in love?"* he said, grinning through his laughter. "That's absurd, Versi."

"But the way you look at her. The way you are when you're around her," Versi said, her demeanour shrinking in light of Marjen's reaction. "You seem so happy."

Marjen's laughter died out and he placed his hands on Versi's shoulders. "That's because I am, my dear friend, but not for the reason you think."

"Then why?" Versi said defensively.

Marjen sighed. He turned away from her and leaned over the bannister, contemplating his answer. "It's strange, but I feel like I know her. From the moment I found her in the Fields, I've felt completely at home in her presence and I... I can't explain why. You know I actually said the boys' names today?"

Versi stilled.

"What?" she whispered so quietly that Carey had to edge a little closer to hear what she said next. "But... you haven't been able to talk about them since..." Versi trailed off.

Marjen ran a hand through his tightly curled hair, letting out a long, tight sigh. "I know, but talking with her, it just... happened. I spoke of them with such ease, so freely that I hadn't realised what I'd said until I'd said it."

Versi shuffled her feet anxiously. "Is it so different with her around?"

Marjen noticed the tone in her voice and when he spoke again it was so softly that Carey had to strain to hear what he said next.

"The other day when I brought her to the city..." he hesitated. Marjen clasped his hands in front of him and leaned his forehead against them. "I haven't told anyone why I was out there. To tell you the truth, I was never intending on returning."

"What?" Versi whispered. "What do you mean? Where were you planning on going? You had no provisions. You wouldn't have even made it to the other—" She gasped, bringing her hands to her mouth. "Marjen, no."

Marjen was silent but he nodded at her revelation. Carey's heart was pounding. What had driven Marjen to such a drastic act?

"The war was over, Versi. The Empire had fallen, the dark witch was gone, and our people finally had the freedom we'd been denied for so long. But I... I had nothing," Marjen said, staring out over his city. Versi listened tensely, as did Carey.

"I was a captain born of war. I knew only pain and bloodshed. I had dreamed of peace like this but once we had it, I didn't know what to do. Zafira and the boys were gone. I found myself wondering if I no longer had anything to fight for then what did I have?

"But then I found her."

"Who? Carey?" Versi said, finally breaking her silence.

"When I came upon her in the Fields, I knew I had to protect her, bring her back to the city. There was something about her, Versi, something that made me realise that all wasn't lost, that there was still hope," Marjen explained. "She gave me hope."

"You Saw it, didn't you?" Versi said softly.

"Yes. I Saw what she was, what she could achieve, and it was far beyond anything I could have imagined. I couldn't leave her once I had Seen all that. I will always love Zafira, you know that, until my dying breath, but Carey... Carey has given me hope again. She has brought a light into my life that I thought had died long ago, and I will fight to protect her as I know she will fight to protect us," Marjen said resolutely.

Carey had heard enough. She turned back towards her room and tip-toed quietly back down the hall. It was much to take in — Marjen's attempted suicide, how he perceived her, the expectations he seemed to have of her — and yet somewhere inside she felt a warm glow. The connection they seemed to share made Carey willing to accept Marjen's convictions. No matter how inadvertent her influences, she was glad to have made such an impact on him, to have been able to help him, for there was no doubt that he had made an impact too. It was a lot to live up to, but his faith in her gave her strength. His confidence in her sparked a fire in her very soul and, as of that moment, Marjen stood amongst her dearest friends. She knew without a shadow of a doubt that, as with Ji or Kat or Rupert, she would fight for him with every fibre of her being. She would make herself worthy of the hope he had seen in her.

*

"Oh Marjen, it's magnificent."

Carey stood before a bench in the armoury, marvelling at a suit of armour Marjen had bestowed upon her for the battle. As with everything else in Hilarus, its craftsmanship was elaborate and elegant.

"The body is made from a leather stronger than dragon hide, almost impossible to pierce, and the plating of the shoulders, tassets at your sides and greaves and sabatons are made from a rare metal mined from the Chalybis Mountains," Marjen explained as he ran his hand over the scales of the tassets. "This was Zafira's. It is a suit worthy of a great warrior, just as she was."

Carey was overwhelmed by this gesture. "Thank you, Marjen. I will take good care of it."

The Vuletian armourer helped her into the suit and after about an hour of tinkering and adjustments, Carey was ready to give it a trial in the training arena.

"It's certainly not something I'm used to," Carey admitted to Marjen as he handed her sword to her. "It's lighter than I expected."

"That's one of the properties of that metal. We don't want to be slowed down too much by bulky armour, not when many of our magical opponents have none," Marjen said as he warmed up his shoulders with wide swings.

"Well, shall we give this a go, then?" Carey said, lifting her sword at the ready.

It only took two swings of Marjen's sword to bring Carey to her knee. She was definitely not used to wearing armour.

"All right, Carey?" Marjen said as he pulled her up. She rotated her shoulder, willing it to stretch and loosen. "Again?"

Carey took a couple of swings over her head and readied her stance. "Ready."

This time it only took three swings for Carey to find herself on the ground once more. She cursed as she hauled herself to her feet once more.

"You need to put a little more force into your movements," Marjen advised. "You'll need to exercise a little more strength than you're used to in order to wield your weapons properly. Let's try again."

Adjusting the tassets at her sides, Carey picked up her sword and gripped it with both hands. *A little more force.*

"Again," she said, and she swung her sword up to block Marjen's attack. Ducking his next swing, Carey brought her sword around a little harder than she would have done so before and found that with the pull from the armour, her sword connected with Marjen's with perfect force.

"Yes! Perfect, Carey!" Marjen shouted as she attacked again.

They continued to spar, and Carey admired Marjen's speed; it was exhilarating trying to keep up with him.

Marjen stepped forward suddenly, throwing Carey off and causing her to stumble.

"Got you," he grinned, the tip of his sword to her chest.

For a moment Carey was reminded of Gerard and inspiration sparked within her.

"Fine. You got me," Carey said, flicking Marjen's sword aside. "Again, then?"

Marjen grinned widely. "Fine by me," he said, and he parried Carey's attempt to catch him off guard.

Remembering the avant-garde style of fighting Gerard had showed her, Carey managed to keep Marjen from gaining the upper hand. She landed blow after blow upon his sword, letting go of the formalities of her training and allowing herself to anticipate his moves rather than calculate them. She felt herself quicken in her paces and when Marjen took another lunge to try and catch her out again, she stepped to the side, spinning as she went down on one knee to thrust her sword upwards.

"Got you," Carey grinned as her sword came to rest at his side.

"Well, that's different," Marjen said, stepping back and reaching out to help her up. "I know for certain that is not part of your training."

"Let's just say that Sir Garrow is not the only one who's had a hand in my instruction," Carey winked.

Marjen was about to say something when someone approached them from the entrance. It was the other commander who had attended the meeting the day before.

"Captain Tutari, the Elders wish to see you," he said, saluting. "Your Highness," he added, bowing to Carey.

Placing a hand on her shoulder reassuringly, Marjen said, "I'll be back soon. Don't go anywhere," before following his commander from the arena.

Carey stood, watching as they left, hoping that it wasn't more bad news. Finding herself alone, she headed to the training pole where she'd met Commander Ueran the day before and took a few swings. Her mind drifted from the arena to the conversation she'd overheard the night before and debated whether to tell Marjen. No doubt it was something extremely personal to him, and she didn't want to embarrass him by confronting him about it, especially if he hadn't planned on telling her. She wondered what it might be like if she was overheard talking about something as intimate and decided that if the moment presented itself, she would say something, otherwise it would be up to Marjen to tell her if he wanted. Besides, it wasn't as though she was an old friend like Versi who deserved his confidence, no matter the bond they seemed to share. Carey resolved to put these matters from her mind and work on adjusting to the armour. They would ride for the Dead Plains that night and she did not want to be ill-prepared.

"Did I miss anything?"

Marjen was back and Carey was startled by his sudden return. "That was quick. Nothing bad I hope?"

"No, but the Elders wish to see us before we ride out tonight," he said as he drew his sword. "A little more practice then?"

~Chapter Twenty-Two~

Confessions and Promises

Walking to the Elders' hall later that afternoon, Carey stretched her arms above her head to relieve the tenseness in her muscles. Their practice had gone well but she now regretted not stopping a little sooner — she had inconveniently lost track of time. They would have kept going too, had Commander Ueran not come to fetch them.

"I'll have Versi bring you something for that," Marjen said sympathetically. "I forgot what it was like to wear armour for the first time."

"I don't think I've ever worked my arms so hard in my life," Carey grunted as she stretched her right arm across her chest. "As much as I enjoy the sword, I'm really missing my magic right now."

They arrived at the hall and entered to find the four Elders, Efren, and the other commander waiting for them. The grandeur of the hall had no less of an impact on Carey the second time around, and she gazed at the lights that rose up around them.

"What are they?" she asked Marjen as they passed one of the lights.

"Futures for the Elders to See," he said.

"But there are so many," murmured Carey, wondering how they could possibly get to them all.

"They are drawn to certain futures. The realms draw them to futures that are important, that have significance. This is how Vuletian Seers See — they are drawn to that which will impact their own lives and destinies. The Elders See that which will impact the lives of all Vuletians. This is their fate, their responsibility," Marjen explained in a hushed voice as they approached the others. "However, sometimes they can choose to See a future, but only the strongest Seers can do that."

"Like Alois Patroni," said Carey, remembering how his visions had helped her reach this realm.

"If Alois Patroni had not perished at the hands of the Empire, he would have been an Elder. His abilities were unrivalled," whispered Marjen, and Carey felt a twinge of guilt in her chest.

"Captain Tutari, Princess Carey, thank you for joining us," Elder Seris said, her arms outstretched. "As you know, we have been unable to See the outcome of this battle you are embarking on and therefore we are unable to aid in your victory, Captain."

"Although we have complete faith in your army, Captain Tutari, you must keep in mind this man's past displays of power and brutality. You must not underestimate him," warned Elder Marak, although Carey doubted Marjen needed such a reminder. "Your priority here is the Princess. Return her to the Centre City at any cost."

Heat rose in her cheeks and Carey wished she could object to such a notion, but she knew it wasn't her place. As she had been told before, the Vuletians' purpose was to protect her city and her family, and she knew there was little she could say or do to change their minds.

"We send you forth with the wisdom and strength of the ancestors," said Elder Ezra reverently. "With futures unknown, you have but one path. May it lead you to victory."

Marjen and the commanders bowed to the four Elders, who bowed in turn. Carey took it that they were dismissed, and she followed Marjen and Efren from the hall. None of them spoke until they were outside in the hallway.

"That was... short," Carey said, failing to find a better description for the strange encounter.

"It is customary for the Elders to bestow a blessing upon the captain and commanders of the army before a battle. I am Commander Daaren Riist, Your Highness," the other commander said, finally introducing himself. "Unless there is a future they need us to be aware of, these meetings are generally short."

"What did Elder Ezra mean by *'futures unknown'* and *'one path'*? Excuse my lack of Seeing knowledge but isn't there only one possible future that they can See and therefore generally only one path?" Carey asked, trying to understand the Elder's final words.

"Sometimes yes and sometimes no," Ueran answered cryptically. "Some futures only have one possible outcome whereas others can be rewritten. This is the talent of Vuletian Seers — they can see every possible choice and moment that leads to the future they See and therefore they can determine what can change that future. That said, there are some futures that are part of a much bigger picture and so, no matter what changes are made, the outcome will always be the same."

"So, some futures can be rewritten?" Carey surmised.

"Exactly," Marjen said. "That is why being unable to See the outcome of this battle concerns them so. If they knew, they could determine whether it could be changed."

"It's Saar who is blocking them, isn't it?" said Carey bitterly. It sounded like something he would be capable of; after all, he'd been able to block Seramina's telepathy, so the idea wasn't entirely absurd.

"Oh, that we know for certain. He did it the last time he was here to cover his true intentions," Marjen said darkly.

Carey remembered what Elder Ezra had said the morning before and it suddenly made sense —*'It is as before. We cannot see him nor what is to become of this,'* — and now he had Sirona and Princess Mizéi's powers, he could easily block the Elders' abilities, especially on such a grand scale.

"Carey?" Marjen said, concerned.

She shook her head. "I'm fine. Just lamenting the idea of Saar having so much power."

"Don't worry, Your Highness. Our army has never been defeated and we are not about to let some ragtag group of Imperials do so, regardless of who may be leading them," Commander Riist said confidently. "This man has no power on the Dead Plains."

We can only hope so, Carey thought to herself as she opened the door to her room. Marjen promised to return later once she had rested. *It's not far now. Marjen will get you back home and you can expose Saar for the traitor that he is*, the voice of optimism reassured her. *They will defeat Saar's army and you will make it back in no time.*

Carey held onto this with all her might, clutching this tiny glimmer of hope tight to her chest. However, try as she might, she couldn't help but imagine everything that could go wrong. Past the Dead Plains she couldn't be sure of what awaited her, and the knot of uncertainty tightened in her stomach. She would try her hardest to refrain from using magic, but beyond the Dead Plains there was still a long way to travel. A long way for something to happen, and there was no one to sacrifice themselves magically for her this time. Marjen would be with her, but with no magic of his own, she wasn't optimistic of a favourable outcome should they come up against Saar. She thought of Seramina and wondered how far her telepathy reached now. Could she risk connecting with her as she approached the city? She could send for help, warn them if she was under attack or alone. It was a thought...

A hot tub of water had been prepared for her upon her return and Carey sighed as she sunk into it. The water lapped at her neck and she delighted in the relief it brought to her sore muscles. She tried to push the impending battle from her thoughts, but it lurked menacingly in the corner of her mind. She knew she was to hold back from the fight, but Marjen would undoubtedly be joining his troops, and having to watch him fight would be close to unbearable. If only she could join him... Exasperated by the Vuletian's stubbornness in protecting her, Carey slid beneath the water's surface and let herself float in the belly of the tub. With the sounds of the world muted by the bath, Carey listened to her heart pounding in her ears. Concentrating on the steady thumping in her chest, she let her thoughts float to the water's surface, dispersing as they emerged. She watched each one as they drifted upwards, tiny markers of her own mortality. She closed her eyes and let her mind wander far from the Dead Plains and Saar. She saw blue eyes and rough brown hair, heard a laugh, and her name in soft tones...

Lungs aching for oxygen, she pushed off the bottom of the tub to resurface. Wiping the water from her eyes, Carey dropped her head back against the bath and allowed herself a smile.

The sun was beginning to set when Marjen knocked on her door, a basket of food under his arm.

"What is this?" Carey asked with a smile.

"I thought you might like something different, something a little less formal," he said, offering his other arm for her to take.

Wondering what he was up to, Carey took his arm and followed his lead.

"Where are you taking me Marjen?" she inquired as he led her down an unfamiliar corridor.

He grinned sideways at her. "You'll see. Through here," he said as he unlocked a heavy wooden door at the end and grabbed a torch from a nearby bracket. Inside was a staircase that wound upwards; the walls of the stairwell were rough, as though the steps were cut straight from the mountain. It was dark except for the flickering light of the torch that threw the jagged nature of the walls into sharp relief. Spiderwebs fluttered as they passed, giving Carey the sense that this was not a well-used passage.

"Marjen?"

"Just a little farther," he answered as they continued to climb.

They turned a corner and found themselves facing a similar door to the one they had entered through. Once he had unlocked it, Marjen held out his hand to Carey. "This is somewhere I go if I want to be alone. It's somewhere I can find peace," he said as they left the stairwell and walked onto a small plateau. "It was a lookout post, once upon a time."

Carey was met with the most wondrous view. They were far above Hilarus now; the passageway they had taken had brought them out at a point that gave them a perfect view of the city below. The high cliffs and peaks rose up around them, giant sentinels guarding silently. Everything was awash with the last light of sunset; deep oranges and faded reds, and as the mountains slipped into darkness, the city below flickered to life. Fires and lamps illuminated windows, creating a soft twinkling in the darkness.

"This is something, Marjen," she breathed, looking down over the ledge.

"It's so beautiful."

He smiled. He pulled a long, dark metal cylinder from the basket and handed it to her. It was a spyglass. Carey looked from it to Marjen.

"Here," he said, moving the spyglass to her eye and placing his hands on her arms, guiding her from behind. "Do you see that, over there?" he pointed over her right shoulder at the horizon.

From this point, Carey could see right over the tops of the mountain range. Looking through the spyglass, she angled it in the direction Marjen was indicating. In the distance she could see a small mass rising to meet the night sky. Her heart skipped a beat.

"Is that the Centre City?" she asked hopefully, her hand tightening on the spyglass.

"That it is," Marjen answered quietly.

Carey's breath caught in her throat. The dark space between Torarn and Hilarus seemed like nothing at that moment. No army, no lurking danger; it was like the spyglass had closed the distance and thrown her a line which she grasped and pulled tight. She longed to be there, to see her family, her friends. Ji…

"Who is it?"

Carey turned her gaze from the light of the Centre City. "Who?"

Marjen smiled sadly. "I think you know."

Carey felt the heat rise in her cheeks. "Why would you think…?"

He looked out towards the Centre City, but Carey could tell he wasn't really looking at all. "Your concept of being destined for a single other person is not one we have among the Vuleta — we are not fated the same way you are. But for me, that is how I felt about Zafira, how I still feel. I know that look, Carey. I know it all too well," he said heavily.

Carey shook her head, conceding. "It's Ji. Ji Binx, but it's… complicated…" she said, dropping the spyglass at her side.

Marjen didn't comment but simply nodded understandingly. He reached down into his basket, pulled out a bread roll of sorts and passed it to her. He sat down on the rough, overgrown stone plateau and motioned for her to join him. "I will get you back there, Carey. I promise."

They sat in silence for some time, quietly eating their rolls and looking out over the city as it carried on peacefully. Carey thought about Marjen and Versi's conversation she had overheard and knew she ought to say something. She swallowed her last piece and cleared her throat.

"I have a confession," she said as lightly as she could.

Her tone didn't fool him, however, and he looked over at her with a concerned frown.

"Oh?"

Carey fidgeted with the hem of her sleeve. "I heard you and Versi talking last night. Out on the bridge. You were talking about me," she forced herself to say.

She watched Marjen's face for his reaction, but he merely looked at her, his expression unchanged. She pushed on.

"Do you really believe in what you said? Do you really see something in me?"

Marjen reached down and took her hand, covering it with both of his. "With every fibre of my being. I have always had a gift of being able to See a person's potential — it is something I inherited from my mother. I see so much in you, Carey. I see a hope which I never thought I would know again in my lifetime. You are the light for these dark times, even if you do not see it yourself."

Carey swallowed, looking down at their clasped hands. She couldn't see what he saw, but his conviction and faith in her was inspiring. His words gripped her and gave her hope that she might one day be able to live up to the image he portrayed.

"And what of knowing me? How can I feel like I know you so well when I've never met you before?" Carey asked almost desperately, hoping he had some insight into this strange bond they shared.

Marjen chuckled to himself. "I wish I knew the answer to that, Carey. Perhaps we were always meant to meet," he said, and her heart dropped with disappointment. "But I am glad that we did," Marjen added, squeezing her hand reassuringly.

Carey squeezed back, smiling. "I am too. And you're not the only one,

261

Marjen. You have no idea how much hope you've given me, too."

She put her arms around his neck; Marjen pulled her into a warm embrace and Carey was truly glad for the silver lining he had proven to be.

"Now how about some more food? You'll need your strength before we ride out tonight," Marjen said as they pulled away from each other.

*

Carey had been staring out of her window for the past two hours, her mind flitting from one thought to another without coming to rest on any one notion. She couldn't focus; she was waiting for Versi to come by and help with her armour and she was on edge. They were set to ride out at midnight and yet it couldn't come any quicker. Carey had tried to get some rest, but her attempt had merely resulted in her staring up at the carvings on the ceiling and wondering whether the woodcarvers had completed them before putting them on the roof or after. She wished she had someone to talk to, someone to take her mind off the time so she wouldn't feel every passing second grind on her nerves. Instead she found herself looking out into the night, watching as the lights below faded one by one. From the moment she had seen the lights of her city, she had felt a desire like no other. She wanted nothing more than to get on the back of a horse and ride hard and fast for those lights. It no longer mattered what Saar might have waiting; there was nothing in this realm that would keep her from reaching that city anymore.

Carey was just about to move from the window when there came a knock at her door; it was Versi.

"I have your armour," she greeted Carey, walking past her and depositing her armour onto the bed.

Versi began helping Carey into her suit without another word, and Carey stood without a word in return. It almost seemed that her conversation with Marjen hadn't changed her mind when she said, "I need to ask you something."

Her question took Carey by surprise and she answered immediately. "Of course. Anything."

Versi started lacing Carey's thick leather bodice. "I will not be riding out with the garrison tonight as I usually do. Instead, I have been ordered to stay behind and defend the city if our army fails. I don't like it, but it is my duty," she said bluntly, pulling tightly on the lacing.

Unsure of where she was going with this, Carey turned and said, "I'm not exactly sure what you are asking of me."

"I want you to look out for Marjen, have his back out there," she answered as she began fixing Carey's pauldrons at her shoulders. "I'm not going to be there, and I need to know he's safe."

"I don't know how much use I will be, Versi. Marjen has practically forbidden me to enter into battle—"

"I know this," Versi cut across Carey's explanation. "But Marjen has such faith in you. You've given him hope and that's saved him already. I want to be able to trust you too, so can you do it?"

Carey didn't want to give her any false hope but the desperation in Versi's voice was tangible, and she found that there was no way she could deny her this request. She nodded.

"I will do my best to watch out for him," she said as Versi finished tightening her armour. "I give you my word."

Versi's mouth twitched into what Carey supposed was an attempt at a smile. "Good."

She finished by pulling the front of Carey's hair into a thin plait on either side, leaving the rest of her hair to fall loose at her shoulders. Carey stood in silence, though now it was a little less awkward than before.

Versi stood back, her face impassive once more. "There. Marjen will be along shortly."

As Versi left, Carey couldn't help but feel that, despite their initial impressions, they had turned a corner with this most recent interaction, and she was almost sorry she didn't have more time with her. Her concern for Marjen was touching, and even though Carey doubted Marjen's need of her protection, she had given Versi her word. Besides, if it came to it, Carey wouldn't hold back, no matter Marjen's intentions.

It wasn't long before she heard Marjen knocking at her door.

"Ready?" he asked encouragingly.

He was wearing armour now; a broad expanse of dark chiselled leather stretched across his chest, and gauntlets wound around his wrists, covering his forearms. High leather boots covered his normally bare feet and he looked distinctly unlike his usual self. He looked like a warrior.

"As ready as ever," she answered, throwing the red cape that accompanied her armour over her shoulders.

Marjen revealed the sword she had been practicing with; the blade Arach. "She's yours now," he said, offering her the hilt.

Carey reached for it and as her hand closed around that brilliant red and black handle, the same thrill she had felt the other day ran through her body. Excitement and anticipation mixed with her anxiety and her heartbeat quickened.

"Carey?"

She placed the sword at her hip and looked up at Marjen. His face was serious now, all pretence of light-heartedness gone. He placed a hand on her shoulder, and with the weight of it seemed to come the true enormity of what they were about to face. Carey grasped his hand with her own.

"I'm so sorry about all of this Marjen," she said despairingly. "If it wasn't for me, we wouldn't be..."

Marjen squeezed her shoulder reassuringly. "Nonsense. There is always some enemy, some Imperial loyalist that we will have to fight. This is just another day, another battle. Besides, I'll always be glad I found you that day. It has been my honour to know you, Carey Lee."

He took her hand and gave it a gentle kiss before pulling her into a final embrace. Overwhelmed, Carey fought back tears.

"Thank you," was all she could manage.

"Come. We need to be going. The garrison is waiting for us," Marjen said, holding the door open for her.

Taking a deep breath, one hand on her Seekers necklace, Carey left her room and any certainty behind.

~Chapter Twenty-Three~

The Dead Plains

Carey followed Marjen down through the city, past onlookers and teary-eyed children. She kept her eyes ahead, not wishing to bear witness to their pain. They approached the lowest level of the city, to the towering gates of Hilarus, which were as beautifully carved as the beams in her room, and found Efren waiting for them. He was resplendent in his own set of armour, a long cloak about his shoulders and a wide fur collar. As they approached, he lifted another cloak, this one a deep royal navy, and he placed it around Marjen's shoulders.

"The garrison is ready, Captain," he said formally. "Commanders Ueran and Riist are awaiting Her Highness."

Marjen acknowledged him then summoned somewhere to his left. Carey turned to see what it was and couldn't help but gasp audibly. Two young men were leading three great wolves towards them. At least, that is what they seemed to be at first, but as Carey continued to stare, she noticed they were unlike any wolves she had seen before. The fur of two was a dark green that faded to white at their underbellies. Their tails were long, the hair dragging at the ground behind them, and as they walked their fur rippled in a way that had nothing to do with any wind. They were easily the size of a horse and infinitely more fearsome. The one that Marjen met was a dark majestic blue and it towered over the other two, whom Carey assumed were for Efren and herself.

"These are Amarog, Carey," Marjen said, running his hand through the fur of his wolf. "They are fearless spirits, born of magic and myth. They fight with us, not for us, as it is their bound duty to fight evil in any form.

They are strong and they do not tire. They will sense your intentions and they have an impeccable sense of direction. Should you need to make for the Centre City by yourself, your Amarog will take you there."

Carey looked uncertainly at the creature before her. "And we're supposed to ride them?" she asked nervously.

Marjen grinned in amusement. "You seem awfully surprised by them, especially for someone with a Pegasus."

"You forget though that I grew up in the Common Realm. I doubt I will ever tire of being surprised by this sort of thing," she responded. "And they're safe?"

"As I said, they can sense your intentions," said Marjen as he climbed onto the back of his Amarog. "You have no reason to be afraid."

With some hesitation, Carey walked up to the Amarog that had been brought to her. It looked at her with great piercing blue eyes, and she had the distinct feeling it was searching for something. She stared back until it seemed satisfied with its appraisal; it dropped to the ground before her and she took this as a sign that it was safe to climb onto its back. There was no saddle, but since she had had plenty of practice riding Firefly bareback, she hoped it wouldn't be too difficult. Its fur was soft beneath her, thick and luscious, and she had to stop herself running her hands through it. As soon as Carey had settled upon the Amarog's back, it rose to its feet and she grabbed fistfuls of fur to keep herself from falling off as it moved to join Marjen and Efren at the gates. The sound of a horn blew from within the city and Carey looked back once more at the Vuletians who were standing silently, bidding them farewell.

"It is time," Marjen said to her quietly, and the gates opened to reveal his garrison.

Marjen's garrison was something to behold; row upon row of immaculately armoured Vuletian warriors awaiting their orders. They sat astride the massive backs of more Amarogs, and even as they passed them to take the lead, not one moved or turned their heads. Commanders Ueran and Riist were already at the front of the army and bowed as the three of them approached.

"You are to stay with the commanders, Carey," Marjen said, his voice more commanding now that he had taken his place at the head of his army. "You must stay with them, out of the battle. If you are given a chance to make for the Centre City, you are to do so, with or without me."

Carey was about to argue but the look on Marjen's face silenced her. Despite his tone there was a pleading look in his eyes; he would not risk her capture and she did not want to make him feel as though he had failed her in his promise. She nodded.

"I understand," she said as the commanders took their places on either side of her.

Without another word, Marjen raised his sword overhead and his Amarog let out a long haunting howl that echoed through the valley. Carey jumped as the rest howled in reply, and Marjen set forth. The other Amarog, including her own, followed suit, and Carey held on tightly as they set off. Her hair flew back from her face as they settled immediately into a smooth gallop. The garrison behind her rode in perfect unison and the effect was quite intimidating. Their armour glinted in the moonlight and the fact it was almost pitch black seemed to neither worry nor hinder them. She looked over at Commander Ueran, who was riding straight backed and confident, and said, "How long will it be before we reach the Dead Plains?"

Without looking sideways, she answered, "We should reach there just before dawn. It will take us until then to clear the mountains. If all goes well, we will reach the Plains just before the Loyalists do."

Just before dawn. Only a few hours and she would be facing Saar.

Carey gripped her wolf tighter; the rocking motion made it very difficult for her to ride comfortably and she felt incredibly uncoordinated. Her armour made her slip about on the wolf's back, and as they sped up, she feared she would fall off. Commander Ueran seemed to notice her discomfort.

"Try not to be so tense," she called over to her. "The Amarog will make sure you don't slip off, but it makes it easier if you relax a bit."

Carey didn't answer; there was no way she'd be able to relax, feeling as though with every movement she was about to be thrown off. However, as

267

they travelled onwards, she realised that the Amarog was moving with her and that any slight shift on her behalf was mimicked by the beast to hold her steady. Carey soon found herself starting to loosen up.

As the night wore on and dawn approached, they wound their way through the mountains and valleys that separated them from the Dead Plains. Carey stared at Marjen's back, his fluttering blue cloak, and wondered what he was thinking. She wished she could talk to him, but she knew, from the moment they had left Hilarus he had assumed his role as Captain, and any casual interaction or banter would be sidelined until the battle was done.

"We're almost there," Commander Riist informed her as they turned a corner.

They had reached the edge of the mountain range and found themselves climbing a long ridge. As they reached the summit, Marjen stopped and signalled for a halt. Carey came up beside him, awed by the sight before them.

A vast forest spread from the bottom of the ridge as far as the eye could see, but it was unlike any forest Carey had ever seen before. The trees were blackened, each one twisting in the same direction in endless agony as the early morning mist enveloped them, curling up around their tortured bodies. There was an immediate sense of foreboding as the tell-tale signs of past horrors were laid bare, stark and bold against the cold landscape. The ground at their deadened roots was burnt and cracked, and there seemed no promise of redemption, nor possibility of renewal. The entire forest was devoid of any life, and Carey could feel the lack of magic as though it had been leeched from the air around her. Even if she wanted to use magic, she felt it being suffocated. Stifled by some great invisible force. There was no turning back from the Dead Plains. There was nothing but the swords at their sides to protect them now.

"Are you all right?" she heard Marjen whisper her way.

"I don't know. This place... it's not what I was expecting," she whispered back.

"Stay with the commanders and hopefully you'll have no need to enter there before the battle is won," he said quietly before leading his Amarog out in front.

He craned his head, looking out over the forest for the loyalist army that was no doubt approaching. Everyone was still, waiting and watching; the only sounds of movement were the slight rustling of the wolves and the shifting of armour.

They remained like this for some time. Carey sat uneasily on her mount as she looked around at Marjen's men. They waited, alert, eyes straight ahead with their weapons gleaming at their sides. Wondering at this slightly unnerving display of military unity, Carey couldn't help but think on who these soldiers were beyond the battlefield. They were all here for her, *because* of her, and yet she'd probably never know a single name.

As though he sensed her inner turmoil, Marjen withdrew his gaze from the horizon and turned to her.

"What's on your mind?"

Carey looked at him and her stomach swooped at the look of concern on his face. "You don't want to know," she said, dropping her gaze from his.

"No, I really do, Carey. What's the matter?" she heard him say.

Carey stared down at her hands gripping the fur of her Amarog and sighed deeply. "I don't know how I keep finding myself in situations like this," she said, still not looking at Marjen.

"Situations like these?" he said. "What, facing an Imperial army on the back of a giant wolf is that common for you?"

Despite herself, Carey gave a small laugh. "Well, not this exact situation. What I mean is situations where people are most likely going to get *hurt* because of me." She was about to say *'killed'* but she couldn't bring herself to say it.

"Carey, look at me," Marjen demanded, his voice serious.

Carey lifted her head and found Marjen watching her sternly.

"Let me tell you something," he began. "Firstly, this is what we do — fight Imperials. At some point we would eventually have found ourselves here, fighting, if not this army then some other. The fact that you may have brought them here just that touch earlier makes no difference to us.

Secondly, if the people you are thinking of were anything like my men, then they certainly did not die *because* of you. I understand, Carey. You did not choose this life, you were born into it. I may have been born with the soul of a warrior, but I chose to be a fighter, to be a soldier. That is the right of every Vuleta, to follow the path of a Seer or a Warrior, or to put that aside and become neither. You are a warrior not because you wanted to be, but because of the choices of your forebears. Accepting that people might die for you must be near impossible. That said, I find it hard to believe that those people would have helped you and fallen for you without faith. I know for certain that Alois Patroni and his family knew the risks associated with helping the Order and yet they still did so without a second thought, because they had faith. They believed in what you stand for, what you represent. And if you want to honour their sacrifices, don't ever believe that they died *because* of you. Don't regret their deaths. They died *for* something, for a greater purpose. Regret their deaths and they will have died in vain."

Marjen leant closer to her now, a hard passion in his voice. "If you want to honour them, then stand up and fight. Become the symbol of hope and freedom they believed in and show them that you are worthy of their sacrifice."

Sacrifice. She stared at back him, her jaw tight; his words echoed within her and she felt something shift. Carey had honestly never considered the deaths of those around her as sacrifices. She had only ever seen them as an unnecessary waste of life, and if it hadn't been for her, those people would have certainly lived. She never considered their feelings, whether they believed as deeply in the rebel cause as she did, whether they wanted to see the Empire defeated just as badly. Perhaps they had, perhaps they hadn't, but she owed it to them, to everyone, to fight. She could no longer regret the consequences of her existence, only ensure that no death was in vain. She could not allow it. Would not allow it.

Carey nodded mutely. He returned her silent agreement with a smile that crinkled the corners of his eyes, and then turned his head back to the foggy horizon.

"Captain," Commander Ueran hissed.

Carey snapped around to face Fiika but the commander's head was turned towards the dead forest, her eyes narrowed as she searched the fog-laden woodlands.

Then Carey heard it — the growing sounds of something large approaching. The distant clanging of weapons, the howling of creatures unknown, and the distinct shuffle of a great many feet; the Vuletian army heard their enemies before they could see them, the fog obscuring their foes. Then, slowly, they began to emerge from the grey. A great army of every creature imaginable stalked towards them; wizards, Örd, flying monsters, and others Carey had never encountered before. There were groups of gangling creatures that resembled men but were sallow skinned and sunken-eyed. Their long green hair was matted and dirty, and their clothes hung in tatters. Scattered amongst the horde were creatures with red eyes, thick barrel-like torsos and short stumpy legs that moved deceptively quick despite their stature. They wore rough armour across their chests and on their heads and carried heavy weaponry that looked as though it could easily crush a man with a single swing. As they came into view, Carey felt her heart sink; the enemy army was at least twice the size of Marjen's. She looked over at Commander Ueran expecting to see fear, but her face was calm, her eyes staring unblinkingly at the oncoming army.

The enemy stopped; those in front planted their swords in the ground. A ripple of movement ran down the centre and from within the mass came a tall shrouded figure astride a snarling griffin, and for a wild moment Carey thought it was Malevolence. But then it spoke.

"Vuletians!" it roared in a deep voice up the ridge. "We have come for the princess. Give her to us and you may retreat!"

The man's voice reverberated around them in a way that made Carey feel ill at ease, but Marjen and his garrison did not move.

"We are not here to negotiate!" Marjen shouted back vehemently. "The princess is our ward. You shall not have her! We will not retreat!"

Carey looked from Marjen to the Imperial, her heart pounding against her ribcage. At Marjen's words, the enemy roared in bloodlust, clearly delighted by the idea of a fight. They rattled their weapons and shook their

271

fists in the air; the gangly creatures shook their heads in anticipation and the towering Örd stared murderously at them. Carey felt the Vuletian soldiers around her tense.

"So be it!" the man on the griffin boomed.

He turned to his army and raised a clenched fist, releasing an intense, guttural roar. At this signal, the loyalist army swarmed forth.

Marjen raised his sword wordlessly and lowered it at the surging mass; in unison, the entire Vuletian garrison rushed past Carey and over the ridge, the captain in the lead. War cries and deafening roars rent the cold air. The din assaulted her senses, fear creeping up her throat and threatening to engulf her. Carey watched as the Vuleta charged head-on into the valley, straight at the oncoming surge of Imperials, and with an almighty crash, the two armies met. The Amarog made short work of the enemy frontline, but it soon became apparent that the sheer number of Imperials would soon overwhelm them despite their superior skill. The blue flashes from the Vuletian weapons illuminated the battle with an eerie glow as they slashed at the Imperials.

Looking up, Carey watched in horror as griffins rose from the ranks into the air. With menacing screeches, they swooped down, picking up unsuspecting Vuletian soldiers and flinging them through the air. An Örd below her stepped forward and swept aside two gigantic Amarog with ease, crushing their riders. The gangly creatures were climbing the dead trees and leaping down onto their prey, their sunken eyes wide and wild. Several of the squat, red-eyed creatures were thrashing about with spike-laden clubs, emitting blood-thirsty screams as they knocked Vuletian guards to the ground. The Amarogs they had been riding reared up on their hind legs and roared with unmistakable rage. They threw themselves on the offending creatures in retaliation, only to be swallowed up by the vicious swarm that besieged them.

Carey looked on as terror and rage thundered through her, each clambering to overpower her as she watched the devastation. Her right hand gripped the hilt of her sword hard as she fought to hold herself back. Marjen's army was drowning under the weight of the Imperial force and she was finding it difficult to stand aside and just watch. Her eyes flitted over the crowd anxiously, searching, when they fell upon Marjen. She found him in the centre of the fray, his sword slashing at the enemy before him. So deft were his movements that it seemed that none could come close. His Amarog clawed and bit at the swarm of loyalists, their efforts to drag him from its back proving futile. Carey followed him closely, hardly breathing as he laid waste to the creatures before him.

Then, from the corner of her eye, she saw something fly at her. One of the gangly green-haired beings had made it through the Vuletian line of defence and had launched itself from a ridge above. Before she could draw her sword, it knocked her from her Amarog, and together they tumbled to the ground, hitting the stone hard. Knees and elbows banging painfully, Carey heard someone scream, "Razut! The Princess!" Turning over, she scrambled for her fallen weapon. The creature flipped over, its wild eyes bulging, and its mouth stretched wide in a crazed grin. It scurried forward and leaped at Carey, who finally managed to find the hilt of her sword, and as the creature screeched in triumph, she swung the blade in front of her. She felt it shudder as the sword found its mark. The green-haired creature fell to the ground again, but this time it did not get up. Her heart beating fast, Carey stared down at what she had just done, but before she could take it in, she heard her name.

"Carey! Watch out!"

It was Commander Riist, and Carey looked up just in time to see more of the creatures descending upon them. They landed between them and the entrance to the valley, effectively cutting them off from their retreat. Carey knew at once that they must have been lying in wait, holding off until the most opportune moment. There were not enough to take on Marjen's army alone, but just enough to hinder their escape should they need it. Carey got to her feet as commanders Riist and Ueran drew themselves up by her side, their weapons raised against the advancing enemy. Carey glanced quickly about — there was nothing for it now. With the two warring armies locked in a vicious battle behind her and their way out now impeded by the swarm of gangly creatures, she would have to fight. Adjusting her grip on her sword, she raised it above her head. This seemed to be what the creatures had been waiting for. They sprang forward and Carey brought her sword down hard.

It was absolute chaos. Screams, screeches, howls and snarls filled Carey's ears as she brought her sword about again and again. One of the creatures dodged her weapon and collided with her shoulder, knocking her sideways. Its long bony fingers grappled for her neck as Carey stumbled, almost dropping her weapon. Frantically, she fought against it, trying desperately to push it off her, but she felt one of its spindly hands find her throat as it pushed her up against a rock wall. Its other hand was trying to force her head back, its wide mouth baring rows of sharp needle-like teeth. Carey found her footing, and as the beast bore down on her, she gripped her sword with two hands and thrust it upwards, driving it through its skeletal frame. The creature let out an ear-splitting screech as its grip on Carey slackened and she pushed it off her with a grunt. As it fell to the ground, a deafening roar rent the air and Carey spun around to see Marjen's Amarog rearing up against one of the griffins, whose talons slashed and scraped violently through the air above it. Transfixed, Carey watched as one of the Örd took advantage of Marjen's preoccupation with the griffin, reaching up and dragging him by his cloak from the great wolf, throwing him to the ground.

"No!" Carey exclaimed, and she jumped down from the ridge, sliding on the loose rock as she skidded down the slope towards the battle.

She could see Marjen ahead; he was on his feet and forcing the Örd back. He did not seem to notice the tall shrouded man advancing through the crowd towards him in a manner that caused panic to rise in Carey's chest. The raging battle held no hindrance to him as he cut a path through the fray, his strides long and purposeful. He pulled a long green sword from his side and lowered his hood. He was strong-jawed and deathly pale, his face framed by long black hair. Carey called out to Marjen in warning, pushing her way past the Vuletian soldiers at the back, but he couldn't hear her over the din. The tall man was almost upon him when he looked over at Carey. She faltered in her steps. His eyes were completely black, merciless and terrifying. He looked at her for a moment then lifted his sword. He took two steps towards Marjen, and just as he turned to defend himself, the black-eyed man brought his sword around and thrust it up between the folds in his armour. Carey watched in horror as the tip of the sword pierced Marjen's side.

"Marjen! No!" she screamed, pushing her way towards him.

With a single look of satisfaction, the man pulled his sword from Marjen and watched him slump to the ground. It felt like slow motion to Carey; everyone else around her, Vuletian and Imperial, seemed to fade into background noise. She saw Marjen hit the ground, grasping at his side, his weapon falling just out of reach. The tall man flicked his sword, droplets of Marjen's blood flying from its tip as he turned to face her.

"Carey... don't..." Marjen called out painfully, but it was too late.

She hadn't seen it; she had been too intent on Marjen to realise that she had run straight into a trap. No Imperial made to attack her now; instead they were busy keeping the surrounding Vuletian soldiers back, hindering their attempts to reach her. A wide berth had been created by the enemy combatants and she found herself in the very centre of the clearing. Gripping her sword tighter, her heart racing, Carey turned slowly to face the towering Imperial.

"Princess," he greeted her in his deep voice. "I believe you are to come with me."

Her blood was pounding in her ears; Marjen was lying on the ground behind him and she knew she would need to fight this man if she was to get to him.

"Not in this lifetime I'm not," she said through gritted teeth, raising her sword.

"Oh, I wouldn't do that," he advised her with the hint of a smile, his black eyes following her sword.

"Is that so!" Carey grunted as she swung at his head. The man deflected her easily.

"You really don't want to do this," he warned her again as Carey brought her sword around over and over, trying to land a blow.

"You tried to kill my friend. I'd say I really do!" she yelled at him as their swords connected.

"I wouldn't say I *tried*. This sword will make sure that he really will die," the man taunted as he fought her back with frustrating ease.

Carey looked up at the green blade and saw it glisten unusually in the dim sunlight.

"What is it? What are you?" she hissed, stepping back from the tall man. She glanced down at Marjen's body; he wasn't moving.

"I am Elathan. I was born of the darkness, as was my sword," he said menacingly as he walked towards her. "You are right to fear me."

Elathan's arrogance and banter was infuriating. They were wasting time and the longer this carried on, the worse it got for Marjen. Carey could hear her name being called and she knew the commanders were coming for her, but she would not run from this man. She tightened her grip on her sword.

"I don't fear you," she spat, and with a roar of fury she launched herself at Elathan.

Her refusal to back down caught him off guard and she found him stumbling backwards slightly. She brought her sword down faster, over and over, but he regained his footing almost instantly and pushed her back, his green blade only just missing her cheek.

"Princess!" Commander Ueran had finally reached her, followed closely by Commander Riist, but they were rebuffed by the loyalists encircling Carey and her aggressor.

"Stay back! Don't come any closer!" Carey yelled at them, and Elathan grinned maliciously.

"I heard this about you, Princess — so very ready to sacrifice yourself. How many others have died for you though? I'm guessing the captain here isn't the first," Elathan goaded. "Well?"

Carey felt her anger rising, a red-hot fury that she hadn't felt in a long time. Adrenalin coursed through her veins as she glared at Elathan, staring into those merciless black eyes. His taunts burned at her but at that moment, her rage was stronger than her guilt. She wasn't going to let this man continue.

She wasn't going to let Marjen die for her. She could feel her fingers tingling, a phantom hope, but the magic that lay inside her was of no use here. All she had was her sword and one last move.

She raised her sword and shifted her weight ever so slightly. Elathan snarled, eyes glinting as he lunged at her. At the last possible second, Carey turned away from his blade; she felt it rush past her as she fell to her knees, and with all the strength she had, all the anger and rage, she thrust her sword upwards. As the tip of her blade plunged into Elathan's side, a shock of magic forced itself from her and exploded outwards. Elathan disintegrated, blown away by the sheer force of it, and Carey fell forwards in astonishment, her sword falling from her hands. She watched as the magic flew through the trees, decimating the enemy army as it went. Their shouts and screams of surprise were cut short as they too were turned to dust, their remains falling over the heads of the Vuleta who stumbled in shock.

As the dust settled, there came a moment of complete silence as all eyes found Carey. Then a roar of triumph erupted from the Vuletian army, rippling through the valley. Carey, who was still on her knees, her sword limp in her hand, tried to understand what had just happened.

"What was that?" she heard Commander Riist say, but all she could do was shake her head. Somehow, she had just used magic in the Dead Plains. Somehow, she had just destroyed an entire army...

Carey heard someone groan behind her.

"Marjen!" she gasped.

She scrambled over to him, cursing; she had been so caught up in the moment that she had momentarily and unforgivably forgotten about him. He was lying on his side, clutching at his armour. Blood was seeping from beneath the leather, mingling with the black ash on the ground. Kneeling beside him, Carey grabbed him by the shoulders, unsure of what she should do. Efren appeared at her side and together they gently rolled him onto his back; Carey cradling his head in her lap. He was deathly pale, and his chest rose and fell with short, sharp breaths. His brown eyes fluttered open and Carey tightened her grip on his shoulders hopefully.

"Hold on, Marjen. Everything's going to be all right. I know a fantastic healer in the Centre City. He'll put you right in no time," she said feverishly, trying to ignore the blood pooling at her knees.

Marjen managed a feeble laugh. "Oh Carey, I don't think I'll make it that far."

Carey shook her head, refusing to believe his words. "Don't say that. We'll make it. You promised you'd get me back to the Centre City, remember?"

Marjen reached for her, his hand shaking. Carey took it in hers, squeezing it reassuringly. "Please Marjen."

He took a shuddering breath. "I know. I know," he winced. A harsh cough wracked his body and a trickle of blood appeared at the corner of his lips. "But you will make it, I am sure of it."

Carey bent over him, resting her forehead against their clasped hands, and she held back a sob that was trying to escape her throat. Regardless of what he had told her, she did not want him dying for her. She did not want his sacrifice — just once, she wanted someone to live. "Please," she whispered. "You can't give up."

"I did give up, long ago, but you... you gave me hope again," Marjen choked, his teeth clenched in anguish, the muscles in his neck taut with pain. "It's more than I could have wished for." Marjen's body trembled and his eyes grew wide. His hand gripped hers tighter still. "Have hope, Carey," he murmured, and with that, his grip relaxed, and Carey watched as his eyes slid out of focus.

Marjen Tutari, Captain of the Vuletian army, was dead.

Carey stared into Marjen's blank eyes. A screaming terror began to buzz within her. She could hear nothing but the pounding of her heart, feel the heat and panic wrapping itself around her, threatening to engulf her. It crept all over her, rushing down her limbs, filling her head, but looking down at Marjen's handsome features, she heard his last words in her head — *Have hope, Carey.* She clenched her jaw resolutely. She forced back the tidal wave of emotion building within her; refused to let it take her. Gradually, it subsided, leaving a hollow, ache in her chest. This was not the time to stop and grieve; she would face that later. Instead, she held Marjen's limp hand in hers for a moment longer before laying it on his chest and closing his eyes. Her hands shook slightly. Anger and rage began to bubble up now, filling that empty chasm within her. Pain and guilt were useless to her right now, but rage… *that* she could use. There would be time for mourning later; she had to get back to the Centre City immediately.

Carey leaned over and kissed Marjen on the forehead, then, carefully moving his head from her lap, got to her feet. She had to finish this. She had thought Saar would be here, but instead he had sent others to fight in his stead. He had not even bothered to show his face, and for that, Carey now saw him for what he truly was — nothing but a coward, only too happy to stand back and pull the strings. Well, if that was how it was, then she would have to force him out and face him herself. No armies, no stooges. A fierce determination joined the rage coursing through her, and as she turned her gaze away from Marjen's body. She knew there was nothing now that would keep her from reaching the Centre City.

"Efren. I'm leaving. I need you to send word to the Centre City. Tell them I was captured by the enemy army and say nothing of what happened here. I need a head start," she said to the lieutenant by her side as she sheathed her sword at her hip.

"In that case, the commanders will escort you. Marjen would've wanted that," he said, summoning Riist and Ueran with a wave of his hand. "Will you be all right?" he added in concern.

"I'm fine. At least, I will be," she said, walking over to Marjen's Amarog. The wolf knelt before her and she mounted its back. She felt nothing but a singular purpose driving her towards what she knew to be the end of all this. Fear, pain, grief — it would all have to wait.

"And Efren," she said in a softer voice, "Tell Versi I'm sorry. I did everything I could."

He nodded in understanding before bowing to her. "I will take care of him. Go safely."

Adjusting her position atop the great beast, Carey turned to the commanders who were now waiting at her side, their own Amarogs standing ready.

"Daaren, Fiika. There's no need to stand on ceremony any longer. We ride hard and we ride fast, and we do not stop until we reach the Centre City. Regardless of what just happened here, I cannot risk Saar tracking me down, so I will not be using my magic again. With any luck, he was not able to sense my use of magic here. However, keep your weapons ready. I don't want to take any chances."

Fiika nodded. "Understood. We shall take a back route. We cannot be sure that no one's watching the main roads. We'll take Turris Pass to the north of Torarn."

Carey nodded. "Then let's ride."

~Chapter Twenty-Four~

Onwards

Carey glanced once more at Efren, who was now at Marjen's side, before giving her Amarog a slight nudge with her heels. "Let's go!"

Marjen's great blue wolf howled, the sound resonating through the scorched forest as they took off at a much faster pace than what they had travelled earlier that morning. The Amarog was mirroring Carey's clear sense of determination; she felt no exhilaration as they ran through the blackened woods, losing no momentum as they dodged great clusters of dead foliage. Had this been any other day she would have marvelled at its speed and agility, but she felt nothing but the deepest desire, born from such absolute rage, to reach the Centre City and find Saar. Carey wasn't sure what she would do when she finally confronted him. Could she kill him? Exact a revenge that was barely equal to anything he had done? Would she be able to show restraint, as Marjen had, and be the better person? Marjen's bloodstained face and wide eyes swam across her mind and her rage boiled inside her.

No. She wasn't sure she could, or if she even wanted to show restraint. Saar deserved no such mercy, for he had surely not shown any on his part. Not to Marjen or his family, not to Torena, Alois and theirs, nor to any of the countless others he had murdered for Malevolence and the Empire. No, she would not show mercy. But would she be able to exact justice if he still held the Dragon's Heart? If he knew what she had just done... she had used magic in the Dead Plains — powerful and terrible magic. Hadn't Marjen said that the only other person to do so had been Malevolence?

Carey knew it was that power, that strange magic within her that felt so disconnected... not her own. She had always feared it and rightly so — she had just managed to kill an entire army. *An entire army.* She'd always felt that it was dark, perhaps even evil, and yet... It was the same magic that helped Kat, Ji and she to escape the Empire when they were young. How many tight spots had she found herself in, only to be given aid through this enigmatic power? And it had been the real reason she'd been able to stop Malevolence...

But it had also killed. All those loyalists... there was no denying what she had just done. And if Saar found out, if he ever managed to steal that magic from her...

It was almost midday by the time the trio reached the edge of the Dead Plains. They stood at its edge momentarily, scanning the horizon.

"It's clear," Daaren said in a low voice. "Follow me."

With Daaren in front, Carey and Fiika followed. They moved away from the well-worn track that ran along the edge of the Plains and up into a long stretch of woodlands that covered the mountains to their right. They rode for some time, moving along a narrow path that wound about the close-standing trees. Carey saw no others, only animals that stared, startled, as they hurtled past on their giant wolves. Deeper and deeper into the woods they found themselves, moving until they were surrounded by nothing but dense green foliage. The mountains reared up alongside them, but the path stayed flat along the foot of the hills, keeping the three in the shadows of their steep facades. The trees grew tall around them and soon the high canopy blocked out the sky completely. The only indication of the passing of time was the gradual diminishing of what little light they could see poking through the heavy canopy.

The forest around them grew ever darker until Carey could barely make out their path, and yet neither the oncoming night, nor the increasingly difficult route slowed the Amarogs. With savage glee, Carey grinned at the possibility of riding through the night. Anything to get there sooner.

Suddenly, her Amarog let out a long howl and skidded to a stop.

"What? What is it?" she hissed, gripping hard at the Amarog's fur to prevent herself from slipping off sideways.

Fiika and Daaren had also stopped. "There's something out there," Fiika answered, looking around. "The Amarog have sensed something."

At Fiika's words, Carey's wolf howled again, this time in the direction of its two fellows, and they leapt forward, on the move once more. They were still moving quickly, but Carey noticed a slight change in their movements — they moved with deliberate caution.

Carey had barely enough time to think on what had caught the Amarogs' attention when there came a number of loud *CRACKS* and she found herself veering sideways off the path. High in the trees, two very familiar creatures appeared. With the black head, chest and forelegs of a massive wolf, and a long, scaly tail lined with lethal barbs, the two Dæmons hung in the air above them, flapping their massive leathery wings as they surveyed their prey. The last time Carey had faced one of these Dæmons, she had managed to defeat it by pure luck, *and* magic. As she looked up into the eyes of the snarling beasts, a thrill of panic ran through her. She didn't want to use magic, and yet she could not see how they would get past the Dæmons without it.

She saw a flash of silver from the corner of her eye and before she could say anything, Fiika and Daaren had drawn their weapons, their Amarog baring their great sharp teeth in anticipation.

"Carey! Keep going! We can handle these!" came Daaren's voice.

Carey wanted to warn them but her Amarog heeded Daaren's command and spun away from the two commanders.

"No! I have to help them!" she screamed at the great wolf, pulling at its hair, but it ignored her pleas and made to run when suddenly it snarled at something up ahead. One of the Dæmons appeared in front of them, blocking their way. It screeched viciously before swooping down at them. Carey lay flat against her Amarog's back as she felt it brush past them, the air rippling her hair as they dodged the creature and slammed against a tree. Her grip slipped and Carey fell onto the moss-covered ground. She grappled for the sword at her side, but it wasn't there; spinning around she found it lying on the ground not far from where they were. She ran for it but her Amarog seized her ankle with its jaw, and she fell hard to the ground. She was about to yell something when the Dæmon appeared before her, landing its great black paws on top of her sword. She suddenly realised that her wolf had sensed the Dæmon, saving her just in time. However, now the Dæmon had a clear shot at her, and Carey was completely defenceless at its feet. With a swish of its great barbed tail, the Dæmon lunged.

As she threw her arms over her head, Carey saw a flash of blue and the Dæmon was knocked sideways — it was Fiika and her Amarog. They had leaped at the creature, blocking Carey from its attack. It screeched in surprise before vanishing in a whiff of smoke and appearing again overhead, just out of reach of the giant wolves below. The two commanders were now battling a Dæmon each, their Amarogs helping them to dodge their attacks with their hyper keen senses. Scrambling forward to finally grab her sword, Carey watched as Fiika's Dæmon disappeared again. With a mighty howl, Fiika's Amarog leaped high into the air, its rider diving sideways onto the ground, sword in hand. As the giant wolf reached full height, the Dæmon appeared and the Amarog clamped its great jaw around the Dæmon's throat before they came crashing to the ground. The Dæmon shook, its body shivering as it tried to disappear again, but the Amarog had too tight of a grip, stopping it from breaking free. The two creatures writhed upon the ground, kicking up dust and slamming into the trees. Fiika raised her sword above her head, its blue edge gleaming in the darkness. She ran at the Dæmon and brought her sword down hard, ramming it into its chest. The Dæmon's body shuddered before exploding into a shower of glittering remains.

There was no time for celebration, however. As Fiika pulled her sword from the ground, a loud cry of pain rang through the trees. Carey and Fiika turned to see Daaren's body land nearby, his Amarog bounding over to his rider as the remaining Dæmon followed. Forgetting about her own Amarog, Carey ran towards Daaren, her sword raised. The Dæmon vanished again and in a blink of an eye, landed on Carey. She fell backwards, but her grip on her sword remained firm. With a victorious howl, the creature lunged at her. With both hands, Carey gripped the hilt of her weapon and thrust it upwards. The Dæmon was so close that she could see the look of surprise in its dark eyes as it spotted her sword, but it had too much momentum by that point and had no time to disappear before the blade plunged into its breast. Carey grunted, straining against the weight of the Dæmon as it shuddered before exploding as the other had.

"Daaren?" she heard Fiika's voice behind her.

Panting with exhaustion, Carey rolled onto her stomach to see the commander crouching a few metres away at her partner's side.

"Daaren? Is he hurt?" Carey asked fearfully, pulling herself up onto her knees.

There came a groan as Daaren stirred, and she breathed a sigh of relief.

"Only my ego. Damned Skeriks," he grunted as Fiika helped him to his feet.

"We need to keep moving, in case there are more out there," Fiika said as she mounted her Amarog, having made sure Daaren truly wasn't hurt.

Carey didn't even answer; adrenalin still pumping through her veins, she jumped to her feet, pulled herself up onto her wolf and nudged its sides with her heels. She kept her sword at the ready, choosing not to sheath it in case they were attacked again. Her Amarog growled and the three leaped forward. Deeper they ran into the forest, and for now there were no signs of any more Dæmons. The adrenalin from the fight continued to course through Carey's body, excusing her from feeling any of the terror she knew lay within. It made her bold, and right now, that was exactly what she needed.

For a moment, the trees thinned, and they found themselves on a cliff. Below was a wide expansive plane; its grass rippling in the silvery moonlight. Beyond that was a copse of trees, but farther still the trees ended and the ground gave way to yet another cliff. It was there in the distance, far below them, that the Centre City could be seen.

"There it is," Carey breathed, unable to tear her eyes away from the shimmering lights of her city.

"If we continue at our current pace, we should make it by mid-morning," Fiika said to her right.

Mid-morning. "Then lead the way, Fiika."

"Wait."

Daaren, who had been silent by her side, raised a hand and placed a finger to his lips. Carey froze, her body tense as she listened hard for what had caught Daaren's attention.

There it was — a distant rustling coming from behind them, then, piercing shrieks.

"What is that?" Fiika whispered, and with the cold dread of realisation, Carey answered, "Daeva."

"Shadow Dæmons!" Daaren translated.

"Go!" Fiika commanded as she drew her sword unnecessarily; Carey was sure the action was merely one of comfort than of actual practicality, but she wasn't about to point that out. She patted her Amarog hastily and they took off down the slope.

The screeching was growing louder, and Carey gripped the fur of her Amarog, knowing desperately that they wouldn't be able to outrun the Daeva. As the three of them hurtled through the forest on their wolves, the sound of the Daeva grew, surrounding them on all sides until Carey was sure they were almost upon them.

"Kiyosei!"

For a moment she thought Fiika was yelling at the Daeva, but then she noticed something happening to the trees around them. At first Carey thought they were moving, but then she saw part of a tree detach itself completely and launch itself upwards. It was a creature, a fairy of sorts, thin and sharp featured as though it was born of the tree from which it had emerged. More and more of them appeared, and for a moment she thought they were about to attack them too, but in a blur of wings, they shot straight past them towards the sound of the Dæva. Hazarding a backwards glance, Carey saw them collide with the oncoming darkness with sudden bursts of light. The forest was soon illuminated by hundreds of light explosions and still more zoomed past Carey and the others as they raced down into a valley.

"They're holding them back! The Kiyosei are holding back the Dæva!"

Fiika called out triumphantly.

The air was now thick with the flying Kiyosei and the resulting glow from their attacks was almost blinding. It was true — the Dæva were falling back, hindered by the light, but they weren't gone just yet.

"Keep going! If we can reach that field, then perhaps the moonlight will keep the Dæva from following us," Daaren shouted over to them.

Carey nodded as the Amarog carried them at breakneck speed through the dense trees. Her hands were aching from gripping its fur so tightly, but she felt as though she would be thrown off if she loosened her grip for even a second. If that were to happen, then the Dæva would most certainly have her and it would be all over. They were so close now that the injustice of such a thought burned deep. She pushed the pain aside and lay low against her Amarog's back, squinting through the rushing wind.

I'm so close. So close, Carey thought repeatedly. The flashes of light from the Kiyosei were now farther away, and Carey almost cried out in elation when a tendril of darkness shot out from her right. Her Amarog only just managed to dodge it as the Dæva shot straight at her. She screamed as she felt herself losing her balance; her Amarog was stumbling, the speed still carrying them forward. Carey could see the field just ahead as she felt her fingers slip from her wolf's fur. Flying through the air, she could see the Dæva now, bearing down on her. As she braced herself, there was a flash of fur and for the briefest of moments she felt a great set of teeth clamp around her body, scraping at her armour. She was flung with such force that it was a blur. She flew past the trees and was met with the bright face of the moon. She hit the ground hard, rolling to a stop amongst foot-high grass. She jumped to her feet, expecting the Dæva to shoot out of the trees to meet her, but it didn't follow. Daaren had been right — the moonlight was too bright for it.

The moments passed and the bursts of light from the Kiyosei continued to flash through the trees, yet no one else emerged from the forest. Carey was beginning to feel fearful when three Amarog and the two commanders leapt into the clearing.

"You escaped!" she cried in relief as her Amarog stopped to let her on.

"That last Dæva must have slipped past the Kiyosei," Daaren said, breathless. "I wasn't sure if you'd made it to the clearing or not."

"That was your Amarog, then? I almost didn't. Thank you," Carey said, holding her armour where the wolf's teeth had scratched along it.

Turning from the forest, she grunted as she jumped back up onto her Amarog, shooting pains making her keenly aware of where Daaren's wolf had held her in its jaw. "Do you think they can hold the Dæva back until we're gone from here?"

"It's possible, but we need to move if we're to give the Kiyosei a chance," Fiika said. "I know the way from here. Come."

They dashed across the open field and were amongst the trees again before they knew it. Compared to where they had just come from, this part of the forest was almost silent except for the bubbling sound of a stream somewhere. Fiika led on, and soon they were by the side of a small river. It was barely a few metres across, but Carey could see that it was deep, its dark waters swirling. She was worried for a second that they would have to swim across when Fiika turned left and continued running alongside it. As they ran, the river grew wider and its bubbly stream began to grow wild as the water splashed about large rocks that rose from its depths. A faint roar met Carey's ears, and for a wild moment, she thought the Dæva were back. However, as they continued, it became apparent that the sound was vastly different to that of the Shadow Dæmons, and she soon realised that it was the rumble of rushing water. As they rounded a bend, the three of them found themselves at the edge of a towering cliff; the water from the river hurtled towards it, rushing over the edge in a haze of mist.

"This way," Fiika called as she led them to a point just by the edge of the cliff.

There, hidden in the face of the cliff, was an impossibly steep path, roughly hewn into the rock by the waterfall. Fiika started down the path, her Amarog moving slowly. Despite its size, the creature was surprisingly nimble and sure-footed on the wet track. As its large tail disappeared from view, Carey took a deep steadying breath and gave her Amarog a soft nudge. As she reached the very edge of the cliff, she risked a quick glance and immediately wished she hadn't; the cliff was sharp and so high that the bottom of the waterfall was barely discernible. She tightened her grip and stared straight ahead as her wolf started its descent down the treacherous path. As they inched down the path, the Amarog's large paws found easy purchase on the slippery rock, and the muted light proved little hindrance to their progress. Despite the wolves' agility, Carey was incredibly glad they weren't being made to go faster, as she doubted they'd be so sure-footed if they did.

The pathway wound itself in and out of the cliff, taking them through short tunnels then out into the open again as it zig-zagged down the rockface. All the while, the waterfall raced past them, showering them with a fine mist until they were completely soaked through. They were silent for a long while until Daaren finally spoke behind her.

"It's supposed to be light soon," he commented, looking upwards.

"Supposed to be?" Carey repeated. She followed the direction of his gaze.

Over their heads a great storm cloud was gathering quickly. It blocked the light from the moon and all too soon they were plunged into an oppressive darkness. Carey stared as the clouds moved impossibly fast. There was something about them that seemed very familiar...

"But there were no clouds before," she heard Fiika say. "Where did they come from?"

It was then that Carey realised where she had seen this type of weather before.

"They're no ordinary clouds," she said with a growing sense of dread. "Someone is making them."

"Making them?" Fiika asked, then in a sharp tone she said, "We need to get down from here. Now."

The Amarogs picked up the pace, but with even less light than before, Carey could feel hers starting to lose its footing on hidden rocks and narrow edges. Lying flat along its back, Carey felt the first of the raindrops. They were barely halfway, and she had a feeling that it was about to get much worse.

There came a loud crack of thunder followed by a torrential downpour.

Carey could barely see the path in front of her, let alone her companions. She felt her Amarog stop and move against the cliff wall. She could sense its fear and confusion. Through the rain, she heard Daaren call out to them as though from a great distance.

"We need to get undercover! One of the tunnels! Keep moving!"

Laying her head against the wet fur of her wolf, Carey stroked its great ear reassuringly. "Please. Just a little further."

Slowly but surely, the Amarog started to move again, but its great paws slipped treacherously on the soaked track and more than once Carey thought they were about to go over the side. They were right next to the waterfall now, and Carey noticed it was starting to lap at the edge of the path. The rain was making it swell, covering the parts of the track closest to it. Fiika had stopped completely, unable to move beyond the rushing water.

"We're trapped," Carey muttered to herself.

"We need to go back!" Fiika shouted dimly through the downpour.

"It's the same! We can't move unless the rain stops!" Carey heard Daaren reply.

Carey shook her head. "He won't stop this! He won't stop until I use magic to get us down!"

"Don't even think about it, Carey!" Fiika warned her. "We'll get you out of this! We'll—"

But her words were lost in a sudden clap of thunder and a loud rumbling overhead.

"Rockslide!"

Carey felt her Amarog slam itself against the cliff in a vain effort to protect them from the falling rocks, but it was no use; a great chunk of rock crashed down on to the path behind them, cutting them off from Daaren and shunting them forward into Fiika and her wolf. Fiika's Amarog stumbled, losing its footing completely, and in a shower of water and rocks, Carey, Fiika and the two great wolves tumbled forward into the waterfall. The raging waters hit Carey with a force unlike anything she'd ever experienced. It knocked the wind from her as she fell, and she was pushed downwards by the water, limp as a ragdoll. She tumbled over and over, unable to bring new air into her lungs. She saw the momentary flash of Fiika's armour, a glimpse of fur, then, with almost bone shattering force, she hit the pool at the base of the falls. The water thrust her beneath the surface and Carey struggled against the flow, trying desperately to find the right way up. She was tossed about by the current, slamming against a large rock. There was a searing pain as it sliced through the bare skin of her arm. Her lungs were now screaming for air and bright white spots blurred her vision. Her head was spinning, and she struck out, hoping it was the right way. Something snagged her cape and began dragging her along; Carey twisted and kicked out feebly, but the lack of oxygen left her feeling heavy and useless. She was utterly spent, and as black spots began to pop in her vision, she felt herself break the surface of the water, the cold sweet air hitting her face.

Gasping and spluttering, she thrashed about, desperate for something solid to hold on to. Her hand connected with something soft and wet and she rolled over to find the great blue Amarog clutching her cape in its teeth. She let it drag her to the shore where she flopped, shivering and exhausted on the rocks. Carey reached out and grasped at the great wolf's fur, immensely grateful for its protection. It lay beside her, alert despite their ordeal, its great eyes watchful as it panted heavily. The rain was still falling but it appeared to be letting up the tiniest bit, and Carey squinted through the haze, searching for the commanders.

"Fiika! Daaren!" she cried feebly, still struggling to pull air into her badly depleted lungs. No one answered.

She knew for sure that Fiika had fallen with her, but she wasn't sure about Daaren. She wanted so much to find them, but the longer she waited, there was a greater chance of someone or something showing up. Saar was responsible for all this, she was sure of it, but Carey didn't want to wait around to see what he sent next.

Shakily, she got to her feet, holding onto the great blue wolf. Blood was pouring from the wound in her arm, and she grasped it hard to staunch the flow. Looking around, she could see no evidence of her companions anywhere; no armour or loose weaponry. Her heart bashed against her chest as she tried not to focus on the worst — perhaps Fiika had been washed farther downstream. Perhaps Daaren was still up on the cliff, trapped until the rain stopped. As much as she wanted to stay and search for them, Carey needed to get out of there and make for the Centre City. It wasn't far, and if her Amarog wasn't injured, they would make good time. Providing Saar didn't get in her way...

Checking her sword was still tight at her waist — it had miraculously survived their fall — Carey pulled herself up onto her Amarog and took one last look about for Fiika, but to no avail. If she managed to get to the city safely and end all of this, she would come back for them, make sure they were all right. They had to be all right...

"To the Centre City," she said in the most commanding tone she could manage, and the great beast sped away from the falls.

Squinting against the rain, they raced through a thin layer of trees before finding themselves on an open plain. There, in the distance, was the Centre City. Carey had never been so glad to see that castle, but she was also aware of how vulnerable she was out in the open. She drew her sword and held it at the ready for extra measure. They had cleared the rain now, and they could finally see the sun rising to their left. As it rose above the horizon, Carey spotted four or five black dots silhouetted against it. They were high in the sky and growing larger by the moment, clearly heading in their direction.

Cursing, Carey watched as they grew closer. Griffons. With sharp talons that glinted in the morning sun, and wicked black eyes, they were gaining on her rapidly. Her Amarog sensed them and growled menacingly as it sped along, although Carey couldn't see how the wolf could defend her against five full-sized griffons. Within minutes they were upon them, their great beating wings thumping loudly. Carey raised her sword and as she did so, they dove, one after the other.

Carey's sword flashed blue as she swung it through the air with all her might. The first two veered out of reach of the weapon, but the others kept coming. Ducking out of the way of the third, Carey's sword connected with the leg of the fourth. The griffon screeched in agony as it hit the ground to their right, thrashing about in the grass. The others shrieked angrily, diving again at Carey and her wolf. One of the griffons came at them head on, only to meet its fate in the teeth of Carey's Amarog. They stumbled for a moment as the griffon was dispatched; it clearly stood no chance against the massive wolf. The remaining three griffons assaulted Carey all at once, their large talons stretching towards her as if to take hold of her. At the last moment, she flattened herself against the back of her Amarog just as it skidded to a halting stop; the three griffons, missing them by barely an inch, crashed into the ground with a sickening crunch. They screeched in pain and fury, their great wings flapping and flailing about as they lay writhing in a heap in the long grass. Dodging past them, Carey didn't turn around to see if they had recovered or not; the Centre City was close now and she could just see the gates in the distance. If she could get within the gates at least, she wouldn't have to worry about any griffons following them through.

Absorbed in this thought, Carey didn't notice the griffon she had wounded with her sword until it was right above her. She only just managed to raise her sword in time, the blade slicing at its underbelly. As it flew past her, plunging to the ground for a second time, one of its talons clipped the side of Carey's head and she screamed in agony. Hot, sticky red blood poured down the side of her face. Her head felt as though it was going to split in two from the pain as she fell forward onto her Amarog, barely holding on. The beast growled; glancing upwards she saw the towering grey walls of the city through the blood and the pain.

Just a little farther. A little farther, she told herself, clutching the wolf's fur. *Almost there...*

~Chapter Twenty-Five~

Truth and Consequences

Voices. They came and went, ebbed and flowed like waves upon the shore. Carey tried to speak; she tried to warn them. Her head felt as though it would burst but she needed to speak. Someone touched her wrist — she reached out, trying to catch hold of them, but she was pushed back down. Her arms felt so heavy. She felt hands on her wrists, someone dabbing gently at her head with a damp washer.

"Please... you must... Acheron... where is h... must know..." she mumbled, struggling to string together a coherent sentence. It was there, all in her head, but her mouth refused to cooperate. She cried out in pain and frustration; the hands on her wrists tightened.

"Carey... Carey, relax. You need to relax..." she heard a familiar voice say, but she couldn't.

"No... you must... it's Acheron... he needs to... be..." she strained to say, but before Carey could finish, she felt herself overcome by a wave of calm. The voices disappeared completely; her body relaxed, a feeling of absolute bliss overwhelmed her and she drifted off into a dreamless sleep...

Princess... Princess... Time to wake up... Wake up!

The light was soft on the backs of her eyelids, her bed warm and soft.

Carey frowned.

She opened her eyes and found herself staring at the ceiling of the Healer's Ward. Only, it wasn't the Healer's Ward at all.

She bolted upright, clutching her head — it was healed, no bandage or graze from the griffon's talon. But she wasn't tired or disorientated. She wasn't either of those things because this wasn't real. She'd been summoned.

"Good morning, Princess."

He was standing at the doorway to the ward, tall and thin and dark, his eyes shining in the morning light drifting through the stained-glass. Carey didn't move, didn't speak as he sauntered towards her, triumph on his face.

"You look... well," Saar said, the ends of his mouth twitching up into a sneer.

Carey gripped the bed sheets tightly in her fists, her knuckles turning white. She needed to get out of here, away from this man and his rancorous lies. She would not listen to him, would not allow him to get his claws in.

Clenching her jaw, Carey closed her eyes against Saar and tried to will herself back to her body. If only she could use her magic...

"You think that wise, Princess?" she heard Saar say in mocking tones, and Carey snapped her eyes open again, glaring at the Imperial at the end of her bed.

"Let me go," she snarled, not bothering to contain her anger.

He cocked his head to the side, as though considering her request. "Now why would I do that?"

She glared murderously up at him. Carey didn't much like sitting in this bed, having Saar look down on her.

"Let. Me. Go," she said again as she swung her legs to the side of the bed and stood up.

'He can't hurt me here,' Carey reminded herself as she took a step towards Saar, her back straight and chin high. 'He can't hurt me...'

He was still looking down at her with a wide grin on his sharp features, as though the whole situation was amusing. He leaned in.

"Not until you give me what I want."

Carey spat a curse at him, but the full meaning of his words made her want to be sick. It didn't matter that she had made it back to the City, that she had defeated an Imperial army and escaped Shadow Dæmons. He was going to keep her here as long as he liked; until she surrendered, he was not letting her go. She had failed. She had failed Marjen and Sirona and everyone else, and he knew it.

Carey's hands balled into fists at her side as she stared back. Fury spiked within her at the thought of his winning, but she simply gritted her teeth and said nothing. Saar took a step closer.

"You can't keep at this forever, Princess," he breathed, barely a foot apart from

her now. "Look what denying me has done so far. I mean, the Vuletian Captain was a great man. If you had only—"

"Don't you dare," Carey hissed, breaking her silence. "Don't you dare talk about Marjen. Not after what you did to his family."

Saar's smile widened. "Marjen, is it now? Don't tell me you were friends?" he said in mock-concern, but Carey didn't answer.

To hear Marjen's name come from his lips made her want to tear at his face. Her heart was pounding furiously now, and all the anger and rage she had harboured for this man was firing through her veins, fuelled by his toxic words.

Saar clicked his tongue, raising an eyebrow. "I might have tried to break him once. Clearly, I failed. But Princess," he leered at her, "At least I wasn't the one who killed him."

"Liar!" Carey bellowed.

His words cut through her, severing her tether to logic and reason.

"You killed him! You sent those monsters, not me! It was all you!"

"Really?" Saar moved right into her space so she had to tilt her head back to look at him. "I gave you a chance. Several, if I remember correctly," he said in a low, dangerous voice. "I offered you something greater than that of a Seeker and you turned me down. If you had joined me, offered your magic freely, you would never have been there. You would never have met the Vuletian Captain. It goes without saying, that had you considered my proposals, he would still be alive. So, tell me, Princess. Tell me that this isn't your fault."

Her rage was simmering. Her body was shaking, and her breathing was shallow and rough at his words. Carey knew it wasn't the truth, that this was all his doing, but his venomous lies were blinding her. She tightened her hands at her sides, feeling her nails cut into her palms.

"I have you now, though," he continued, lifting a hand and running one of his fingers along her jaw. "And I am not letting go. Your healer friend has you tucked safe and warm in the Healer's Ward in the castle, and your parents have retired for the night. No one has questioned why the quiet and unassuming Lord Acheron is sitting at your side, not when they trust him so."

Saar was sneering down at her, revelling in the effect his words had on Carey. "So, here or there, I. Have. You."

Carey stared at him seething; fear and fury crashing about within her. She stepped back a few paces, her eyes on his, her jaw set.

"Let me go," she muttered again, barely in control.

She could feel her magic trying to escape, the power that always came to her rescue. Carey relished in the idea of obliterating Saar as she had done to that Imperial army; any sense of morality blown away by the power roiling about inside of her. She flexed her fingers experimentally. If he would not let her go...

Saar approached her slowly now, a predator stalking its prey. "Then give me what I want," he snarled, slow and deliberate.

He was upon her now, and she wanted nothing more than to destroy him, take his poisonous words and cut him down. Her magic was building to a peak within her, and she strained to control it as desire and fear battled each other. Saar was right before her now, trapping her against the wall.

"Then they will all die," he said, his manic eyes gleaming.

She snapped.

Carey had no control. All the hatred and anger she felt towards Saar surged from her in powerful waves. Blinding white filled the ward, wiping out the illusion in a blaze of fiery light. Her magic pulled at her centre, tugged at her very core, and she was pulled from Saar's presence. His exultant smile was the last thing to disappear from her view.

She was travelling back to her body, the black swirling about her as magic engulfed her senses, blurring thought and sight.

Carey gasped.

Something cold was reaching inside her chest. Icy tendrils stifled the warmth of her magic, wrapping themselves around it and digging in claws. Then, with an almighty wrench, it was torn from her body. She let out a feeble cry as her eyes flew open.

"Well, that was easy," came Saar's voice, his tone filled with savage amusement.

Carey rolled her head to the side, her eyes flooding with tears, sobbing and clutching at her chest. She was in the Healer's Ward, and there at her side was Lord Acheron, Saar's silver eyes burning at her through the darkness. She coughed, unable to speak; what had been there a moment ago was now completely gone, and she was left with a void that was raw and painful. She watched as Saar reached into his robes and pulled out the blood-red Dragon's Heart. It was glowing brightly. He reached over and stroked her cheek gently; Carey was frozen at his touch.

"If only you'd joined me when I'd asked. Now we shall see what your magic is truly capable of," he leered, and his hand snaked around to grab her by the nape of her neck.

Before she could react, they were already gone. The world rushed past them, Saar's grip tight and painful. The air grew colder around them and she found herself kneeling in the snow. They had reached their destination. No sudden stops or interruptions this time. They were exactly where Saar meant for them to be. Carey lifted her head, still clutching at her breast, and felt her world shatter.

Before them was a great stone arch, its face etched with unintelligible markings. On one side stood the woman holding a bow, and on the other, the man wielding a great sword. Looking up towards the centre of the archway, Carey could see the nymph, just like at the gateway to the Common realm. It was the same, except that it stood in the middle of a snowy clearing between two steep inclines. At that moment the gateway looked through to the other side of the field — there was no white mist like the other gateway, no other world. Yet...

Before the gateway were two shapes hunched against the freezing winds whipping through the valley.

"Come, Princess," Saar said, hauling her to her feet, his hand still at her neck. "It is time you joined us."

Trudging through the snow, Saar dragged Carey to the foot of the gateway and threw her beside the other two bodies. Gasping from the cold, Carey wrapped her arms around her body. Her breath rose in clouds from her lips and she could already feel the tips of her fingers starting to go numb. She glanced sideways to find that the two figures were none other than Lady Sirona and Princess Mizéi. Her heart leapt with relief at seeing them alive. Sirona was awake and alert, huddled under a thin shawl, but Princess Mizéi was still, her eyes closed, and head bowed to the ground. As Saar walked by her, he pointed to her, a thin stream of gold winding its way around her body. As the magic faded, Mizéi's eyes flew open and she gasped. She looked around frantically, momentarily dazed.

"You dozed off there, Princess," Saar said derisively. "Our final guest has arrived. Time to start the show."

He turned his back on the three women and crouched down at the base of the archway. Sirona leaned towards Carey and whispered, "Carey, what happened? Did you make it back? Did you manage to get back to the Centre City?"

Carey swallowed dryly. "I did but... I didn't get a chance to warn anyone..." she murmured haltingly, stumbling over the pain in her chest where her magic used to be.

Sirona's face fell. "And then?"

Carey managed to shake her head, shame now burning at her cheeks. "I lost control—"

"Indeed," Saar cut across, turning away from the arch. He'd clearly been listening. "And now I have the best of you. Magic of all three." He held up the Dragon's Heart victoriously. "And to think you were going to pass up this opportunity."

"Opportunity?" Princess Mizéi spat contemptuously, her voice shaking from the cold. "To help you rebuild the Empire and terrorise yet another realm of people? I care not that this gateway has been found, particularly if its opening will bring about more misery. I would have preferred it remained lost."

Saar raised an eyebrow unenthusiastically. "Again, Mizéi, you bore me with your sanctimonious opinions. You should see this as an honour. You will be part of history."

Mizéi snorted derisively. "As accomplices to the subjugation of an entire realm? Call me old fashioned, but I don't see the honour in that."

"Yes, and yet you will still be remembered for it regardless because the time has come, and since no white knights have arrived to save the day —" he motioned to the empty clearing with outstretched arms "— it seems I am free to open it."

Hopelessly wishing she could use magic to get herself out of this mess, Carey watched as Saar placed a hand on the Dragon's Heart. He closed his eyes and grinned as burning red tendrils of magic flowed from the stone into his hands. A rush of magic flurried about them, whipping up snow and creating a column of icy wind. Carey turned her head against it, trying desperately to keep her eyes on Saar, but the wind only intensified, burning her cheeks and thrashing at her exposed skin. Through the haze she could just make out the bright red glow of the magic flowing from the Dragon's Heart.

Then the wind died as suddenly as it had begun, and the Dragon's Heart glowed no more. Saar looked triumphant, and Carey couldn't help thinking with an infinite amount of horror that Saar was now possibly even stronger than Malevolence had ever been.

"Aah, now *this* is power," he sighed, stretching his fingers.

"You can wield our magic, but you will never be able to open that gateway," Sirona hissed. "The Gadælic scholars were the only ones who knew how to open a gateway, and if I remember rightly, your Empire destroyed much of that history."

Saar gave a humourless bark of laughter as he walked coolly over to stand before her. "Ah, see that is where you are wrong, My Lady. We only made it seem that way. The Dark Empress was never so short-sighted as to dispose of anything truly important. But of course, even if we had, you undoubtedly know how it is done, don't you?" he said, suddenly deadly serious, all traces of ill-humour gone.

"Sirona," Carey said nervously, "What does he mean? How do you open the gateway?"

"Since the Lady Sirona was so kind to point it out, she shall be helping me with this task today. Let us put that pesky problem of your immortality to the test, shall we?" Saar said menacingly.

He began to raise his arm, reaching out towards Sirona; at the same time, she lifted from the snow, her face defiant but fearful. Slowly, she began to drift towards him, her toes dragging along the top of the snow until she was right before him. With a licentious grin upon his lips, Saar wrapped his arm around her shoulders, pressing Sirona's back against his chest. With his other hand he pulled a long silver dagger from within his cloak. Carey and Mizéi stumbled to their feet in alarm, all thoughts of the cold gone, but they were forced back to their knees with a single look from Saar.

"What!? You can't be serious?!" Carey cried out, unable to move. "Sirona!"

"Acheron, stop! This is madness!" screamed Mizéi in horror.

"Oh, there is nothing mad about it," Saar said casually as he raised the dagger to Sirona's throat. "My Princess here," he nodded in Carey's direction "knows exactly the lengths I will go to."

"Saar," Sirona pleaded. "Please."

"Hmm, I don't think so."

Petrified, Carey gazed up into Sirona's eyes; they were filled with a desperate fear that pierced her very soul.

And then, there was nothing.

"No..." Mizéi uttered despairingly.

Dagger dripping with blood, Saar threw Sirona's lifeless body to the ground before the gateway. Carey stared incomprehensibly at Sirona's motionless form.

"Come on, Sirona" she mumbled, remembering the way Sirona had been revived on the pirate ship. "Please heal. Please come back."

But as the moments slid by, Sirona's face grew paler and paler. Carey bit back a sob as blood stained the snow about Sirona's body; a red blight upon the landscape.

How was this possible? She was supposed to be immortal, eternal, but now... It was as though she had never been any greater than the rest of them. Carey wanted to know how, wanted to know why Death had finally been able to recognise her. Had it been because without her magic, she was no longer a witch? Had stripping her powers made her vulnerable? With a shuddering breath, Carey turned her head away from her fallen friend. Whatever the reason, it didn't matter now — it was clear with every passing minute that Sirona was not coming back.

Tears welling in her eyes, Carey looked up at Saar with utter contempt. He was wiping the blood from his weapon onto his hand, grinning manically as he did so.

"It would seem the power of the Dragon's Heart is absolute. Mortal after all," he said dispassionately, and he turned from them.

He walked over to the guardian on the right. Reaching up, he smeared some of Sirona's blood on the stone; he then walked to the other side and did the same. Walking to the centre of the archway, he lifted both hands skywards in offering. Saar began to mutter something inaudible, and Carey watched as magic shot from his outstretched hands and hit the Nymph above him. It rebounded and ricocheted within the archway, creating a great glittering spiderweb of magic. Then, with a great burst of light and a thunderous roar, the gateway exploded into life, showering them with golden sparks. Saar was silhouetted against the light of the archway, his arms outstretched gleefully, his face contorted in savage delight as his robes swirled around him.

"No," Carey breathed, still on her hands and knees in the freezing snow.

Saar turned back to them. Without saying a word, he raised his hands again and lifted Carey from the ground just as he had done with Sirona. Mizéi cried out as Saar closed his hand around Carey's neck. His lips widened into a grin as he slowly tightened his grip, cutting at her windpipe. Carey gagged and spluttered; she grasped at his wrist with her hands, but her attempts were futile. He was too strong. As she struggled, she saw the Dragon's Heart fall from the folds of Saar's robes to rest openly on his chest. If only she could reach it...

"I so hoped we could have done this together," Saar whispered in her ear. "Goodbye, dear Princess..."

Saar lifted the stained dagger to her throat.

"Carey!"

"What—"

Distracted, Saar's hand slackened on Carey's throat. A shot of bright red sparks flew past their heads. Both eyes locked on the Dragon's Heart, Carey snatched at the stone, her fingers wrapping around the pendant. Noticing her attempt, Saar made to slash at her with the dagger, but was hit on the shoulder by a red curse. Flesh smouldering, he roared in pain, dropping

Carey to the ground. The Dragon's Heart broke from its chain and Carey held it to her chest as she landed hard upon the snow. Looking up, she saw Ji, Kat, and her father running towards them, curses flying at Saar. Stumbling back towards the gateway and clutching his shoulder, Saar dove for the white swirling smoke. Carey reached out towards him.

"No!" she shouted, but he was already gone, whisked away to the other side.

~Chapter Twenty-Six~

Into the Flames

"Carey! Carey, are you all right?"

Her father skidded to her side, but Carey was already on her feet, trying to push past him to the gateway. Her surprise at seeing any of them there was overridden by the immediate urge to pursue Saar.

"We need to go after him! We need to catch him," Carey said urgently.

She was not about to let Saar get away, but Robert stopped her, grabbing her by the shoulders.

"Carey, no. Wait. You can't," he said gently, holding her back.

"Why not? He's probably just on the other side there!" she cried in frustration. "We have to go after him!"

She tried to push past her father again, but he held her back.

"First of all, we don't know what kind of world is on the other side. We could go running into something we are completely unprepared for," her father said calmly. "Also, he took your powers from you. We know about the necklace," he added in explanation at her look of surprise. "How do you expect to go after him?"

Carey thrust out her hand; the scarlett pendant of the Dragon's Heart was nestled in her palm. "I have it here. I have my powers back—"

"Carey, wait."

Mizéi was getting to her feet with Ji's help. "You managed to get it back?"

Carey held it out for the others to see. "I grabbed it from him just before he disappeared. I have my powers back—"

Mizéi shook her head. "Not quite. You can access them through the stone, but they will never fully be part of you again. If you lose it, then you will also lose your powers. It also means that I cannot use mine unless I possess the stone myself. My people know the Lore of the Dragon's Heart well."

Looking down at the stone, blood pounding in her ears, Carey asked, "Is there any way we can retrieve our powers from the stone?"

"Yes, but only one. We must return it to where it came from."

Ji cleared his throat. "And where might that be, exactly?" he asked.

Carey had a feeling she was not going to like Mizéi's answer.

"The village is now gone but the bush remains," Mizéi said slowly. "In the heart of Dragon country."

Robert Lee exhaled deeply. "On the edge of the Darklands."

Mizéi confirmed this with a nod. "I am afraid so."

Carey's father was silent for a moment. "Then we will make plans. Go once the two of you are strong enough."

"What? Wait!" Carey said incredulously. She pulled out of her father's grip, her breathing heavy and her body buzzing with impatience. "No, we need to go as soon as possible. I can't be without my powers."

"But Carey—"

Carey shook her head stubbornly. "No. We have the stone now. As careful as we can be, I'm not going to risk losing it, or worse."

Robert considered it for a moment before nodding in agreement. "Fine. Are you able? Is there anything you need healing first?"

"No. I'm fine," Carey said immediately.

Her body was aching, pain pinching and burning all over, but the anticipation of having her magic back was enough to make her forget it all. She was not about to give up now. Not after what had just happened.

"As am I," Mizéi added.

"Then I will return to the Centre City with Lady Sirona," Carey's father said, helping Carey up out of the snow. "Kat, Ji, go with Carey and Princess Mizéi."

"But, how?" Carey asked, suddenly realising she had no idea of how they had gotten there in the first place.

Ji smiled. "We may not be so well versed in Wayfaring, but we had a little help," he said, indicating over his shoulder.

Standing some way away from the action was a small thin figure, but Carey knew that shock of red hair anywhere. "Of course."

Carey watched as her father bent down at the foot of the gateway and gently lifted Sirona's limp form up into his arms. Her head was curled against Robert's chest, and Carey set her jaw against the tightness in her chest as he walked towards Seramina. She watched sadly as he said something to her, wondering if Sirona had known what the Dragon's Heart could do. Perhaps she did and that's why she knew of it. Perhaps that is why she seemed so scared before her death. She knew there was no coming back from it this time.

Seramina reached up and gently touched Robert on the arm; he disappeared, leaving behind a slight haze in the air that soon vanished too.

Kat came up beside her as they trudged towards Seramina through the snow. It took every fibre of Carey's being to not turn around and run through the gateway. A deep desire for revenge was pulsing through her, but logic held her back. She would find Saar again — she would not stop until she had. But first she needed her magic back.

"I'm sorry we took so long to get here," Kat said in a low voice. "We could have saved you all if we'd been faster."

"You found out about Saar, then?" Carey said. "You managed to get close to him?"

Kat nodded. "It's a long story, but yes."

"How did you know we were here?" Mizéi asked, her face drawn but determined.

Again, Ji nodded in Seramina's direction. "The moment she stood in the Healer's Ward she knew exactly where they'd gone. Don't ask me how she does it — she's a wizarding genius, that one."

"Please tell me you're not talking about me again, Ji," Seramina said coyly as they approached.

"I'm only telling the truth," he said with a grin.

Shaking her head shyly, Seramina blushed. "I'm just trying to help. That's all."

306

Letting go of Kat's arm, Carey rushed over and gave the young girl a warm hug. "You've done so much more than that. Thank you."

Seramina's cheeks turned an even darker shade of red. "So where are we going?" she said, diverting the conversation.

Carey held out the Dragon's Heart, her pulse racing. "The Darklands. We need to return this so that Mizéi and I can regain our powers. Can you take us there?"

Seramina frowned. "I've never been so I don't think I could take you exactly where you need to go. I only managed to get here because I followed you and Lord Acheron," she said regretfully.

Mizéi stepped forwards. "What if I could tell you? I know the Lore; I could probably get us fairly close."

As Mizéi described the location, Carey looked sideways at Ji. After all that distance and the sleepless nights, he was finally there, standing at her side. She took his hand in her own and gave it a small squeeze.

"Thank you for coming," she said quietly to him.

His face was a mixture of confusion and surprise, and he was about to reply when Seramina cut across. Carey quickly released his hand.

"All right everyone. I need you all to hold onto my arm. It might be a bit bumpy with all of us at once so hold on tight," she said, proffering her arm.

The four of them took hold of her, and before Carey could look back towards the gateway, they found themselves racing away from the freezing mountainside.

*

Carey stumbled a little; the ground beneath their feet was hard and uneven, infinitely different to that from which they had just come. Seramina was on her hands and knees beside her, gasping for breath.

"Seramina!"

Carey and Kat pulled her up off the ground; her face was ashen.

"What's the matter?" Carey said, her eyes roving over her, searching for a wound.

"I don't know. There's something different," she said weakly.

"Wayfaring doesn't usually do this to someone," Mizéi said concernedly. "Something's wrong."

"I say let's get that stone back to where it came from so we can get her back to the Centre City," Ji said as they settled her down on more even ground.

Kat was staring out past Ji's shoulder "Um, everyone? I think we're in the right place."

They found themselves standing on an outcrop of blackened and burnt rock overlooking a vast gorge. The surroundings were desolate; even darker and wilder than that of the Dead Plains. The skeletal remains of burnt trees and animals littered the landscape. Large, sharp rock formations jutted out of the ground, slicing their way through the surface. Smoke rose from several small fires, mixing with the humid, bitter air. The sky was monstrously dark; the black clouds were tinted red and hung low over the canyon, and everywhere shrieks and booming roars rent the air.

Dragons.

They meandered through the skies above and roamed the plains below. Mizéi pointed out each of the different species. The great red and gold ones which strode through the wasteland spewing fire as they went were Sorth. The Bazzalth — long, thin dragons with inky black bodies — slithered about, fighting over half eaten carcases. Vanlith were giant green monsters with long sharp spines that ran down their backs; they flew about lazily, looking down over the valley with piercing yellow eyes. And finally, there were the Niadhogr, colossal electric blue dragons that looked more like great snakes, with a shock of white fur that lined their backs. They snaked and curled their way through the air, their brothers curled upon the blackened ground below, thin streams of smoke rising constantly from their nostrils.

The group ducked low and crawled out to the edge of the outcrop. From there they had a perfect overview of the entire canyon.

"There. See it? Right in the middle of the canyon," Mizéi said, pointing to the middle of the gorge.

Squinting, Carey made out a large bush with dark green foliage. "It's not burnt."

"Its magic protects it, which is lucky for us, I suppose," said Mizéi.

"And of course, it's in the very centre," Ji said dryly. "So, what's the plan? Mizéi?"

"The Lore is very specific but simple. We need to return the stone to the tree to have our powers restored," she explained.

"I can Guide you there," Seramina said faintly, to the protests of the others.

"Not a chance, Ser," Ji said with a shake of his head. "We need you to get us back to the Centre City. Stay here and try to recover. You're no good to us if you wipe yourself out."

"Ji's right. You need to stay here and keep a lookout," Kat agreed, and Seramina nodded unhappily.

"Can Ji and I do it for you?" Kat now asked hopefully, yet Carey had a sneaking suspicion it wouldn't be so simple. She was right; Mizéi shook her head.

"If only. Unfortunately, Carey and I must be there when it's returned otherwise our magic will disperse and it will be lost forever."

Carey bit her bottom lip. She wasn't at all eager to tackle an entire horde of dragons without her magic. She would've given anything to at least have her Vuletian sword with her.

"All right, this is how we'll do it," Kat said, taking charge. "I'll go with Mizéi. Ji, go with Carey. Stay close and try not to get split up."

Everyone nodded in agreement and Mizéi and the three Seekers began descending the steep decline.

"Stay close," Ji murmured to Carey as they ducked behind a tall shard of rock at the bottom.

"You don't have to tell me twice," she replied as they took a moment to survey the landscape.

"The bush is that way," Kat pointed past a fallen tree. "We'll go first and then signal for you to follow."

Kat and Mizéi dashed out from behind the rock; as Carey watched them go, she noticed Ji blinking rapidly.

"Ji, what is it? Why are you doing that?"

He waved away her concern. "It's nothing. The atmosphere here is just a little funny. I can see outlines, vibrations, but they're a little less defined than usual."

She grabbed him by the shoulder and turned him around to face her. "Are you sure? I don't want you getting hurt."

Ji managed a smile and gripped her hand. "I'm sure."

Kat waved from behind the tree, and Ji and Carey made a run for it. They were almost at the tree when an ear-piercing shriek rent the air. A blue Niadhogr rose from behind a nearby rock, its eyes glowing viciously. It had been hiding, unseen by the four wizards until now, and the noise had alerted the other dragons. Carey could see more of them starting to turn their way.

"Ji! Carey! Run!"

Ji reached out and grabbed Carey's hand, and they ran for the others. The Niadhogr was now advancing on them, snaking along the ground, its claws gouging deep marks in the earth.

"Get behind me!" Kat shouted as she held out her hands.

The Niadhogr slammed against the shield of magic she produced, but it was strong, and Kat buckled under its force. Ji wheeled around and shot a bright red curse which hit the dragon on the back, singeing its fur and making it screech in pain. As it flailed about, Kat, Carey, Mizéi and Ji bolted out from behind the tree, dashing between rocks until the Niadhogr was far behind them.

"Keep going!" Mizéi shouted, taking the lead. "It's this—"

A great golden tail swung out from nowhere and caught Mizéi in the stomach, throwing her backwards into the other three. They fell hard onto the scorched earth as the glimmering Sorth came into view, its every movement sending tremors through the ground. Scrambling to their feet, they noticed a second dragon approaching from behind: a sleek black Bazzalth, and it was eyeing them hungrily.

"Carey! You have the stone. You can use our powers!" Mizéi screeched.

Shoving her hand into her pocket, she withdrew the blood-red stone, cursing herself for not thinking of it sooner. Kat and Ji were now standing back-to-back, firing off a volley of curses, but the golden Sorth was undeterred, and the black Bazzalth was lithe and quick, dodging the burning red sparks. Carey held the stone tight and at once felt the magic within flowing from the stone into her. It was beyond anything she had ever felt; more than she'd ever experienced. The landscape before her, the dragons and fiery sky were suddenly infinitely brighter, and her senses were immediately heightened. She saw the Bazzalth duck a curse and dive at them, black eyes glinting hungrily. Without hesitation, Carey dropped to one knee and released a blast of magic, knocking the dragon to the ground, unconscious. The Sorth roared with rage as its brother fell, and opened its mighty jaws, spewing fire at the wizards. Ji managed to shield them, causing the fire to splash against the invisible barrier while the others ran for cover. The Sorth attempted to follow them but Carey rebuffed it, her magic bouncing off its tough scales with enough force to send it stumbling backwards.

They had now caused enough of a scene to attract quite a bit of unwanted attention. Carey looked up to see at least nine different dragons flying towards them, and the ground shook with the arrival of several more. They were not going to wait around; they took off again, running past startled dragons and ducking behind a large pile of rocks as another Sorth let loose a jet of flames in their direction.

As they waited for it to stop, a bright green Vanlith appeared to their right, catching them unawares. It swung its great spiked tail around, catching Ji on the arm and knocking him to the ground.

"No!" Carey screamed, knocking out the Vanlith with a curse in response as she ran to Ji's side.

His face was contorted with pain as he clutched his arm, blood seeping out from between his fingers.

"It's not too bad. You need to get going," he muttered through gritted teeth.

"Not likely. We're not leaving you," Carey said, trying to think of what to do.

Beside her, Kat shouted as another Bazzath slithered around the corner,

311

advancing warily. Carey gripped the bottom of her shirt, ripped a strip of material from the waist and wrapped it quickly around Ji's arm. She had never mended a wound magically, and this hardly seemed the time to attempt it.

"There. It's definitely not of the same calibre as Rupert's work but it should do for now," she said, tying it off.

"Good. Now let's go!" Kat shouted, shunting back the Bazzath that had tried to take advantage of their distraction.

With the bleeding staunched, Ji got to his feet and followed Mizéi, who had taken the lead again. Kat was bringing up the rear, trying her best to stun the persistent Bazzath behind them. Another Vanlith roared overhead and to their right a Niadhogr slithered in and out of rock formations as it followed them. The Vanlith dove suddenly, landing with a thud upon the ground in front of Mizéi. Its outstretched wings blocked their way; its great belly gurgling with the sound of distant thunder. Smoke curled at its nostrils and Carey knew she wouldn't get there in time...

Over the roar of the Vanlith, Carey called out, "Mizéi! Stone!" and launched the Dragon's Heart into the air towards the Princess.

Mizéi caught it deftly, and as the dragon spewed forth a fountain of fire, Mizéi raised her hands. Carey gasped in horror as the flames enveloped her, for a moment thinking that she'd not been fast enough, but then the fire began to swirl faster and faster around the princess. It grew brighter and hotter... the dragons began to back away, unsure of what was happening, then with a force greater than anything the dragons had shown, the flames shot back at the Vanlith, engulfing it in flames. As the creature howled and shrieked, the Bazzath turned and fled; the Niadhogr retreated into the shadows and stayed there, its eyes glowing through the darkness. Mizéi appeared from within the fire, untouched and clutching the stone, much to Carey's relief.

"What just happened?" Kat asked, panting as she watched the other dragons flee and the Vanlith continue to roar.

It stumbled away, screeching in agony, its own flames consuming it.

"So that's the kind of thing you can do," Carey said, unlikely to forget the ghastly sight of the burning dragon anytime soon.

"Using its power against it? Yes," Mizéi said gravely, her breathing shallow and tight. "You need not wonder why I don't tell many people about it. But now we are free to continue. The bush is not far now. Come."

After the spectacle of the burning Vanlith, it seemed the rest of the dragon population were happy to keep their distance. However, Carey suspected that this wouldn't last long, and as the bush came into view, they noticed the blue Niadhogr from before beginning to creep back out of the shadows.

"Ah, ladies…" Ji said nervously as another Bazzalth stuck its head out from behind a pile of rocks.

The dragons were quickly regaining their confidence.

"Go!" Kat screamed as a Sorth soared low overhead.

Her cry triggered an onslaught and dragons appeared on all sides, roaring and shrieking. As the four of them ran for the bush, the dragons advanced, slithering, flying, and snaking their way towards them. Mizéi reached the bush first and held up the crystal. As the others skidded to her side, they saw a thin vine curl up from the centre of the bush; it wound its way around the Dragon's Heart, reclaiming it.

"Mizéi…?" Carey said nervously as the dragons grew closer and closer. "Look…"

The Dragon's Heart was glowing again, bright red against the gloom. Long tendrils curled from the crystal, flitting round and round, searching. The dragons were almost on top of them, and the magic stretching from the stone paused, then it shot forth. Carey gasped as it converged with her chest, flowing through her body.

With a collective roar, the dragons pounced on the wizards…

Fire split the air as magic burned behind her eyes…

"Time to go," a voice said, and someone grabbed her by the arm.

~Chapter Twenty-Seven~

Out of Balance

The sky was dark despite it only being midday. The cold winds were at odds with the toxic black clouds; the red lining them bright and angry. It had snowed during the night, creating a layer of slush that lined the streets of the Centre City. Carey stood on a balcony overlooking the courtyard, a fur shawl wrapped around her shoulders. It had only been a day since Seramina had brought them back after the dragon onslaught, yet it felt infinitely longer. Down in the courtyard castle, craftsmen worked on the rose statue, carving the names Carey had brought back with her. She had no news yet of Fiika or Daaren, but she fervently hoped their names wouldn't be added to the memorial. Sirona's people had arrived in the early morning to collect her, draped in black and speechless with grief. A young man accepted Carey's explanation in silence, yet she felt no judgment or resentment on their behalf; their sorrow was rooted wholly in their love and respect for the impossible woman who had been their protector and friend for so long. As she had watched them disappear into the distance, Carey felt yet another piece of her wither and die. Another friend, another ally…

She heard footsteps behind her, and Kat leaned on the balcony beside her.

"They just announced that they'll be closing the gateway to the Common Realm," she said flatly, watching the workers below. "At least that will put an end to this mad weather and the balance will be restored."

"That's what Ji and Seramina were affected by, wasn't it?" Carey asked, only half interested.

"Apparently if you have just two of the gateways open it throws out the balance of magic between the realms," Kat said, turning her back to the courtyard and leaning back on the railing. "It's either one gateway or all three, and since we have no idea where the gateway between the Common Realm and the Third World are, it makes sense just to close the one to the Common Realm for now."

"Well we're certainly not closing the one we just opened," Carey said bitterly.

She had every intention of going after Saar and considering what it had cost them to open that gateway, there was no way she was going to see it closed again.

"Well I don't think that was really ever an option," Kat said pointedly.

"As soon as we have this sorted, I'm going after him," Carey said, balling her hands into fists, her fingernails cutting into her palms. "He has bigger plans, Kat. Like I said to my parents last night, this was just one part of a bigger plan. He wants to bring back the Empire, that's for sure, but that's not all. I got the feeling there was something else. Something he never said aloud..."

She waited for Kat to speak, but she was remained still. They stood in silence for a time and Carey continued to watch the workers below.

"How did you find out Acheron was Saar?" she heard herself ask, listening to the clink of metal on stone.

Kat pursed her lips, letting her head flop backwards as she gazed up at the sky.

"The night of the ball, when you didn't come back, we looked everywhere. Seramina began to notice something strange about Acheron — she said it was like his memories were mixed up with someone else's all of a sudden."

Carey frowned. "I know he'd been employing magic against her to block his true thoughts and feelings — maybe he was losing control over it."

"Or maybe Seramina was getting stronger," Kat suggested, which Carey supposed was probably the more likely scenario. "In any case, that was enough for us to suspect him in having a hand in your disappearance."

"And you received my warning?" Carey asked, looking up from the courtyard below.

315

"What? That tiny note on the strange disappearing paper?" Kat smiled slightly. "It only made us more suspicious. It was the day before we received word of your being in Hilarus that we confirmed Acheron was Saar."

"How?"

"My abilities are apparently… much more pronounced than we originally thought," Kat said slowly. "It would seem that I can read people without needing to touch them."

"But I wasn't gone that long," Carey said, raising her eyebrows. "You managed to develop your power to that extent in such a short time?"

"I think Rupert explains it well enough. He thinks that I just didn't know I *could* do it, that I'd been so focused on the physical aspect of it that I hadn't even tried. Wanting to find you seemed to prove suitable motivation, however."

Carey scoffed, impressed. "Just, don't read me, no matter how tempting," she said, and Kat pouted comically.

"Well, you're no fun."

"Did you tell my parents once you knew it was him?" Carey continued, suppressing a laugh.

At this, Kat's smile turned downwards. "We did, but only because we knew that when the time came, we'd be easily outmatched if we tried to take on Saar ourselves. We held back, watching him, waiting for the moment that it would be safe to expose him. We all knew that if we tried to approach him too early, he would disappear, and you with him."

"So," Carey drew out the vowel, "You essentially used me as bait."

Kat looked at her sheepishly, but Carey gave her a shrug. "I understand. It's the only way you could have caught him out."

"Yes, only we didn't catch him…"

The two of them fell into silence as they contemplated the consequences of this statement.

"It'll only be a matter of time," Carey murmured, the dark desire of revenge curling in her chest. "We'll be after him soon enough."

She shook her head; she couldn't think about that right now.

"How is Ji, by the way?"

Kat gave an exasperated sigh. "Trust him to get hit by a dragon. I just spoke to Rupert on my way here. He said he should be out by tomorrow morning. Why don't you go see him?" she suggested. "He's still in the Healer's Ward and the rest of the Council are still in session."

Ever since their return, Carey had been wondering when she'd get a chance to talk to Ji alone. It had been niggling at the corner of her mind, and despite the intensity of her feelings for him, when she tried to tell him, she found herself lost. How was she supposed to broach the subject? It wasn't exactly something you throw into casual conversation. She would just have to hope that the moment would eventually present itself.

Knocking on the doorway to the Healer's Ward, Carey steadied herself, laughing nervously at the ridiculousness of the situation. Dragons? Not a problem. Full-blown battle? A cinch. Telling Ji how she felt? Good luck with that.

The door opened and Rupert stuck his head through the crack. Despite her nerves, Carey couldn't help but grin at his head of bright turquoise hair. He noticed her eyeing his bright new hairdo and ran a hand through it confidently.

"My stylist though' I needed a new look. Like it?" he winked, giving Carey a warm hug.

"I think your sister has fantastic taste," she grinned before adding a little more seriously, "Ji?"

He nodded and led her into the ward. There, lying in the bed next to his brother's, was Ji, looking a little worse for wear. His face was paler than usual and there were dark bags under his eyes. He squinted as they approached and said, "Carey?"

As Rupert returned to his room at the end of the ward, Carey took a seat by Ji's bed. "Are your senses still out of sorts?"

Sitting up, Ji nodded. "At least Seramina doesn't seem to be as suffering as badly from it as I am. She was out of here last night in no time at all."

"So, it's the instability between the realms that knocked her about, then?" Carey asked as she thought back to the dragon's valley and how ashen-faced Seramina had appeared. "I was worried that it was the effort of using her

317

Wayfaring abilities with so many at once."

Ji tutted in disbelief. "It seems to be the only thing that disturbs her. As far as she knows, she had no issue with the Wayfaring. The opening of the Third Realm threw her off a bit when she used her powers to get us there, made her a bit dizzy, but as soon as that dissipated, she came to our aid."

"And not a second too soon," Carey said with a shudder at the thought of what would have happened had Seramina not got them out of there when she had. Dragon's dinner at the very least, that's for sure. The sooner they closed the gateway to the Common Realm, the better.

"Did you hear? Kat said they're going to close the gateway to the Common Realm. I wonder how they're going to do that," Ji pondered.

"As long as it's nothing like what it took to open the other one..." Carey said, her chest tightening.

Ji patted her on the arm reassuringly and her stomach did a nervous little flip at his touch.

"If it is, I'd say the Council would rather leave it open than resort to such measures."

"How... how will we work it out?" she stammered slightly. "Saar said Malevolence took the records that detailed how it all works."

"You would think someone knows something about it. Perhaps one of the older Council members, or even one of our parents?" Ji said, shrugging. "I guess someone does, if they've decided to close it."

"Hmm, I suppose you're right," Carey concurred. "Sirona knew about it."

Ji shook his head in wonder. "I can't believe she was really as old as you say. Could you imagine what she knew? What she'd seen?"

"I have a feeling she found it very lonely," Carey said, thinking back to their time on the pirate ship. "To watch all you loved slowly disappear..."

"I suppose it would be both a blessing and a curse," Ji said pensively. "To never change while everything else did. I think I would've gone mad..."

"Perhaps she did at one point," Carey said imagined. "A thousand years is a long time..."

Ji grunted as he rested his head against the headboard. "That it is..."

Carey observed him for a moment, letting her eyes linger on his soft brown hair and his sharp, handsome features. She realised that she'd never allowed herself just to look, to take him in, and Carey saw that he was no longer the boy she'd seen in the marketplace in Monaghan. He was lean and strong, his face fuller and more defined than it had been back then. His eyelashes fanned over his high cheekbones as he lay there, eyes closed, and his lips bowed in the centre, soft and relaxed.

How had she never noticed any of this before? It was like she'd been looking at Ji through a frosted window, seeing him but not really. He took a long deep breath, and Carey leaned over and lightly touched his bandaged arm.

"How is it, by the way? You're looking a little pale."

Ji laughed. "Thanks! No, I'm fine. Rupert's just trying to determine whether there was any venom in that dragon's barbs. He says he has a number of remedies to fix that so I should be fine," he said dismissively.

"Venom?" Carey said uneasily. "That doesn't sound like something to not worry about."

"*Possible* venom," he corrected her. "And I'm sure I'll be fine. Honestly, I don't feel as bad I look. Promise."

He crossed his heart and gave her a smile that did not entirely convince her.

"Honestly! Rupert is the best healer we have. If it turns out there is, you can be sure that he'll have me fixed in no time," Ji said as she raised an eyebrow.

"Yes, well he better," she said emphatically. "Or he'll have me to answer to."

It was Ji who raised an eyebrow this time, although it was neither sceptical nor sarcastic. She had said that last thing without even thinking, inadvertently providing herself the exact moment she'd been looking for. Her heart pounding in her ears, she reached over to take Ji's hand.

"Carey, darling!"

Ji's parents, Oliver and Meela, were walking down the ward towards them, smiles upon their faces. Carey dropped her hand back to her lap in disappointment but recovered as they approached. She looked away from

Ji, avoiding his gaze.

"Oliver. Meela," she acknowledged, standing up. "I was… just about to leave." She could feel Ji's eyes on her back and heat rose in her cheeks.

"Oh," Meela said as she took a seat at the end of Ji's bed. "Won't you stay?"

Shaking her head, Carey made to leave; she could feel her face burning. If only they had stayed away a few minutes longer…

"No, I must find… my parents," she lied. "I'll see you later, Ji." She gave him a quick glance and immediately regretted doing so; the look on his face was one of confusion and disappointment and she had a suspicion that he, too, knew exactly the importance of that one lost moment.

Carey left as quickly as she could with no intention of finding her parents. She made her way to her room and flopped down on her bed, burying her face in her pillow. That moment kept running through her mind, over and over; her face burned with embarrassment as she imagined what Ji must be thinking. Breathing in the smell of the pillow's down, she debated whether to go back to the Healer's Ward and just come straight out and tell him, but something was keeping her rooted to the bed. It was as though her body was filled with lead and refused to move.

The sun dropped ever lower in the sky as she lay there with her heart and mind racing. She punched her pillow in frustration. She already knew how he felt; it had always been so evident despite her own confusion, so why was it so difficult for her to say what she wanted, now she felt the same?

Carey cast her mind back to that day on the deck with Sirona, when it had all become so clear. Clear that Ji was her Other and that was the truth of it. There was nothing else to it, only that. It had always been Ji.

Carey jumped to her feet. She felt that pull once more, that sense of urgency she'd felt on the deck of the pirate ship, and she knew what she must do.

"It's all in my head," she said firmly to herself. "I need to just go in there," she strode over to the door "and say it."

Carey marched herself back down the hallway, fighting an intense urge to run back to her room the entire way. When she reached the Healer's Ward, she pushed the door open a small way and peered inside; her heart dropped a little when she realised Ji's parents were still there. They were deep in conversation, their voices inaudible from that distance, but Carey could tell that it was something serious. Pulling herself back behind the door until she could just see them through the crack, she watched as Meela hugged her son with impassioned fervour, her body wracked with silent sobbing. His father ran his hand through Ji's hair fondly, his expression one of intense pride. Carey couldn't see Ji's face, and she honestly didn't want to. Her heart was pounding so hard that she was afraid it would give her away. What had happened between when she'd left and now? She strained her ears, trying to catch even a word of their conversation, but they were talking so softly that it was impossible.

Ji pulled away from his mother; his face was one of fierce determination and intense sadness. His expression tore at Carey's heart as her mind raced with unimaginable possibilities. She wanted to storm in there and demand to know what had happened. Perhaps it was something she could help with. Anything to take that look from Ji's face.

Instead she turned from the ward and she ran. She ran so hard and so fast, as though by doing so she could outstrip her own thoughts, run far enough from the scene she had just witnessed that she would no longer see it in her mind's eye. She was so consumed by her desire to flee the ward that she almost collided with her father, who was waiting outside her room.

"Carey!" he said in alarm, catching her by the shoulders.

"Oh, Father! I'm sorry... I didn't see you..." she stammered, quickly recovering.

"Is something the matter?" Robert asked, his eyes searching her face. "You came flying around that corner..."

Carey took a deep breath and rearranged her face into one of a happier disposition. "No. Nothing's the matter. I was just running back here to get something... for Kat," she finished rather lamely.

Luckily her father seemed happy with this explanation as he beckoned her to follow him without any further questioning. They entered her room and he took a seat by her bed; Carey sat on the edge of the bedspread, silently wondering what her father wanted while trying not to think of Ji. Her heart was still pounding.

"Carey, you've probably heard by now that we're going to close the gateway to the Common Realm," Robert started seriously, his hands clasped as he leaned forward. "We've put together a group of Council members that will travel to the gateway, and we'd like you to be part of it."

"Me?" His request surprised her so much that her anxiety over Ji was momentarily forgotten. "Does this have anything to do with my part in opening the new gateway?"

Robert shook his head. "No. I understand why you might think that, but no. You have significant power, Carey, and it would be prudent of you to be there in case it is needed."

Carey wondered if her father really knew the extent of her powers but was not about to enlighten him. Not at that moment, in any case.

"Of course," she said with a nod. "Who else will be going?"

"Your mother will be joining you. I will need to stay behind for the city," he said, referring to the need to have at least one of the royal family within the city at all times. "Meela, Oliver, Lord Carron and Lady Marksis of the Council, Katrina... and Ji."

Ji's name was almost an afterthought, and Carey wondered if it was because of his recent injuries that her father seemed hesitant in adding him.

"You will be departing tomorrow morning. Preparations are being made," Robert added. "You'll take Firefly and the others will be on horseback."

Robert stood up and placed a hand on her shoulder. "If this seems too much, you can always stay behind," he said gently. Carey shook her head fervently.

"No. This feels like something I need to see through," she said firmly. "So much of this is my fault, regardless of what everyone keeps telling me," Carey added as her father made to contradict her, "and I need to do my part."

Robert gave her shoulder as squeeze. "I'm sure you will."

*

There hadn't been another chance to speak to Ji that evening; by the time she had returned to the Healer's Ward, Ji's parents had left, and he was resting. Heavy rain had begun to fall, and large raindrops slapped hard against the long windows above his bed. Carey had stood for a moment in the doorway, watching his chest rise and fall peacefully, hoping tomorrow she would get another chance to speak with him.

It was not long after sunrise that Carey found herself standing in the courtyard, staring at the rose memorial, her eyes fixed on one name. Marjen's commanders still hadn't been found and Carey still held hope that they were merely travelling back to Hilarus and hadn't had been able to reach anyone just yet. It was, after all, almost a three-day ride and, as Carey kept reminding herself, it was better to have hope than to concede the worst. It was better not to have to add anymore names to the rose.

Carey heard someone approaching and turned to see Princess Mizéi walking towards her. She greeted her warmly.

"So, you're leaving, then?" Carey said, pulling back from her embrace.

"My people need me."

Mizéi stood back and surveyed her. "Try not to be too hard on yourself, Carey. We stood very little chance against the power of the Dragon's Heart. It is not your fault," she said as though reading Carey's mind.

Carey grimaced. "It's not only that. Friends of mine are dead, and I keep wondering that perhaps if I'd noticed Saar's deception earlier..." her voice cracked, unable to continue.

"Listen to me, Carey," Mizéi said sternly. "You can blame yourself all you like, go back and forth over everything and dwell on the what-ifs, but all that would do is keep you from moving on. You would be stuck in the past, and sooner or later you will start doubting yourself, if you haven't already started, and if what I saw the other day is anything to go on, you have absolutely nothing to doubt. Saar is to blame here and no one else. You cannot ever know how things would have gone had you done things differently, so it is best to simply learn from what has happened and move forward. I doubt anyone you have lost would have wanted you to stay stuck in the past."

Carey looked over at the memorial again and remembered what Marjen had said about not regretting the lives of those who had passed, of how she should fight instead to ensure their legacy. She could easily sink into a state of regret and self-pity, or she could be strong, take the harder route and face those demons. Yes, that's what she would do, what she *had* to do, if not for herself then for Sirona and for Marjen. She would not allow herself to wallow in the pain of the past but would instead use it to find the strength to go on.

Carey turned back to Princess Mizéi. "Thank you," she said graciously. "For everything."

Mizéi grasped Carey's shoulder briefly before saying, "Should you ever need anything, you have only to ask. Take care, Carey Lee."

With a smile, she walked beyond the castle gates to where a black Sleipnir was waiting for her, two of her own guard by its side atop their own. She mounted the horse-like creature lightly, and with a final wave, was away.

"So Mizéi has left," Carey heard Kat say from behind her.

"Her people need her more than ours do," Carey said as they watched the princess ride off into the distance.

"Ready, then?"

Carey shrugged. "I suppose. I guess I just want it done."

"Hmm. Well at least it's not far. The others are coming. Want to head to the stables?" Kat suggested, and they made their way around the side of the castle.

Firefly was bounding with happiness at the sight of her and Carey laughed.

"Hey girl," she said, patting her fondly on the muzzle. "I missed you too."

Carey climbed onto Firefly's back then joined Kat outside. "Come on. Let's go finish this."

They waited for the others back in the courtyard, and before long, they were on their way to the gateway. Ji was looking much better, thanks to Rupert, but for most of the journey he kept to himself, deep in thought. Kat tried to coax a few words from him but the most he could do was mumble something incoherent after which Kat shrugged and gave up. Carey wondered if it had anything to do with what she had seen the day before.

She took to the sky for a bit, the wind and freedom of flight alleviating some of her worries for a time. She flew low, as the clouds, even after the storm the night before, were still dark and heavy. There was something sinister about the way they rolled through the sky, lined with red. After some time, the wind began to pick up, and for fear of being blown about by the gusts now rippling through the clouds, Carey and Firefly were forced back to the ground. By the time they reached the gateway, it was blowing fiercely, but the party managed to find an outcrop of rock under which to take shelter, and they lit a fire.

"You wouldn't think it was just after noon," Kat said, gazing out over the darkened plains. "I wonder if it was like this all the time before the first gateway was opened."

"As far as the scholars knew, this gateway has always been open," Lady Marksis said, overhearing her. "I read once that there was nothing to suggest a time before it. Or perhaps it was just so long ago that it was before the dawn of written history."

"So, you know about the gateways, then?" Carey asked.

"Well, when you spend as much time in the archives as we have, you tend to know a thing or two about almost everything," she said with a small smile.

"My sister. Ever so humble," Lord Carron said, giving his sibling a nudge to the shoulder.

Kat sat up, intrigued. "Of course. And you know Gadælic which means you'd have read some of the older works before they were destroyed."

"Oh, yes. Why do you think the Empire was so interested in trying to catch us? They didn't just want us for our daring and good looks," Lord Carron joked, and Carey was reminded of the many stories of intrigue and escape she had heard about the two.

"We did, however, come across some history tomes on the gateways before Malevolence came into power," Lady Marksis said, giving her brother a reproving look as she continued. "They were some of the first works to go under the Empire."

"Well, if they had been planning to find and open the gateway to the Third

Realm, then they wouldn't want anyone else knowing how. That could be where Saar got his information," Kat said with a meaningful look towards Carey.

Carey was about to ask Lady Marksis how they were going to close the gateway when her mother called across to them. Ji was already sitting with his parents — he had been keeping his distance since they'd arrived, and Carey had the distinct feeling that he was trying to avoid them. Between that and his silent disposition the whole way there, she couldn't help but feel a little despondent. Surely it wasn't all because of last night. If so, she felt it was a tad childish of him, given she was trying her best to make it right.

They sat around the fire they had built, shielding it from the wind that was now blowing in icy gusts. Jenny cleared her throat.

"We all know why we are here," she began. "We need to close this gateway and restore balance to the realms. Even though many of our People still exist in the Common Realm, this is our only choice now. If we can open it again in the future, then we most certainly will. We will not leave our People who remain in the Common realm stranded, but for now this is all we can do. The man we knew as Lord Acheron has left us with no other alternative.

"Lord Carron and Lady Marksis have detailed how we must close the gateway. We have two choices: the first is a blood sacrifice—"

"No!" Carey cried out suddenly, shocked that her mother would even voice such a thing. After everything that had happened with Sirona, she wouldn't allow it. Her mother laid a reassuring hand on her knee.

"You needn't worry, Carey," she said soothingly, "There is no way we would even consider it. I was merely enumerating the ways, not the course we would take."

Carey flushed red at her outburst. "Of course, you wouldn't..." she mumbled.

"The second," Jenny continued in a louder voice, "and therefore our only course of action, is to have someone on the other side. Lady Marksis, if you could explain..."

"Of course, Your Majesty. The scholars explained that to open or close a gateway, magic must be present on both sides. If this is not the case, then the more powerful alternative is a blood sacrifice combined with a trifecta of magic from one side only," Lady Marksis said as though she was reciting from a text. "To close with magic present on both sides, the recitations required must be said on both sides, thus successfully closing the gateway. Magic from only one side will not close it without the offering of a life."

Listening to her explanation, Carey frowned. "But…"

"That means someone will have to be on the other side. They'll be stuck in the Common Realm," Kat finished.

Confused, Carey looked around the circle. Was one of them intending on being that person?

"Who's going through?" Kat asked, perplexed, sounding Carey's confusion.

Everyone had gone quiet. For a moment the only sounds were the howling of the wind and the crackle of the fire. Then, slowly, Ji got to his feet.

"I am."

~Chapter Twenty-Eight~

Truth Will Out

Carey stared at Ji, speechless. Surely, she hadn't heard him right. Had Ji just volunteered to go through to the other side? Hadn't he heard what Lady Marksis had said? He would be stuck, unable to cross back through, and who knew if it would ever be opened again... As the moments passed and no one else said anything, the creeping feeling of panic began to grip her. She felt sick — her body felt light and her throat constricted with the feeling of something trying to force its way out. No one else seemed even vaguely surprised by this revelation — Ji's mother and father were quiet, but were looking up at him with fierce pride, and suddenly it all made complete sense. They had obviously made this decision last night when she had seen them in the ward, after the Council had made its decision. And this morning, when he had been so quiet... it was no wonder now what he had been thinking of. But for the life of her, Carey could not think of why Ji was so compelled to do this. She looked sideways at Kat and saw that her friend's face mirrored her shock. Her mouth was hanging open and she was clearly struggling to find something to say. Ji was standing resolute, his expression hard and determined.

"Thank you, Ji, for volunteering to do this," Carey's mother said solemnly. "We know how much of a sacrifice this is, and for that we will be eternally grateful..."

She then began to discuss the exact details of the closing, but Carey heard none of it. All she could do was stare at Ji as he retook his seat, her heart in her throat.

No, this is wrong, she thought adamantly. *He can't do this. He can't just leave us.*

Kat couldn't look at him anymore; her eyes were fixed furiously on a rock by her feet. What on earth had he been thinking when he agreed to do this? Surely his parents wouldn't let him go just like that. But as Jenny continued speaking, Oliver sat stoic and impassive and Meela held her son's hand gently, her fingers grazing his knuckles soothingly. There was no distress in their actions, just calm acceptance. Carey couldn't stand it.

Finally, Jenny finished speaking and the group began to disperse. Ji gave his mother's hand a pat before releasing it and getting up from the group. As he began walking away, Carey jumped to her feet and called out to him.

"Ji! Wait!"

He continued walking.

"Ji, stop. Wait!" she said again, running after him.

They were out in the open now, the cold air whipping around them, and yet he kept walking. The raw feeling of burning in her chest urged her to catch up with him.

"Ji—"

Ji whipped around. "What is it, Carey?" he said, his face set with an unreadable expression. His voice was cold and distant.

Taken aback, Carey dropped her gaze. Her breath was short, caught in her throat and not truly reaching her lungs. She choked as she tried to speak but she was rendered suddenly speechless under his hard glare. Silently, he turned to leave. Carey was startled by this harsh reaction as he seemed so unaffected by her obvious distress.

"Ji, please. Stop!" she pleaded, her voice rasping but at least found.

Again, he waited, but this time he stood with his back to her. Carey took a deep gulp of air, trying to steady herself, fighting off a nervous wave of dizziness.

"What are you thinking? Why... why are you doing this?" she stammered, talking to his back. "Why have you agreed to do this, to be the one... the one who has to..."

She couldn't bring herself to say it; she was already fighting back tears, and to finish that sentence would've been unbearable.

Expressionlessly, Ji turned to her. His face was blank, devoid of any emotion which made Carey feel nervous. "Because I am a Keeper of the Realms. That is my title, my duty, and as such, it is my responsibility to protect my people should the occasion call for it."

"What?" Carey spluttered in disbelief. "But..."

"But what?" Ji said coldly.

"What do you mean *your duty?*"

"Exactly that," he said dispassionately. "I have a duty as a Seeker and as Keeper of the Realms to do this"

"But to do this, surely you're not the only one who can?"

"If not me then who? Why shouldn't I fulfil the duties of my position? Or do you think this title was one I was given just to make me feel useful? That I shouldn't take it seriously?" Ji said accusingly and Carey shrank back.

"That's... that's not what I was going to say..." Carey stuttered, trying to find the words. "I just... this means... you do know what this means, don't you?"

"Of course I do, Carey, but if it is not my responsibility than whose is it?" he said. His words were exasperated and slightly hysterical. "Ever since *this*," he indicated his smoky blue eyes with a careless wave, "Ever since then, I can't seem to be anything, *do* anything right. I couldn't even stop that dragon..." He clutched at his injured arm angrily. "This has to be done, and if it has to be someone, then surely, this... this I can do."

He was rambling, struggling to find the words to convince her.

"But surely there is someone else! Why you?" she blurted out. "What about your parents? And Zacharia? Have you really thought this over?"

Ji looked down at her with such an expression as she had never seen on his face before but there, for the briefest of moments, was another emotion: pain. When he finally spoke, his voice was soft and low, as though he could barely breathe the words he uttered.

"Please don't delude yourself into thinking I haven't considered them, the pain this decision will cause them. It is almost more than I can bear. But knowing this, knowing this pain, what this will do to them, how can I then expect someone else to take my place? Do you really think me so selfish?"

Ji's words bit at her and Carey flinched at their implication.

"I'd never think that," she said in barely a whisper.

Ji must have heard the apparent horror in her voice for he took an involuntary step towards her, his face finally releasing any hostility, only to be replaced by a sad, pained look.

"Then you must know that I can't let anyone else do it. I could use them as a reason not to, use them as an excuse, but then what kind of person would that make me?" he said almost imploringly.

"Someone who can't bear to leave their family," Carey said, willing him to consider it.

She couldn't let him leave. She had to try and convince him to stay.

"What do you propose, then?" Ji said quietly, his clouded eyes searching.

Carey took both of his hand in hers; she felt him flinch slightly, but she didn't release her grip. "There has to be something else... someone else..."

Ji pulled his hands from hers and stepped back away from her. "Someone more disposable..."

She heard the edge to his voice and shook her head. "No, that's not... you just can't... what about..." Carey stammered, flustered. She couldn't find the words.

He looked away from her, his eyes upon the ground at her feet.

"No, it has to be me. I have to... please..."

He turned to leave again.

"Then don't leave... don't leave *me*..." she said, reaching out to him.

The words had forced themselves from her mouth, as though the panic building inside her had wrenched them from her chest.

Ji stopped. "What did you say?" he said in barely a whisper.

Throwing all caution to the wind, Carey took a deep breath. "I said don't leave me. I... I don't want you to go."

His face was impassive. "Why?"

Tears had begun to streak down her face. "I wish it was more obvious. But I let it go on too long," she gasped. "I couldn't understand what was happening, it was just so *confusing*. But then Sirona helped me to see, helped me realise..." Carey looked fearfully up into Ji's face, her heart racing painfully. "It's always been you, Ji. Always. But now... please..." her voice was shaking now. "Please tell me I'm not too late. Please..."

They stood there, the silence filling the space between them until it felt like there would never be anything else. For one horrible moment, Carey thought she might indeed be too late, that she had lost him, and her heart began to break...

Ji lowered his head and Carey heard him give a small, incredulous laugh. "Oh, Carey."

Before she could say anything else, he had closed the gap with two long strides. Ji wrapped an arm around her waist and pulled her close, his lips spread in a wide smile and his eyes blazing.

"Never," he said, and Carey threw her arms around his neck as his lips met hers.

Never had she felt anything like this before. The world around her shattered into a million pieces as their lips touched, and magic and passion fired through their veins. A brilliant ecstasy erupted in her chest and Carey closed her eyes, the feeling warming her all over. They pulled each other close, one of Ji's hands pressing at the small of her back, the other at the base of her neck. His lips were hot against her own and Carey tangled her fingers in his hair, holding him against her, never wanting to let go. This was where they'd always been heading — this was where they were meant to be. They clung to each other, unwilling to relent, all soft touches and warm breath. Ji spoke her name through smiling lips, a whisper that curled around her ear, and Carey felt as if they would drown in this swirling never-ending bliss...

At some point during that evening it had begun to snow, but when or for how long, Carey failed to notice. She and Ji had found shelter within a small secluded cave, and they sat in the mouth of it, watching the world around them turn white. Carey knew now what knowing her Other truly meant — she had felt that undeniable magic, the universe binding them as they came together. It was a promise, the hope of eternity in one brilliant, shining moment, and it was wonderful.

Carey sat with her back against Ji's chest, her fingers entwined with his.

She could feel his heartbeat, strong and comforting, the warmth of his arms around her. She was no longer afraid or nervous; instead, for the first time in a long while, all she felt was an abounding sense of happiness. They talked as they had never talked before, their conversation unimpeded by the awkwardness that had plagued them, and they stayed awake long into the night, long after the others had fallen asleep.

As Carey watched the snowflakes fall, she lifted his hand to her lips and kissed it softly. She heard him sigh softly at her touch and she smiled. She turned to Ji and held his face in her hands.

"Why did I wait so long?" she said as she brushed his hair back from his face. "I'm so sorry."

Ji reached up and took her hand in his. "You don't need to say that. There is nothing to apologise for."

"But I was so…" Carey said with a frown, but Ji silenced her with a shake of his head.

"You knew when you were meant to," he said gently, running the pad of his thumb along her bottom lip. "Besides, it doesn't matter anymore. I would've waited, no matter how long."

He pulled her into him and gave her a long, gentle kiss, and she felt as those her heart might burst.

Laying back down on his chest, Carey said, "Can I ask you… when did you realise?"

"Hmm," Ji thought for a moment, tangling his fingers in hers once more. "It was that day at the market, back before you knew who we were. Remember? You gave us what was possibly the filthiest look that day."

"Oh, I remember!" Carey said with a smirk. "Of course, that was back when I thought I was one of those 'strait-laced and upstanding' kind of citizens, unlike you ruffians."

"Yes, and look at you now," Ji joked.

"That was so long ago. Almost a lifetime," Carey said, turning her head so that her cheek rested in the crook of his neck.

"And yet I'm glad I did know then. It helped me through so much," he said quietly.

Carey knew he was thinking of darker times, but when she went to say something, he stopped her.

"Not now," he said with a shake of his head. "Let us just have this moment without any of that."

The snow was getting heavier now, so much so that they could no longer see the black and red clouds above. Carey tucked herself into Ji's chest and he wrapped his arms around her tighter.

"I could stay like this forever..." she said wistfully, her eyelids growing heavy.

"Mmm," Ji said, stroking her hair. "Forever would be nice..."

"You will though, won't you?" Carey muttered, feeling herself starting drift off.

Ji replied, but his words were lost in the swirling snow and the warmth of their embrace...

*

Carey woke the next morning to find the surrounding area blanketed in a thick layer of brilliant white snow. It had stopped falling during the night and the black clouds were again visible, creating a strange juxtaposition of dark and light. The fire they had lit was now a pile of smoking embers, a thin ribbon of smoke curling up from within the coals.

It took a moment for Carey to realise that she was all alone; she was lying against a large rock with Ji's coat draped over her. Ji was nowhere to be seen.

Ji's absence dragged Carey from her sleepy state, and she climbed to her feet. The others were already awake and talking quietly not far from her, but she couldn't see Ji among them. Stepping out from the rocky outcrop into the snow, Carey went to search for him. Just around the corner was a small copse of trees; it was there she found him, leaning up against one of the trunks. He turned his head as he heard her approaching but he didn't move from his spot, one shoulder against the tree, his arms crossed against his chest.

Placing his coat over his hunched shoulders, Carey looked up into his face. His brow was furrowed and there were dark shadows under his eyes. His expression softened as she came around, but Carey couldn't help but notice a hint of sadness. She reached up and swept her hand over his brow, trying to discern what was troubling him. He continued to stand in silence as she unwrapped his arms and held his hands.

Suddenly, his grip on her hands tightened and he pulled her into a tight embrace, drawing her face to his. Carey felt the urgency and desperation in his kiss, and she pulled away, alarmed. Heart beating fast, she held his face in her hands and gazed searchingly into his eyes.

"You're still going."

Ji didn't answer and Carey felt her stomach drop sickeningly. He was still intending on leaving, she could see it in his face.

"But... what about last night?" she said breathlessly. "What about... us...?"

Ji shook his head and closed his eyes as though he was trying to shut her out, but Carey was having none of it. She grabbed him by the shirt roughly and shook him, shock giving way to anger. "Don't you do this, Ji Binx, you hear me? Talk to me. Please tell me you aren't going through with this!"

They heard Jenny calling from back at the camp and Ji grabbed her briefly by the hand.

"I have to," was all he said, and he turned, leaving her standing in the snow alone.

She could feel the world crashing down around her as she watched him walk away. Her heart felt as though it was being ripped from her body. Clutching at her chest, Carey gasped in pain, her head spinning. This wasn't happening, this couldn't be... she clung to the tree, gulping at the air, feeling like she couldn't breathe. She fell to the ground and her hands sunk deep into the snow, but she felt nothing, not the sting of ice on bare skin... nothing. She could hear her mother calling for her and she realised that it must be time.

Soft hands took her by the shoulders and lifted her from the snow. She heard a familiar voice speaking soothingly to her, but she couldn't discern their meaning. Kat's face swam into view as Carey felt herself being gently steered away from the trees. Again, she heard her name being called.

"Come on, Carey. We can do this," she heard Kat say softly. "You can do this."

Taking a couple of steadying breaths, Carey whispered, "Ji..."

"This way," Kat said, not noticing the strain in her voice.

Slowly, they made their way back to the others. She was still shaking uncontrollably, and Carey felt unendurably sick, as though she had been suddenly struck down by a high fever. Her head felt heavy and her heart banging against her ribs was excruciating. She looked over to where Ji was standing with his mother and father. They were speaking in low voices; his father grasped his shoulder bracingly as Meela held Ji's face in her hands. Tears streamed down her cheeks as she spoke, gazing lovingly up at him. Carey watched numbly as they embraced, Oliver's arms enveloping all three of them, their heads bowing together in one last moment.

Ji then moved to bid farewell to the others, to Lady Marksis and Lord Carron, then Carey's mother. When he reached Kat, she dropped her arm from Carey's shoulders and flung herself around his neck, sobbing in a rare display of emotion. As he held her tightly, he whispered something in her ear that Carey couldn't hear. When they parted, Kat was nodding as though accepting something.

And then he was there. Standing in front of Carey, he pulled her into his arms and for the longest moment, they simply stood there, holding each other close. She clung to him, feeling that if she let go, the world would disappear from beneath her and she would fall, endlessly, hopelessly. She took note of his scent, the way his arms pulled her in tightly and yet gently, and how he buried his head into her shoulder. Finally, reluctantly, he pulled away, and with the hint of a smile said, "Be strong. Be happy."

He turned for the gateway. As he walked up the steps towards the swirling smoke, Carey called out his name desperately, and forgetting about everyone else, forgetting everything, she rushed up to him. Whipping around, Ji caught her up in his arms and lifted her off the ground. She was holding onto him like she was never going to let go, kissing him unabashedly. Their breathing short and rapid, they pulled apart, but only just. Ji was so close that Carey could see a single tear caught in his eyelashes.

Carey struggled to say what needed to be said. How could she convey a million feelings in just a few words? "Ji..." she said in a strained voice.

"I know..." he breathed, nodding. "I love you, too..."

Then he kissed her one last time before letting her down gently. Their hands slipping from each other's grasp, he moved towards the gateway. He stopped just as he reached the threshold and with a final glance, he gave Carey a small, sad smile. Then he lifted a foot and stepped through the gateway.

Shaking, Carey backed away as Lady Marksis and Lord Carron began to chant. Kat rushed to her side, grabbing her by the shoulders as her knees gave way. The smoke swirled faster and faster within the stone archway, the light burning her eyes as the siblings' chanting grew louder. Tears blurring her vision, Carey scrunched up her eyes against the unbearable glare of the gateway, and then, just as the chanting reached its climax, it was gone.

Carey opened her eyes hesitantly, afraid of what she would see.

The last wisps of smoke dissipated with the wind, and where the opening had been moments before, now was nothing but a slab of smooth grey rock. She reached out to where Ji had disappeared and felt hot tears rolling down her face. Beside her she could feel Kat quaking with silent sobs.

Stumbling to her feet, Carey approached the now solid gateway. Placing a hand on the cool rock, she closed her eyes and took a deep breath.

I love you, too.

Epilogue

Carey wasn't sure how she got back in the Centre City. She remembered fragments, as though she was awakening from a dream and it was slowly slipping from her memory. There had been Kat, helping her on to Firefly's back at the gateway... the castle from the air as they made to land... her father holding her... Everything else was a painful blur, thoughts and memories she wanted to both remember and forget at the same time. Somehow, she found herself walking back to her room alone. She distinctly recalled lying to her father, saying she just needed rest. What she really wanted more than anything was to be by herself. She doubted she would have made very good company in any case.

Carey opened the door to her room, the doorknob cold and unwelcoming. She leaned against it as it closed, sliding down onto the floor. Running her hands through her hair, she fought back more tears. She knew if she relinquished to the urge, she would find it impossible to stop, so she sat there on the cold hard floor, her head in her hands and her heart in her mouth.

Something glistened in the corner of her eye.

She lifted her head and looked around her room, searching for the source. There, on the table by her bed, was a small glass box; it was shining, or rather, whatever was inside it was shining, and it threw brilliant white spots of light about the room. Slowly getting to her feet, Carey realised there was something else on the table.

A letter.

Dashing across to it, she snatched up the folded piece of paper. On the front was a single word: Carey. She recognised the script immediately — it was Ji's writing. Sitting on the edge of her bed, she ran her hand over the letters, her hand shaking. She turned it over and found a seal. Her fingers hovered over the red splotch of wax. Did she really want to read this? Carey felt that if she read it then it would feel all too real, that it would make his absence that much more tangible, but…

"I have to," she said, running a finger under the seal and opening the letter.

Dear Carey,

I suppose by the time you read this, I will have already passed through to the other realm and for this, I am truly sorry. I know the pain I must be causing you and it breaks my heart knowing that I'm responsible. I know what you must be thinking, but this decision was just as hard for me to make as it must be for you to understand. It is true that it is my duty to do this, to fulfil my role as Keeper of the Realm, and I will have told you this already. But there is one thing I believe to be truer than anything else and that is you. The thing is, your destiny is far greater than mine. Your horizons spread wider and farther than anything I could ever imagine, and that is why I had to go. I fear that if I were to stay then I would only keep you from fulfilling the destiny that awaits you. I am not the man I once was, and I could never bear the embarrassment if I were to hinder your destiny. Despite what I told you, the injury I sustained from that dragon has weakened me even further, and I did not want you to have to choose between me and what you must do. You may disagree with me (as I know you will), but I know for sure that I would be nothing more than a distraction and a burden, which, in the end, made my decision that much easier.

The devastating truth is that I love you. I love you more than anything in all the realms, always have and always will. That gateway may close, but from what I've seen, there is so much out there that we are yet to discover, and with the hope that there is another way, I will wait for the day that I will see you again.

I have one thing to ask of you though. Be strong. I know it is a tall order, given everything I have just put you through, but this world needs your strength. Carry on. Live your life as best you can. Do what you've always done. Be wonderful. And above all else, be you. Be proud of who you are and what you can do, for you are capable of amazing things. You did not start this war, but I have no doubt that you will be the one to end it.

With this letter is a glass case. Within this case is a star. Your star. You can keep it, or you can let it go. It is to you what you are to me - you were my light in my darkest hours and for me, you are the only true light I will ever know.

My heart belongs to you, now and forever.

Forgive me,

Ji

Carey stared at the last word and felt a small bubble of anger rise through the pain. He wouldn't have been a burden; how could he know that? Did he not have faith in her abilities to at least give her a chance? Of course, she knew why he hadn't told her all of this before he left — she would've told him he was being stupid. Ridiculous. Despite all his injuries, everything he had endured, he'd always pushed beyond it, shown that they were nothing but a nuisance. The very idea that he himself would have been a distraction, a liability, was preposterous.

And then the bubble burst, and all that anger drifted away as she realised it was useless. Ji wasn't there for her to be angry with, and no matter how indignant she felt about his decision, it would not bring him back. She had but his last request, and his final gift...

Carey looked over at the small glass box. *Her star,* as he had called it. She recalled his words from that night on the hill and her heart swelled. For so long he had believed in her, believed that she was destined for something bigger. Perhaps it was time she started believing in herself too. With enormous effort, she pushed aside the despair and the fear that was weighing on her chest and reached for the star. As her hand closed around the small case, its light escaping through her fingers, Carey vowed to honour Ji's last request.

She would carry on.

And she would see him again.

About the Author

Alysha King is a Young Adult fiction author who lives in Canberra, Australia with her husband, two young children, a very large dog, and a sneaky white cat. She began writing the Rose Chronicles in high school after being inspired by such writers as Eoin Colfer and Isobelle Carmody. She revels in fantasy and sci-fi and has a soft spot for Enid Blyton, citing her works as some of her all-time favourites and of which she has quite a large collection of in her home library. Alysha also enjoys historical fiction and is currently collecting research for a number of future novels.

When she is not writing or collecting vintage copies of works by famous English writers, Alysha can be found indulging in any number of her other hobbies which include cosplay costuming with her son and daughter, baking overly sweet treats, and collecting Harry Potter paraphernalia.

Alysha can be found on social media and via her website www.alyshaking.com.